HELEN
BIANCHIN

Latin Lovers

D0716572

HELEN BIANCHIN

COLLECTION

February 2016

March 2016

April 2016

May 2016

June 2016

July 2016

HELEN BIANCHIN

Latin Lovers

MILLS & BOON

First Published in Great Britain 2016
By Mills & Boon, an imprint of HarperCollins*Publishers*
1 London Bridge Street, London, SE1 9GF

LATIN LOVERS © 2016 Harlequin Books S.A.

A Convenient Bridegroom © 1999 Helen Bianchin
In the Spaniard's Bed © 2003 Helen Bianchin
The Martinez Marriage Revenge © 2008 Helen Bianchin

ISBN: 978-0-263-92147-2

09-0316

Harlequin (UK) Limited's policy is to use papers that are natural, renewable and recyclable products and made from wood grown in sustainable forests. The logging and manufacturing processes conform to the legal environmental regulations of the country of origin.

Printed and bound in Spain
by CPI, Barcelona

A CONVENIENT
BRIDEGROOM
HELEN BIANCHIN

Helen Bianchin was born in New Zealand and travelled to Australia before marrying her Italian-born husband. After three years they moved, returned to New Zealand with their daughter, had two sons and then resettled in Australia.

Encouraged by friends to recount anecdotes of her years as a tobacco sharefarmer's wife living in an Italian community, Helen began setting words on paper and her first novel was published in 1975.

Currently Helen resides in Queensland, the three children now married with children of their own. An animal lover, Helen says her two beautiful Birman cats regard her study as much theirs as hers, choosing to leap onto her desk every afternoon to sit upright between the computer monitor and keyboard as a reminder they need to be fed...like right now!

CHAPTER ONE

'Night, *cara*. You will be staying over, won't you?'

Subtle, very subtle, Aysha conceded. It never ceased to amaze that her mother could state a command in the form of a suggestion, and phrase it as a question. As if Aysha had a choice.

For as long as she could remember, her life had been stage-managed. The most exclusive of private schools, extra-curricular private tuition. Holidays abroad, winter resorts. Ballet, riding school, languages…she spoke fluent Italian and French.

Aysha Benini was a product of her parents' upbringing. Fashioned, styled and presented as a visual attestation to family wealth and status.

Something which must be upheld at any cost.

Even her chosen career as an interior decorator added to the overall image.

'Darling?'

Aysha crossed the room and brushed her lips to her mother's cheek. 'Probably.'

Teresa Benini allowed one eyebrow to form an elegant arch. 'Your father and I won't expect you home.'

Case closed. Aysha checked her evening purse, selected her car key, and turned towards the door. 'See you later.'

'Have a good time.'

5

What did Teresa Benini consider a *good time*? An exquisitely served meal eaten in a trendy restaurant with Carlo Santangelo, followed by a long night of loving in Carlo's bed?

Aysha slid in behind the wheel of her black Porsche Carrera, fired the engine, then eased the car down the driveway, cleared the electronic gates, and traversed the quiet tree-lined street towards the main arterial road leading from suburban Vaucluse into the city.

A shaft of sunlight caught the diamond-studded gold band with its magnificent solitaire on the third finger of her left hand. Brilliantly designed, horrendously expensive, it was a befitting symbol representing the intended union of Giuseppe Benini's daughter to Luigi Santangelo's son.

Benini-Santangelo, Aysha mused as she joined the flow of city-bound traffic.

Two immigrants from two neighbouring properties in a northern Italian town had travelled in their late teens to Sydney, where they'd worked two jobs every day of the week, saved every cent, and set up a cement business in their mid-twenties.

Forty years on, Benini-Santangelo was a major name in Sydney's building industry, with a huge plant and a fleet of concrete tankers.

Each man had married a suitable wife, sadly produced only one child apiece; they lived in fine homes, drove expensive cars, and had given their children the best education that money could buy.

Both families had interacted closely on a social and personal level for as long as Aysha could remember. The bond between them was strong, more than friends. Almost family.

The New South Head Road wound down towards Rose Bay, and Aysha took a moment to admire the view.

At six-thirty on a fine late summer's evening the ocean resembled a sapphire jewel, merging with a sky clear of cloud or pollution. Prime real estate overlooked numerous coves and bays where various sailing craft lay anchored. Tall city buildings rose in differing architectural design, structured towers of glass and steel, providing a splendid backdrop to the Opera House and the wide span of the Harbour Bridge.

Traffic became more dense as she drew close to the city, and there were the inevitable delays at computer-controlled intersections.

Consequently it was almost seven when she drew into the curved entrance of the hotel and consigned her car to valet parking.

She could, *should* have allowed Carlo to collect her, or at least driven to his apartment. It would have been more practical, sensible.

Except tonight she didn't feel *sensible*.

Aysha nodded to the concierge as she entered the lobby, and she hadn't taken more than three steps towards the bank of sofas and single chairs when a familiar male frame rose to full height and moved forward to greet her.

Carlo Santangelo.

Just the sight of him was enough to send her heart racing to a quickened beat. Her breath caught in her throat, and she forced herself to monitor the rise and fall of her chest.

In his late thirties, he stood three inches over six feet and possessed the broad shoulders and hard-muscled body of a man who coveted physical fitness. Sculpted raw-boned facial features highlighted planes and angles, accenting a powerful jaw, strong chin, and a sensuously moulded mouth. Well-cut thick dark brown hair was stylishly groomed, and his eyes were incredibly dark, almost black.

Aysha had no recollection of witnessing his temper. Yet there could be no doubt he possessed one, for his eyes could darken to obsidian, the mouth thin, and his voice assume the chill of an ice floe.

'Aysha.' He leant down and brushed his mouth against her own, lingered, then he lifted his head and caught both of her hands in his.

Dear God, he was something. The clean male smell of him teased her nostrils, combining with his subtle aftershave.

Her stomach executed a series of somersaults, and her pulse hammered heavily enough to be almost audible. Did she affect him the way he affected her?

Doubtful, she conceded, aware of precisely where she fitted in the scheme of things. Bianca had been his first love, the beautiful young girl he'd married ten years ago, only to lose her in a fatal car accident mere weeks after the honeymoon. Aysha had cried silent tears at the wedding, and wept openly at Bianca's funeral.

Afterwards he'd flung himself into work, earning

a reputation in the business arena as a superb strategist, able to negotiate with enviable skill.

He had dated many women, and selectively taken what they offered without thought of replacing the beautiful young girl who had all too briefly shared his name.

Until last year, when he'd focused his attention on Aysha, strengthening the affectionate bond between them into something much more personal, more intimate.

His proposal of marriage had overwhelmed her, for Carlo had been the object of her affection for as long as she could remember, and she could pinpoint the moment when teenage hero-worship had changed and deepened into love.

A one-sided love, for she was under no illusion. The marriage would strengthen the Benini-Santangelo conglomerate and forge it into another generation.

'Hungry?'

At the sound of Carlo's drawled query Aysha offered a winsome smile, and her eyes assumed a teasing sparkle. 'Starving.'

'Then let's go eat, shall we?' Carlo placed an arm round her waist and led her towards a bank of elevators.

The top of her head came level with his shoulder, and her slender frame held a fragility that was in direct contrast to strength of mind and body.

She could, he reflected musingly as he depressed the call button, have turned into a terrible brat. Yet for all the pampering, by an indulgent but fiercely protective mother, Aysha was without guile. Nor did she have an inflated sense of her own importance. Instead, she was a warm, intelligent, witty and very attractive young woman whose smile transformed her features into something quite beautiful.

The restaurant was situated on a high floor offering magnificent views of the city and harbour. Expensive, exclusive, and a personal favourite, for the chef was a true artiste with an expertise and flair that had earned him fame and fortune in several European countries.

The lift doors slid open, and she preceded Carlo into the cubicle, then stood in silence as they were transported with electronic speed.

'That bad, hmm?'

Aysha cast him a quick glance, saw the musing cynicism apparent, and didn't know whether to be amused or resigned that he'd divined her silence and successfully attributed it to a ghastly day.

Was she that transparent? Somehow she didn't think so. At least not with most people. However, Carlo was an entity all on his own, and she'd accepted a long time ago that there was very little she could manage to keep hidden from him.

'Where would you like me to begin?' She wrinkled her nose at him, then she lifted a hand and proceeded to tick off each finger in turn. 'An irate client, an even more irate floor manager, imported fabric caught up in a wharf strike, or the dress fitting from hell?' She rolled her eyes. 'Choose.'

The elevator slid to a halt, and she walked at his side to the restaurant foyer.

'Signor Santangelo, Signorina Benini. Welcome.'
The maître d' greeted them with a fulsome smile,
and accorded them the deference of valued patrons.
He didn't even suggest a table, merely led them to
the one they preferred, adjacent the floor-to-ceiling
window.

There was, Aysha conceded, a certain advantage
in being socially well placed. It afforded impeccable
service.

The wine steward appeared the instant they were
seated, and Aysha deferred to Carlo's choice of white
wine.

'Iced water, please,' she added, then watched as
Carlo leaned back in his chair to regard her with
interest.

'How is Teresa?'

'Now there's a leading question, if ever there was
one,' Aysha declared lightly. 'Perhaps you could be
more specific?'

'She's driving you insane.' His faint drawling
tones caused the edges of her mouth to tilt upwards
in a semblance of wry humour.

'You're good. Very good,' she acknowledged with
cynical approval.

One eyebrow rose, and there was gleaming amusement evident. 'Shall I try for excellent and guess the
current crisis?' he ventured. 'Or are you going to tell
me?'

'The wedding dress.' Visualising the scene earlier
in the day brought a return of tension as she vividly
recalled Teresa's calculated insistence and the seam-
stress's restrained politeness. Dammit, it should be

so easy. They'd agreed on the style, the material. The fit was perfect. Yet Teresa hadn't been able to leave it alone.

'Problems?' He had no doubt there would be many, most of which would be of Teresa's making.

'The dressmaker is not appreciative of Mother's interference with the design.' Aysha experienced momentary remorse, for the gown was truly beautiful, a vision of silk, satin and lace.

'I see.'

'No,' she corrected. 'You don't.' She paused as the wine steward delivered the wine, and went through the tasting ritual with Carlo, before retreating.

'What don't I see, *cara*?' Carlo queried lightly.

'That Teresa, like most Italian *mammas*, wants the perfect wedding for her daughter. The perfect venue, caterers, food, wine, *bomboniera*, the cake, limousines. And the dress must be outstanding.'

'You've forgotten the flowers,' Aysha reminded him mildly. 'The florist is at the end of his tether. The caterer is ready to quit because he says *his* tiramisu is an art form and he will not, *not*, you understand, use my grandmother's recipe from the Old Country.'

Carlo's mouth formed a humorous twist. 'Teresa is a superb cook,' he complimented blandly.

Teresa was superb at everything; that was the trouble. Consequently, she expected others to be equally superb. The *trouble* as such, was that while Teresa Benini enjoyed the prestige of employing the *best* money could buy, she felt bound to check every little detail to ensure it came up to her impossibly high standard.

Retaining household staff had always been a problem for as long as Aysha could remember. They came and left with disturbing rapidity due to her mother's refusal to delegate even the most minor of chores.

The waiter arrived with the menu, and because he was new, and very young, they listened in silence as he explained the intricacies of each dish, gave his considered recommendations, then very solicitously noted their order before retreating with due deference to relay it to the kitchen.

Aysha lifted her glass and took a sip of chilled water, then regarded the man seated opposite over the rim of the stemmed goblet.

'How seriously would you consider an elopement?'

Carlo swirled the wine in his goblet, then lifted it to his lips and savoured the delicate full-bodied flavour.

'Is there any particular reason why you'd want to incur Teresa's wrath by wrecking the social event of the year?'

'It would never do,' she agreed solemnly. 'Although I'm almost inclined to plug for sanity and suffer the wrath.'

One eyebrow slanted, and his dark eyes assumed a quizzical gleam.

The waiter delivered their starters; minestrone and a superb linguini with seafood sauce.

'Two weeks, *cara*,' Carlo reminded her.

It was a lifetime. One she wasn't sure she'd survive intact.

She should have moved out of home into an apartment of her own. Would have, if Teresa hadn't dismissed the idea as ridiculous when she had a wing in the house all to herself, complete with gym, sauna and entertainment lounge. She had her own car, her own garage, and technically she could come and go as she pleased.

Aysha picked up her fork, deftly wound on a portion of pasta and savoured it. Ambrosia. The sauce was *perfecto*.

'Good?'

She wound on another portion and held it to his lips. 'Try some.' She hadn't intended it to be an intimate gesture, and her eyes flared slightly as he placed his fingers over hers, guided the fork, and then held her gaze as he slid the pasta into his mouth.

Her stomach jolted, then settled, and she was willing to swear she could hear her own heartbeat thudding in her ears.

He didn't even have to try, and she became caught up with the alchemy that was his alone.

A warm smile curved his lips as he dipped a spoon into his minestrone and lifted it invitingly towards her own. 'Want to try mine?'

She took a small mouthful, then shook her head when he offered her another. Did he realise just how difficult it was for her to retain a measure of sangfroid at moments like these?

'We have a rehearsal at the church tomorrow evening,' Carlo reminded her, and saw her eyes darken.

Aysha replaced her fork, her appetite temporarily diminished. 'Six-thirty,' she concurred evenly. 'After which the wedding party dine together.'

Both sets of parents, the bride and groom to-be, the bridesmaids and their attendants, the flower girls and page boys and *their* parents.

Followed the next day by a bridal shower. Hardly a casual affair, with just very close friends, a few nibblies and champagne. The guest list numbered fifty, it was being catered, and Teresa had arranged entertainment.

To add to her stress levels, she'd stubbornly refused to begin six weeks' leave of absence from work until a fortnight before the wedding.

On the positive side, it kept her busy, her mind occupied, and minimised the growing tension with her mother. The negative was hours early morning and evening spent at the breathtaking harbourside mansion Carlo had built, overseeing installation of carpets, drapes, selecting furniture, co-ordinating colours. And doing battle with Teresa when their tastes didn't match and Teresa overstretched her advisory capacity. Something which happened fairly frequently.

'Penny for them.'

Aysha glanced across the table and caught Carlo's teasing smile.

'I was thinking about the house.' That much was true. 'It's all coming together very well.'

'You're happy with it?'

'How could I not be?' she countered simply, visualising the modern architectural design with its five sound-proofed self-contained wings converging onto a central courtyard. The interior was designed for light and space, with a suspended art gallery, a small theatre and games room. A sunken area featured spa and sauna, and a jet pool.

It was a showcase, a place to entertain guests and business associates. Aysha planned to make it a home.

The wine waiter appeared and refilled each goblet, followed closely by the young waiter, who removed their plates prior to serving the main course.

Carlo ate with the enjoyment of a man who consumed nourishment wisely but well, his use of cutlery decisive.

He was the consummate male, sophisticated, dynamic, and possessed of a primitive sensuality that drew women to him like a magnet. Men envied his ruthlessness and charm, and knew the combination to be lethal.

Aysha recognised each and every one of his qualities, and wondered if she was woman enough to hold him.

'Would you care to order dessert, Miss Benini?'

The young waiter's desire to please was almost embarrassing, and she offered him a gentle smile. 'No, thanks, I'll settle for coffee.'

'You've made a conquest,' Carlo drawled as the waiter retreated from their table.

Her eyes danced with latent mischief. 'Ah, you say the nicest things.'

'Should I appear jealous, do you think?'

She wanted to say, *only if you are*. And since that was unlikely, it became easy to play the game.

'Well, he *is* young, and good-looking.' She pretended to consider. 'Probably a university student working nights to pay for his education. Which would indicate he has potential.' She held Carlo's dark gleaming gaze and offered him a brilliant smile. 'Do you think he'd give up the room he probably rents, sell his wheels…a Vespa scooter at a guess…and be a kept toy-boy?'

His soft laughter sent shivers over the surface of her skin, raising fine body hairs as all her nerve-endings went haywire.

'I think I should take you home.'

'I came in my own car, remember?' she reminded him, and saw his eyes darken, the gleam intensify.

'A bid for independence, or an indication you're not going to share my bed tonight?'

She summoned a winsome smile, and her eyes shone with wicked humour. 'Teresa is of the opinion catering to your physical needs should definitely be my priority.'

'And Teresa knows best?' His voice was silky-smooth, and she wasn't deceived for a second.

'My mother believes in covering all the bases,' Aysha relayed lightly.

His gaze didn't shift, and she was almost willing to swear he could read her mind. 'As you do?'

Her expression sobered. 'I don't have a hidden agenda.' Did he know she was in love with him? Had loved him for as long as she could remember? She hoped not, for it would afford him an unfair advantage.

'Finish your coffee,' Carlo bade gently. 'Then we'll leave.' He lifted a hand in silent summons, and the waiter appeared with the bill.

Aysha watched as Carlo signed the slip and added a generous tip, then he leaned back in his chair and surveyed her thoughtfully.

She was tense, but covered it well. His eyes narrowed faintly. 'Do we have anything planned next weekend?'

'Mother has something scheduled for every day until the wedding,' she declared with unaccustomed cynicism.

'Have Teresa reorganise her diary.'

Aysha looked at him with interest. 'And if she won't?'

'Tell her I've surprised you with airline tickets and accommodation for a weekend on the Gold Coast.'

'Have you?'

His smile held humour. 'I'll make the call the minute we reach my apartment.'

Her eyes shone, and she broke into light laughter. 'My knight in shining armour.'

Carlo's voice was low, husky, and held amusement. 'Escape,' he accorded. 'Albeit brief.' He stood to his feet and reached out a hand to take hold of hers. His gleaming gaze seared right through to her heart. 'You can thank me later.'

Together they made their way through the room to the front desk.

The maître d' was courteously solicitous. 'I'll arrange with the concierge to have your cars brought to the front entrance.'

Both vehicles were waiting when they reached the lobby. Carlo saw her seated behind the wheel of her Porsche, then he crossed to his Mercedes to fire the engine within seconds and ease into the line of traffic.

Aysha followed, sticking close behind him as he traversed the inner city streets heading east towards Rose Bay and his penthouse apartment.

When they reached it she drove down into the underground car park, took the space adjoining his private bay, then walked at his side towards the bank of lifts in companionable silence.

They didn't *need* a house, she determined minutes later as she stepped into the plush apartment lobby.

The drapes weren't drawn, and the view out over the harbour was magnificent. Fairy lights, she mused as she crossed the lounge to the floor-to-ceiling glass stretching across one entire wall.

City buildings, street lights, brightly coloured neon vying with tall concrete spires and an indigo sky.

Aysha heard him pick up the phone, followed by the sound of his voice as he arranged flights and accommodation for the following weekend.

'We could have easily lived here,' she murmured as he came to stand behind her.

'So we could.' He put his arms around her waist and pulled her back against him.

She felt his chin rest on the top of her head, sensed the warmth of his breath as it teased her hair, and was unable to prevent the slight shiver as his lips sought the vulnerable hollow beneath the lobe of one ear.

She almost closed her eyes and pretended it was real. That *love* not lust, and *need* not want, was Carlo's motivation.

A silent groan rose and died in her throat as his mouth travelled to the edge of her neck and nuzzled, his tongue, his lips erotic instruments as he tantalised the rapidly beating pulse.

His hands moved, one to her breast as he sought a sensitive peak, while the other splayed low over her stomach.

She wanted to urge him to quicken the pace, to dispense with her clothes while she feverishly tore every barrier from his body until there was nothing between them.

She wanted to be lifted high in his arms and sink down onto him, then clutch hold of him as he took her for the ride of her life.

Everything about him was too controlled. Even in bed he never lost that control completely, as she did.

There were times when she wanted to cry out that while she could accept Bianca as an important part of his past, *she* was his future. Except she never said the words. Perhaps because she was afraid of his response.

Now she turned in his arms and reached for him, her mouth seeking his as she gave herself up completely to the heat of passion.

He caught her urgency and effortlessly swept her into his arms and carried her into the bedroom.

Aysha's fingers worked on his shirt buttons, unfastened the buckle on his belt, then pulled his shirt free.

His nipples were hard, and she savoured each one in turn, then used her teeth to tease, aware that Carlo had deftly removed most of her clothes.

She heard his intake of breath seconds ahead of the soft thud as he discarded one shoe and the other, then dispensed with his trousers.

'Wait.' His voice was low and slightly husky, and she ran her hands over his ribcage, searched the hard plane of his stomach and reached for him.

'So you want to play, hmm?'

CHAPTER TWO

CARLO caught hold of her arms and let his hands slide up to cup her shoulders as he buried his mouth in the vulnerable hollow at the edge of her neck.

Her subtle perfume teased his senses, and he nuzzled the sensitive skin, tasted it, nipped ever so gently with his teeth, and felt the slight spasm of her body's reaction to his touch.

She was a generous lover. Passionate, with a sense of adventure and fun he found endearing.

He trailed his lips down the slope of her breast and suckled one tender peak, savoured, then moved to render a similar supplication to its twin.

Did he know what he did to her? Aysha felt a stab of pain at the thought that his lovemaking might be contrived. A practised set of moves that pushed all the right buttons.

Once, just once she wanted to feel the tremors of need shake his body…for her, only her. To know that she could make him so crazy with desire that he had no restraint.

Was it asking too much to want *love*? She wore his ring. Soon *she* would bear his name. It should be enough.

She wanted to mean so much more to him than just a satisfactory bed partner, a charming hostess.

Take what he's prepared to give, and be grateful,

a tiny voice prompted. *A cup half-full is better than one that is empty.*

Her hands linked at his nape and she drew his head down to hers, exulting in the feel of his mouth as he shaped her own.

She let her tongue slide against his, then conducted a slow, sweeping circle before initiating a probing dance that was almost as evocative as the sexual act itself.

His hand shaped her nape and held fast her head, while the other slipped low over one hip, cupped her bottom and drew her close in against him.

She wanted him *now*, hard and fast, without any preliminaries. To be able to feel the power, the strength, without caution or care. As if he couldn't bear to wait a second longer to effect possession.

The familiar slide of his fingers, the gentle probing exploration as he sought the warm moistness of her feminine core brought a gasping sigh from her lips.

Followed by a despairing groan as he began an evocative stimulation. It wasn't fair that he should have such intimate knowledge and be aware precisely how to wield it to drive a woman wild.

His mouth hardened, and his jaw took control of hers, moving it in rhythm with his own.

She clutched hold of his shoulders and held on as his fingers probed deeper, and just as she thought she could bear it no longer he shifted position.

A cry rose and died in her throat as he slid into her in one long, thrusting movement.

Dear God, that felt good. So good. She murmured

her pleasure, then gave a startled gasp as he tumbled her down onto the bed and withdrew.

His mouth left hers, and began a seeking trail down her throat, tasting the vulnerable hollows at the base of her neck, the soft, quivering flesh of each breast, the indentation of her navel.

She knew his intention, and felt the flame lick along every nerve-end, consuming every sensitised nerve-cell until she was close to conflagration.

Her head tossed from one side to the other as sensation took hold of her whole body. Part of her wanted to tell him to stop before it became unbearable, but the husky admonition sounded so low in her throat as to be indistinguishable.

He was skilled, so very highly skilled in giving a woman pleasure. The slight graze of his teeth, the erotic laving of his tongue. He knew just where to touch to urge her towards the edge. And how to hold her there, until she begged for release.

Aysha thought she cried out, and she bit down hard as Carlo feathered light kisses over her quivering stomach, then paused to suckle at her breast,

His mouth closed on hers, and she arched up against him as he entered her in one surging movement, stretching delicate tissues to their utmost capacity.

He began to move, slowly at first, then with increasing depth and strength as she became consumed with the feel of him.

His skin, her own, was warm and slick with sweat, and the blood ran through her veins like quicksilver.

It was more than a physical joining, for she gifted

him her heart, her soul, everything. She was *his*. Only his. At that moment she would have died for him, so complete was her involvement.

Frightening, shattering, she reflected a long time later as she lay curled into the warmth of his body. For it almost destroyed her concept of who and what she had become beneath his tutelage.

The steady rise and fall of his chest was reassuring, the beat of his heart strong. The lazy stroke of his fingers along her spine indicated he wasn't asleep yet, and the slight pressure against the indentations of each vertebrae was soothing. She could feel his lips brush lightly over her hair as she drifted into a peaceful sleep.

It was the soft, hazy aftermath of great lovemaking. A time for whispered avowals of love, Aysha thought as she woke, the affirmation of commitment.

Aysha wanted to utter the words, and hear them in return. Yet she knew she would die a silent death if he didn't respond in kind. She pressed a light butterfly kiss to the muscled ridge of his chest and traced a gentle circle with the tip of her tongue.

He tasted of musk, edged with a faint tang that was wholly male. She nipped the hard flesh with her teeth and bestowed a love-bite, then she soothed it gently before moving close to a sensitive male nipple.

She trailed her fingers over one hip, lingered near his groin, and felt his stomach muscles tense.

'That could prove dangerous,' Carlo warned as she began to caress him with gentle intimacy.

The soft slide of one finger, as fleeting as the tip of a butterfly's wing, in a careful tactile exploration. Incredible how the male organ could engorge and enlarge in size. Almost frightening, its degree of power as instrument to a woman's pleasure.

Aysha had the desire to tantalise him to the brink of madness, and unleash everything that was wild and untamed, until there were no boundaries. Just two people as one, attuned and in perfect accord on every level. Spiritual, mental and physical.

A gasp escaped her throat as he clasped both hands on her waist and swept her to sit astride him.

Excitement spiralled through her body as he arched his hips and sent her tumbling down against his chest.

One hand slid to her nape as he angled her head to his, then his mouth was on hers, all heat and passion as he took possession.

The kiss seared her heart, branding her in a way that made her *his*…totally. Mind, body, and soul. She had no thought for anything but the man and the storm raging within.

It made anything she'd shared before seem less. Dear Lord, she'd ached for his passion. But this…this was raw, primitive. Mesmeric. Ravaging.

She met and matched his movements, driven by a hunger so intense she had no recollection of time or place.

Aysha wasn't even aware when he reversed positions, and it was the gentling of his touch, the gradual loss of intensity that intruded on her conscious mind and brought with it a slow return to sanity.

There was a sense of exquisite wonderment, a sensation of wanting desperately to hold onto the moment in case it might fracture and fragment.

She didn't feel the soft warmth of tears as they slid slowly down her cheeks. Nor was she aware of the sexual heat emanating from her skin, or the slight trembling of her body as Carlo used his hands, his lips to bring her down.

He absorbed the dampness on one cheek, then pressed his lips against one closed eyelid, before moving to effect a similar supplication on the other. His hands shifted as he gently rolled onto his back, carrying her with him so she lay cradled against the length of his body.

Slight tremors shook her slim form, and he brought her mouth to his in a soft, evocative joining. His fingers trailed the shape of her, gently exploring the slim supple curves, the slender waist, the soft curve of her buttocks.

It was Carlo who broke contact long minutes later, and she trailed a hand down the edge of his cheek.

'I get first take on the shower. You make the coffee,' she whispered.

His slow smile caused havoc with her pulse-rate. 'We share the shower, then I'll organise coffee while you cook breakfast.'

'Chauvinist,' Aysha commented with musing tolerance.

His lips caressed her breast, and desire arrowed through her body, hot, needy, and wildly wanton. 'We can always miss breakfast and focus on the shower.'

His arousal was a potent force, and her eyes danced with mischief as she contemplated the option. 'As much as the offer attracts me, I need *food* to charge my energy levels.' She placed the tip of a finger over his lips, then gave a mild yelp as he nipped it with his teeth. 'That calls for revenge.'

Carlo's hands spanned her waist and he shifted her to one side, then he leaned over her. 'Try it.'

She rose to the challenge at once, although the balance of power soon became uneven, and then it hardly seemed to matter any more who won or lost.

Afterwards she had the quickest shower on record, then she dressed, swept her hair into a twist at her nape, added blusher, eye colour and mascara.

She looked, Carlo noted with respect, as if she'd spent thirty minutes on her grooming instead of the five it had taken her.

'Sit down and eat,' he commanded as he slid an omelette onto a plate. 'Coffee's ready.'

'You're a gem among men,' Aysha complimented as she sipped the coffee. Pure nectar on the palate, and the omelette was perfection.

'From chauvinist to gem in the passage of twenty minutes,' he drawled with unruffled ease, and she spared him a wicked grin in between mouthfuls.

'Don't get a swelled head.'

She watched as he poured himself some coffee then joined her at the table. The dark navy towelling robe accented his breadth of shoulder, and dark curling hair showed at the vee of the lapels. Her eyes slid down to the belt tied at his waist, and lingered.

'You don't have time to find out,' he mocked lazily, and she offered a stunning smile.

'It's my last day at work.' She rose to her feet and gulped the last mouthful of coffee. 'But as of tomorrow...'

'Promises,' Carlo taunted, and she reached up to brush her lips to his cheek, except he moved his head and they touched his mouth instead.

'Got to rush,' she said with genuine regret. 'See you tonight.'

Her job was important to her, and she loved the concept of using colour and design to make a house a home. The right furnishings, furniture, fittings, so that it all added up to a beautiful whole that was both eye-catching and comfortable. She'd earned a reputation for going that extra mile for a client, exploring every avenue in the search to get it right.

However, there were days when phone calls didn't produce the results she wanted, and today was one of them. Added to which she had to run a final check over all the orders that were due to come in while she was away. An awesome task, just on its own.

Then there was lunch with some of her fellow staff, and the presentation of a wedding gift...an exquisite crystal platter. The afternoon seemed to fly on wings, and it was after six when she rode the lift to Carlo's penthouse.

'Ten minutes,' she promised him as she entered the lounge, and she stepped out of heeled pumps *en route* to the shower.

Aysha was ready in nine, and he snagged her arm as she raced towards the door.

'Slow down,' he directed, and she threw him an urgent glance.

'We're late. We should have left already.' She tugged her hand and made no impression. 'They'll be waiting for us.'

He pulled her close, and lowered his head down to hers. 'So they'll wait a little longer.'

His mouth touched hers with such incredible gentleness her insides began to melt, and she gave a faint despairing groan as her lips parted beneath the pressure of his.

Minutes later he lifted his head and surveyed the languid expression softening those beautiful smoky grey eyes. Better, he noted silently. Some of the tension had ebbed away, and she looked slightly more relaxed.

'OK, let's go.'

'That was deliberate,' Aysha said a trifle ruefully as they rode the lift down to the underground car park, and caught his musing smile.

'Guilty.'

He'd slowed her galloping pace down to a relaxed trot, and she offered a smile in silent thanks as they left the lift and crossed to the Mercedes.

'How was your day?' she queried as she slid into the passenger seat and fastened her belt.

'Assembling quotes, checking computer print-outs, checking a building site. Numerous phone calls.'

'All hands-on stuff, huh?'

The large car sprang into instant life the moment he turned the key, and he spared her a wry smile as they gained street level.

'That about encapsulates it.'

The church was a beautiful old stone building set back from the road among well-tended lawns and gardens. Symmetrically planted trees and their spreading branches added to the portrayed seclusion.

There was an air of peace and grace apparent, meshing with the mystique of blessed holy ground.

Aysha drew a deep breath as she saw the several cars lining the curved driveway. Everyone was here.

Attending someone else's wedding, watching the ceremony on film or television, was a bit different from participating in one's own, albeit this was merely a rehearsal of the real thing.

'I want to carry the basket,' Emily, the youngest flower girl, insisted, and tried to wrest it from Samantha's grasp.

'I don't want to hold a pillow. It looks sissy,' Jonathon, the eldest page boy declared.

Oh, my. If he thought carrying a small satin lace-edged pillow demeaned his boyhood, then just wait until he had to get dressed in a miniature suit, satin waistcoat, buttoned shirt and bow-tie.

'Sissy,' the youngest page boy endorsed.

'You have to,' Emily insisted importantly.

'Don't.'

'Do so.'

Aysha didn't know whether to laugh or cry. 'What if Samantha carries the basket of rose petals, and Emily carries the pillow?'

It was almost possible to see the ensuing mental tussle as each little girl weighed the importance of each task.

'I want the pillow,' Samantha decided. Rings held more value than rose-petals to be strewn over the carpeted aisle.

'You can have the basket.' Emily, too, had done her own calculations.

Teresa rolled her eyes, the girls' respective mothers attempted to pacify, and when that failed they tried bribery.

The four bridesmaids looked tense, for they'd each been assigned a child to care for during the formal ceremony.

'OK.' Aysha lifted both hands in a gesture of expressive defeat. 'This is how it's going to be. Two baskets, so Emily and Samantha get to carry one each.' She cast both boys a stern look. 'Two pillows.'

'Two?' Teresa queried incredulously, and Aysha inclined her head.

'Two.'

The little girls beamed, and both boys bent their heads in sulky disagreement.

Maybe it would have been wiser not to give the children a rehearsal at all, and simply tell them what to do on the day and hope they'd concentrate so hard there wouldn't be the opportunity for error.

Celestial assistance was obviously going to be needed, Aysha mused as she listened to the priest's instructions.

An hour later they were all seated at a long table in a restaurant nominated as children-friendly. The food was good, the wine did much to relax fraught nerves, and Aysha enjoyed the informality of it all as she leaned back against Carlo's supporting arm.

'Tired?'

She lifted her face to his, and her eyes sparkled with latent intimacy. 'It's been a long day.'

He leaned in close and brushed his lips to her temple. 'You can sleep in in the morning.'

'Generous of you. But I need to be home early to help Teresa with preparations for the bridal shower. Remember?'

It was almost eleven when everyone began to make a move, and a further half-hour before Aysha and Carlo were able to leave, for the bridesmaids lingered and Teresa had last-minute instructions to impart.

The witching hour of midnight struck as she preceded Carlo into the penthouse, and she slipped off her shoes, took the clip from her hair and shook it loose, then she padded through to the kitchen.

'Coffee?'

Aysha sensed rather than heard him move behind her, and she murmured her approval as his hands kneaded tense shoulder muscles.

'Good?'

Oh, yes. So good, she was prepared to beg him to continue. 'Please. Don't stop.' It was bliss, almost heaven, and she closed her eyes as his fingers worked a magic all on their own.

'Any ideas for tomorrow night?'

She heard the lazy quality in his voice and smiled. 'You mean we have a free evening?'

'I can book dinner.'

'Don't,' she said at once. 'I'll pick up something.'

'I could do this much better if you lay down on the bed.'

Her senses were heightened, and her pulse began to quicken. 'That might prove dangerous.'

'Eventually,' Carlo agreed lazily. 'But there are advantages to a full body massage.'

Aysha's blood pressure moved up a notch. 'Are you seducing me?'

His soft laughter sounded deep and husky close to her ear. 'Am I succeeding?'

'I'll let you know,' she promised with wicked intent. 'In about an hour from now.'

'An hour?'

'The quality of the massage will govern your reward,' Aysha informed him solemnly, and he laughed as he swept her into his arms and carried her through to the bedroom.

To lay prone on towels as Carlo slowly smoothed aromatic oil over every inch of her body was sensual torture of the sweetest kind.

Whatever had made her think she'd last an hour? After thirty minutes the pleasure was so intense, it was all she could do not to roll onto her back and beg him to take her.

'I think,' she said between gritted teeth, 'that's enough.'

His fingertips smoothed up her thighs and lingered a hair's breadth away from the apex, then shaped each buttock before settling at her waist.

'You said an hour,' Carlo reminded her, and gently rolled her onto her back.

Aysha looked at him from beneath long-fringed

lashes. 'I'll make you pay,' she promised as liquid heat spilled through her veins.

He leaned down and took her mouth in a brief hard kiss. 'I'm counting on it.'

The sweet sorcery of his touch nearly sent her mad, and afterwards it was she who drove him to the brink, aware of those dark eyes watching her with an almost predatory alertness that gradually shifted and changed as she tried to break his control.

Desire, raw and primitive, tore through her body, and she felt bare, exposed, as her own fragile control shredded into a thousand pieces.

Aysha had no recollection of the tears that slowly spilled down each cheek until Carlo cupped her face and erased them with a single movement of his thumb.

His lips brushed hers, gently, back and forth, then angled in sensual possession.

Afterwards he simply held her until her breathing slowed and steadied into a regular beat, then he gently eased her to lie beside him and held her close through the night.

She barely stirred when he rose at eight, and he showered in a spare bathroom, then dressed and made breakfast.

The aroma of freshly brewed coffee stirred Aysha's senses, and she fought through the final mists of sleep into wakefulness.

'The tousled look suits you,' Carlo teased as he placed the tray down onto the bedside pedestal. Her cheeks were softly flushed, her eyes slumberous, the dilated pupils making them seem too large for her face.

'Hi.' She made an attempt to pull the sheet a little higher, and incurred his husky laughter.

'Your modesty is adorable, *cara*.'

'Breakfast in bed,' she murmured appreciatively. 'You've excelled yourself.'

He lowered his head and bestowed an open-mouthed kiss to the edge of her throat, teased the tender skin with his teeth, then trailed a path to the gentle swell of her breast.

'I aim to please.'

Oh, yes, he did that. She retained a very vivid memory of just how well he'd managed to please her. Not that it had been entirely one-sided… She'd managed to take him further towards the edge than before. One of these days…*nights*, she amended, she planned to tip him over and watch him free-fall.

'Naturally, your mind is more on food than me at this point, hmm?'

Go much lower, and I won't get to the food. 'Of course,' she offered demurely. 'I'm going to need stamina to make it through the day.'

'The bridal shower,' he mused. His eyes met hers, and she regarded him solemnly.

'Teresa wants the occasion to be memorable.'

Carlo sank down onto the bed. 'There's orange juice, and caffeine to kick-start the day.'

Together with toast, croissants, fruit preserve, cheese, wafer-thin slices of salami and prosciutto. A veritable feast.

Aysha slid up in the bed, paying careful attention

to keep the sheet tucked beneath her arms, and took the glass of juice from Carlo's extended hand. Next came the coffee, then a croissant with preserve, followed by a piece of toast folded in half over a layer of cheese and prosciutto.

'More coffee?'

She hesitated, checked the time, then shook her head. 'I said I'd be home around nine.'

Carlo stood to his feet and collected the tray. 'I'll take this downstairs.'

Ten minutes later she had showered, dressed and was ready to face the day. Light blue jeans sheathed her slim legs, hugged her hips, and she wore a fitted top that accentuated the delicate curve of her breasts.

She skirted the servery, reached up and planted a light kiss against the edge of his jaw. 'Thanks for breakfast.'

He caught her close and slanted his mouth over hers with a possession that wreaked havoc with her equilibrium. Then he eased the pressure and brushed his lips over the swollen contours of her own, lingered at one corner, then gently released her.

'I consider myself thanked.'

Her eyes felt too large, and she quickly blinked in an effort to clear her vision. That had been... 'cataclysmic' was a word that came immediately to mind. And passionate, definitely passionate.

Maybe she was beginning to scratch the surface of his control after all.

That thought stayed with her as she took the lift down to the underground car park, and during the few kilometres to her parents' home.

CHAPTER THREE

AYSHA'S four bridesmaids were the first to arrive, followed by Gianna and a few of Teresa's friends. Two aunts, three cousins, and a number of close friends.

There were beautifully wrapped gifts, much laughter, a little wine, some champagne, and the exchange of numerous anecdotes. Entertainment was provided by a gifted magician whose expertise in pulling at least a hundred scarves from his hat and jacket pockets had to be seen to be believed.

Coffee was served at three-thirty, and at four Teresa was summoned to the front door to accept the arrival of an unexpected guest.

The speed with which Lianna, Aysha' chief bridesmaid, joined Teresa aroused suspicion, and there was much laughter as a good-looking young man entered the lounge.

'You didn't—' Aysha began, and one look at Lianna, Arianne, Suzanne and Tessa was sufficient to determine that her four bridesmaids were as guilty as sin.

A portable tape-recorder was set on a coffee table, and when the music began he went into a series of choreographed movements as he began to strip.

It was a tastefully orchestrated act, as such acts went. The young man certainly had the frame, the

38

body, the muscles to execute the traditional bump-and-grind routine.

'You refused to let us give you a ladies' night out, so we had to do something,' Lianna confided with an impish grin as everyone began to leave.

'Fiend,' Aysha chastised with affectionate remonstrance. 'Wait until it's your turn.'

'What'll you do to top it, Aysha? Hire a group of male strippers?'

'Don't put thoughts into my head,' she threatened direly.

The caterers tidied and cleaned up, then left fifteen minutes later, and Aysha crossed to the table where a selection of gifts were on display.

From the intensely practical to the highly decorative, they were all beautiful and reflected the giver's personality. A smile curved her lips. Lianna's gift of a male stripper had been the wackiest.

'You had no idea of Lianna's surprise?' Teresa queried as she crossed to her side.

'None,' Aysha answered truthfully, and curved an arm around her mother's waist. 'Thanks, Mamma, for a lovely afternoon.'

'My pleasure.'

Aysha grinned unashamedly. 'Even the stripper?' she teased, and glimpsed the faint pink colour in her mother's cheeks.

'No comment.'

She began to laugh. 'All right, let's change the subject. What shall we do with these gifts?'

They set them on a table in one of the rooms Teresa had organised for displaying the wedding presents, and when that was done Aysha went up-stairs and changed into tailored trousers and matching silk top.

It was after six when she entered Carlo's pent-house apartment, and she crossed directly into the kitchen to deposit the carry-sack containing a selection of Chinese takeaways she'd collected *en route* from home.

'Let me guess. Chinese, Thai, Malaysian?' Carlo drawled as he entered the kitchen, and she directed him a winsome smile.

'Chinese. And I picked up some videos.'

'You have plans to spend a quiet night?'

She opened cupboards and extracted two plates, then collected cutlery. 'I think I've had enough excitement for the day.' And through last night.

'Care to elaborate on the afternoon?'

Her eyes sparkled with hidden devilry. 'Lianna ordered a male stripper.' She decided to tease him a little. 'He was young, *built*, and gorgeous.' She wrinkled her nose at him. 'Ask Gianna; she was there.'

'Indeed?' His eyes speared hers. 'Perhaps I need to hear more about this gorgeous hunk.'

Carlo had her heart, her soul. It never ceased to hurt that she didn't have his.

'Well...' She deliberated. 'There was the body to die for.' She ticked off each attribute with teasing relish. 'Longish hair, tied in this cute little ponytail, and when he let it free...wow, so sexy. No apparent body hair.' Her eyes sparkled with devilish humour. 'Waxing must be a pain...literally. And he had the cutest butt.'

Carlo's eyes narrowed fractionally, and she gave him an irrepressible grin. 'He stripped down to a thong bikini brief.'

'I imagine Teresa and Gianna were relieved.'

She tried hard not to laugh, and failed as a chuckle emerged. 'They appeared to enjoy the show.'

His lips twitched. 'An unexpected show, unless I'm mistaken.'

'Totally,' she agreed, and viewed the various cartons she'd deposited on the servery. 'Let's be *really* decadent,' she suggested lightly. 'And watch a video while we eat.'

The first was a thriller, the acting sufficiently superb to bring an audience to the edge of their seats, and the second was a comedy about a wedding where everything that could go wrong, did. It was funny, slapstick, and over the top, but in amongst the frivolity was a degree of reality Aysha could identify with.

In between videos she'd tidied cartons and rinsed plates, made coffee, and now she carried the cups through to the kitchen.

She felt pleasantly tired as she ascended the stairs to the main bedroom, and after a quick shower she slid between the sheets to curl comfortably in the circle of Carlo's arms with her head pillowed against his chest.

Within minutes she fell asleep, and she was unaware of the light touch as Carlo's lips brushed the top of her head, or the feather-light trail of his fingers as they smoothed a path over the surface of her skin.

They woke late, lingered over breakfast, then took

Giuseppe's cabin cruiser for a day trip up the
Hawkesbury River. They returned as the sun set in a
glorious flare of fading colour and the cityscape
sprang to life with a myriad of pin-prick lights.

Magic, Aysha reflected, as the wonder of nature
and manmade technology overwhelmed her.

Tomorrow the shopping would begin in earnest as
Teresa initiated the first of her many lists of Things
to Do.

'Mamma, is this really necessary?'

As shopping went, it had been a profitable day
with regard to acquisitions. Teresa, it appeared, was
bent on spending money... *Serious* money.

'You're the only child I have,' Teresa said simply.
'Don't deny me the pleasure of giving my daughter
the best wedding I can provide.'

Aysha tucked her hand through her mother's arm
and hugged it close. 'Don't rain on my parade, huh?'

'Exactly.'

'OK. The dress, if you insist. But...' She paused,
and cast Teresa a stern look. 'That's it,' she admonished.

'For today.'

They joined the exodus of traffic battling to exit
choked city streets, and made it to Vaucluse at five-
thirty, leaving very little time to shower, change and
be ready to leave the house at six thirty.

'You go on ahead,' Teresa suggested. 'I'll put
these in the room next to yours. We can sort through
them tomorrow.'

Aysha raced upstairs to her bedroom, then discarded her clothes and made for the shower. Minutes later she wound a towel round her slim curves, removed the excess moisture from her hair and wielded the hairdrier to good effect.

Basic make-up followed, then she crossed to the walk-in robe, cast a quick discerning eye over the carefully co-ordinated contents, and extracted a figure-hugging gown in black.

The hemline rested at mid-thigh, the overall length extended slightly by a wide border of scalloped lace. The design was sleeveless, backless, and cunningly styled to show a modest amount of cleavage. Thin shoulder straps ensured the gown stayed in place.

Sheer black pantyhose? Or should she settle for bare legs and almost non-existent thong bikini briefs? And very high stiletto-heeled pumps?

Minimum jewellery, she decided, and she'd sweep her hair into a casual knot atop her head.

Half an hour later she descended the stairs to the lower floor and entered the lounge. Teresa and Giuseppe were grouped together sharing a light aperitif.

Her father turned towards her, his expression a comedic mix of parental pride and male appreciation. Any hint of paternal remonstrance was absent, doubtless on the grounds that his beloved daughter was safely spoken for, on the verge of marriage, and therefore he had absolutely nothing to worry about.

Teresa, however, was something else. One glance was all it took for those dark eyes to narrow fractionally and the lips to thin. *Appearance* was everything, and tonight Aysha did not fit her mother's required image.

'Don't you think that's a little...?' Teresa paused delicately. 'Bold, darling?'

'Perhaps,' Aysha conceded, and directed her father a teasing glance. 'Papà?'

Giuseppe was well versed in the ways of mother and daughter, and sought a diplomatic response. 'I'm sure Carlo will be most appreciative.' He gestured towards a crystal decanter. 'Can I fix you a spritzer?'

She hadn't eaten much throughout the day, just nibbled on fresh fruit, sipped several glasses of water, and taken three cups of long black coffee. Alcohol would go straight to her head. 'I stopped by the kitchen when I arrived home and fixed some juice,' she declined gently. 'I'm fine.'

'Unless I'm mistaken, that's Carlo now.'

The light crunch of car tires, the faint clunk of a door closing, followed by the distant sound of melodic door chimes heralded his arrival, and within seconds their live-in housekeeper ushered him into the lounge.

Aysha crossed the room and caught hold of his hand, then offered her cheek for his kiss. It was a natural gesture, one that was expected, and only she heard the light teasing murmur close to her ear. 'Stunning.'

His arm curved round the back of her waist and he drew her with him as he moved to accept Teresa's greeting.

'A drink, Carlo?'

'I'll wait until dinner.'

It would be easy to lean in against him, and for a moment she almost did. Except there was no one to impress, and the evening lay ahead.

Giuseppe swallowed the remainder of his wine, and placed his glass down onto the tray. 'In that case, perhaps we should be on our way. Teresa?'

At that moment the phone rang, and Teresa frowned in disapproval. 'I hope that's not going to make us late.'

Not unless the call heralded something of dire consequence; there wasn't a chance. Aysha bit back on the mockery, and sensed her mother's words even before they were uttered.

'You and Carlo go on ahead. We won't be far behind you.'

Sliding into the passenger seat of the car was achieved with greater decorum than she expected, and she was in the process of fastening her seatbelt when Carlo moved behind the wheel.

A deft flick of his wrist and the engine purred to life. Almost a minute later they had traversed the curved driveway and were heading towards the city.

'Am I correct in assuming the dress is a desire to shock?'

Aysha heard the drawling voice, sensed the underlying cynicism tinged with humour, and turned to look at him. 'Does it succeed?'

She was supremely conscious of the amount of bare thigh showing, and she fought against the temptation to take hold of the hemline and attempt to tug it down.

He turned slightly towards her, and in that second

she was acutely aware of the darkness of his eyes, the faint curve of his mouth, the gleam of white teeth.

'Teresa didn't approve.'

'You know her so well,' she indicated wryly. 'Papà seemed to think you'd be appreciative.'

'Oh, I am,' Carlo declared. 'As I'm sure every other man in the room will be.'

She directed him a stunning smile. 'You say the nicest things.'

'Careful you don't overdo it, *cara*.'

'I'm aiming for brilliance.'

For one brief second her eyes held the faintest shadow, then it was gone. He lifted a hand and brushed light fingers down her cheek.

'A few hours, four at the most. Then we can leave.'

Yes, she thought sadly. And tomorrow it will start all over again. The shopping, fittings, social obligations. Each day it seemed to get worse. Fulfilling her mother's expectations, having her own opinions waved aside, the increasing tension. If only Teresa wasn't bent on turning everything into such a *production*.

Suburban Point Piper was a neighbouring suburb and took only minutes to reach.

Carlo turned between ornate wrought-iron gates and parked behind a stylish Jaguar. Four, no, five cars lined the curved driveway, and Aysha experienced a moment's hesitation as she moved towards the few steps leading to the main entrance.

There had been countless precedents of an evening

such as this, Aysha reflected as she accepted a light wine and exchanged pleasantries with fellow guests.

Beautiful home, gracious host and hostess. The requisite mingling over drinks for thirty minutes before dinner. Any number between ten to twenty guests, a splendid table. An exquisite floral centrepiece. The guests carefully selected to complement each other.

'Carlo, *darling*.'

Aysha heard the greeting, recognised the sultry feminine purr, and turned slowly to face one of several women who had worked hard to win Carlo's affection.

Now that the wedding was imminent, most had retired gracefully from the hunt. With the exception of Nina di Salvo.

The tall, svelte fashion consultant was a *femme fatale*, wealthy, widowed, and selectively seeking a husband of equal wealth and social standing.

Nina was admired, even adored, by men. For her style, beauty and wit. Women recognised the predatory element existent, and reacted accordingly.

'Aysha,' Nina acknowledged. 'You look…' The pause was deliberate. 'A little tired. All the preparations getting to you, darling?'

Aysha summoned a winsome smile and honed the proverbial dart. 'Carlo doesn't permit me enough sleep.'

Nina's eyes narrowed fractionally, then she leaned towards Carlo, brushed her lips against his cheek, and lingered a fraction too long. 'How are you, *caro*?'

'Nina.' Carlo was too skilful a strategist to give anything away, and too much the gentleman to do other than observe the social niceties.

He handled Nina's overt affection with practised ease and minimum body contact. Although Nina more than made up for his reticence, Aysha noted, wondering just how he regarded the glamorous brunette's attention.

She saw his smile, heard his laughter, and felt the tender care of his touch. Yet how much was a façade?

'Do get me a drink, *caro*,' Nina commanded lightly. 'You know what I like.'

Oh, my, Aysha determined as Carlo excused himself and made his way to the bar. This could turn into one hell of an evening.

'I hope you don't expect fidelity, darling,' Nina warned quietly. 'Carlo has...' she paused fractionally '...certain needs not every woman would be happy to fulfil.'

Cut straight to the chase, a tiny voice prompted. 'Really, Nina? I'll broach that with him.'

'What will you broach, and with whom?'

Speak of the devil... Aysha turned towards him as he handed Nina a slim flute of champagne.

Quite deliberately she tilted her chin and gazed into his dark gleaming eyes with amused serenity. She'd had plenty of *smile* practice, and she proffered one of pseudo-sincerity. 'Nina expressed her concern regarding my ability to fulfil your needs.'

Carlo's expression didn't change, and Aysha

dimly registered that as a poker player he would be almost without equal.

'Really?'

It seemed difficult to comprehend a single word could hold such a wealth of meaning. Or the quiet tone convey such a degree of cold anger.

The tension was evident, although Carlo hadn't moved so much as a muscle. Anyone viewing the scene would assume the three of them were engaged in pleasant conversation.

'Perhaps Nina and I should get together and compare notes,' Aysha declared with wicked humour.

Nina lifted the flute to her lips and took a delicate sip. 'What for, darling? My notes are bound to be far more extensive than yours.'

Wasn't that the truth? She caught a glimpse of aqua silk and saw Teresa and Giuseppe enter the room, and wasn't sure whether to be relieved or disappointed at their appearance.

Her mother would assess Nina's presence in an instant, and seek to break up their happy little threesome.

Aysha began a silent countdown… Three minutes to greet their hosts, another three to acknowledge a few friends.

'There you are, darling.'

Right on cue. Aysha turned towards her mother and proffered an affectionate smile. 'Mamma. You weren't held up too long, after all.' She indicated the tall brunette. 'You remember Nina?'

Teresa eyes sharpened, although her features bore

a charming smile. 'Of course. How nice to see you again.'

A lie, if ever there was one. Polite society, Aysha mused. Good manners hid a multitude of sins. If she were to obey her base instincts, she'd tell Nina precisely where to go and how to complete the journey.

There was an inherent need to show her claws, but this wasn't the time or place.

'Shall we go in to dinner?'

A respite, Aysha determined with a sense of relief. Unless their hostess had chosen unwisely and placed Nina in close proximity.

The dining room was large, the focal point being the perfectly set table positioned beneath a sparkling crystal chandelier of exquisite design.

The scene resembled a photograph lifted out of the social pages of a glossy magazine. It seemed almost a sacrilege for guests to spoil the splendid placement precision.

Although there were, she noted, a waiter and waitress present to serve allotted food portions at prearranged intervals. Likewise the imported wine would flow, but not at a rate that was considered too free.

Respectability, decorum, an adherence to exemplary good manners, with carefully orchestrated conversational topics guaranteed to stimulate the guests' interest.

Aysha caught Nina's gleam of silent mockery, and had an insane desire to disrupt it. A little, just a little.

Nothing overt, she decided as she selected a spoon

and dipped it into the part-filled bowl of mushroom soup.

The antipasto offered a superb selection, and the serving of linguini with its delicate cream and mushroom sauce couldn't be faulted.

'Could you have the waiter pour me some wine, darling?' Aysha cast Carlo a stunning smile. She rarely drank alcohol, and he knew it. However, she figured she had sufficient food in her stomach to filter the effect if she sipped it slowly.

Her request resulted in a slanted eyebrow, and she offered him the sweetest smile. 'Please.'

If he hesitated, or attempted to censure her in any way, she'd kill him.

A glance was all it took for the waiter to fill her glass, and seconds later she lifted the crystal flute to her lips and savoured the superb Chablis.

Giuseppe smiled, and lifted his own glass in a silent salute.

A few glasses of fine wine, good food, pleasant company. It took little to please her father. He was a man of simple tastes. He had worked hard all his life, achieved more than most men; he owned a beautiful home, had chosen a good woman as his wife, and together they had raised a wonderful daughter who was soon to be married to the son of his best friend and business partner. His life was good. Very good.

Dear Papà, Aysha thought fondly as the wine began to have a mellowing effect. He was everything a father should be, and more. A man who had managed to blend the best of the Old Country with the best of the new. The result was a miscible blend of wisdom and warmth tempered with pride and passion.

The main course was served...tender breast of chicken in a delicate basil sauce with an assortment of vegetables.

Her elbow touched Carlo's arm, and she lowered her hand to her lap as she unconsciously toyed with her napkin. His thigh was close to her own. Very close.

Slowly, very slowly, she moved her leg until it rested against his. It would be so easy to glide her foot over his. With extreme care, she cautioned silently. Stiletto heels as fine as hers should almost be registered as a dangerous weapon. The idea was to arouse his attention, not cause him an injury.

Gently she positioned the toe of her shoe against his ankle, then inched it slowly back and forth without moving her heel, thereby making it impossible for anyone to detect what she was doing.

This could be fun, she determined as she let her fingers slide towards his thigh. A butterfly touch, fleeting.

Should she be more daring? Perhaps run the tip of her manicured fingernail down the outer seam of the trousered leg so close to her own? Maybe even...

Ah, that brought a reaction. Slight, but evident, nonetheless. And the slight but warning squeeze of his fingers as they caught hold of her own.

Aysha met his gaze fearlessly as he turned towards her, and she glimpsed the musing indolence apparent beneath the gleaming warmth of those dark brown depths.

Without missing a beat, he lifted her hand to his lips and kissed each finger in turn, watching the way her eyes dilated in startled surprise. Then he returned her hand to rest on his thigh, tracing a slow pattern over the fine bones, aware of her slight tremor as he deliberately forestalled her effort to pull free.

It was fortunate they were between courses. Aysha looked at the remaining wine in her glass, and opted for chilled water. Wisdom decreed the need for a clear head. Each brush of his fingers sent flame licking through her veins, and she clenched her hand, then dug her nails into hard thigh muscle in silent entreaty.

She experienced momentary relief when Carlo released her hand, only to suppress a faint gasp as she felt his fingers close over her thigh.

CHAPTER FOUR

AYSHA reached for her glass and took a sip of iced water, and cast the table's occupants a quick, encompassing glance.

Her eyes rested briefly on Nina, witnessed her hard, calculating glance before it was quickly masked, and felt a shiver glide down the length of her spine.

Malevolence, no matter how fleeting, was disconcerting. Envy and jealousy in others were unenviable traits, and something she'd learned to deal with from a young age. It had accelerated with her engagement to Carlo. Doubtless it would continue long after the marriage.

She wanted love...desperately. But she'd settle for fidelity. Even the thought that he might look seriously at another woman made it feel as if a hand took hold of her heart and squeezed until it bled.

'What do you think, Aysha?'

Oh, hell. It wasn't wise to allow distraction to interfere with the thread of social conversation. Especially not when you were a guest of honour.

She looked at Carlo with a silent plea for help, and met his humorous gaze.

'Luisa doesn't agree I should keep our honeymoon destination a surprise.'

A second was all it took to summon a warm smile.

'I need to pack warm clothes.' Her eyes gleamed and a soft laugh escaped her lips. 'That's all I know.'

'Europe. The snowfields?' The older woman's eyes twinkled. 'Maybe North America. Canada?'

'I really have no idea,' Aysha declared.

Dessert comprised individual caramelised baskets filled with segments of fresh fruit served with brandied cream.

'Sinful,' Aysha declared quietly as she savoured a delectable mouthful.

'I shouldn't, but I will,' Luisa uttered ruefully. 'Tomorrow I'll compensate with fresh juice for breakfast and double my gym workout.'

Teresa, she noted, carefully removed the cream, speared a few segments of fruit, and left the candied basket. As mother of the bride, she couldn't afford to add even a fraction of a kilo to her svelte figure.

It was half an hour before the hostess requested they move into the lounge for coffee.

Aysha declined the very strong espresso brew and opted for a much milder blend with milk. The men took it short and sweet, added *grappa*, and converged together to exchange opinions on anything from *bocce* to the state of the government.

Argue, Aysha amended fondly, all too aware that familiar company, good food, fine wine all combined to loosen the male Italian tongue and encourage reminiscence.

She loved to listen to the cadence of their voices as they lapsed into the language of their birth. It was expressive, accompanied by the philosophical shrug of masculine shoulders, the hand movements to emphasise a given point.

'Giuseppe is in his element.'

Aysha mentally prepared herself as she turned to face Nina. One glance was all it took to determine Nina's manner was the antithesis of friendly.

'Is there any reason why he shouldn't be?'

'The wedding is a major coup.' The smile didn't reach her eyes. 'Congratulations, darling. I should have known you'd pull it off.'

Aysha inclined her head. 'Thank you, Nina. I'll take that as a compliment.'

There was no one close enough to overhear the quiet exchange. Which was a pity. It merely offered Nina the opportunity to aim another poisoned dart.

'How does it feel to be second-best? And know your inherited share in the family firm is the sole reason for the marriage?'

'Considering Carlo is due to inherit his share in the family firm, perhaps you should ask him the same question.'

Successfully fielded. Nina didn't like it. Her eyes narrowed, and the smile moved up a notch in artificial brilliance.

'You're the one who has to compete with Bianca's ghost,' Nina offered silkily, and Aysha waited for the punchline. 'All cats are alike in the dark, darling. Didn't you know?'

Oh, my. This was getting dirty. 'Really?' Her cheeks hurt from keeping a smile pinned in place. 'Perhaps you should try it with the lights on, some time.'

As scores went, it hardly rated a mention. And the victory was short-lived, for it was doubtful Nina would allow anyone to gain an upper hand for long.

'Aysha.' Luisa appeared at her side. 'Teresa has just been telling me about the flowers for the church. Orchids make a lovely display, and the colour combination will be exquisite.'

She was a guest of honour, the focus her wedding day. It was easy to slip into animated mode and discuss details. Only the wedding dress and the cake were taboo.

Except talking and answering questions merely reinforced how much there still was to do, and how essential the liaison with the wedding organiser Teresa had chosen to co-ordinate everything.

The invitation responses were all in, the seating arrangements were in their final planning stage. According to Teresa, any one of the two little flower girls and two page boys could fall victim to a malicious virus, or contract mumps, measles or chicken pox. Alternately, one or all could become paralysed with fright on the day and freeze half-way down the aisle.

At ages three and four, anything was possible.

'My flower girl scattered rose petals down the aisle perfectly at rehearsal, only to take three steps forward on the day, tip the entire contents of the basket on the carpet, and run crying to her mother,' recalled one of the guests.

Aysha remembered the incident, and another wedding where the page boy had carried the satin ring-cushion with such pride and care, then refused to give it up at the appropriate moment. A tussle had ensued, followed by tears and a tantrum.

It had been amusing at the time, and she really didn't care if one of the children made a mistake, or missed their cue. It was a wedding, not a movie which relied on talented actors to perform a part.

Her mother, she knew, didn't hold the same view.

Aysha glanced towards Carlo, and felt the familiar pull of her senses. Dark, well-groomed hair, a strong shaped head. Broad shoulders accentuated by perfect tailoring.

A slight inclination of his head brought his profile into focus. The wide, sculpted bone structure, the strong jaw. Well-defined cheekbones, and the glimpse of his mouth.

Fascinated, she watched each movement, her eyes clinging to the shape of him, aware just how he felt without the constriction of clothes. She was familiar with his body's musculature, the feel and scent of his skin.

At this precise moment she would have given anything to cross to his side and have his arm curve round her waist. She could lean in against him, and savour the anticipation of what would happen when they were alone.

He was fond of her, she knew. There were occasions when he completely disconcerted her by appearing to read her mind. But that special empathy between two lovers wasn't there. No matter how desperately she wanted it to be.

Did he know she could tell the moment he entered a room? She didn't have to see him, or hear his voice. A developed sixth sense alerted her of his presence, and her body reacted as if he'd reached out and touched her.

All the fine hairs moved on the surface of her skin, and the back of her neck tingled in recognition.

Damnable, she cursed silently.

It was after eleven when the first of the guests took their leave, and almost midnight when Teresa and Giuseppe indicated an intention to depart.

Aysha thanked their hosts, smiled until her face hurt, and quivered slightly when Carlo caught hold of her hand as they followed her parents down the steps to their respective cars.

'Goodnight, darling.' Teresa leaned forward and brushed her daughter's cheek.

Aysha stood as Carlo unlocked the car, then she slid into the passenger seat, secured her belt, and leaned back against the headrest as Carlo fired the engine.

'Tired?'

She was conscious of his discerning glance seconds before he set the car in motion.

'A little.' She closed her eyes, and let the vehicle's movement and the quietness of the night seep into her bones.

'Do you want me to take you home?'

A silent sigh escaped her lips, and she effected a rueful smile. 'Now there's a question. Which home are you talking about? Yours, mine or ours?'

'The choice is yours.'

Was it? The new house was completely furnished, and awaiting only the final finishing touches. Her own bedroom beckoned, but that was fraught with implication Teresa would query in the morning.

Besides, she coveted the touch of his hands, the feel of his body, his mouth devastating her own.

Then she could pretend that good lovemaking was a substitute for *love*. That no one was meant to have it all, and in Carlo, their future together, she had more than her share.

'The penthouse.'

Carlo didn't comment, and she wondered if it would have made any difference if she'd said *home*.

An ache started up in the pit of her stomach, and intensified until it became a tangible pain as he slowed the car, de-activated the security system guarding entrance to the luxury apartment building, then eased down into the underground car park and brought the vehicle to a halt in his allotted space.

They rode the lift to the top floor in silence, and inside the apartment Aysha went willingly into his arms, his bed, an eager supplicant to anything he chose to bestow.

It was just after nine when Aysha eased the Porsche into an empty space in an inner city car park building, and within minutes she stepped off the escalator and emerged onto the pavement.

It was a beautiful day, the sky a clear azure with hardly a cloud in sight, and the sun's warmth bathed all beneath it with a balmy summer brilliance. Her needs were few, the purchases confined to four boutiques, three of which were within three blocks of each other.

Two hours, tops, she calculated, then she'd meet her bridesmaids for lunch. At two she had a hair appointment, followed by a manicure, and tonight she was attending an invitation-only preview of the first in a series of foreign films scheduled to appear over the next month.

Each evening there was something filling their social engagement diary. Although last night when Carlo had suggested dining out she'd insisted they eat in...and somehow the decision hadn't got made one way or the other. She retained a vivid recollection of *why*, and a secret smile curved her lips as she slid her sunglasses into place.

Selecting clothes was something she enjoyed, and she possessed a natural flair for colour, fashion and design.

Aysha had three hours before she was due to join her bridesmaids for lunch, and she intended to utilise that time to its fullest potential.

It was nice to be able to take time, instead of having to rush in a limited lunch-hour. Selective shopping was fun, and she gradually added to a growing collection of glossy carry-bags.

Bags she should really dispense with before meeting the girls...which meant a walk back to the car park to deposit her purchases in the boot of her car.

Lianna, Arianne, Suzanne and Tessa were already seated when Aysha joined them. Two brunettes, a redhead, and a blonde. They'd attended school together, suffered through piano and ballet lessons, and, although their characters were quite different from each other, they shared an empathy that had firmed over the years as an unbreakable bond.

'You're late, but we forgive you,' Lianna began before Aysha was able to say a word. 'Of course, we do understand.' She offered one of her irrepressible smiles. 'You have serious shopping on the agenda.' She leaned forward. 'And your penance is to relay every little detail.'

'Let me order a drink first,' Aysha protested, and gave her order to a hovering waiter. 'Mineral water, slice of lemon, plenty of ice.'

'What did you buy to change into after the wedding?' Arianne quizzed, and Lianna pulled a face.

'Sweetheart, she won't *need* anything to wear after the wedding except skin.'

'Sure. But she should have something sheer and sexy to start off with,' Suzanne interceded.

'Honest, girls, can you see Carlo helping Aysha out of the wedding gown and into a nightgown? Come on, let's get real here!'

'Are you done?' Aysha queried, trying to repress a threatening laugh.

'Not yet,' Lianna declared blithely. 'You need to suffer a little pain for all the trouble we're going to for you.' She began counting them off on each finger. 'Dress fittings, shoe shopping, church rehearsals, child chaperoning, in church and out of it, organising the bridal shower, not to mention make-up sessions and hair stylists practising on our hair.' Her eyes sparkled with devilish laughter. 'For all of which our only reward is to kiss the groom.'

'Who said you get to do that?' Aysha queried with

mock seriousness. 'Married men don't kiss other women.'

'No kiss, we decorate the wedding car,' Lianna threatened.

'Are you ladies ready to order?'

'Yes,' they agreed in unison, and proceeded to completely confuse the poor young man who'd been assigned to their table.

'You're incorrigible,' Aysha chastised as soon as he'd disappeared towards the kitchen, and Lianna gave a conciliatory shrug.

'This is a *feel-good* moment, darling. The last of the great single-women luncheons. Saturday week you join the ranks of married ladies, while we, poor darlings, languish on the sideline searching for the perfect man. Of which, believe me, there are very few.' She paused to draw breath. 'If they look good, they sound terrible, or have disgusting habits, or verge towards violence, or, worst of all, have no money.'

Suzanne shook her head. 'Cynical, way too cynical.'

They ordered another round of drinks, then their food arrived.

'So, tell us, darling,' Lianna cajoled. 'Is Carlo as gorgeous in bed as he is out of it?'

'That's a bit below the belt,' Arianne protested, and Lianna grinned.

'Got it in one. Hey, if Aysha ditches him, I'm next in line.' She cast Aysha a wicked wink. 'Aren't you glad I'm your best friend?'

'Yes,' she responded simply. Loyalty and integrity

mattered, and Lianna possessed both, even if she was an irrepressible motor-mouth. The fun, the generous smile hid a childhood marred by tragedy.

'You haven't told us what you bought this morning.'

'You didn't give me a chance.'

'I'm giving it to you now,' Lianna insisted magnanimously, and Aysha laughed.

She needed the levity, and it was good, so good to relax and unwind among friends.

'What social event is scheduled for tonight? Dinner with family, the theatre, ballet, party? Or do you just get to stay home and go to bed with Carlo?'

'You have the cheek of old Nick,' Aysha declared, and caught Lianna's wicked smile.

'You didn't answer the question.'

'There's a foreign film festival on at the Arts Centre.'

'Ah, eclectic entertainment,' Arianne sighed wistfully. 'What are you going to wear?'

'Something utterly gorgeous,' Lianna declared, her eyes narrowing speculatively. 'Long black evening trousers or skirt, matching top, shoestring straps, and that exquisite beaded evening jacket you picked up in Hong Kong. Minimum jewellery.'

'OK.'

'*OK?* I'm in fashion, darling. What I've just described is considerably higher on the scale of gorgeous than just *OK*.'

'All right, I'll wear it,' Aysha conceded peaceably.

They skipped dessert, ordered coffee, and Aysha barely made her hair appointment on time.

'No dinner for me, Mamma. I'll just pick up some fruit. I had a late lunch,' she relayed via the mobile phone prior to driving home. With the way traffic was moving, it would be six before she reached Vaucluse. Which would leave her just under an hour to shower, dress, tend to her hair and make-up, and be at Carlo's apartment by seven-fifteen.

'*Bella,*' he complimented warmly as she used her key barely minutes after the appointed time.

Aysha could have said the same, for he looked devastatingly attractive attired in a dark evening suit, snowy white cotton shirt, and black bow tie. Arresting, she added, aware of her body's reaction to his appreciative appraisal. Heat flooded her veins, activating all her nerve-ends, as she felt the magnetic pull of the senses. It would be so easy just to hold out her arms and walk into his, then lift her face for his kiss. She wanted to, badly.

'Would you like a drink before we leave?'

Alcohol on a near-empty stomach wasn't a good idea, and she shook her head. 'No. Thanks.'

'How was lunch with the girls?'

A smile lifted the edges of her mouth, and her eyes gleamed with remembered pleasure. 'Great. Really great.'

Carlo caught hold of her hand and lifted it to his lips. 'I imagine Lianna was at her irrepressible best?'

'It was nice just to sit, relax and laugh a little.' Her smile widened, and her eyes searched his. 'Lianna is looking forward to kissing the groom.'

Carlo pulled back the cuff of his jacket and checked his watch. 'Perhaps we should be on our way. Traffic will be heavy, and parking probably a problem.'

It was a gala evening, and a few of the city's social scions numbered among the guests. The female contingent wore a small fortune in jewels and French designer gowns vied with those by their Italian equivalent.

Aysha mingled with fellow guests, nibbled from a proffered tray of hors d'oeuvres, and sipped orange juice with an added dash of champagne.

'Sorry I'm a little late. Parking was chaotic.'

Aysha recognised the light feminine voice and turned to greet its owner. 'Hello, Nina.'

The brunette let her gaze trail down to the tips of Aysha's shoes, then slowly back again in a deliberately provocative assessment. 'Aysha, how—pretty, you look. Although black is a little stark, darling, on one as fair as you.'

She turned towards Carlo, and her smile alone could have lit up the entire auditorium. '*Caro*, I really need a drink. Do you think you could organise one for me?'

Very good, Aysha silently applauded. Wait for the second Carlo is out of earshot, and…any minute now—

'I doubt you'll satisfy him for long.'

Aysha met that piercing gaze and held it. She even managed a faint smile. 'I'll give it my best shot.'

'There are distinct advantages in having the wedding ring, I guess.'

'I get to sleep with him?'

Nina's eyes glittered. 'I'd rather be his mistress

than his wife, darling. That way I get most of the pleasure, all of the perks, while you do the time.'

The temptation to throw the contents of her glass in Nina's face was almost irresistible.

'Champagne?' Carlo drawled, handing Nina a slim flute.

The electronic tone summoning the audience to take their seats came as a welcome intrusion, and she made her way into the theatre at Carlo's side, all too aware of Nina's presence as the usherette pointed them in the direction of their seats.

Now why wasn't she surprised when Nina's seat allocation adjoined theirs? Hardly coincidence, and Aysha gritted her teeth when Nina very cleverly ensured Carlo took the centre seat. Grr.

The lights dimmed, and her fingers stiffened as Carlo covered her hand with his own. Worse was the soothing movement of his thumb against the inside of her wrist.

So he sensed her tension. Good. He'd sense a lot more before the evening was over!

The theatre lights went out, technicolor images filled the screen, and the previews of forthcoming movies showed in relatively quick sequence. The main feature was set in Paris, the French dubbed into English, and it was a dark movie, *noir*, with subjective nuances, no comedy whatsoever. Aysha found it depressing, despite the script, directorship and acting having won several awards.

The final scene climaxed with particular violence, and when the credits faded and the lights came on she saw Nina withdraw a hand from Carlo's forearm.

Aysha threw her an icy glare, glimpsed the glittering satisfaction evident, and wanted to scream.

She turned towards the aisle and moved with the flow of exiting patrons, aware, as if she was a disembodied spectator, that Nina took full advantage of the crowd situation to press as close to Carlo as decently possible.

They reached the auditorium foyer, and Aysha had to stand with a polite smile pinned to her face as the patrons were served coffee, offered cheese and biscuits or minuscule pieces of cake.

'Why don't we go on to a nightclub?' Nina suggested. 'It's not late.'

And watch you attempt to dance and play kissy-face with Carlo? Aysha demanded silently. Not if I have anything to do with it!

'Don't let us stop you,' Carlo declined smoothly as he curved an arm along the back of Aysha's waist. Tense, definitely tense. He wanted to bend his head and place a placating kiss to the curve of her neck, then look deep into those smoky grey eyes and silently assure her she had nothing whatsoever to worry about.

A slight smile curved his lips. Nina saw it, and misinterpreted its source.

'The music is incredible.' She tucked her hand through his arm, and cajoled with the guile of a temptress. 'You'll enjoy it.'

'No,' he declined in a silky voice as he carefully disengaged her hand. 'I won't.'

Nina recognised defeat when she saw it, and she

lifted her shoulders with an elegant shrug. 'If you must miss out...'

His raised eyebrow signalled her departure, and she swept him a deep sultry glance. 'Another time, maybe.'

Aysha drew a deep breath, then released it slowly. Of all the nerve! She lifted her cup and took a sip of ruinously strong coffee. It would probably keep her awake half the night, but right at this precise moment she didn't give a damn.

'Carlo, *come stai*?'

A business acquaintance, whose presence she welcomed with considerable enthusiasm. The man looked mildly stunned as she enquired about his wife, his children, their schooling and their achievements.

'You overwhelmed him,' Carlo declared with deceptive indolence, and she fixed him with a brilliant smile.

'His arrival was timely,' she assured him sweetly. 'I was about to hit you.'

'In public?'

She drew in a deep breath, and studied his features for several long seconds. 'This is not a time for levity.'

'Nina bothers you?'

Aysha forced herself to hold his gaze. 'She never misses an opportunity to be wherever we happen to go.'

His eyes narrowed fractionally. 'You think I don't know that?'

'Were you ever lovers?' she demanded, and a faint

chill feathered across the surface of her skin as she waited for his response.

'No.'

The words tripped out before she could stop them. 'You're quite sure about that?'

Carlo was silent for several seconds, then he ventured silkily, 'I've never been indiscriminate with the few women who've shared my bed. Believe me, Nina didn't number among them.' He took her cup and placed it together with his own on a nearby table. 'Shall we leave?'

He was angry, but then so was she, and she swept him a glittering look from beneath mascaraed lashes. 'Let's do that.'

Their passage to the car wasn't swift as they paused momentarily to chat to fellow patrons whom they knew or were acquainted with.

'Your silence is ominous,' Carlo remarked with droll humour as he eased the Mercedes into the flow of traffic.

'I'm going with the saying…*if you can't find anything nice to say, it's better to say nothing at all.*'

'I see.'

No, you don't. You couldn't possibly know how terrified I am of not being able to hold your interest. Petrified that one day you'll find someone else, and I'll be left a broken shell of my former self.

The drive from the city to Rose Bay was achieved in a relatively short space of time, and Carlo cleared security at his apartment underground car park, then manoeuvred the car into his allotted space.

Aysha released the door-clasp, slid to her feet,

closed the door, and moved the few steps to her car.

'What are you doing?'

'I would have thought that was obvious. I'm going home.'

'Your keys are in the apartment,' Carlo said mildly.

Dammit, so they were. 'In that case, I'll go get them.'

She turned and stalked towards the bank of lifts, stabbed the call button, and barely contained her impatience as she waited for it to arrive.

'Don't you think you're overreacting?'

There was something in his voice she failed to recognise, although some deep, inner sixth sense did and sent out a red alert. 'Not really.'

The doors slid open and she stepped into the cubicle, jabbed the top panel button, and stood in icy silence as they were transported to the uppermost floor.

Carlo unlocked the apartment door, and she swept in ahead of him, located the keys where she'd put them on a table in the foyer, and collected them.

'Your parents aren't expecting you back tonight.'

It didn't help that he was right. 'So I'll ring them.'

He noted the proud tilt of her chin, the firm set of her mouth. 'Stay.'

Her eyes flared. 'I'd prefer to go home.' Nina's vitriolic words had provided too vivid an image to easily dispel.

'I'll drive you.'

The inflexibility evident in his voice sent chills

scudding down the length of her spine. 'The hell you will.'

His features hardened, and a muscle tensed at the side of his jaw. 'Try to walk out of this apartment, and see how far you get.'

Aysha allowed her gaze to travel the length of his body, and back again. He had the height, the sheer strength to overcome any evasive tactics she might employ.

'Brute force, Carlo? Isn't that a little drastic?'

'Not when your well-being and safety are at stake.'

Her chin tilted in a gesture of defiance. 'Somehow that doesn't quite add up, does it?' She held up her hand as he began to speak. 'Don't.' Her eyes held a brilliant sheen that was a mixture of anger, pride, and pain. 'At least let there be honesty between us.'

'I have never been dishonest with you.'

She felt sick inside, a dreadful gnawing emptiness that ripped away any illusions she might have had that affection and caring on his part were enough.

Without a further word she turned and walked towards the front door, released the locking mechanism, then took the few steps necessary to reach the bank of lifts.

Please, *please* let there be one waiting, she silently begged as she depressed the call button.

The following twenty seconds were among the longest in her life, and she gave an audible sigh of relief when the heavy stainless steel doors slid open.

Aysha stepped inside and turned to jab the appropriate floor panel, only to gasp with outraged indignation as Carlo stepped into the cubicle.

'Get out.'

Dark eyes lanced hers, mercilessly hard and resolute. 'I can drive you, or follow behind in my car.' The ruthlessness intensified. 'Choose.'

The lift doors slid closed, and the cubicle moved swiftly down towards the car park.

'Go to hell.'

His smile held little humour. 'That wasn't an option.'

'Unfortunately.'

The flippant response served to tighten his expression into a grim mask, and his anger was a palpable entity.

'Believe you wouldn't want me to take you there.' His drawl held a silky threat that sent shivers scudding down the length of her spine.

The doors whispered open, and without a word she preceded him into the huge concrete cavern. Her car was parked next to his, and she widened the distance between them, conscious of her heels clicking against the concrete floor.

Carlo crossed to the Mercedes, unlocked the passenger door, and held it open. 'Get in.'

Damned if she'd obey his dictum. 'I'll need my car in the morning.'

His expression remained unchanged. 'I'll collect you.'

Aysha felt like stamping her foot. 'Or I can have Teresa drop me, or take a cab, or any one of a few other options.' Her eyes were fiery with rebellion. 'Don't patronise me, dammit!'

It had been a long night, fraught with moments of sheer anger, disillusionment, and introspective rationalisation. None of which had done much to ease the heartache or the sense of betrayal. Each of which she'd examined in detail, only to silently castigate herself for having too high an expectation of a union based solely in reality.

Worse, for allowing Nina's deviousness to undermine her own ambivalent emotions. Nina's success focused on Aysha's insecurity, and it irked unbearably.

Carlo watched the fleeting emotions chase across her expressive features and divined each and every one of them.

'Get in the car, *cara*.'

His gentle tone was almost her undoing, and she fought against the sudden prick of tears. Damn him. She wanted to maintain her anger. Lash out, verbally and physically, until the rage was spent.

Conversely, she needed his touch, the soothing quality of those strong hands softly brushing her skin, the feel of his mouth on hers as the sensual magic wove its own spell.

She wanted to re-enter the lift and have it transport them back to his apartment. Most of all, she wanted to lose herself in his loving, then fall asleep in his arms with the steady beat of his heart beneath her cheek.

Yet pride prevented her from taking that essential

step, just as it locked the voice in her throat. She felt raw, and emotionally at odds.

Did most brides suffer this awful ambivalence? *Get real*, a tiny voice reminded her. You don't represent *most* brides, and while you have the groom's affection, it's doubtful he'll ever gift you his unconditional love.

With a gesture indicating silent acquiescence she slid into the passenger seat, reached for the safety belt as Carlo closed the door, and fastened it as he crossed in front of the vehicle. Seconds later he fired the engine and cruised up the ramp leading to street level.

'Call your parents.'

Aysha reached into her purse and extracted the small mobile phone, and keyed in the appropriate digits.

Giuseppe answered on the third ring. 'Aysha? Something is wrong?'

'No, Papà. I'll be home in about fifteen minutes. Can you fix security?'

Thank heavens it wasn't Teresa who'd answered, for her mother would have fired off a string of questions to rival the Spanish Inquisition.

Aysha ignored Carlo's brief encompassing glance as the car whispered along the suburban street, and she closed her eyes against the image of her mother slipping on a robe in preparation for a maternal chat the instant Aysha entered the house.

A silent laugh rose and died in her throat. At this precise moment she didn't know which scenario she preferred... The emotive discussion she'd just had with Carlo, or the one she was about to have with Teresa.

Aysha had no sooner stepped inside the door than her mother launched into a series of questions, and it was easier to fabricate than spell out her own insecurities.

She justified her transgression by qualifying Teresa had enough on her plate, and nothing could be achieved by the confidence.

'Are you sure there is nothing bothering you?' Teresa persisted.

'No, Mamma.' Inspiration was the mother of invention, and she used it shamelessly. 'I forgot to take the samples I need to match up the shoes tomorrow, so I thought I'd come home.'

'You didn't quarrel with Carlo?'

Quarrel wasn't exactly the word she would have chosen to describe their altercation. 'Why would I do that?' Aysha countered.

'I'll make coffee.'

All she wanted to do was go to bed. 'Don't bother making it for me.'

'You're going upstairs now?'

'Goodnight, Mamma,' she bade gently. 'I'll see you in the morning.'

'Gianna and I will meet you for lunch tomorrow.' She mentioned a restaurant. 'I'll book a table for one o'clock.'

She leaned forward and brushed lips to her mother's cheek. 'That sounds nice.'

Without a further word she turned and made for the stairs, and in her room she slowly removed her clothes, cleansed her face of make-up, then slid in between the sheets.

CHAPTER FIVE

'I'LL be there in half an hour,' Carlo declared as Aysha took his call early next morning. 'Don't argue,' he added before she had a chance to say a word.

Conscious that Teresa sat within hearing distance as they shared breakfast she found it difficult to give anything other than a warm and friendly response.

'Thanks,' she managed brightly. 'I'll be ready.' She replaced the receiver, then drained the rest of her coffee. 'That was Carlo,' she relayed. 'I'll go change.'

'Will you come back here, or go straight into the city?'

'The city. I need to choose crockery and cutlery for the house.' Pots and pans, roasting dishes. Each day she tried to accumulate some of the necessities required in setting up house. 'I may as well make an early start.'

In her room, she quickly shed shorts and top and selected a smart straight skirt in ivory linen, added a silk print shirt and matching jacket, slid her feet into slim-heeled pumps, tended to her hair and make-up, and was downstairs waiting when Carlo's Mercedes slid to a halt outside the front door.

Aysha drew a calming breath, then she walked out to the car and slipped into the passenger seat. 'There was no need for you to collect me,' she assured him, conscious of the look of him, the faint aroma of his cologne.

'There was every need,' he drawled silkily as he sent the car forward.

'I don't want to fight with you,' she said ingenuously, and he spared her a swift glance.

'Then don't.'

A disbelieving laugh escaped her throat. 'Suddenly it doesn't seem that easy.'

'Nina is a woman who thrives on intrigue and innuendo.' Carlo's voice was hard, his expression an inscrutable mask.

Oh, yes, Aysha silently agreed. And she's so very good at it. 'She wants *you*.'

'I'm already spoken for, remember?'

'Ah, now there's the thing. Nina abides by the credo of *all being fair in love and war*.'

'And this is shaping up as war?'

You'd better believe it! 'You're the prize, *darling*,' she mocked, and incurred his dark glance.

'Yours.'

'You have no idea how gratifying it is to hear you say that.'

'Cynicism doesn't suit you.' Carlo slanted her a slight smile, and she raised one eyebrow in mocking acquiescence.

'Shall we change the subject?'

He negotiated an intersection, then turned into Rose Bay.

'I've booked a table for dinner tonight. I'll collect you at six.'

They'd had tickets for tonight's première performance by the Russian *corps de ballet* for a month. How could she not have remembered?

The remainder of the short drive was achieved in silence, and Carlo deposited her beside her car, then left as she slid in behind the wheel of the Porsche.

City traffic was horrific at this hour of the morning, and it was after nine when Aysha emerged onto the inner city street.

First stop was a major department store two blocks distant, and she'd walked less than half a block when her mobile phone rang.

She automatically retrieved the unit from her bag and heard Teresa's voice, pitched high in distress.

'Aysha? I've just had a call from the bridal boutique. Your headpiece has arrived from Paris, but it's the wrong one!'

She closed her eyes, then opened them again. It had taken a day of deliberation before making the final choice… How long ago? A month? Now the order had been mixed up. Great. 'OK, Mamma. Let's not panic.'

Her mother's voice escalated. 'It was perfect, just perfect. There wasn't another to compare with it.'

'I'll go sort it out.' A phone call from the boutique to the manufacturer in Paris, and the use of a courier service should see a successful result.

Aysha should have known it couldn't be that simple.

'I've already done that,' the boutique owner relayed. 'No joy, unfortunately. They don't have another in stock. The design is intricate, the seed pearls needed are held up heaven knows where, and the gist of it is, we need to choose something else.'

'OK, let's do it.' It took an hour to select, ascertain the order could be filled and couriered within the week.

'That's definite,' the vendeuse promised.

Now why didn't that reassure her? Possibly because she'd heard the same words before.

An hour later she had to concede there were diverse gremlins at work, for the white embroidered stockings ordered hadn't arrived. The lace suspender belt had, but it didn't match the garter belt, as it was supposed to do.

Teresa would consider it a catastrophe. Aysha merely drew in a deep breath, ascertained the order might be correctly filled in time, decided *might* wasn't good enough, and opted to select something else with a guaranteed delivery.

It was after midday when she collected the last carry-bag and added it to the collection she held in each hand. Shoes? Did she have time if she was to meet Teresa and Gianna at Double Bay for lunch at one? She could always phone and say she'd be ten or fifteen minutes late.

With that thought in mind she entered the Queen Victoria building and made her way towards the shoe shop.

It was a beautiful old building, historically preserved, and undoubtedly heritage-listed. Aysha loved the ambience, the blend of old and modern, and she admired a shop display as she rode the escalator to the first floor.

She'd only walked a few steps when an exquisite bracelet showcased in a jeweller's window caught her eye, and she paused to admire it. The gold links were of an unusual design, and each link held a half-carat diamond.

'I'm sure you'll only have to purr prettily in Carlo's ear, and he'll buy it for you.'

Aysha recognised the voice and turned slowly to face the young woman at her side. 'Nina,' she acknowledged with a polite smile, and watched as Nina's expression became positively feline.

She took in the numerous carry-bags and their various emblazoned logos. 'Been shopping?'

Aysha effected a faint shrug. 'A few things I needed to collect.'

'I was going to ring and invite you to share a coffee with me. Can you manage a few minutes now?'

The last thing she wanted was a tête-à-tête with Nina…with or without the coffee. 'I really don't have time. I'm meeting Teresa and Gianna for lunch.'

'In that case…' She slid open her attaché case, extracted a large square envelope and slipped it into one of Aysha's carry-bags. 'Have fun with these. I'm sure you'll find them enlightening.' Closing the case, she proffered a distinctly feline smile. '*Ciao*. See you tomorrow night at the sculpture exhibition.'

Given the social circle in which they both moved, their attendance at the same functions was inevitable. Aysha entertained the fleeting desire to give the evening exhibition a miss, then dismissed the idea. Bruno would never forgive their absence.

Aysha caught the time on one of the clocks featured in the jeweller's window, and hurriedly made for the bank of escalators.

Five minutes later she joined the flow of traffic and negotiated a series of one-way streets before hitting the main arterial one that would join with another leading to Double Bay.

Teresa and Gianna were already seated at a table when she entered the restaurant, and she greeted them both warmly, then sank into a chair.

'Shall we order?'

'You were able to sort everything out with the bridal boutique?'

It was easier to agree. Afterwards she could go into detail, but right now, here, she didn't want Teresa to launch into a long diatribe. 'Yes.'

'*Bene.*' Her mother paused sufficiently long for the waiter to take their order. 'You managed to collect everything?'

'Except shoes, and I'm sure I'll find something I like in one of the shops here.' Double Bay held a number of exclusive shops and boutiques. 'I'll have a look when we've finished lunch.'

It was almost two when they emerged onto the pavement, and Aysha left both women to complete their shopping while she tended to the last few items on her list.

A rueful smile played at the edges of her mouth. In a little over a weeek all the planning, the shopping, the organising…it would all be over. Life could begin to return to normal. She'd be Aysha Santangelo, mistress of her own home, with a husband's needs to care for.

Just thinking about those needs was enough to send warmth coursing through her veins, and put wickedly sensuous thoughts in her head.

During the next two hours she added to the number of carry-bags filling the boot of her car. The envelope Nina had slid into one of them drew her attention, and she pulled it free, examined it, then, curious as to its contents, she undid the flap.

Not papers, she discovered. Photographs. Several of them. She looked at the first, and saw a man and a woman embracing in the foyer of a hotel.

Not any man. Carlo. And the woman was Nina.

Aysha's insides twisted and began to churn as she put it aside and looked at the next one, depicting the exterior and name of a Melbourne hotel, the one where Carlo had stayed three weeks ago when he'd been there for a few days on business. Supposedly business, for the following shot showed Carlo and Nina entering a lift together.

Aysha's fingers shook as she kept flipping the photographs over, one by one. Nina and Carlo pausing outside a numbered door. About to embrace. Kissing.

The evidence was clear enough. Carlo was having an affair...with Nina.

Her legs suddenly felt boneless, and her limbs began to shake. How dared he abuse her trust, her love...everything she'd entrusted in him?

If he thought she'd condone a mistress, he had another think coming!

Anger rose like newly ignited flame, and she thrust

the photographs back into the envelope, closed the boot, then slid in behind the wheel of her car.

There were many ways to hurt someone, but betrayal was right up there. She wanted to march into his office and instigate a confrontation. *Now.*

Except she knew she'd yell, and say things it would be preferable for no one else to overhear.

Wait, an inner voice cautioned as she negotiated peak hour traffic travelling the main east suburban road leading towards Vaucluse.

The car in front braked suddenly, and only a split-second reaction saved her from running into the back of it.

All her fine anger erupted in a stream of language that was both graphic and unladylike. Horns blared in rapid succession, car doors slammed, and there were voices raised in conflict.

Traffic banked up behind her, and it was ten minutes before she could ease her car forward and slowly clear an intersection clogged with police car, ambulance, tow-truck.

Consequently it was after five when she parked the car out front of her parents' home, and she'd no sooner entered the house than Teresa called her into the kitchen.

'I'll be there in a few minutes,' Aysha responded. 'After I've taken everything up to my room.'

A momentary stay of execution, she reflected as she made her way up the curved staircase. The carry-bags could be unpacked later. The photographs were private, very private, and she tucked them beneath her pillow.

She took a few minutes to freshen up, then she retraced her steps to the foyer. The kitchen was redolent with the smell of herbs and garlic, and a small saucepan held simmering contents on the ceramic hotplate.

Teresa stood, spoon in hand, as she added a little wine, a little water, before turning to face her daughter.

'You didn't tell me what happened at the bridal boutique.'

Aysha relayed the details, then waited for her mother's anticipated reaction. She wasn't disappointed.

'Why weren't they couriered out? Why weren't we told before this there might be a problem? I'll never use that boutique again!'

'You won't have to,' Aysha said drily. 'Believe me, I've no intention of doing a repeat performance in this lifetime.'

'We should have used someone else.'

'As most of the bridal boutiques get all their supplies from the same source, I doubt it would have made a difference.'

'You don't know that,' Teresa responded sharply. 'I should have dealt with it myself. Can't they get anything right? Now we learn the wedding lingerie doesn't match.'

'I'm sure Carlo won't even notice.'

Teresa gave her a look which spoke volumes. 'It doesn't matter whether he notices or not. You'll know. *I'll* know. And so will everyone else when you lift your dress and he removes the garter.' The volume of her voice increased. 'We spent hours selecting each individual item. Now nothing matches.'

'Mother.' *Mother* was bad. Its use forewarned of frazzled nerves, and a temper stretched close to breaking point. 'Calm down.' One look at Teresa's face was sufficient to tell a verbal explosion was imminent, and she took a deep breath and released it slowly. 'I'm just as disappointed as you are, but we have to be practical.' Assertiveness probably wasn't a good option at this precise moment. 'I've already chosen something I'm happy with and they've guaranteed delivery within days.'

'I'll check it out in the morning.'

'There's no need to do that.'

'Of course there is, Aysha.' Teresa was adamant. 'We've put a great deal of business their way.'

If she stayed another minute, she'd spit the dummy and they'd have a full-scale row. 'I haven't got time to discuss it now. I have to shower and change, and meet Carlo in less than an hour.'

It was a cop-out, albeit a diplomatic one, she decided as she quickly ascended the stairs. Differences of opinion were one thing. All-out war was another. Teresa was *Teresa*, and she was unlikely to change.

Damn Nina and her Mission. She was a bitch of the first order. Desperate, and dangerous.

The worst kind, Aysha determined viciously as she stripped off her clothes and stepped beneath the cascade of water.

Five minutes later she emerged, wound a towel around her slender curves and crossed into the bedroom bent on selecting something mind-blowing to wear.

Dressed to kill. What a marvellous analogy, she decided. One look at her mirrored reflection revealed a slender young woman in a black beaded gown that was strapless, backless, with a hemline that fell to her ankles. A long chiffon scarf lay sprawled across the bed and she draped it round her neck so both ends trailed down her back.

Make-up was, she determined, a little overstated. Somehow it seemed appropriate. Warriors painted themselves before they went into battle, didn't they? And there would be a battle fought before the night was over. She could personally guarantee it.

Teresa was setting the table in the dining room. 'Mamma, I'm on my way.'

Was it something in her voice that caused her mother to cast her a sharp glance? When it came to maternal instincts, Teresa's were second to none. 'Have a good time.'

That was entirely debatable. Dinner *à deux* followed by an evening at the ballet had definitely lost its appeal. 'Thanks.'

Fifteen minutes later she garaged her car in the underground car park, then rode the lift to Carlo's apartment. The envelope containing the photographs was in her hand, and the portrayed images on celluloid almost scorched her fingers.

He opened the door within seconds, and she saw his pupils widen in gleaming male appreciation. A shaft of intense satisfaction flared, and she took in the immaculate cut of his dark suit, the startling white cotton shirt, the splendid tie.

The perfectly groomed, wildly attractive fiancé. Loving, too, she added a trifle viciously as he drew her close and nuzzled the sensitive curve of her neck.

The right touch, the expert moves. It was almost too much to expect him to be faithful as well. His love, she knew, would never be hers to have. But fidelity... That was something she intended to insist on.

'What's wrong?'

Add *intuitive*, Aysha accorded. At least some of his senses were on track. She moved back a step, away from the traitorous temptation of his arms. It would be far too easy to lean in against him and offer her mouth for his kiss. But then she'd kiss him back, and that wouldn't do at all.

'What makes you think that?' she queried with deliberate calm, and saw his eyes narrow.

'We've never played guessing games, and we're not going to start now.'

Games, subterfuge, deception. They were one and the same thing. 'Really?'

His expression sharpened, accentuating the broad facial bone structure with its strong angles and planes. 'Spit it out, Aysha. I'm listening.'

Aysha rang the tip of one fingernail along the edge of the envelope. Eyes like crystallised smoke burned with a fiery heat as she thrust the envelope at him. 'You've got it wrong. You talk. I get to listen.'

He caught the envelope, and a puzzled frown creased his forehead. 'What the hell is this about?'

'*Hell* is a pretty good description. Open the damned thing. I think you'll get the picture.' She certainly had!

His fingers freed the flap and she watched him carefully as he extracted the sheaf of photos and examined them one by one.

His expression barely altered, and she had to hand it to him... He had tremendous control. Somehow his icy discipline had more effect than anger.

'Illuminating, wouldn't you agree?'

His gaze speared hers, dark, dangerous and as hard as granite. 'Very.'

Her eyes held his fearlessly. 'I think I deserve an explanation.'

'I stayed in that hotel, and, yes, Nina was there. But without any prior knowledge or invitation on my part.'

How could she believe him when Nina continued to drip poison at every turn?

'That's it?' She was so cool it was a wonder the blood didn't freeze in her veins.

'As far as I'm concerned.'

'I guess Nina just happened to be standing outside your room?' She swept his features mercilessly. 'I don't buy it.'

'It happens to be the truth.' His voice was inflexible, and Aysha's eyes were fearless as she met his.

'I'm fully aware our impending marriage has its base in mutual convenience,' she stated with restrained anger. 'But I insist on your fidelity.'

Carlo's eyes narrowed and became chillingly

calm. There was a leashed stillness apparent she knew she'd be wise to heed.

Except she was past wisdom, beyond any form of rationale. Did he have any conception of what she'd felt like when she'd sighted those photos? It was as if the tip of a sword pierced her heart, poised there, then thrust in to the hilt.

'My fidelity isn't in question.'

'Isn't it?'

'Would you care to rephrase that?'

'Why?' Aysha countered baldly. 'What part didn't you understand?'

'I heard the words. It's the motive I find difficult to comprehend.'

With admirable detachment she raked his large frame from head to toe, and back again. 'It's simple. In this marriage, there's only room for two of us.' She was so angry, she felt she might self-destruct. 'There's no way I'll turn a blind eye to you having a mistress on the side.'

'Why would I want a mistress?' Carlo queried with icy calm.

Her eyes flashed, a brilliant translucent grey that had the clarity and purity of a rare pearl. 'To complement my presence in the marital bed?'

His gaze didn't waver, and she fought against being trapped by the depth, the intensity. It was almost hypnotic, and she had the most uncanny sensation he was intent on dispensing with the layers that guarded her soul, like a surgeon using a scalpel with delicate precision.

'Nina has done a hatchet job, hasn't she?' Carlo

offered in a voice that sounded like silk being razed by tempered steel. 'Sufficiently damaging, that any assurance I give you to the contrary will be viewed with scepticism?' He reached out a hand and caught hold of her chin between thumb and forefinger. 'What we share together,' he prompted. 'What would you call that?'

She was breaking up inside, slowly shattering into a thousand pieces. *Special*, a tiny voice taunted. So special, the mere thought of him sharing his body with someone else caused her physical pain.

'Good sex?' Carlo persisted dangerously.

Her stance altered slightly, and her eyes assumed a new depth and intensity. 'Presumably not good enough,' she declared bravely.

It was possible to see the anger build, and she watched with detached fascination as the fingers of each hand clenched into fists, watched the muscles bunch at the edge of his jaw, the slight flaring of nostrils, and the darkening of his eyes.

He uttered a husky oath, and she said with deliberate facetiousness, 'Flattery isn't appropriate.'

Something moved in the depths of his eyes. An emotion she didn't care to define.

'Nina,' Carlo vented emotively, 'has a lot to answer for.'

Didn't she just! 'On that, at least, we agree.'

'Let's get this quite clear,' he said with dangerous quietness. 'You have my vow of fidelity, just as I have yours. Understood?'

She wanted to lash out, then pick up something

and smash it. The satisfaction would be immensely gratifying.

'Aysha?' he prompted with deadly quietness, and she forced herself to respond.

'Even given that Nina is a first-class bitch, I find it a bit too much of a coincidence for you both to be in Melbourne at the same time, staying in the same hotel, the same floor.' Aysha drew in a deep breath. 'Photographic proof bears considerable weight, don't you think?'

He could have shaken her within an inch of her life. For having so little faith in him. So little trust.

'Did it not occur to you to consider it strange that a photographer just happened to be in the hotel lobby at the time Nina and I entered it…coincidentally together? Or that her suite and mine were very conveniently sited opposite each other?' It hadn't taken much pressure to discover Nina had bribed the booking receptionist to reshuffle bookings. 'Perhaps a little too convenient the same photographer was perfectly positioned to take a shot Nina had very carefully orchestrated?'

'You were kissing her!'

'Correction,' he drawled with deliberate cynicism. 'She was kissing me.'

Nina's words rose to the forefront of Aysha's mind. Vicious, damaging, and incredibly pervasive. 'Really? There didn't seem a marked degree of distinction to me.'

He extended his hands as if to catch hold of her shoulders, only to let them fall to his sides. 'A few seconds either way of that perfectly timed shot, and the truth would have been clearly evident.'

'According to Nina,' Aysha relayed bitterly, 'you represent the ultimate prize in the *most suitable husband* quest. Rich, handsome, and, as reputation has it...*a lover to die for.*' Her smile was a mere facsimile. 'Her words, not mine.'

Something fleeting darkened his eyes. A quality that was infinitely ruthless.

'An empty compliment, considering it's completely false.'

The celluloid print of that kiss rose up to haunt her. 'A willing, voluptuous female well-versed in every sexual trick in the book.' Her eyes swept his features, then focused on the unwavering depth of those dark eyes. 'You mean to say you refused what was so blatantly offered?' It took considerable effort to keep her voice steady. 'How noble.'

Carlo reached forward and caught hold of her chin, increasing the pressure as she attempted to twist out of his grasp.

'Why would I participate in a quick sexual coupling with a woman who means nothing to me?'

He was almost hurting her, and her eyes widened as he slid a hand to her nape and held it fast.

'A moment's aberration when your libido took precedence?' she sallied, hating the way his cologne teased her nostrils and began playing havoc with her equilibrium.

Oh, God, she didn't know anything any more. There were conflicting emotions warring inside her head, some of which hardly made any sense.

'Aysha?'

Her eyes searched his, wide, angry, and incredibly hurt. 'How would you feel if the situation were reversed?'

A muscle bunched at the side of his jaw, and something hot and terrifyingly ruthless darkened his eyes.

'I'd kill him.'

His voice was deadly quiet, yet it held the quality of tempered steel, and she felt as if a hand took hold of her throat and squeezed until it choked off her breath.

Her chest tightened and her heart seemed to beat loud, the sound a heavy, distant thud that seemed to reverberate inside her ears.

'A little extreme, surely?' Aysha managed after several long seconds.

'You think so?'

'That sort of action would get you long service, perhaps even life, in gaol.'

'Not for the sort of death I have in mind.' His features assumed a pitiless mask.

He had the power, the influence, to financially ruin an adversary. And he would do it without the slightest qualm.

A light shivery sensation feathered over the surface of her skin. She needed time out from all the madness that surrounded her. Somewhere she could gain solitude in which to think. A place where she had an element of choice.

'I'm going to move into the house for a few days.'

The words emerged almost of their own accord, and she saw his eyes narrow fractionally.

'It's the house, or a hotel,' Aysha insisted, meaning every word.

He wanted to shake her. Paramount was the desire to wring Nina's neck. Anger, frustration, irritation…each rose to the fore, and he banked them all down in an effort to conciliate.

'If that's what it takes.'

'Thank you.'

She was so icily polite, so remote. Pain twisted his gut, and he swore beneath his breath.

'We're due at the ballet in an hour.'

'Go alone, or don't go at all, Carlo. I really don't care.'

Aysha walked into the bedroom and caught up a few essentials from drawers, the wardrobe, aware that Carlo stood watching her every move from the doorway.

For one tragic second she felt adrift, homeless. Which was ridiculous. The thought made her angry, and she closed the holdall, then slung the strap over one shoulder.

'Aysha.'

She'd taken only a token assortment of clothing. That fact should have been reassuring, yet he'd never felt less assured in his life.

Clear grey eyes met his, unwavering in their clarity. 'Right now, there isn't a word you can say that will make a difference.'

She walked to the doorway, stepped past him, and made her way through the apartment to the front door. She half expected him to stop her, but he didn't.

The lift arrived swiftly, and she rode it down to the car park, unlocked her car, then drove it up onto the road.

Carlo leaned his back against the wall and stared sightlessly out of the wide plate-glass window. After a few tense minutes, he picked up the receiver, keyed in a series of digits, then waited for it to connect.

The private detective was one of the best, and with modern technology he should have the answer Carlo needed within days.

He made three more calls, offered an obscene amount of money to ensure that his requests... *orders*, he amended with grim cynicism, were met within a specified time-frame.

Now, he had to wait. And continue to endure Aysha's farcical pretence for a few days. Then there would be no more room for confusion.

He moved away from the wall, prowled the lounge, then in a restless movement he lifted a hand and raked fingers through his hair.

Yet strength wasn't the answer. Only proof, irrefutable proof.

In business, it was essential to cover all the bases, and provide back-up. He saw no reason why it wouldn't work in his personal life.

CHAPTER SIX

AYSHA was hardly aware of the night, the flash of headlights from nearby vehicles, as she traversed the streets and negotiated the Harbour Bridge. She handled the car with the movements of an automaton, and it was something of a minor miracle she reached suburban Clontarf.

Celestial guidance, she decided wryly as she activated the wrought-iron gates guarding entrance to the architectural masterpiece Carlo had built.

Remote-controlled lights sprang on as she reached the garage doors, and she checked the alarm system before entering the house.

It was so quiet, so still, and she crossed into the lounge to switch on the television, then cast a glance around the perfectly furnished room.

Beautiful home, luxuriously appointed, every detail perfect, she reflected; except for the relationship of the man and woman who were to due to inhabit it.

A weary sigh escaped her lips. Was she being foolish seeking a temporary escape? What, after all, was it going to achieve?

Damn. Damn Nina and the seeds she'd deliberately planted.

A slight shiver shook her slender frame, and she resolutely made her way to the linen closet. It was late, she was tired, and all she had to do was fetch fresh linen, make up the bed, and slip between the sheets.

She looked at the array of linen in their neat piles, and her fingers hovered, then shifted to a nearby stack.

Not the main bedroom. The bed was too large, and she couldn't face the thought of sleeping in it alone.

A guest bedroom? Heaven knew there were enough of them! She determinedly made her way towards the first of four, and within minutes she'd completed the task.

In a bid to court sleep she opted for a leisurely warm shower. Towelled dry, she caught up a cotton nightshirt and slid into bed to lie staring into the darkness as her mind swayed every which way but loose.

Carlo. Was he in bed, unable to sleep? Or had he opted to attend the ballet, after all?

What if Nina was also there? The wretched woman would be in her element when she discovered Carlo alone. Oh, for heaven's sake! Be sensible.

Except she didn't *feel* sensible. And sleep was never more distant.

Perhaps she did fall into a fitful doze, although it seemed as if she'd been awake all night when dawn filtered through the drapes and gradually lightened the room.

She lifted her left wrist and checked the time. A few minutes past six. There was no reason for her to rise this early, but she couldn't just lie in bed.

Aysha thrust aside the covers and padded barefoot

to the kitchen. The refrigerator held a half-empty bottle of fruit juice, a partly eaten sandwich, and an apple.

Not exactly required sustenance to jump-start the day, she decided wryly. So, she'd go shopping, stop off at a café for breakfast, then come back, change, and prepare to meet Teresa at ten. Meantime she'd try out the pool.

It was almost seven when she emerged, and she blotted off the excess moisture, then wrapped the towel sarong-wise and re-entered the house.

Within minutes the phone rang, and she reached for it automatically.

'You slept well?'

Aysha drew in a deep breath at the sound of that familiar voice. 'Did you expect me not to?'

There was a faint pause. 'Don't push it too far, *cara*,' Carlo drawled in husky warning.

'I'm trembling,' she evinced sweetly.

'So you should be.' His voice tightened, and acquired a depth that sent goosebumps scudding over the surface of her skin.

'Intimidation isn't on my list.'

'Nor is false accusation on mine.'

With just the slightest lack of care, this could easily digress into something they both might regret.

With considerable effort she banked down the anger, and aimed for politeness. 'Is there a purpose to your call, other than to enquire if I got any sleep?' She thought she managed quite well. 'I have a host of things to do.'

'*Grazie.*'

She winced at the intended sarcasm. *'Prego,'* she concluded graciously, and disconnected the phone.

On reflection, it wasn't the best of days, but nor was it the worst. Teresa was in fine form, and so consumed with her list of Things to Do, Aysha doubted her own preoccupation was even noticed. Which was just as well, for she couldn't have borne the string of inevitable questions her mother would deem it necessary to ask.

'You're looking a little peaky, darling. You're not coming down with something, are you?'

'A headache, Mamma.' It wasn't too far from the truth.

Teresa frowned with concern. 'Take some tablets, and get some rest.'

As if *rest* was the panacea for everything! 'Carlo and I are attending the sculpture exhibition at the Gallery tonight.'

'It's just as well Carlo is whisking you away to the Coast for the weekend. The break will do you good.'

Somehow Aysha doubted it.

The Gallery held a diverse mix of invited guests, some of whom attended solely to be seen and hopefully make the social pages. Others came to admire, with a view to adding to their collection.

Carlo and Aysha fell into a separate category. A close friend was one of the exhibiting artists and they wanted to add their support.

'Ciao, bella,' a male voice greeted, and Aysha

turned to face the extraordinarily handsome young man who'd sent his personal invitation.

'Bruno!' She flung her arms wide and gave him an enthusiastic hug. 'How are you?'

'The better for seeing you.' He lowered his head and bestowed a kiss to each cheek in turn. 'Damn Carlo for snaring you first.' He withdrew gently and looked deeply into those smoky grey eyes, then he turned towards Carlo and lifted one eyebrow in silent query. 'Carlo, *amici. Come stai?*'

Something passed between both men. Aysha glimpsed it, and sought to avert any swing in the territorial parameters by tucking one hand through Carlo's arm.

'Come show us your exhibits.'

For the next half-hour they wandered the large room, pausing to examine and comment, or converse with a few of the fellow guests.

Aysha moved towards a neighbouring exhibit as Carlo was temporarily waylaid by a business acquaintance.

'Your lips curve wide with a generous smile, yet your eyes are sad,' said Bruno. 'Why?'

'The wedding is a week tomorrow.' She gave a graceful shrug. 'Teresa and I have been shopping together every day, and nearly every night Carlo and I have been out.'

'Sad, *cara*,' Bruno reiterated. 'I didn't say tired. If Carlo isn't taking care of you, he will answer to me.'

She summoned a wicked smile and her eyes sparkled with hidden laughter. 'Swords at dawn? Or should that be pistols?'

'I would take pleasure in breaking his nose.'

She turned to check on the subject of their discussion, and stiffened. Bruno, acutely perceptive, shifted his head and followed her gaze. 'Ah, the infamous Nina.'

The statuesque brunette looked stunning in red, the soft material hugging every curve like a well-fitting glove.

Bruno leant down and said close to Aysha's ear, 'Shall we go break it up?'

'Let's do that.' The smile she proffered didn't reach her eyes, and her heart hammered a little in her chest as she drew close.

Nina's tapered red-lacquered nails rested on Carlo's forearm, and Aysha watched those nails conduct a gentle caressing movement back and forth over a small area of his tailored jacket.

Nina's make-up was superb, her mouth a perfect glossy red bow.

'Want me to charm her?' Bruno murmured, and Aysha responded equally quietly.

'Thanks, but I can fight my own battles.'

'Take care, *cara*. You're dealing with a dangerous cat.' He paused as they reached Carlo's side. 'Your most precious possession,' Bruno said lightly, and inclined his head with deliberate mockery, 'Nina.' Then he smiled, and moved through the crowd.

Wise man, Aysha accorded silently, wishing she could do the same.

'Darling, do get me a drink. You know what I like.'

Aysha began a mental countdown the moment Carlo left to find a waitress.

'I imagine you've checked the photographs?' Nina raised one eyebrow and raked Aysha's slender frame. 'Caused a little grief, did they?'

'Wasn't that your purpose?' Aysha was cold, despite the warmth of the summer evening.

'How clever of you,' Nina approved. 'Have you decided to condone his transgressions? I do hope so.' Her smile was seductively sultry. 'I would hate to have to give him up.'

Her heart felt as if it was encased in ice. 'You've missed your vocation,' she said steadily.

'What makes you say that, darling?'

She needed the might of a sword, but a verbal punch-line was better than nothing. 'You should have been an actress.' A smile cost her almost every resource she had, but she managed one beautifully, then she turned and threaded her way towards one of Bruno's sculptures.

'Who won?'

Bruno could always be counted on, and she cast him a wry smile. 'You noticed.'

'Ah, but I was looking out for you.' He curved an arm around the back of her waist. 'Now, tell me what you think about this piece.'

She examined it carefully. 'Interesting,' she conceded. 'If I say it resembles my idea of an African fertility god, would it offend you?'

'Not at all, because that's exactly what it is.'

'You're just saying that to make me feel good.'

He placed a hand over his heart. 'I swear.'

She began to laugh, and he smiled down at her. 'Why not me, *cara*?' he queried softly, and hugged her close. 'I'd treat you like the finest porcelain.'

'I know,' she said gently, and with a degree of very real regret.

'You love him, don't you?'

'Is it that obvious?'

'Only to me,' he assured her quietly. 'I just hope Carlo knows how fortunate he is to have you.'

'He does.'

Aysha heard that deep musing drawl, glimpsed the latent darkness in his eyes, and gently extricated herself from Bruno's grasp. 'I was admiring Bruno's sculpture.'

Carlo cast her a glittering look that set her nerves on edge. How dared he look at her like that when he'd been playing *up close and personal* with Nina?

'Don't play games, *cara*,' Carlo warned as soon as Bruno was out of earshot.

'Practise what you preach, *darling*,' she said sweetly. 'And *please* get me a drink. It'll give Nina another opportunity to waylay you.'

He bit off a husky oath. 'We can leave peaceably, or not,' he said with deceptive quietness. 'Your choice.' He meant every word.

'Bruno will be disappointed.'

'He'll get over it.'

'I could make a scene,' Aysha threatened, and his expression hardened.

'It wouldn't make any difference.'

It would, however, give Nina the utmost pleasure

to witness their dissension. 'I guess we get to say goodnight,' she capitulated with minimum grace.

Ten minutes later she was seated in the Mercedes as it purred across the Harbour Bridge towards suburban Clontarf.

She didn't utter a word during the drive, and she reached for the door-clasp the instant Carlo drew the car to a halt. It would be fruitless to tell him not to follow her indoors, so she didn't even try.

'Bruno is a friend. A good friend,' she qualified, enraged at his high-handedness. 'Which is more than I can say for Nina.'

'Neither Bruno nor Nina are an issue.'

Her chin tilted as she glared up at him. 'Then what the hell is the issue?'

'We are,' he vouchsafed succinctly.

'Well, now,' Aysha declared. 'There's the thing. Nina is quite happy for you to marry me, just as long as she gets to remain your mistress.'

His eyes filled with chilling intensity. 'Nina has one hell of an imagination.'

She'd had enough. 'Go home, Carlo.' Her eyes blazed with fury. 'If you don't, I'll be tempted to do something I might regret.'

She wasn't prepared for the restrained savagery evident as his mouth fastened on hers, forcing it open and controlling it as his tongue pillaged the inner sweetness. It was a deliberate ravishment of her senses. Claim-staking, punishing. She lost all sensation of time as one hand slid through her hair to hold fast her head, while the other curved low down her back.

Then the pressure eased, and the punishing quality changed to passion, gradually dissipating to a sensuous gentleness that curled round her inner core and tugged at her emotions, seducing until she was weak-willed and malleable.

From somewhere deep inside she dredged sufficient strength to tear her mouth free, and her body trembled as he traced the edge of his thumb across the swollen contours of her lips.

'Nina is nothing to me, do you understand? She never has been. Never will be.'

She didn't say a word. She just looked at him, glimpsed the faint edge of regret, and was incapable of moving.

He pulled her close and buried her head in the curve of his shoulder, then he pressed his lips to her hair.

Aysha could feel the power in that large body, the strength, and she felt strangely ambivalent. 'I don't want you to stay.'

'Because you'll only hate me in the morning?'

She drew a shaky breath. 'I'll hate myself even more.'

All he had to do was kiss her, and she'd change her mind. Part of her wanted him so much it was an impossible ache. Yet if she succumbed she'd be lost, and that wouldn't achieve a thing.

He held her for what seemed an age, then he turned her face to his and brushed his lips across her own, lingered at one corner and angled his mouth into hers in a kiss that was so incredibly evocative it dispensed with almost all her doubts.

Almost, but not quite. He sensed the faint barrier, and gently put her at arm's length.

'I'll pick you up at seven, OK?'

It was easy to simply nod her head, and she watched as he turned and walked to the door. Seconds later she heard his car's engine start, and she checked the lock, then activated security before crossing to her room.

Sleep seemed a distant entity, and she switched on the television in the hope of discovering something which would occupy her interest. Except channel-hopping provided nothing she wanted to watch, and she retired to her bedroom, then lay staring at the ceiling for what seemed hours before finally slipping into a restless slumber in which vivid dreams assumed nightmarish proportion as Nina took the role of vamp.

CHAPTER SEVEN

AYSHA woke early, padded barefoot to the kitchen, poured herself some fresh orange juice, then headed outdoors to swim several laps of the pool.

After fifteen minutes or so she emerged, towelled off the excess moisture, then retreated indoors to change and make breakfast.

The ambivalence of the previous evening had disappeared, and in the clear light of day it seemed advantageous for she and Carlo to spend the weekend apart.

With that thought in mind she crossed to the phone and punched in his number. The answering machine picked up, and she replaced the receiver down onto the handset.

He was probably in the shower, or, she determined with a glance at her watch, he could easily have left. She keyed in the digits that connected with his mobile, and got voicemail.

Damn. It would have been less confrontational to cancel via the phone than deal with him in person.

It was almost seven when Carlo walked into the kitchen, and his eyes narrowed at the sight of her in cut-off denims and skimpy top.

'You're not ready.'

'No.' Her response was matter-of-fact. 'I think we both need the weekend apart.'

His expression was implacable. 'I disagree. Go change and get your holdall. We don't have much time.'

'Give me one reason why I should go?' she demanded, tilting her chin at him in a way that drove him crazy, for he wanted to kiss her until all that fine anger melted into something he could deal with.

'I can give you several. But right now you're wasting valuable time.'

Without a word he strode through the lounge and ascended the stairs. She followed after him, watching as he entered the bedroom, opened a cupboard, extracted a leather holdall and tossed it down onto the bed, then he riffled through her clothes, selected, discarded, then opened drawers and took a handful of delicate underwear and dumped it in the holdall.

'What in hell do you think you're doing?'

A pair of heeled pumps followed sandals.

'I would have thought it was obvious.'

He moved into the *en suite* bathroom, collected toiletries and make-up, and swept them into a cosmetic case. He lifted his head long enough to spare her a searching look.

'You might want to change.'

Her eyes flashed fire. 'I might not,' she retaliated swiftly.

He shrugged his shoulders, pressed everything into the holdall, then closed the zip fastener.

'OK, let's go.'

'Don't you *listen*?' His implacability brought her to a state of rage. 'I am not going anywhere.'

Carlo was dangerously calm. Too calm. 'We've already done this scene.'

Aysha was too angry to apply any caution. 'Well, *hell*. Let's do it again.'

'No.' He slung the holdall straps over one shoulder, then he curved an arm round her waist and hoisted her over one shoulder with an ease that brought forth a gasp of outrage.

'You fiend! What do you think you're doing?'

'Abducting you.'

'In the name of God... *Why?*'

Carlo strode out of the room and began descending the short flight of stairs. 'Because we're flying to the Coast, as planned.'

She struggled, and made no impression. In sheer frustration she pummelled both hands against his back. 'Put me down!'

He didn't alter stride as he negotiated the stairs, and she aimed for his ribs, his kidneys, anywhere that might cause him pain. All to no avail, for he didn't so much as grunt when each punch connected.

'If you don't put me down this *instant*, I'll have you arrested for attempted kidnapping, assault, and anything else I can think of!'

Carlo reached the impressive foyer, took three more steps, then lowered her to stand in front of him.

'No, you won't.'

He was bigger, broader, taller than her, yet she refused to be intimidated. 'Want to bet?'

'Cool it, *cara*.'

'I am not your darling.'

His mouth curved with amusement, and she poked him several times in the chest.

'Don't you *dare* laugh!'

He curled his hands over her shoulders and held her still. 'What would you have me do? Kiss you? Haul you across one knee and spank your deliciously soft *derrière*?'

'Soft?' She worked out, and while her butt might be curved, it was tight.

'If you keep opposing me, I'll be driven to effect one or the other.'

'Lay a hand on me, and I'll—'

He was much too swift, and any further words she might have uttered were lost as his mouth closed over hers in a deep, punishing kiss which took hold of her anger and turned it into passion.

Aysha wasn't conscious when it changed, only that it did, and the fists she lashed him with gradually uncurled and crept up to his nape to cling as emotion wrought havoc and fragmented all her senses.

Carlo slowly eased the heat, and his mouth softened as he gently caressed the swollen contours of her lips, then pressed light butterfly kisses along the tender curve to one corner and back again.

When he lifted his head she could only look at him with drenched eyes, and he traced a forefinger down the slope of her nose.

'Now that I have your full attention… A weekend at the Coast will remove us from all the madness. No pressures, no demands, no social engagements.'

And no chance of accidentally bumping into Nina.

'Last call, Aysha,' Carlo indicated with a touch of mockery. 'Stay, or go. Which is it to be?'

It wasn't the time for deliberation. 'Go,' she said decisively, and heard his husky laughter.

They made the flight with ten minutes to spare, and touched down at Coolangatta Airport just over an hour later. It was almost ten when they checked into the hotel, and within minutes of entering into their suite Aysha crossed to the floor-to-ceiling glass window fronting the Broadwater, and released the sliding door.

She could hear the muted sound of traffic, voices drifting up from the pool area. Adjacent was an enclosed man-made beach with a secluded cave and waterfall.

In the distance she could see the architecturally designed roof resembling a collection of sails atop an exclusive shopping centre fronting a marina and connected by a walkway bridge to an exclusive ocean-front hotel.

A few minutes later she sensed rather than heard him move to stand behind her.

'Peaceful.'

It was, and she said so. 'Yes.'

His arms curved round her waist and he pulled her close. 'What do you want to do with the day?'

There was a desperate need to get out of the hotel suite, and lose herself among the crowds. 'A theme park?' She said the first one that came into her head. 'Dreamworld.'

He hid a wry smile. 'I'll organise it.'

'Just like that?'

'We can hire a car and drive into the mountains, take any one of several cruises.' His shoulders shifted as he effected a lazy shrug. 'You get to choose.'

'For today?'

'All weekend,' he said solemnly.

'Give me too much power, and it might go to my head,' Aysha teased, suddenly feeling more in control.

'I doubt it.'

He knew her too well. 'After dinner we go to the Casino, then tomorrow we do Movieworld.' Crowds, lots of people. Which left only the hours between midnight or later and dawn spent in this beautiful suite, with its very large, prominently positioned bed.

Dreamworld was fun. They played tourist and took a bus there, went on several rides, ate hot dogs and chips as they wandered among the crowd. Aysha laughed at the white tigers' antics, viewed the Tower of Terror and voiced an emphatic *no* to Carlo's suggestion they take the ride.

It was almost six when the bus deposited them outside the hotel.

'I'll have first take on the shower,' Aysha indicated as they rode the lift to their designated floor.

'We could share.'

'I don't think that's a good idea,' she said evenly. Just remembering how many showers they'd shared and their inevitable outcome set all her fine body hairs on edge.

The lift slid to a stop and she turned in the direction of their suite.

Inside, she collected fresh underwear and entered

the large bathroom. The water was warm and she
adjusted the dial, undressed, then stepped into the
tiled stall.

Seconds later the door slid open and her eyes widened as Carlo joined her.

'What do you think you're doing?'

'Sharing a shower isn't necessarily an invitation to
have sex,' he said calmly, and took the soap from
her nerveless fingers.

He was too close, but there was no further room
to move.

'Want me to shampoo your hair?'

'I can do it,' she managed in a muffled voice, and
she missed his slight smile as he uncapped the courtesy bottle and slowly worked the gel into her hair.

His fingers began a gentle massage, and she closed
her eyes, taking care to stifle a despairing groan as
he rinsed off the foam.

Not content, he palmed the soap and proceeded to
smooth it over her back, her buttocks, thighs, before
tending to her breasts, then her stomach.

'Don't,' Aysha begged as he travelled lower, and
she shook her head in mute denial when he placed
the soap in her hand, then guided it over his chest.

Her fingers scraped the curling hair there, and she
felt the tautness of his stomach, then consciously
held her breath as he'd traversed lower.

His arousal was a potent force, and she began to
shake with the need for his possession. It would be
so easy to let the soap slip from her hand and reach
for him. To lift her face to his, and invite his mouth
down to hers.

Then he turned and his voice emerged as a silky drawl. 'Do my back, *cara*.'

She thrust the soap onto its stand, and slid open the door. 'Do it yourself.'

Aysha escaped, only because he let her, she was sure, and she caught up a towel, clutched hold of her underwear, and moved into the bedroom.

It was galling to discover her hands were trembling, and she quickly towelled herself dry, then wound the towel turban-wise round her head.

By the time Carlo emerged she was dressed, and she re-entered the bathroom to utilise the hairdrier, then tend to her make-up.

White silk evening trousers, a gold-patterned white top, minimum jewellery, and white strapped heeled pumps made for a matching outfit.

Black trousers and a white chambray shirt emphasised his dark hair and tanned skin. He'd shaved, and his cologne teased her nostrils, creating a havoc all its own with her senses.

'Ready?'

They caught a taxi to the Casino, enjoyed a leisurely meal, then entered the gambling area.

Aysha's luck ran fickle, while Carlo's held, but she refused to use his accumulated winnings, choosing instead to watch him at the blackjack table. Each selection was calculated, his expression impossible to read. Much like the man himself, she acknowledged silently.

It was after one when they returned to the hotel. Aysha felt pleasantly tired, and in their suite she slipped out of her clothes, cleansed her face of make-up, then slid into bed to lie quietly with her eyes closed, pretending sleep.

Moments later she felt the mattress depress as Carlo joined her, and she measured her breathing into a slow, steady rise and fall. Grateful, she told herself, that Carlo's breathing gradually acquired a similar pattern.

Why was it that when you didn't want something, you felt cheated when you didn't receive it? Aysha queried silently. The size of the bed precluded any chance of accidentally touching, and she didn't feel inclined to instigate the contrived kind...

'Come on, sleepyhead, rise and shine.'

Aysha heard the voice and opened her eyes to brilliant sunshine and the aroma of freshly brewed coffee. It was *morning* already?

'Breakfast,' Carlo announced. 'You have three quarters of an hour to eat, shower and dress before we need to take the bus to Movieworld.'

What had happened to the night? You slept right through it, a tiny voice taunted. Wasn't that what you wanted?

They boarded the bus with a few minutes to spare, and there were thrills and spills and fun and laughter as the actors went through their paces. The various stuntmen and women earned Aysha's respect and admiration as more than once a scene made her catch her breath in awe of the sensitive degree of timing and expertise involved.

They caught the early evening-flight out of Coolangatta Airport, and arrived in Sydney after nine. Carlo collected the car, then headed towards the city.

For one brief moment Aysha was tempted to choose the apartment, except Carlo pre-empted any decision by driving to Clontarf.

She told herself fiercely that she wasn't disappointed as he checked the house and re-set the alarm.

His kiss was brief, a soft butterfly caress that left her aching for more. Then he turned and retraced his steps to the car.

Half an hour later Carlo crossed to the phone and punched in a series of digits, within minutes of entering his apartment.

Samuel Sloane, a legal eagle of some note, picked up on the seventh ring, and almost winced at the grim tone of the man who'd chosen to call him at such an hour on a Sunday evening at home. He listened, counselled and advised, and wasn't in the least surprised when he was ignored.

'I don't give a damn for the what-if's and maybes protecting my investments, my interests. I'm not consulting you for advice. I'm instructing you what to do. Draw up that document. I'll be in your office just before five tomorrow. Now, do we understand each other?'

The impulse to slam the receiver down onto the handset was uppermost, and Carlo barely avoided the temptation to do so.

Aysha spent the morning organising the final soft furnishing items she'd ordered several weeks previously. A message alerting her of their arrival had been on her answering machine when she'd checked it on her return from the Coast.

At midday she stood back and surveyed the results, and was well pleased with the effect. It was perfect, and just as she'd envisaged the overall look.

It was amazing how a few cushions, draped pelmets in matching fabric really set the final touch to a room.

All it needed, she decided with a critical eye, was a superbly fashioned terracotta urn in one corner to complete the image she wanted. Maybe she'd have time to locate the urn before she was due to meet Teresa at one.

Aysha made it with minutes to spare, and together they spent the next few hours with the dressmaker, checked a few minor details with the wedding organiser, then took time to relax over coffee.

'You haven't forgotten we're dining with Gianna and Luigi tonight?'

Aysha uttered a silent scream in sheer frustration. She didn't want to play the part of soon-to-be-married adoring fiancée. Nor did she want to dine beneath the watchful eyes of their respective parents.

When she arrived at the house she checked the answering machine and discovered a message from Carlo indicating he'd collect her at six. An identical message was recorded on her mobile phone.

Her fingers hovered over the telephone handset as she contemplated returning his call and cancelling out, only to retreat in the knowledge that she had no choice but to see the evening through.

A shower did little to ease the tension, and she

deliberately chose black silk evening trousers and matching halter-necked top, added stiletto pumps, twisted her hair into a simple knot atop her head, and kept make-up to a minimum.

She was ready when security alerted her that the front gate had been activated, and she opened the front door seconds ahead of Carlo's arrival.

He was a superb male animal, she conceded as she caught her first glimpse of him. Tall, broad frame, honed musculature, and he exuded a primitive alchemy that was positively lethal.

Expensively tailored black trousers, dark blue shirt left unbuttoned at the neck, and a black jacket lent a sophistication she could only admire. 'Shall we leave?' Aysha asked coolly, and saw those dark eyes narrow.

'Not yet.'

Her stomach executed a slow somersault, and she tensed involuntarily. 'We don't want to be late.'

He was standing too close, and she suppressed the need to take a backward step. She didn't need him close. It just made it more difficult to maintain a mental distance. And she needed to, badly.

He brushed his fingers across one cheek and pressed a thumb to the corner of her mouth. 'You're pale.'

She almost swayed towards him, drawn as if by a magnetic force. Dammit, how could she love him, yet hate him at the same time? It was almost as if her body was detached from the dictates of her brain.

'A headache,' she responded evenly, and his expression became intensely watchful.

'I'll ring and cancel.'

It was easier to handle him when he was angry. At least then she could rage in return. Now, she merely felt helpless, and it irked her that he knew.

'That isn't an option, and you know it,' she refuted, and lifted a hand in expressive negation.

'You've taken something for it?'

'Yes.'

'Povera piccola,' he declared gently as he lowered his head and brushed his lips against her temple.

Sensation curled inside her stomach as his mouth trailed down to the edge of her mouth, and she turned her head slightly, her lips parting in denial, only to have his mouth close over hers.

He caught her head between both hands, and his tongue explored the inner tissues at will, savouring the sweetness with such erotic sensuousness that all rational thought temporarily fled.

His touch was sheer magic, exotic, intoxicating, and left her wanting more. Much more.

It's just a kiss, she assured herself mentally, and knew she was wrong. This was seductive claim-staking at its most dangerous.

Aysha pushed against his shoulders and tore her mouth from his, her eyes wide and luminous as they caught the darkness reflected in his. Her mouth tingled, and her lips felt slightly swollen.

'Let's go.' Was that her voice? It sounded husky, and her mouth shook slightly as she moved away from him and caught up her evening bag.

In the car she leaned her head back against the

cushioned rest, and stared sightlessly out of the window.

Summer daylight saving meant warm sunshine at six in the evening, and peak-hour traffic crossing the Harbour Bridge had diminished, ensuring a relatively smooth drive to suburban Vaucluse.

Aysha didn't offer anything by way of conversation, and she was somewhat relieved when Carlo brought the Mercedes to a halt behind Teresa and Giuseppe's car in the driveway of his parents' home.

'Showtime.'

'Don't overdo it, *cara*,' he warned quizzically, and she offered him a particularly direct look.

Did he know just how much she hurt deep inside? Somehow she doubted it. 'Don't patronise me.'

She saw one eyebrow lift. 'Not guilty,' Carlo responded, then added drily, 'on any count.'

Now there was a *double entendre* if ever there was one. 'You underestimate yourself.'

His eyes hardened fractionally. 'Take care, Aysha.'

She reached for the door-clasp. 'If we stay here much longer, our parents will think we're arguing.'

'And we're not?'

'Now you're being facetious.' She opened the door and stood to her feet, then summoned a warm smile as he crossed to her side.

Gianna Santangelo's affectionate greeting did much to soothe Aysha's unsettled nerves. This was *family*, although she was under no illusions, and knew that both mothers were attuned to the slightest nuance that might give hint to any dissension.

Dinner was an informal meal, although Gianna had gone to considerable trouble, preparing *gnocchi* in a delicious sauce, followed by chicken pieces roasted in wine with rosemary herbs and accompanied by a variety of vegetables.

Gianna was a superb cook, with many speciality dishes in her culinary repertoire. Even Teresa had the grace to offer a genuine compliment.

'*Buona*, Gianna. You have a flair for *gnocchi* that is unsurpassed by anyone I know.'

'*Grazie*. I shall give Aysha the recipe.'

Ah, now there was the thing. Teresa's recipe versus that of Gianna. Tricky, Aysha concluded. Very tricky. She'd have to vary the sauce accordingly whenever either or both sets of parents came to dinner. Or perhaps not serve it at all? Maybe she could initiate a whole new range of Italian cuisine? Or select a provincial dish that differed from Trevisian specialities?

'I won't have time for much preparation except at the weekends.' She knew it was a foolish statement the moment the words left her mouth, as both Teresa and Gianna's heads rose in unison, although it was her mother who voiced the query.

'Why ever not, *cara*?'

Aysha took a sip of wine, then replaced her glass down onto the table. 'Because I'll be at work, Mamma.'

'But you have finished work.'

'I'm taking a six-week break, then I'll be going back.'

'Part-time, of course.'

'Full-time.'

Teresa stated the obvious. 'There is no need for you to work at all. What happens when you fall pregnant?'

'I don't plan on having children for a few years.'

Teresa turned towards Carlo. 'You agree with this?'

It could have been a major scandal they were discussing, not a personal decision belonging to two people.

'It's Aysha's choice.' He turned to look at her, his smile infinitely warm and sensual as he took hold of her hand and brushed his lips to each finger in turn. His eyes gleamed with sensual promise. 'We both want a large family.'

Bastard, she fumed silently. He'd really set the cat among the pigeons now. Teresa wouldn't be able to leave it alone, and she'd receive endless lectures about caring for a husband's needs, maintaining an immaculate house, an excellent table.

Aysha leaned forward, and traced the vertical crease slashing Carlo's cheek. His eyes flared, but she ignored the warning gleam. 'Cute, plump little dark-haired boys,' she teased as her own eyes danced with silent laughter. 'I've seen your baby pictures, remember?'

'Don't forget I babysat you and changed your nappies, *cara*.'

Her first memory of Carlo was herself as a four-year-old being carried round on his shoulders, laughing and squealing as she gripped hold of his hair for dear life. She'd loved him then with the innocence of a child.

Adoration, admiration, respect had undergone a subtle change in those early teenage years, as raging female hormones had labelled intense desire as sexual attraction, infatuation, lust.

He'd been her best friend, confidant, big brother, all rolled into one. Then he'd become another girl's husband, and it had broken her heart.

Now she was going to marry him, have his children, and to all intents and purposes live the fairy tale dream of happy-ever-after.

Except she didn't have his heart. That belonged to Bianca, who lay buried beneath an elaborate bed of marble high on a hill outside the country town in which she'd been born.

Aysha had wanted to hate her, but she couldn't, for Bianca had been one of those rare human beings who was so genuinely kind, so *nice*, she was impossible to dislike.

Carlo caught each fleeting expression and correctly divined every one of them. His mouth softened as he leant forward and brushed his lips to her temple.

She blinked rapidly, and forced herself to smile. 'Hands-on practice, huh? You do know you're going to have to help with the diapering?'

'I wouldn't miss it for the world.'

Aysha almost believed him.

'I'll serve the *cannoli*,' Gianna declared. 'And afterwards we have coffee.'

'You women have the *cannoli*,' Luigi dismissed with the wave of one hand. 'Giuseppe, come with me. We'll have a brandy. With the coffee, we'll have *grappa*.' He turned towards his son. 'Carlo?'

Women had their work to do, and it was work which didn't involve men. Old traditions died hard, and the further they lived away from the Old Country, Aysha recognised ruefully, the longer it took those traditions to die.

Carlo rose to his feet and followed the two older men from the room.

Aysha braced herself for the moment Teresa would pounce. Gianna, she knew, would be more circumspect.

'You cannot be serious about returning to work after the honeymoon.'

Ten seconds. She knew, because she'd counted them off. 'I enjoy working, Mamma. I'm very good at what I do.'

'Indeed,' Gianna complimented her. 'You've done a wonderful job with the house.'

'*Ecco*,' Teresa agreed, and Aysha tried to control a silent sigh.

Her mother invariably lapsed into Italian whenever she became passionate about something. Aysha sank back in her chair and prepared for a lengthy harangue.

She wasn't disappointed. The use of Italian became more frequent, as if needed to emphasise a point. And even Gianna's gentle intervention did little to stem the flow.

'If you had to work, I could understand,' Teresa concluded. 'But you don't. There are hundreds, thousands,' she corrected, 'without work, and taking money from the government.'

Aysha gave a mental groan. Politics. They were in for the long haul. She cast a pleading glance at Carlo's mother, and received a philosophical shrug in response.

'I'll make coffee,' Gianna declared, and Aysha stood to her feet with alacrity.

'I'll help with the dishes.'

It was only a momentary diversion, for the debate merely shifted location from the dining room to the kitchen.

Aysha's head began to throb.

'Zia Natalina has finished crocheting all the baskets needed for the *bomboniera*,' Gianna interceded in a bid to change the subject. 'Tomorrow she'll count out all the sugared almonds and tie them into tulle circles. Her daughter Giovanna will bring them to the house early on the day of the wedding.'

'*Grazie*, Gianna. I want to place them on the tables myself.'

'Giovanna and I can do it, if it will help. You will have so much more to do.'

Teresa inclined her head. 'Carlo has the wedding rings? Annalisa has sewn the ring pillow, but the rings need to be tied onto it.' A frown furrowed her brow. 'I must phone and see if she has the ribbon ready.' She gathered cups and saucers together onto the tray while Gianna set some almond biscuits onto a plate.

'The men won't touch them, but if I don't put a plate down with something Luigi will complain.' She lifted a hand and let it fall to her side. 'Yet when I produce it, he'll say they don't want biscuits with coffee.' Her humour was wry. 'Men. Who can understand them?' She cast a practised eye over the tray. 'We have everything. Let's join them, shall we?'

All three men were grouped together in front of the television engrossed in a televised, soccer match.

Luigi was intent on berating the goal keeper for presumably missing the ball, Aysha determined, and her father appeared equally irate.

'Turn off the set,' Gianna instructed Luigi as she placed the tray down onto a coffee table. 'We have guests.'

'Nonsense,' he grumbled. 'They're family, not guests.'

'It is impossible to talk with you yelling at the players.' She cast him a stern glance. 'Besides, you are taping it. When you replay you can yell all you like. Now we sit down and have coffee.'

'*La moglie.*' He raised his eyes heavenward.

'*Dio madonna.* A man is not boss in his own house any more?'

It was a familiar by-play, and one Aysha had heard many times over the years. Her father played a similar verbal game whenever Gianna and Luigi visited.

Her eyes sought Carlo's, and she glimpsed the faint humorous gleam evident as they waited silently for Gianna to take up the figurative ball.

'Of course you are the boss. You need me to tell you this?'

Luigi cast the tray an accusing glance. 'You

brought biscuits? What for? We don't need biscuits with coffee. It spoils the taste of the *grappa*.'

'Teresa and Aysha don't have *grappa*,' she admonished. 'You don't think maybe we might like biscuits?'

'After *cannoli* you eat biscuits? You won't sleep with indigestion.'

'I won't sleep anyway. After *grappa* you snore.'

'I don't snore.'

'How do you know? Do you listen to yourself?'

Luigi spread his hands in an expansive gesture. 'Ah, *Mamma*, give it up, huh? We are with friends. You cooked a good dinner. Now it is time to relax.' He held out a beckoning hand to Aysha. 'Come here, *ma tesora*.'

She crossed to his side and rested against the arm he curved round her waist.

'When are you going to invite us to dinner at the new house?'

'After they get back from the honeymoon,' Gianna declared firmly. 'Not before. It will bring bad luck.'

Luigi didn't take any notice. 'Soon there will be *bambini*. Maybe already there is one started, huh, and you didn't tell us?'

'You talk too much,' his wife chastised. 'Didn't you hear Aysha say she intends to wait a couple of years? Aysha, don't listen to him.'

'Ah, grandchildren. You have a boy first, to kick the soccer ball. Then a girl. The brother can look after his sister.'

'Two boys,' Giuseppe insisted, joining the conversation. 'Then they can play together.'

'Girls,' Aysha declared solemnly. 'They're smarter, and besides they get to help me in the house.'

'A boy and a girl.'

'If you two *vecchios* have finished planning our children,' Carlo intruded mildly as he extricated Aysha from his father's clasp. 'I'm going to take Aysha home.'

'*Vecchios*? You call us old men?' Giuseppe demanded, a split second ahead of Luigi's query,

'What are you doing going home? It's early.'

'Why do you think they're going home?' Gianna disputed. 'They're young. They want to make love.'

'Perhaps we should fool them and stay,' Aysha suggested in an audible aside, and Carlo shook his head.

'It wouldn't make any difference.'

'But I haven't had my coffee.'

'You don't need the caffeine.'

'Making decisions for me?'

'Looking out for you,' Carlo corrected gently. 'A few hours ago you had a headache. Unless I'm wrong, you're still nursing one.'

So he deserved full marks for observation. Without a further word she turned towards Luigi and pressed a soft kiss to his cheek, then she followed suit with her father before crossing to Teresa and Gianna.

Saying goodbye stretched out to ten minutes, then they made it to the car, and seconds later Carlo eased the Mercedes through the gates and out onto the road.

CHAPTER EIGHT

'You threw me to the lions.'

'Wrong century, *cara*,' he informed her wryly. 'And the so-called lions are pussy cats at heart.'

'Teresa doesn't always sheath her claws.' It was an observation, not a condemnation. 'There are occasions when being the only chick in the nest is a tremendous burden.'

'Only if you allow it to be.'

The headache seemed to intensify, and she closed her eyes. 'Intent on playing amateur psychologist, Carlo?'

'Friend.'

Ah, now there's a descriptive allocation, Aysha reflected. *Friend*. It had a affectionate feel to it, but affection was a poor substitute for love. The all-encompassing kind that prompted men to kill and die for it.

She lapsed into silence as the car headed down towards Double Bay.

'How's the headache?'

It had become a persistent ache behind one eye that held the promise of flaring into a migraine unless she took painkillers very soon. 'There,' she informed succinctly, and closed her eyes against the glare of oncoming headlights.

Carlo didn't offer another word during the drive

to Clontarf, for which she was grateful, and she reached for the door-clasp as soon as the car drew to a halt outside the main entrance to the house.

Aysha turned to thank him, only to have the words die in her throat at his bleak expression.

'Don't even think about uttering a word,' he warned.

'Don't tell me,' she dismissed wearily. 'You're intent on playing nurse.'

His silence was an eloquent testament of his intention, and she slid from the car and mounted the few steps to the front door.

Within minutes he'd located painkillers and was handing them to her together with a tumbler of water.

'Take them.'

She swallowed both tablets, then spared him a dark glance. 'Yessir.'

'Don't be sassy,' he said gently.

Damn him. She didn't need for him to be considerate. Macho she could handle. His gentleness simply undid her completely.

Aysha knew she should object as he took hold of her hand and led her to one of the cushioned sofas, then pulled her down onto his lap, but it felt so *good* her murmur of protest never found voice.

Just close your eyes and enjoy, a tiny imp prompted.

It would take ten minutes for the tablets to begin to work, and when they did she'd get to her feet, thank him, see him out of the door, then lock up and go to bed.

In a gesture of temporary capitulation she tucked

her head into the curve of his neck and rested her cheek against his chest. His arms tightened fractionally, and she listened to the steady beat of his heart.

She'd lain against him like this many times before. As a young child, friend, then as a lover.

Memories ran like a Technicolor film through her head. A fall and scraped knees as a first-grade kid in school. When she'd excelled at ballet, achieved first place at a piano recital. But nothing compared with the intimacy they'd shared for the past three months. That was truly magical. So mesmeric it had no equal.

She felt the drift of his lips against her hair, and her breathing deepened to a steady rise and fall.

When Aysha woke daylight was filtering into the room.

The main bedroom. And she was lying on one side of the queen-size bed; the bedcovers were thrown back on the other. She conducted a quick investigation, and discovered all that separated her from complete nudity was a pair of lacy briefs.

Memory was instant, and she blinked slowly, aware that the last remnants of her headache had disappeared.

The bedroom door opened and Carlo's tall frame filled the aperture. 'You're awake.' His eyes met hers, their expression inscrutable. 'Headache gone?'

'You stayed.' Was that her voice? It sounded breathless and vaguely unsteady.

He looked as if he'd just come from the shower. His hair was tousled and damp, and a towel was hitched at his waist.

'You were reluctant to let me go.'

Oh, God. Her eyes flew to the pillow next to her own, then swept to meet his steady gaze. Her lips parted, then closed again. Had they…? No, of course they hadn't. She'd remember…wouldn't she?

'Carlo—'

Her voice died in her throat as he discarded the towel and pulled on briefs, then thrust on a pair of trousers and slid home the zip.

Each movement was highlighted by smooth rippling muscle and sinew, and she watched wordlessly as he shrugged his arms into a cotton shirt and fastened the buttons.

He looked up and caught her watching him. His mouth curved into a smile, and his eyes were warm, much too warm for someone she'd chosen to be at odds with.

'Mind if I use a comb?'

Her lips parted, but no sound came out, and with a defenceless gesture she indicated the *en suite* bathroom. 'Go ahead.'

She followed his passage as he crossed the room, and she conducted a frantic visual search for something to cover herself with so she could make it to the walk-in wardrobe.

Carlo emerged into the bedroom as she was about to toss aside the bedcovers, and she hastily pulled them up again.

'I'll make coffee,' he indicated. 'And start breakfast. Ten minutes?'

'Yes. Thanks,' she added, and wondered at her faint edge of disappointment as he closed the door behind him.

What had she expected? That he'd cross to the bed and attempt to kiss her? *Seduce* her?

Yet there was a part of her that wanted him to…badly.

With a hollow groan she tossed aside the covers and made for the shower.

Ten minutes later she entered the kitchen to the aroma of freshly brewed coffee. Carlo was in the process of sliding eggs onto a plate, and there were slices of toasted bread freshly popped and ready for buttering.

'Mmm,' she murmured appreciatively. 'You're good at this.'

'Getting breakfast?'

Dressed, she could cope with him. 'Among other things,' she conceded, and crossed to the coffee-maker.

Black, strong, with two sugars. There was nothing better to kick-start the day. 'Shall I pour yours?'

'Please.' He took both plates and placed them on the servery. 'Now, come and eat.'

Aysha took a seat on one of four bar stools and looked at the food on her plate. 'You've given me too much.'

'Eat,' bade Carlo firmly.

'You're as bad as Teresa.'

He reached out a hand and captured her chin. 'No,' he refuted, turning her head towards him. 'I'm not.'

His kiss was sensuously soft and incredibly sensual, and she experienced real regret when he gently put her at arm's length.

'I have to leave. Don't forget we're attending the

Zachariahs' party tonight. I'll call through the day and let you know a time.'

With only days until the wedding, the pressure was beginning to build. Teresa seemed to discover a host of last-minute things that needed organising, and by the end of the day she began to feel as if the weekend at the Coast had been a figment of her imagination.

The need to feel supremely confident was essential, and Aysha chose a long, slim-fitting black gown with a sheer lace overlay. The scooped neckline and ribbon shoulder straps displayed her lightly tanned skin to advantage, and she added minimum jewellery: a slender gold chain, a single gold bangle on one wrist, and delicate drop earrings. Stiletto-heeled evening pumps completed the outfit, and she spared her reflection a cursory glance.

Black was a classic colour, the style seasonally fashionable. She looked OK. And if anyone noticed the faint circles beneath her eyes, she had every excuse for their existence. A bride-to-be was expected to look slightly frazzled with the surfeit of social obligations prior to the wedding.

Carlo's recorded message on the answering machine had specified he'd collect her at seven-thirty. The party they were to attend was at Palm Beach, almost an hour's drive from Vaucluse, depending on traffic.

She would have given anything not to go. The thought of mixing and mingling with numerous social friends and acquaintances didn't appeal any more than having to put on an act for their benefit.

Security beeped as Carlo used the remote module

to release the gates, and Aysha's stomach executed a series of somersaults as she collected her evening purse and made her way down to the lower floor.

She opened the front door as he alighted from the car, and she crossed quickly down the few steps and slid into the passenger seat.

His scrutiny was swift as he slid in behind the wheel, encompassing, and she wondered if he was able to define just how much effort it cost her to appear cool and serene.

Inside, her nerves were stretched taut, and she felt like a marionette whose body movements were governed by a disembodied manipulator.

She met his dark gaze with clear distant grey eyes. No small acting feat, when her body warmed of its own accord, heating at the sight of him and his close proximity.

His elusive cologne invaded her senses, stimulating them into active life, and every nerve-end, every fibre seemed to throb with need.

The *wanting* didn't get any better. If anything, each passing hour made it worse. Especially the long, empty nights when she hungered for his touch.

'How are you?'

Three words spoken in a commonplace greeting, yet they had the power to twist Aysha's stomach into a painful knot.

'Fine.' She didn't aim to tell him anything different.

Carlo eased the car forward, past the gates, then he accelerated along the suburban street with controlled ease.

She directed her attention beyond the windscreen and didn't see the muscle bunch at the edge of his jaw.

Would Nina be an invited guest? Dear Lord, she hoped not. Yet it was a possibility. A probability, she amended, aware that with each passing day the wedding drew closer. Which meant Nina would become more desperate to seize the slightest opportunity.

Aysha cursed beneath her breath at the thought of playing a part beneath Nina's watchful gaze. Worse, having to clash polite verbal swords with a woman whose vindictiveness was aimed to maim.

The harbour, with its various coves and inlets provided a scenic beauty unsurpassed anywhere in Australia, and she focused on the numerous small craft anchored at various moorings, cliff-top mansions dotted in between foliage.

Peak hour traffic had subsided, although it took the best part of an hour to reach their destination. A seemingly endless collection of long minutes when polite, meaningless conversation lapsed into silence.

'I guess our presence tonight is essential?'

Carlo cast her a direct look. 'If you're concerned Nina might be there…don't be. She won't have the opportunity to misbehave.'

'Do you really think you'll be able to stop her?' Aysha queried cynically.

He met her gaze for one full second, then returned his attention to the road. 'Watch me.'

'Oh, I intend to.' It could prove to be an interesting evening.

They reached the exclusive Palm Beach suburb at

the appointed time, and Aysha viewed the number of cars lining the driveway with interest. At a guess there were at least thirty guests.

Fifty, she re-calculated as their host drew them through the house and out onto the covered terrace.

It was strictly smile-time, and she was so well versed in playing the part that it was almost second nature to circulate among the guests and exchange small-talk.

A drink in one hand, she took a sip of excellent champagne and assured the hostess that almost every wedding detail was indeed organised, Claude, the wedding organiser, was indeed a gem, and, yes, she was desperately looking forward to the day.

Details she repeated many times during the next hour. She was still holding on to her first glass of champagne, and she took a hot savoury from a proffered platter, then reached for another.

'You missed dinner?'

Aysha spared Carlo a slow, sweet smile. 'How did you guess?'

His mouth curved, and his dark eyes held a musing gleam. 'You should have told me.'

'Why?'

The need to touch her was paramount, and he brushed fingertips down her cheek. 'We could have stopped somewhere for a meal.'

Her eyes flared, then dilated to resemble deep grey pools. 'Please don't.'

'Am I intruding on a little tiff?'

Aysha heard the words, recognised the feminine voice, and summoned a credible smile.

'Nina.'

Nina avidly examined Aysha's features, then fastened on the object of her obsession. She pressed exquisitely lacquered nails against the sleeve of Carlo's jacket. 'Trouble in paradise, *caro*?'

'What makes you think there might be?' His voice was pleasant, but there was no mistaking the icy hardness in his eyes as he removed Nina's hand from his arm.

Her pout was contrived to portray a sultry sexiness. 'Body language, darling.'

'Really?' The smile that curved his lips was a mere facsimile. 'In that case I would suggest your expertise is sadly lacking.'

Oh, my, Aysha applauded silently. If she could detach herself emotionally, the verbal parrying was shaping into an interesting bout.

'You know that isn't true.'

'Only by reputation. Not by personal experience.'

His voice was silk-encased steel, tempered to a dangerous edge. Only a fool would fail to recognise the folly of besting him.

'Darling, *really*. Your memory is so short?'

'We've frequented the same functions, sat at the same table. That's all.'

Nina spared Aysha a cursory glance. 'If you say so.' She gave a soft laugh and shook her head in telltale disbelief. 'The question is…will Aysha believe you?'

Aysha glimpsed the vindictive smile, registered the malevolence apparent in Nina's sweeping glance, before she turned back towards Carlo.

'*Ciao*, darlings. Have a happy life.'

Aysha watched Nina's sylph-like frame execute a deliberately evocative sway as she walked across the terrace.

'I think I need some fresh air.' And another glass of champagne. It might help dull the edges, and diminish the ugliness she'd just been witness to.

Strong fingers closed over her wrist. 'I'll come with you.'

'I'd rather go alone.'

'And add to Nina's satisfaction?'

Bright lights lit the garden paths, and there were guests mingling around the pool area. Music filtered through a speaker system, and there was the sound of muted laughter.

'Believe me, Nina's satisfaction is the last thing I want to think about.'

His grip on her hand tightened fractionally. 'I've never had occasion to lie to you, *cara*.' His eyes speared hers, fixing them mercilessly.

'There's always a first time for everything.'

Carlo was silent for several long seconds. 'I refuse to allow Nina's malicious machinations to destroy our relationship.'

The deadly softness of his voice should have warned her, but she was beyond analysing any nuances.

'Relationship?' Aysha challenged. 'Let's not delude ourselves our proposed union is anything other than a mutually beneficial business partnership.' She was on a roll, the words tripping easily, fatalistically, from her tongue. 'Cemented by holy matrimony in a bid to preserve a highly successful business empire for the next generation.' Her smile was far too bright, her voice so brittle she scarcely recognised it as her own.

Carlo's appraisal was swift, and she was totally unprepared as he lifted her slender frame over one shoulder.

An outraged gasp left her throat. 'What in *hell* do you think you're doing?'

'Taking you home.'

'Put me down.'

His silence was uncompromising, and she beat a fist against his ribcage in sheer frustration. With little effect, for he didn't release her until they reached the car.

'You *fiend*!' Aysha vented, uncaring of his ruthless expression as he unlocked the passenger door.

'Get in the car,' Carlo said hardily.

Her eyes sparked furiously alive. 'Don't you *dare* give me orders.'

He bit off a husky oath and pulled her in against him, then his head lowered and his mouth took punishing possession of her own.

Aysha struggled fruitlessly for several seconds, then whimpered as he held fast her head. His tongue was an invasive force, and she hated her traitorous body for the way it began to respond.

The hands which beat against each shoulder stilled and crept to link together at his nape. Her mouth softened, and she leaned in to him, uncaring that only seconds before anger had been her sole emotion.

She sensed the slight shudder that ran through his

large body, felt the hardening of his desire, and experienced the magnetising pulse of hunger in response.

Aysha felt as if she was drowning, and she temporarily lost any sense of time or where they were until Carlo gradually loosened his hold.

His lips trailed to the sensitive hollow at the edge of her neck and caressed it gently, then he lifted his head and bestowed a light, lingering kiss to her softly swollen mouth.

Sensation spiralled through her body, aching, poignant, making her aware of every nerve-centre, each pleasure spot.

Aysha didn't feel capable of doing anything but subsiding into the car, and she stared sightlessly out of the window as Carlo crossed to the driver's side and slid in behind the wheel.

She didn't offer a word for much of the time it took to reach Clontarf, for what could she say that wouldn't seem superfluous? The few occasions Carlo broached a query, her answer was monosyllabic.

Nina's image rose like a spectre in her mind, just as her voice echoed as the words replayed again and again.

CHAPTER NINE

THE Mercedes pulled off the main street and eased into a parking space. Carlo switched off the engine and undid his seatbelt.

Aysha looked at him askance. 'Why have you stopped?'

He reached sideways and unclasped her seatbelt. 'You didn't eat dinner, remember?'

The thought of food made her feel ill. 'I don't feel hungry.'

'Then we'll just have coffee.'

She looked at him in exasperation, and met the firm resolve apparent in his stance, the angle of his jaw.

'Do I get to have any say in this? Or will you employ strong-arm tactics?'

'You've dropped an essential kilo or two, you're pale, and you have dark circles beneath your eyes.'

'And I thought I was doing just fine,' Aysha declared silkily.

'It's here, or we raid the kitchen fridge at home.'

That meant him entering the house, making himself at home in the kitchen, and afterwards... She didn't want to contemplate *afterwards*. Having him stay was akin to condoning...

Oh, *damn*, she cursed wretchedly, and reached for the door-clasp.

The restaurant was well-patronised, and they were led to a centre table at the back of the room. Aysha heard the music, muted Mediterranean melancholy plucked from a boujouki, and the sound tugged something deep inside.

Carlo ordered coffee, and she declined. Greek coffee was ruinously strong.

'Tea. Very weak,' she added, and rolled her eyes when Carlo ordered moussaka from the menu. 'I don't want anything to eat.'

Moussaka was one of her favoured dishes, and when it arrived she spared it a lingering glance, let the aroma tease her nostrils. And she didn't argue when Carlo forked a portion and proffered a tempting sample.

It was delicious, and she picked up a spare fork and helped herself. Precisely as he'd anticipated she would do, she conceded wryly.

There was hot crusty bread, and she accepted a small glass of light red wine which she sipped throughout the meal.

'Better?'

It wasn't difficult to smile, and she could almost feel the relaxing effect of the wine releasing the knots of tension that curled tightly around her nerve-ends. 'Yes.'

'More tea?'

Aysha shook her head.

'Do you want to stay for a while, or shall we leave?'

She looked at him carefully, and was unable to define anything from his expression. There was a waiting, watchful quality apparent, a depth to his eyes that was impossible to interpret.

She spared a glance to the dance floor, and the few couples sharing it. Part of her wanted the contact, the closeness of his embrace. Yet there was another part that was truly torn.

Nina's accusations were too fresh in her mind, the image too vivid for it not to cloud her perspective.

Everything was wedding-related. And right now, the last thing she wanted to think about, let alone discuss, was the wedding.

'I adore the music. It's so poignant.'

Was she aware just how wistful she sounded? Or the degree of fragility she projected? Carlo wanted to smite a fist onto the table, or preferably close his hands around Nina's neck.

More than anything, he wanted to take Aysha to bed and make love with her until every last shred of doubt was removed. Yet he doubted she'd give him the opportunity. At least, not tonight.

Now, he had to be content to play the waiting game. Tomorrow, he assured himself grimly, he'd have everything he needed. And damned if he was going to wait another day.

He leaned across the table and caught hold of her hand, then lifted it to his lips.

It was an evocative gesture, and sent spirals of sensation radiating through her body. Her eyes dilated, and her lips shook slightly as he kissed each finger in turn.

'Dance with me.'

The shaking seemed to intensify, and she couldn't

believe it was evident. Dear God, dared she walk willingly into his arms?

And afterwards? What then? Let him lead her into the house, and into bed? That wouldn't resolve anything. Worse, the lack of a resolution would only condone her acquiescence to the status quo.

'Is dancing with me such a problem?' Carlo queried gently, and watched her eyes dilate to their fullest extent.

'It's what happens when I do.'

His eyes acquired a faint gleam, and the edges of his mouth tilted. 'Believe it's mutual.'

Aysha held his gaze without any difficulty at all. An hour ago she'd been furious with him. And Nina. *Especially* Nina.

'Pheromones,' she accorded sagely, and he uttered a soft laugh as he stood and drew her gently to her feet.

'The recognition by one animal of a chemical substance secreted by another,' Aysha informed him.

'You think so?'

She could feel her whole body begin to soften, from the inside out. A melting sensation that intensified as he brushed his lips against her temple.

'Yes.'

Would it always be like this? A smile, the touch of his mouth soothing the surface of her skin? *Is it enough*? a tiny voice taunted. Affection and sexual satisfaction, without love.

Many women settled for less. Much less.

He led her onto the dance floor and into his arms, and she didn't think about anything except the moment and the haunting, witching quality of the music as it stirred her senses and quickened the pace of her pulse.

Aysha wanted to close her eyes and think of nothing but the man and the moment.

For the space of a few minutes it was almost magic, then the music ceased as the band took a break, and she preceded Carlo back to the table.

'Another drink?'

'No, thanks,' she refused.

He picked up the account slip, summoned the waitress, paid, then led the way out to the car.

It didn't take long to reach Clontarf, and within minutes Carlo activated the gates, then drew the Mercedes to a halt outside the main entrance.

Aysha reached for the door-clasp as he released his seatbelt and opened the car door.

'There's no need—'

He shot her a glance that lost much of its intensity under cover of night. 'Don't argue,' he directed, and slid out from the car.

Indoors she turned to face him, and felt the sexual tension apparent. There was a slumberous quality in the depths of his eyes that curled all her nerve-ends, and she looked at him, assessing the leashed sensuality and matching it with her own.

'All you have to do is ask me to stay,' Carlo said quietly, and she looked at him with incredibly sad eyes.

It would be so easy. Just hold out her hand and follow wherever he chose to lead.

For a moment she almost wavered. To deny him

was to deny herself. Yet there were words she needed to say, and she wasn't sure she could make them sound right.

'I know.'

He lifted a hand and brushed his knuckles gently across her cheekbone. 'Go to bed, *cara*. Tomorrow is another day.'

Then he released her hand and turned towards the door.

Seconds later she heard the refined purr of the engine, and saw the bright red tail-lights disappear into the night.

He'd gone, when she'd expected him to employ unfair persuasion to share her bed. There was an ache deep inside she refused to acknowledge as disappointment.

If he'd pressed to stay, she'd have told him to leave. So why did she feel cheated?

Oh, for heaven's sake, this was ridiculous!

With a mental shake she locked the door and activated security, then she set the alarm and climbed the stairs to her room.

'Mamma,' Aysha protested. 'I don't *need* any more lingerie.'

'Nonsense, darling,' Teresa declared firmly. 'Nonna Benini sent money with specific instructions for you to buy lingerie.'

Aysha spared a glance at the exquisite bras, briefs and slips displayed in the exclusive lingerie boutique. Pure silk, French lace, and each costing enough money to feed an average family for a week.

After a sleepless night spent tossing and turning in her lonely bed, which had seen her wake with a headache, the last thing she needed was a confrontational argument with her mother.

'Then I guess we shouldn't disappoint her.'

Each garment had to be tried on for fit and size, and it was an hour before Aysha walked out of the boutique with bras and briefs in ivory, peach and black. Ditto slips, cobweb-fine pantyhose, and, the *pièce de resistance*, a matching nightgown and negligee.

'Superfluous,' she'd assured her mother when Teresa had insisted on the nightgown, and had stifled a sigh at her insistent glance.

Now, she tucked a hand beneath Teresa's arm and led her in the direction of the nearest café. 'Let's take five, Mamma, and share a cappuccino.'

'And we'll revise our list.'

Aysha thought if she heard the word *list* again, she'd scream. 'I can't think of a single thing.'

'Perfume. Something really special,' Teresa enthused. 'To wear on the day.'

'I already have—'

'I know. And it suits you so well.'

They entered the café, ordered, then chose a table near the window.

'But you should wear something subtly different, that you'll always associate with the most wonderful day of your life.'

'Mamma,' she protested, and was stalled in any further attempt as Teresa caught hold of her hands.

'A mother dreams of her child's wedding day from

the moment she gives birth. Especially a daughter. I want yours to be perfect, as perfect as it can be in every way.' Her eyes shimmered, and Aysha witnessed her conscious effort to control her emotions. 'With Carlo you'll have a wonderful life, enjoying the love you share together.'

A one-sided love, Aysha corrected silently. Many a successful marriage had been built on less. Was she foolish to wish for more? To want to be secure in the knowledge that Carlo had eyes only for her? That *she* was the only one he wanted, and no one else would do?

Chasing rainbows could be dangerous. If you did catch hold of one, there was no guarantee of finding the elusive pot of gold.

'Your father and I had a small wedding by choice,' Teresa continued. 'Our parents offered us money to use however we chose, and it was more important to use it towards the business.'

Aysha squeezed her mother's hand. 'I know, Mamma. I appreciate everything you've done for me.' Their love for each other wasn't in question, although she'd give almost anything to be able to break through the parent-child barrier and have Teresa be her friend, her equal.

However, Teresa was steeped in a different tradition, and the best she could hope for was that one day the balance of scales would become more even.

It was after eleven when they emerged into the arcade. Inevitably, Teresa's list had been updated to include perfume and a complete range of cosmetics and toiletries.

Aysha simply went with the flow, picked at a chicken salad when they paused for lunch, took two painkillers for her headache, and tried to evince interest in Teresa's summary of the wedding gifts which were beginning to arrive at her parents' home.

At three her mobile phone rang, and when she answered she heard Carlo's deep drawl at the other end of the line.

'Good day?'

Her heart moved up a beat. 'We're just about done.'

'I'll be at the house around seven.'

She was conscious of Teresa's interest, and she contrived to inject her tone with necessary warmth. 'Shall I cook something?'

'No, we'll eat out.'

'OK. *Ciao*.' She cut the connection and replaced the unit into her bag.

'Carlo,' Teresa deduced correctly, and Aysha inclined her head. 'He's a good man. You're very fortunate.'

There was only one answer she could give. 'I know.'

It was almost five when they parted, slipped into separate cars, and entered the busy stream of traffic, making it easy for Aysha to hang back at an intersection, then diverge onto a different road artery.

If Teresa discovered her daughter and prospective son-in-law were temporarily occupying separate residences, it would only arouse an entire host of questions Aysha had no inclination to answer.

The house was quiet, and she made her way upstairs, deposited a collection of brightly-coloured carry-bags in the bedroom, then discarded her clothes, donned a bikini and retraced her steps to the lower floor.

The pool looked inviting, and she angled her arms and dived into its cool depths, emerging to the surface to stroke several lengths before turning onto her back and lazily drifting.

Long minutes later she executed sufficient backstrokes to bring her to the pool's edge, then she levered herself onto the ledge and caught up a towel. Standing to her feet, she blotted excess moisture from her body, then she crossed to a nearby lounger and sank back against its cushioned depth.

The view out over the harbour was sheer magic, for at this hour the sea was a dark blue, deepening almost to indigo as it merged in the distance with the ocean.

There were three huge tankers drawing close to the main harbour entrance, and in the immediate periphery of her vision hundreds of small craft lay anchored at moorings.

It was a peaceful scene, and she closed her eyes against the strength of the sun's warmth. It had a soporific effect, and she could feel herself drifting into a light doze.

It was there that Carlo found her more than an hour later, after several minutes of increasing anxiety when he'd failed to locate her anywhere indoors.

His relief at seeing her lying supine on the lounger was palpable, although he could have shaken her for putting him through a few minutes of hell.

He slid open the door quietly, and stood watching her sleep. She looked so relaxed it was almost a shame to have to wake her, and he waited a while, not willing to disturb the moment.

A soft smile curved his mouth. He wanted to cross to her side and gently tease her into wakefulness. Lightly trail his fingers over the length of her body, brush his lips to her cheek, then find her mouth with his own. See her eyelids flutter then lift in wakefulness, and watch the warmth flood her eyes as she reached for him.

Except as things stood, the moment her lashes swept open her eyes were unlikely to reflect the emotion he wanted.

CHAPTER TEN

'AYSHA.'

She was dreaming, and she fought her way through the mists of sleep at the sound of her name.

The scene merged into reality. The location was right, so was the man who stood within touching distance.

It was the circumstances that were wrong.

She moved fluidly into a sitting position. 'Is it that late?' She swung her legs onto the ground and rose to her feet.

He looked impressive dressed in tailored trousers, pale blue cotton shirt, tie and jacket. She kept her eyes fixed on the knot of his tie. 'I'll go shower and change.'

He let her go, then followed her into the house. He crossed to the kitchen, extracted a cool drink from the refrigerator and popped the can, then he prowled around the large entertainment area, too restless to stand or sit in one place for long.

There were added touches he hadn't noticed before. Extra cushions on the chairs and sofas, prints hanging on the walls. The lines were clean and muted, but the room had a comfortable feeling; it was a place where it would be possible to relax.

Carlo checked his watch, and saw that only five minutes had passed. It would take her at least another thirty to wash and dry her hair, dress and apply make-up.

Forty-five, he accorded when she re-entered the room.

The slip dress in soft shell-pink with a chiffon overlay and a wide lace border on the hemline heightened her lightly tanned skin, emphasised her dark blonde hair, and clever use of mascara and shadow deepened the smoky grey of her eyes.

She'd twisted her hair into a knot atop her head, and teased free a tendril that curled down to the edge of her jaw.

Aysha found it easy to return his gaze with a level one of her own. Not so easy was the ability to slow the sudden hammering of her heart as she drew close.

'Shall we leave?' Her voice was even, composed, and at total variance to the rapid beat of her pulse.

'Before we do, there's something I want you to read.' Carlo reached for the flat manila envelope resting on the nearby table and handed it to her.

The warm and wonderful girl of a week ago no longer existed. Except in an acted portrayal in the presence of others.

Alone, the spontaneity was missing from her laughter, and her eyes were solemn in their regard. Absent too was the generous warmth in her smile.

The scene he'd initiated with Nina earlier in the day had been damaging, but he didn't give a damn. The woman's eagerness to accept his invitation to lunch had sickened him, and he hadn't wasted any time informing her exactly what he planned to do should she ever cause Aysha a moment's concern.

He'd gone to extraordinary lengths in an attempt to remove Aysha's doubts. Now he needed to tell her, *show* her.

'Read it, Aysha.'

'Can't it wait until later?'

He thrust a hand into a trouser pocket, and felt the tension twist inside his gut. 'No.'

There was a compelling quality evident in those dark eyes, and she glimpsed the tense muscle at the edge of his jaw.

She was familiar with every one of his features. The broad cheekbones, the crease that slashed each cheek, the wide-spaced large eyes that could melt her bones from just a glance. His mouth with its sensually moulded lips was to die for, and the firm jawline hinted at more than just strength of character.

'Please. Just read it.'

Aysha turned the envelope over, and her fingers sought the flap, dealt with it, then slid out the contents.

The first was a single page, sworn and signed with a name she didn't recognise. Identification of the witness required no qualification, for Samuel Sloane's prominence among the city's legal fraternity was legend.

Her eyes skimmed the print, then steadied into a slower pace as she took in the sworn affidavit testifying Nina di Salvo had engaged the photographic services of William Baker with specific instructions to capture Carlo Santangelo and herself in compromising positions, previously discussed and outlined, for the agreed sum of five hundred dollars per negative.

Aysha mentally added up the photographic prints Nina had shown her, and had her own suspicions confirmed. Carlo had been the target; Nina the arrow.

Her eyes swept up to meet his. 'I didn't think she'd go to these lengths.'

Carlo's eyes hardened as he thought of Nina's vitriolic behaviour. 'It's doubtful she'll bother either of us again.' He'd personally seen to it.

'Damage control,' Aysha declared, and saw his eyes darken with latent anger.

'Yes.'

It was remarkable how a single word could have more impact than a dozen or so. 'I see.'

She was beginning to. But there was still a way to go. 'Read the second document.'

Aysha carefully slipped the affidavit to one side. There were several pages, each one scripted in legalese phrased to confuse rather than clarify. However, there was no doubt of Carlo's instruction.

Any assets in whatever form, inherited from either parents' estates, were to remain solely in her name for her sole use. At such future time, Carlo Santangelo would assume financial responsibility for Benini-Santangelo.

There was only one question. 'Why?'

'Because I love you.'

Aysha heard the words, and her whole body froze. The stillness in the room seemed to magnify until it became a tangible entity.

Somehow she managed to dredge up her voice,

only to have it emerge as a sibilant whisper. 'If this is a trick, you can turn around and walk out of here.'

Her eyes became stricken with an emotion she couldn't hide, and his expression softened to something she would willingly give her life for.

He caught both her hands together with one hand, then lifted the other to capture her nape.

'I love you. *Love*,' he emphasised emotively. 'The heart and soul that is *you*.' He moved his thumb against the edge of her jaw, then slowly swept it up to encompass her cheekbone. His eyes deepened, and his voice lowered to an impassioned murmur. 'I thought the love Bianca and I shared was irreplaceable. But I was wrong.' He lowered his forehead down to rest against hers. 'There was you. Always you. Affection, from the moment you were born. Respect, as you grew from child to woman. Admiration, for carving out your own future.'

His hands moved to her shoulders, then curved down her back to pull her close in against him.

It would be all too easy to lean in and lift her mouth to meet his. As she had in the past. This time she wanted sanity unclouded by emotion or passion.

Aysha lifted her hands to his chest and tried to put some distance between them. Without success. 'I can't think when you hold me.'

Those dark eyes above her own were so deeply expressive, she thought she might drown in them.

'Is it so important that you think?' he queried gently, and she swallowed compulsively.

'Yes.' She was conscious of every breath she took, every beat of her heart.

Carlo let his hands drop, and his features took on a quizzical warmth.

What she wanted, she hardly dared hope for, and she looked at him in silence as the seconds ticked by.

His smile completely disarmed her, and warmth seeped into her veins, heating and gathering force until it ran through her body.

'You want it all, don't you?'

Her mouth trembled as she fought to control her emotions. She was shaking, inwardly. Very soon, she'd become a trembling mass. 'Yes.'

Carlo pushed both hands into his trouser pockets, and she was mesmerised by his mouth, the way it curved and showed the gleam of white teeth, the sensuous quirk she longed to touch.

'I knew marriage between us could work. We come from the same background, we move in the same social circles, and share many interests. We had the foundation of friendship and affection to build on.'

The vertical crease slashed each cheek as he smiled, and his eyes... She felt as if she could drown in their depths.

'In the beginning I was satisfied that it was enough. I didn't expect to have those emotions develop into something more, much more.'

She had to ask. 'And now?'

'I need to be part of your life, to have you need me as much as I need you. As my wife, my friend, the other half of my soul.' He released his hands and reached out to cup her face. 'To love you, as you deserve to be loved. With all my heart. For the rest of my life.'

Aysha felt the ache of tears, and blinked rapidly to dispel them. At that precise moment she was incapable of uttering a word.

Did she realise how transparent she was? Intimacy was a powerful weapon, persuasive, invasive, and one he could use with very little effort. It would be so easy to lower his head, pull her close and let her *feel* what she did to him. His hands soothing her body, the possession of his mouth on hers...

He did none of those things.

'Yes.'

He heard the single affirmative, and every muscle, every nerve relaxed. Nothing else mattered, except their love and the life they would share together. 'No qualifications?'

She shook her head. 'None.'

'So sure,' Carlo said huskily. He reached for her, enfolding her into the strength of his body as his mouth settled over hers. Gently at first, savouring, tasting, then with a passionate fervour as she lifted her arms and linked her hands together at his nape.

Aysha felt his body tremble as she absorbed the force of his kiss and met and matched the mating dance of his tongue as it explored and ravaged sensitive tissue.

His hands shaped and soothed as they sought each pleasure spot, stroking with infinite care as the fire ignited deep within and burst into flame.

It seemed an age before he lifted his head, and she

could only stand there, supported by the strength of his arms.

'Do you trust me?'

She heard the depth in his voice, sensed his seriousness, and raised her eyes to meet his. There was no question. 'Yes,' she said simply.

'Then let's go.'

'OK.'

'Such docility,' Carlo teased gently as he brushed his lips against one temple.

Aysha placed a hand either side of his head and tilted it down as she angled her mouth into his in a kiss that was all heat and passion.

His heart thudded into a quickened beat, and she felt a thrill of exhilaration at the sense of power, the feeling of control.

Carlo broke the contact with emotive reluctance. 'The temptation to love you now, *here*, is difficult to resist.'

A mischievous smile curved her mouth. 'But you're going to.'

His hands slid to her shoulders and he gave her a gentle shake. 'Believe it's merely a raincheck, *cara*.' He released her and took hold of her hand.

'Are you going to tell me *where* we're going?'

'Someplace special.'

He led her outside, then turned to the side path leading to the rear of the grounds.

'Here?' Aysha queried in puzzlement, as they traversed the short set of steps leading down to the gazebo adjacent the pool area.

Lights sprang to life as if by magic, illuminating

the gazebo and casting a reflected glow over the newly planted garden, the beautiful free-form pool.

Her eyes widened as she saw a man and two women standing in front of a small rectangular pedestal draped with a pristine white lace-edged cloth. Two thick candles displayed a thin flicker and a vaporous plume, and there was the scent of roses, beautiful white tight-petalled buds on slender stems.

'Carlo?'

Even as she voiced the query she saw the answer in those dark eyes, eloquent with emotive passion. And love.

'This is for us,' he said gently, curving an arm across the back of her waist as he pulled her into the curve of his body. 'Saturday's production will fulfil our parents' and the guests' expectations.'

She was melting inside, the warmth seeping through her body like molten wax, and she didn't know whether to laugh or cry.

An hour ago she'd been curled up on a soft-cushioned sofa contemplating her shredded emotions.

'OK?' Carlo queried gently.

Her heart kicked in at a quickened beat, and she smiled. A slow, sweet smile that mirrored her inner radiance. 'Yes.'

Introductions complete, Aysha solemnly took her position at Carlo's side.

If the celebrant was surprised at the bride and groom's attire, she gave no indication of it. Her manner appeared genuine, and the words she spoke held a wealth of meaning during the short service.

Carlo slipped a diamond-encrusted ring onto her

finger, and Aysha slid a curved gold band onto his, listening in a haze of emotions as they were solemnly pronounced man and wife.

She lifted her mouth to meet his, and felt the warmth, the hint of restrained passion as he savoured the sweetness and took his fill.

Oh, my, this was about as close to heaven as it was possible to get, Aysha conceded as he reluctantly loosened his hold.

The heat was there, evident in the depth of his eyes, banked down beneath the surface. Desire, and promised ecstasy.

She cast him a witching smile, glimpsed the hunger and felt anticipation arrow through her body.

There was champagne chilling in an ice bucket, and Carlo loosened the cork, then filled each flute with slightly frothy sparkling liquid.

The bubbles tingled her tastebuds and teased the back of her throat as she sipped the excellent vintage.

Each minute seemed like an eternity as she conversed with the celebrant and two witnesses, and accepted the toast.

With both official and social duties completed, the celebrant graciously took her leave, together with the couple who had witnessed the marriage.

Aysha stood in the circle of Carlo's arms, and she leaned back against him, treasuring the closeness, the sheer joy attached to the moment.

Married. She could hardly believe it. There were so many questions she needed to ask. But not yet. There would be time later to work out the answers.

For now, she wanted to savour the moment.

Carlo's lips teased her sensitive nape, then nuzzled an earlobe. 'You're very quiet.'

'I feel as if we're alone in the universe,' she said dreamily. Her mouth curved upwards. 'Well, almost.' A faint laugh husked low in her throat. 'If you block out the cityscape, the tracery of street lights, the suburban houses.'

'I thought by now you'd have unleashed a barrage of questions,' he said with quizzical amusement.

She felt the slide of his hand as he reached beneath her top and sought her breast. The familiar kick of sensation speared from her feminine core, and she groaned emotively as his skilled fingers worked magic with the delicate peak.

She turned in his arms and reached for him, pulling his head down to hers as she sought his mouth with her own in a kiss that wreaked havoc with her tenuous control.

Aysha was almost shaking when he gently disengaged her, and her lips felt faintly swollen, her senses completely swamped with the feel, the taste of him.

'Let's get out of here,' Carlo directed huskily as he caught hold of her hand and led her towards his car.

'Where are we going?'

'I've booked us into a hotel suite for the night. Dinner at the restaurant. Champagne.'

'Why?' she queried simply. 'When everything we need is right here?'

'I want the night to be memorable.'

'It will be.' Without a doubt, she promised silently.

'You don't want the luxurious suite, a leisurely meal with champagne?' he teased.

'I want *you*. Only you,' Aysha vowed with heart-felt sincerity. 'Saturday we get to go through the formalities.' The elegant bridal gown, the limousines, the church service, the extravagant reception, she mused silently. Followed by the hotel bridal suite, and the flight out the next morning to their honeymoon destination.

A bewitching smile curved her generous mouth, and her eyes sparkled with latent humour. 'Tonight we can please ourselves.'

Carlo pressed a light kiss to the edge of her lips. 'Starting now?'

'Here?' she countered wickedly. 'And shock the neighbours?'

He swept an arm beneath her knees and carried her into the house. He traversed the stairs without changing stride, and in the main bedroom he lowered her down to stand in front of him.

Slowly, with infinite care, he released her zip. Warm fingers slid each strap over her shoulders, then shaped the soft slip down over her hips, her thighs, to her feet. Only her briefs and bra remained, and he dispensed with those.

She ached for his touch, his possession, and she closed her eyes, then opened them again as he lightly brushed his fingers across her sensitised skin.

He followed each movement with his lips, each single touch becoming a torture until she reached for him, her fingers urgent as they released shirt buttons and tugged the expensive cotton from his muscular frame.

His eyes dilated as she undid the buckle of his belt, and he caught his breath as she worked the zip fastening.

'Not quite in control, huh?' she offered with a faintly wicked smile, only to gasp as his mouth sought a vulnerable hollow at the edge of her neck.

He had the touch, the skill to evoke an instant response, and she trembled as his tongue wrought renewed havoc.

His hands closed over hers, completing the task, and she clutched hold of his waist as he dispensed with the remainder of his clothes.

The scent of his skin, the slight muskiness of *man* intermingled with the elusive tones of soap and cologne. Tantalising, erotic, infinitely tempting, and inviting her to savour and taste.

Aysha felt sensation burgeon until it encompassed every nerve-cell. The depth, the magnitude overwhelmed her. Two souls melding, seamlessly forging a bond that could never be broken.

She lifted her arms and wound them round his neck as he lowered her down onto the bed and followed her, protecting her from the full impact of his weight.

His mouth closed over hers, devastatingly sensual, in a kiss that drugged her mind, her senses, until she hardly recognised the guttural pleas as her own.

She was on fire, the flames of desire burning deep within until there was no reason, no sensation of anything other than the man and the havoc he was causing as he led her through pleasure to ecstasy and beyond.

Now, she wanted him *now*. The feel of him inside her, surging again and again, deeper and deeper, until she absorbed all of him, and their rhythm became as one, in tune and in perfect accord as they soared together, clung momentarily to the sexual pinnacle, then reached the ultimate state of nirvana.

Did she say the words? She had no idea whether they found voice or not. There was only the journey, the sensation of spiralling ecstasy, the scent of sexual essence, and the damp sheen on his skin.

She was conscious of her own response, *his*, the shudder raking that large body as he spilled his seed, and she exulted in the moment.

The sex between them had always been good. Better than good, she accorded dimly as she clung to him. But this, this was more. Intoxicating, exquisite, wild. And there was *love*. That essential quality that transcended physical expertise or skill.

There was no contest, Aysha acknowledged with lazy warmth a long time later as she lay curled against a hard male body.

Neither had had the will to indulge in leisurely lovemaking the first time round. It had been hard and fast, each one of them *driven* by a primal urge so intense it had been electrifying, wanton, and totally impassioned.

Afterwards they had shared the Jacuzzi, then towelled dry, they'd returned to bed for a lingering aftermath of touching, tasting…a *loving* that had had no equal in anything they'd previously shared.

'Are we going to tell our parents?'

Carlo brushed his chin against the top of her head. 'Let a slight change in wording to *reaffirmation* of vows do it for us on the day.'

CHAPTER ELEVEN

AYSHA woke to the sound of rain, and she took a moment to stretch her limbs, then she checked the bedside clock. A few minutes past seven.

Any time soon Teresa would knock on her door, and the day would begin.

If she was fortunate, she had an hour, maybe two, before Teresa began checking on everything from the expected delivery time of flowers…to the house, the church, the reception. Followed by a litany of reminders that would initiate various supervisors to recheck arrangements with their minions. The wedding co-ordinator was doubtless on the verge of a nervous breakdown.

Aysha slid out from the bed and padded barefoot across the carpet to the draped window. A touch to the remote control module activated the mechanism that swept the drapes open, and she stifled a groan at the sight of heavy rain drenching the lawn.

Her mother, she knew, would consider it an omen, and probably not a propitious one.

Aysha selected shorts and a top, discarded her nightshirt, then quickly dressed. With a bit of celestial help she might make it downstairs to the dining room—

Her mobile phone rang, and she reached for it.

'Carlo?'

'Who else were you expecting?'

His deep voice did strange things to her senses, and the temptation to tease him a little was difficult to resist. 'Any one of my four bridesmaids, your mother, Nonna Benini, phoning from Treviso to wish me *buona fortuna*, Sister Maria Teresa...' she trailed off, and was unable to suppress a light laugh. 'Is there any particular reason you called?'

'Remind me to exact retribution, *cara*,' he mocked in husky promise.

The thought of precisely how he would achieve it curled round her central core, and set her heart beating at a quickened pace.

'You weren't there when I reached out in the night,' Carlo said gently. 'There was no scent of you on my sheets, no drift of perfume to lend assurance to my subconscious mind.' He paused for a few seconds. 'I missed you.'

She closed her eyes against the vivid picture his words evoked. She could feel her whole body begin to heat, her emotions separate and shred. 'Don't,' she pleaded with a slight groan. 'I have to get through the day.'

'Didn't sleep much, either, huh?' he queried wryly, and she wrinkled her nose.

'An hour or two, here and there,' Aysha admitted.

'Are you dressed?'

'Yes.' Her voice was almost prim, and he laughed.

'Pity. If I can't have you in the flesh, then the fantasy will have to suffice.'

'And you, of course, have had a workout, showered, shaved, and are about to eat breakfast?'

Carlo chuckled, a deep, throaty sound that sent shivers slithering down her spine. 'Actually, no. I'm lying in bed, conserving my energy.'

Just the thought of that long muscular body resting supine on the bed was enough to play havoc with her senses. Imagining how he might or might not be attired sent her pulse beating like a drum.

'I don't think we'd better do this.'

'Do *what*, precisely?'

'Phone sex.'

His voice held latent laughter. 'Is that what you think we're doing?'

'It doesn't compensate for the real thing.'

His soft laughter was almost her undoing. 'I doubt Teresa will be impressed if I appear at the door and sweep you into the bedroom before breakfast.'

A firm tattoo sounded against the panelled door. 'Aysha?'

The day was about to start in earnest. 'In a moment, Mamma.'

'Don't keep me waiting too long at the church, *cara*,' Carlo said gently as she crossed the room.

'To be five minutes late is obligatory,' she teased, twisting the knob and drawing back the door. '*Ciao.*'

Teresa stood framed in the doorway. '*Buon giorno*, darling.' Her eyes glanced at the mobile phone. 'You were talking to Carlo?' She didn't wait for an answer as she walked to the expanse of plate glass window with its splendid view of the harbour and northern suburbs. 'It's raining.'

'The service isn't scheduled until four,' Aysha attempted to soothe.

'Antonio has spent so much time and effort on the gardens these past few weeks. It will be such a shame if we can't assemble outside for photographs.'

'The wedding organiser has a contingency plan, Mamma.' Photographs in the conservatory, the massive entry foyer, the lounge.

'Yes, I know. But the garden would be perfect.'

Aysha sighed. The problem with a perfectionist was that rarely did *anything* meet their impossibly high expectations.

'Mamma,' she began gently. 'If it's going to rain, it will, and worrying won't make it different.' She crossed to the *en suite* bathroom. 'Give me a few minutes, then we'll go downstairs and share breakfast.'

It was the antithesis of a leisurely meal. The phone rang constantly, and at nine the first of the day's wedding gifts arrived by delivery van.

'Put them in here,' Teresa instructed, leading the way into a sitting room where a long table decorated with snowy white linen and draped tulle held a large collection of various sized wrapped and beribboned packages.

The doorchimes sounded. 'Aysha, get that, will you, darling? It'll probably be Natalina or Giovanna.'

The first in line of several friends who had offered their services to help.

'Aysha, you look so calm. How is that?'

Because Carlo loves me. And we're already married. The words didn't find voice, but they sang through her brain like the sweetest music she'd ever heard.

'Ask me again a few hours from now,' she said with a teasing smile.

Organisation was the key, although as the morning progressed the order changed to relative chaos and went downhill from there.

The florist delivered the bridal bouquets, exquisitely laid out in their boxes...except there was one missing. The men's buttonholes arrived with the bouquets, instead of being delivered to Gianna's home.

Soon after that problem was satisfactorily resolved Teresa received a phone call from one of the two women who'd offered to decorate the church pews...they couldn't get in, the church doors were locked, and no one appeared to be answering their summons.

Lunch was hardly an issue as time suddenly appeared to be of the essence, with the arrival of Lianna, Arianne, Suzanne and Tessa.

'*Très* chic, darling,' Lianna teased as she appraised Aysha from head to toe and back again. 'Bare feet, cut-off jeans and a skimpy top. The ultimate in avant-garde bridal wear. Just add the veil, and you'll cause a sensation,' she concluded with droll humour.

'Mamma would have a heart attack.'

'Not something to be countenanced,' Lianna agreed solemnly. 'Now,' she demanded breezily, 'we're all showered and ready to roll. Command, and we'll obey.'

Together they went over the *modus operandi*, which went a little haywire, as the hairdresser arrived early and the make-up artist was late.

There followed a lull of harmonious activity until

it became volubly clear Giuseppe was insistent on wearing navy socks instead of black, and an argument ensued, the pitch of frazzled voices rising when Teresa laddered new tights.

'Ah, your *mamma*...' Giuseppe sighed eloquently as he entered the dining room where the hairdresser was putting the finishing touches to Aysha's hair.

'I love you, Papà,' Aysha said softly, and saw his features dissolve into gentleness.

'*Grazie.*' His eyes moistened, and he blinked rapidly. 'The photographer, he will be here soon. Better you go upstairs and get into that dress, or we'll both have your Mamma to answer to, hmm.'

She gave him a quick hug, touched her fingers to his cheek, and smiled as he caught hold of them and bestowed a kiss to her palm. 'A father couldn't wish for a more beautiful daughter. Now go.'

When she reached her bedroom Teresa was fussing over the bridesmaids' gowns in a bid to ensure every detail was perfect.

Lianna rolled her eyes in silent commiseration, then exhibited the picture of genteel grace. 'When are the little terrors due to arrive?'

'My God,' Teresa cried with pious disregard as she swept to face Aysha. 'The rose petals. Did you see a plastic container of rose petals in the florist's box?'

Aysha shook her head, and Teresa turned and all but ran from the room.

'For heaven's sake, darling,' Lianna encouraged. 'Get into that fairy floss of a dress, we'll zip you up, stick on the headpiece and veil—' An anguished wail rent the air. 'Guess the rose petals were a no-show, huh?' she continued conversationally. 'I'll go offer my assistance before dear Teresa adds a nervous breakdown to the imminent heart attack.'

Ten minutes later she was back, and Aysha merely lifted one eyebrow in silent query.

'One container of rose petals found safe and sound at Gianna's home. As we need *two*, Giuseppe has been despatched to denude Antonio's precious rose bushes.'

'Whose idea was that?' Aysha shook her head in a silent gesture of mock despair. 'Don't tell me. Yours, right?'

Lianna executed a sweeping bow. 'Of course. What the hell else were we going to do?' She inclined her head, then gave a visible shudder. 'Here come the cavalry of infants.'

Aysha removed her wedding dress from its hanger, then with the girls' help she carefully stepped into it and eased it gently into place. The zip slid home, and she adjusted the scalloped lace at her wrist.

The fitted bodice with its overlay of lace was decorated with tiny seed pearls, and the scooped neckline displayed her shoulders to perfection. A full-length skirt flowed in a cluster of finely gathered pleats from her slender waist and fell in a cascade of lace. The veil was the finest tulle, edged with filigree lace and held in place by an exquisite head piece fashioned from seed pearls and tiny silk flowers.

'Wow,' Lianna, Arianne, Suzanne and Tessa accorded with reverence as she turned to face them, and Lianna, inevitably the first to speak, declared, 'You're a princess, sweetheart. A real princess.'

Lianna held out her hand, and, in the manner of a surgeon requesting instruments, she demanded, 'Shoes? Garter in place? Head piece and veil.' That took several minutes to fix. 'Something borrowed?' She tucked a white lace handkerchief into Aysha's hand. 'Something blue?' A cute bow tucked into the garter. 'Something old?'

Aysha touched the diamond pendant on its thin gold chain.

Teresa re-entered the room and came to an abrupt halt. 'The children are waiting downstairs with the photographer.' Her voice acquired a betraying huskiness. '*Dio Madonna*, I think I'm going to cry.'

'No, you're not. Think of the make-up,' Lianna cajoled. 'Then we'd have to do it over, which would make us late.' She made a comical face. 'The mother of the bride gets to cry *after* the wedding.' She patted Teresa's shoulder with theatrical emphasis. 'Now's the time you launch yourself into your daughter's arms, assure her she's the most beautiful girl ever born, and any other mushy stuff you want to add. Then,' she declared with considerable feeling, 'we smile prettily while the photographer does his thing, and get the princess here to the church on time.'

Teresa's smile was shaky, definitely shaky, as she crossed to Aysha and placed a careful kiss on first one cheek, then the other. 'It's just beautiful.' She swallowed quickly. 'You're beautiful. Oh, dear—'

'Whoa,' Lianna cautioned. 'Time to go.'

The photographer took almost an hour, utilising indoor shots during a drizzling shower. Then miraculously the sun came out as they took their seats in no fewer than three stretch limousines parked in line on the driveway.

'Well, Papà, this is it,' Aysha said softly. 'We're on our way.'

He reached out and patted her hand. 'You'll be happy with Carlo.'

'I know.'

'Did I tell you how beautiful you look?'

Aysha's eyes twinkled with latent humour. 'Mamma chose well, didn't she?'

His answering smile held a degree of philosophical acceptance. 'She has planned this day since you were a little girl.'

The procession was slow and smooth as the cavalcade of limousines descended the New South Head Road.

Stately, Aysha accorded silently as the first of the cars slowed and turned into the church grounds.

There were several guests waiting outside, and there was the flash of cameras as Giuseppe helped her out from the rear seat.

Lianna and Arianne checked the hem of her gown, smoothed the veil, then together they made their way to the church entrance, where Suzanne and Tessa were schooling the children into position.

The entire effect came together as a whole, and Aysha took a moment to admire her bridal party.

Each of the bridesmaids wore burgundy silk off-the-shoulder fitted gowns and carried bouquets of ivory orchids. The flower girls wore ivory silk full-length dresses with puffed sleeves and a wide waistband, tied at the back in a large bow, with white shoes completing their attire, while the two page boys each wore a dark suit, white shirt with a paisley silk waistcoat and black bow-tie.

Teresa arrived, and Aysha watched as her mother distributed both satin ring cushions and supervised the little girls with their baskets of rose petals.

This was as much Teresa's day as it was hers, and she smiled as she took Giuseppe's arm. 'Ready, Papà?'

He was giving her into the care of another man, and it meant much to him, Aysha knew, that Carlo met with his full approval.

The organ changed tempo and began the 'Bridal March' as they entered the church, and Aysha saw Carlo standing at the front edge of the aisle, flanked by his best man and groomsmen.

Emily and Samantha strewed rose petals on the carpet in co-ordinated perfection. Neither Jonathon nor Gerard dropped the ring cushions.

As she walked towards Carlo he flouted convention and turned to face her. She saw the glimpse of fierce pride mingling with admiration, love meshing with adoration. Then he smiled. For her, only for her.

Everything else faded to the periphery of her vision, for she saw only him, and her smile matched his own as she moved forward and stood at his side.

Carlo reached for her hand and covered it with his own as the priest began the ceremony.

The substitution *reaffirmation* of their vows seemed to take on an electric significance as the guests assimilated the change of words.

Renewed pledges, the exchange of rings, and the

long, passionate kiss that undoubtedly would become a topic of conversation at many a dinner table for months to come.

There was music, not the usual hymn, but a poignant song whose lyrics brought a lump to many a guest's throat. A few feminine tears brought the use of fine cotton handkerchiefs when the groom leaned forward and gently kissed his bride for the second time.

Then Aysha took Carlo's arm and walked out of the church and into the sunshine to face a barrage of photographers.

It was Lianna who organised the children and cajoled them to behave with decorum during the photographic shoot. Aysha hid a smile at the thought they were probably so intimidated they didn't think to do anything but obey.

'She's going to drive some poor man mad,' Carlo declared with a musing smile, and Aysha laughed, a low, sparkling sound that was reflected in the depths of her eyes.

'And he'll adore every minute of it,' she predicted.

The shift to the reception venue was achieved on schedule, and Aysha turned to look at Carlo as their limousine travelled the short distance from the church.

'You were right,' she said quietly. 'I wouldn't have missed the church service for the world.'

His smile melted her bones, and her stomach executed a series of crazy somersaults as he took her hands to his lips and kissed each one in turn.

'I'll carry the image of you walking towards me down the aisle for the rest of my life.'

She traced a gentle finger down the vertical crease of his cheek and lingered at the edge of his mouth. 'Now we get to cut the cake and drink champagne.'

'And I get to dance with my wife.'

'Yes,' she teased mercilessly. 'After the speeches, the food, the photographs…'

'Then I get to take you home.'

Oh, my. She breathed unsteadily. How was she going to get through the next few hours?

With the greatest of ease, she reflected several hours later as they circled the guests and made their farewells.

Teresa deserved tremendous credit, for without doubt she had staged the production of her dreams and turned it into the wedding of the year. Press coverage, the media, the church, ceremony, catering, cake… Everything had gone according to plan, except for a few minor hiccups.

A very special day, and one Aysha would always treasure. But it was the evening she and Carlo had exchanged their wedding vows that would remain with her for the rest of her life.

Saying goodbye to her parents proved an emotional experience, for among their happiness and joy she could sense a degree of sadness at her transition from daughter to wife.

Tradition died hard, and Aysha hugged them tight and conveyed her appreciation not only for the day and the night, but for the care and devotion they'd accorded her from the day she was born.

There was confetti, rice, and much laughter as they escaped to the limousine. A short drive to an inner city hotel, and then the ascent by lift to the suite Carlo had booked for the night.

Aysha gave a startled gasp as he released the door then swept her into his arms and carried her inside.

'Now,' he began teasingly, as he pulled her close. 'I get to do this.'

This was a very long, intensely passionate kiss, and she just held on and clung as she met and matched his raw, primitive desire.

Then he gently released her and crossed to the table, where champagne rested on ice.

Aysha watched as Carlo loosened the cork on the bottle of champagne.

Froth spilled from the neck in a gentle spume, and she laughed softly as he picked up a flute to catch the foaming liquid.

'I've done that successfully at least a hundred times.' He partly filled another, then he handed her one, and touched the rim with his own. 'To us.'

Her mouth curved to form a generous smile, and her eyes... A man could drown in those luminous grey depths, at times mysterious, winsome, wicked. Today they sparkled with warmth, laughter and love. He wanted to reach out and pull her into his arms. Hold and absorb her until she was part of him, and never let go.

'Happiness, always,' said Aysha gently, and sipped the fine champagne.

He placed the bottle and the flute down onto the

coffee table, then he gently cradled her face between both hands.

'I love you.' His mouth closed over hers in a soft, open-mouthed kiss which reduced her to a quivering boneless mass.

'Have I told you how beautiful you looked today?' Carlo queried long minutes later.

After three times she'd stopped counting. 'Yes,' she teased, pressing a finger against the centre of his lower lip. Her eyes dilated as he took the tip into his mouth and began to caress it slowly with his tongue.

Heat suffused her veins, coursing through her body until she was on fire with need.

'There's just one thing.'

He buried his mouth in its palm. 'Anything.'

'Fool,' she accorded gently, and watched in fascination as his expression assumed a seriousness that was at variance with the day, the hour, the moment.

'Anything, *cara*,' he repeated solemnly. 'Any time, anywhere. All you have to do is ask.'

She closed her eyes, then slowly opened them. It frightened her to think she had so much power over this man. It was a quality she intended to treat with the utmost respect and care.

'I have something for you.'

'I don't need anything,' Carlo assured her. 'Except *you*.'

She kissed him briefly. 'I'm not going anywhere.' What she sought reposed within easy reach, and she took the few steps necessary to extract the white envelope, then she turned and placed it in his hand.

'*Cara*? What is this?'

A telephone call, specific instructions, a lecture on the necessity to protect her interests, and time out in a very hectic schedule to attach her signature in the presence of her legal advisor.

'Open and read it.'

Carlo's eyes sharpened as he extracted the neatly pinned papers, and as he unfolded and began to scan the affidavit it became apparent what she'd done.

He lowered the papers and regarded her carefully. 'Aysha—'

'I love you. I always have, for as long as I can remember.' She thought she might die from the intensity of it. 'I always will.'

It was a gift beyond price. 'I know.' Carlo's voice was incredibly gentle. Just as his love for her would endure. It was something he intended to reinforce every day for the rest of his life.

'Come here,' he bade softly, extending his arms, and she went into them gladly, wrapping her own round his waist as he enfolded her close.

The papers fluttered to the floor as his lips covered hers, and she gave herself up to the sensual magic that was theirs alone.

Heaven didn't get much better than this, Aysha mused dreamily as he swept an arm beneath her knees and strode towards the stairs.

'*Ti amo,*' she whispered. '*Ti amo.*'

Carlo paused and took possession of her mouth with his own in a kiss that held so much promise she almost wept. '*In eterno.*' Eternity, and beyond.

IN THE SPANIARD'S BED

HELEN BIANCHIN

CHAPTER ONE

'I'M ON my way.' Cassandra released the intercom, caught up her evening purse, keys, exited her apartment and took the lift down to the foyer where her brother was waiting.

At twenty-nine he was two years her senior, and he shared her blond hair, fair skin and blue eyes. Average height in comparison to her petite frame.

'Wow,' Cameron complimented with genuine admiration, and she responded with an affectionate smile.

'Brotherly love, huh?'

The ice-pink gown moulded her slender curves, its spaghetti straps showing silky skin to an advantage, and the diagonal ruffled split to mid-thigh showcased beautifully proportioned legs. A gossamer wrap in matching ice-pink completed the outfit, and her jewellery was understated.

'Seriously cool.'

She tilted her head to one side as she tucked a hand through his arm. 'Let's go slay the masses.'

Tonight's fundraiser was a prestigious event whose guests numbered among Sydney's social élite. Held in the ballroom of a prominent city hotel, it was one of several annual soirées Cassandra and

5

her brother attended on their father's behalf after a heart attack and stroke two years ago forced him into early retirement.

Guests were mingling in the large foyer when they arrived, and she summoned a practised smile as she acknowledged a few acquaintances, pausing to exchange a greeting with one friend or another as she selected iced water from a hovering drinks waiter.

Observing the social niceties was something she did well. Private schooling and a finishing year in France had added polish and panache. The Preston-Villers family held a certain social standing of which her father was justly proud.

While Cameron had been groomed to enter the Preston-Villers conglomerate from an early age, Cassandra chose to pursue gemmology and jewellery design, added the necessary degree, studied with a well-known jeweller and she was now beginning to gain a reputation for her work.

Mixing and mingling was part of the social game, and she did it well.

Committee members conferred and worked the room in a bid to ensure the evening's success. The hotel ballroom was geared to seat a thousand guests, and it was rumoured there had been a waiting list for last-minute ticket cancellations.

'There's something I need to discuss with you.'

Cassandra met Cameron's gaze, examined his expression, and restrained a faint frown as she glimpsed the slight edginess apparent.

'Here, now?' she queried lightly, and waited for his usual carefree smile.

'Later.'

It couldn't be anything serious, she dismissed, otherwise he would have mentioned it during the drive in to the city.

'Darling, how are you?'

The soft feminine purr evoked a warm smile as she turned to greet the tall, slender model. 'Siobhan.' Her eyes sparkled. They'd attended the same school, shared much, and were firm friends. 'I'm fine, and you?'

'Flying out to Rome tomorrow, then it's Milan followed by Paris.'

Cassandra uttered a subdued chuckle in amusement. 'It's a hard life.'

Siobhan grinned. 'But an interesting one,' she conceded. 'I have a date with an Italian count in Rome.'

'Ah.'

'Old money, and *divine*.'

The musing twinkle in those gorgeous green eyes brought forth a husky laugh as Cassandra shook her head. 'You're wicked.'

'This time it's serious,' Siobhan declared as Cassandra's smile widened.

'It always is.'

'Got to go. The parents are in tow.'

'Have fun.'

'I shall. In Italy.' She leaned forward and pressed her cheek against Cassandra's in a gesture of affection.

'Take care.'

'Always.'

Soon the ballroom doors would be open, and guests would be called to take their seats. There would be the introductory and explanatory speeches, the wine stewards would do their thing, and the first course served.

Speaking of which, she was hungry. Lunch had been yoghurt and fruit snatched between the usual weekend chores.

Cameron appeared deep in conversation with a man she presumed to be a business associate, and she sipped chilled water from her glass as she debated whether to join him.

At that moment she felt the warning prickle of awareness as her senses went on alert, and she let her gaze skim the guests.

There was only one man who had this particular effect on her equilibrium.

Innate instinct? An elusive knowledge based on the inexplicable?

Whatever, it was crazy. Maddening.

Maybe this time she had it wrong. Although all it took was one glance at that familiar dark head to determine her instinct was right on target.

Diego del Santo. Successful entrepreneur, one of the city's nouveau riche…and her personal nemesis.

Born in New York of Spanish immigrant parents, it was reported he'd lived in the wrong part of town, fought for survival in the streets, and made his money early, so it was rumoured, by means beyond legitimate boundaries of the law.

He took risks, it was said, no sensible man would touch. Yet those risks had paid off a million-fold several times over. Literally.

In idle fascination she watched as he turned towards her, then he murmured something to his companion and slowly closed the distance between them.

'Cassandra.'

The voice was low, impossibly deep with the barest trace of an accent, and possessed of the power to send tiny shivers feathering the length of her spine.

Tall, broad-framed, with the sculptured facial features of his Spanish ancestors. Dark, well-groomed hair, dark, almost black eyes, and a mouth that promised a thousand delights.

A mouth that had briefly tasted her own when she'd disobeyed her father and persuaded Cameron to take her to a party. Sixteen years old, emerging hormones, a sense of the forbidden combined with a desire to play grown-up had proved a volatile mix. Add her brother with his own agenda, a few sips too many of wine, a young man who seemed intent on leading her astray, and she could easily have been in over her head. Except Diego del Santo had materialised out of nowhere, intervened, read her the Riot Act, then proceeded to show her precisely what she should be wary of when she heedlessly chose to flirt. Within minutes he had summoned Cameron and she found herself bundled into her brother's car and driven home.

Eleven years had passed since that fateful episode, ten of which Diego had spent in his native New York creating his fortune.

Yet she possessed a vivid recollection of how it felt to have his mouth savour her own. The electric primitiveness of his touch, almost as if he had reached down to her soul and staked a claim.

Diego del Santo had projected a raw quality that meshed leashed savagery with blatant sensuality. A dangerously compelling mix, and one that attracted females from fifteen to fifty.

Now there were no rough edges, and he bore the mantle of power with the same incredible ease he wore his designer clothes.

In his mid-to-late thirties, Diego del Santo was a seriously rich man whose property investments and developments formed a financial portfolio that edged him close to billionaire status.

As such, his return to Australia a year ago had soon seen him become an A-list member of Sydney's social élite, receiving invitations to each and every soirée of note. His acceptance was selective, and his donations to worthy charities, legend.

Preston-Villers' involvement with similar charity events and her father's declining health meant they were frequently fellow guests at one function or another. It was something she accepted, and dealt with by presenting a polite façade.

Only she knew the effect he had on her. The way her pulse jumped and thudded to a rapid beat. No one could possibly be aware her stomach curled into a painful knot at the mere sight of him, or how one glance at his sensual mouth heated the blood in her veins in a vivid reminder of the way it felt to have that mouth possess her own.

The slow sweep of his tongue, the promise of passion, the gentle, coaxing quality that caught her tentative response and took it to an undreamt-of dimension.

Eleven years. Yet his kiss was hauntingly vivid…a taunting example by which she'd unconsciously measured each kiss that followed it. None matched up, no matter how hard she tried to convince herself imagination had merely enhanced the memory.

There were occasions when she thought she should dispense with her own curiosity and accept one of his many invitations. Yet each time something held her back, an innate knowledge such a step would put her way out of her depth.

His invitations and her refusals had become something akin to a polite game they each played. What would he do, she mused, if she surprised him by accepting?

Are you *insane?* a tiny voice queried insidiously.

'Diego,' Cassandra acknowledged coolly, meeting his compelling gaze with equanimity, watching as he inclined his head to her brother.

'Cameron.'

For a millisecond she thought she glimpsed some unspoken signal pass between the men, then she dismissed it as fanciful.

'A successful evening, wouldn't you agree?'

Tonight's event was a charity fundraiser aiding state-of-the-art equipment for a special wing of the city's children's hospital.

Without doubt there were a number of guests with a genuine interest in the nominated charity. However, the majority viewed the evening as a glitz-and-glamour function at which the women would attempt to outdo each other with designer gowns and expensive jewellery, whilst the men wheeled and dealed beneath the guise of socialising.

Diego del Santo didn't fit easily into any recognisable category.

Not that she had any interest in pigeon-holing him. In fact, she did her best to pretend he didn't exist. Something he seemed intent on proving otherwise.

He could have any woman he wanted. And probably did. His photo graced the social pages of numerous newspapers and magazines, inevitably with a stunning female glued to his side.

There was a primitive quality evident. A hint of something dangerous beneath the surface should anyone dare to consider scratching it.

A man who commanded respect and admiration in the boardroom. Possessed of the skill, so it was whispered, and the passion to drive a woman wild in the bedroom.

It was a dramatic mesh of elemental ruthlessness and latent sensuality. Lethal.

Some women would excel at the challenge of taming him, enjoying the ride for however long it lasted. But she wasn't one of them. Only a fool ventured into the devil's playground with the hope they wouldn't get burnt.

Eluding Diego was a game she became adept at playing. If they happened to meet, she offered a polite smile, acknowledged his presence, then moved on.

Yet their social schedule was such, those occasions were many. If she didn't know better, she could almost swear he was intent on playing a game of his own.

'If you'll excuse me,' Cassandra ventured. 'There's someone I should catch up with.' A time-worn phrase, trite but true, for there were always a few friends she could greet by way of escape.

Cameron wanted to protest, she could tell, although Diego del Santo merely inclined his head.

Which didn't help at all, for she could *feel* those dark eyes watching her as she moved away.

Sensation feathered the length of her spine, and something tugged deep inside in a vivid reminder of the effect he had on her composure.

Get over it, she chided silently as she deliberately sought a cluster of friends and blended seamlessly into their conversation.

Any time soon the doors into the ballroom would open and guests would be encouraged to take their seats at designated tables. Then she could rejoin Cameron, and prepare to enjoy the evening.

'You had no need to disappear,' Cameron chastised as she moved to his side.

'Diego del Santo might be serious eye candy, but he's not my type.'

'No?'

'No.' She managed a smile, held it, and began threading her way towards their table.

'Do you know who else is joining us?' Cassandra queried lightly as she slid into one of four remaining seats, and took time to greet the six guests already seated.

'Here they are now.'

She registered Cameron's voice, glanced up from the table…and froze.

Diego del Santo and the socialite and model, Alicia Vandernoot.

No. The silent scream seemed to echo inside her head.

It was bad enough having to acknowledge his presence and converse for a few minutes. To have to share a table with him for the space of an evening was way too much!

Had Cameron organised this? She wanted to rail against him and demand *Why?* Except there wasn't the opportunity to do so without drawing unwanted attention.

If Diego chose the chair next to hers, she'd scream!

Of course he did. It was one of the correct dictums of society when it came to seating arrangements. Although she had little doubt he enjoyed the irony.

Cassandra murmured a polite greeting, and her faint smile was a mere facsimile.

This close she was far too aware of him, the clean smell of freshly laundered clothes, the subtle aroma of his exclusive cologne.

Yet it was the man himself, his potent masculinity and the sheer primitive force he exuded that played havoc with her senses.

A few hours, she consoled herself silently. All she had to do was sip wine, eat the obligatory three courses set in front of her, and make polite conversation. She could manage that, surely?

Not so easy, Cassandra acknowledged as she displayed intent interest in the charity chairperson's introduction prior to revealing funding endeavours, results and expectations.

Every nerve in her body was acutely attuned to Diego del Santo, supremely conscious of each move he made.

'More water?'

He had topped up Alicia's goblet, and now offered to refill her own.

'No, thank you.' Her goblet was part-empty, but she'd be damned if she'd allow him to tend to her.

Did he sense her reaction? Probably. He was too astute not to realise her excruciating politeness indicated she didn't want anything to do with him.

Uniformed waiters delivered starters with practised efficiency, and she forked the artistically arranged food without appetite.

'The seafood isn't to your satisfaction?'

His voice was an accented drawl tinged with amusement, and she met his dark gaze with equanimity, almost inclined to offer a negation just to see what he'd do, aware he'd probably summon the waiter and insist on a replacement.

'Yes.'

The single affirmative surprised her, and she deliberately widened her eyes. 'You read minds?'

The edge of his mouth curved, and there was a humorous gleam apparent. 'It's one of my talents.'

Cassandra deigned not to comment, and deliberately turned her attention to the contents on her plate, unsure if she heard his faint, husky chuckle or merely imagined it.

He was the most irritating, impossible man she'd

ever met. Examining why wasn't on her agenda. At least that's what she told herself whenever Diego's image intruded...on far too many occasions for her peace of mind.

It was impossible to escape the man. He was *there,* a constant in the media, cementing another successful business deal, escorting a high-profile female personality to one social event or another. Cameron accorded him an icon, and mentioned him frequently in almost reverent tones.

Tonight Diego del Santo had chosen to invade her personal space. Worse, she had little option but to remain in his immediate proximity for a few hours, and she resented his manipulation, hated him for singling her out as an object for his amusement.

For that was all it was...and it didn't help that she felt like a butterfly pinned to the wall.

Cassandra took a sip of wine, and deliberately engaged Cameron in conversation, the thread of which she lost minutes later as the waiter removed plates from their table.

She was supremely conscious of Diego's proximity, the shape of his hand as he reached for his wine goblet, the way his fingers curved over the delicate glass...and couldn't stop the wayward thought as to how his hands would glide over a woman's skin.

Where had that come from?

Dear heaven, the wine must have affected her

brain! The last thing she wanted was any physical contact with a man of Diego del Santo's ilk.

'Your speciality is gemmology, I believe?'

Think of the devil and he speaks, she alluded with silent cynicism as she turned towards him. 'Polite conversation, genuine interest,' she inclined, and waited a beat. 'Or an attempt to alleviate boredom?'

His expression didn't change, although she could have sworn something moved in the depths of those dark eyes. 'Let's aim for the middle ground.'

There was a quality to his voice, an inflexion she preferred to ignore. 'Natural precious gemstones recovered in the field by mining or fossiking techniques are the most expensive.' Such facts were common knowledge. 'For a jewellery designer, they give more pleasure to work with, given there's a sense of nature and the process of their existence. It becomes a personal challenge to have the stones cut in such a way they display maximum beauty. The designer's gift to ensure the design and setting reflect the stone's optimal potential.' A completed study of gemmology had led to her true passion of jewellery design.

Diego saw the way her mouth softened and her eyes came alive. It intrigued him, as *she* intrigued him.

'You are not in favour of the synthetic or simulants?'

Her expression faded a little. 'They're immensely popular and have a large market.'

His gaze held hers. 'That doesn't answer the question.' He lifted a hand and fingered the delicate argyle diamond nestling against the hollow at the base of her throat. 'Your work?' It was a rhetorical question. He'd made it his business to view her designs, without her knowledge, and was familiar with each and every one of them.

She flinched at his touch, hating his easy familiarity almost as much as she hated the tell-tale warmth flooding her veins.

If she could, she'd have flung the icy contents of her glass in his face. Instead, she forced her voice to remain calm. 'Yes.'

A woman could get lost in the depths of those dark eyes, for there was warm sensuality lurking just beneath the surface, a hint, a promise, of the delights he could provide.

Sensation feathered the length of her spine, and she barely repressed a shiver at the thought of his mouth on hers, the touch of his hands…how it would feel to be driven wild, beyond reason, by such a man.

'Have dinner with me tomorrow night.'

'The obligatory invitation?' Her response was automatic, and she tempered it with a gracious, 'Thank you. No.'

The edge of his mouth lifted. 'The obligatory refusal…because you have to wash your hair?'

'I can come up with something more original.'

She could, easily. Except she doubted an excuse, no matter how legitimate-sounding, would fool him.

'You won't change your mind?'

Cassandra offered a cool smile. 'What part of *no* don't you understand?'

Diego reached for the water jug and refilled her glass. The sleeve of his jacket brushed her arm, and her stomach turned a slow somersault at the contact.

It was as well the waiters began delivering the main course, and she sipped wine in the hope it would soothe her nerves.

Chance would be a fine thing! She was conscious of every move he made, aware of the restrained power beneath the fine Armani tailoring, the dangerous aura he seemed to project without any effort at all.

Another two hours. Three at the most. Then she could excuse herself and leave. If Cameron wanted to stay on, she'd take a cab home.

Cassandra drew a calming breath and regarded the contents on her plate. The meal was undoubtedly delicious, but her appetite had vanished.

With determined effort she caught Cameron's attention, and deliberately sought his opinion on something so inconsequential that afterwards she had little recollection of the discussion.

There were the usual speeches, followed by light entertainment as dessert and coffee were served. Never had time dragged quite so slowly, nor could she recall an occasion when she'd so badly wanted the evening to end.

To her surprise, it was Cameron who initiated the desire to leave, citing a headache as the reason, and Cassandra rose to her feet, offered a polite good-night to the occupants of their table, then preceded her brother out to the foyer.

'Are you OK?'

He looked pale, too pale, and a slight frown creased her brow as they headed towards the bank of lifts. 'Headache?' She extended her hand as he retrieved his car keys. 'Want me to drive?'

CHAPTER TWO

MINUTES later she slid behind the wheel and sent the car up to street level to join the flow of traffic. It was a beautiful night, the air crisp and cool indicative of spring.

A lovely time of year, she accorded silently as she negotiated lanes and took the route that led to Double Bay.

Fifteen, twenty minutes tops, and she'd be home. Then she could get out of the formal gear, cleanse off her make-up, and slip into bed.

'We need to talk.'

Cassandra spared him a quick glance. 'Can't it wait until tomorrow?'

'No.'

It was most unlike Cameron to be taciturn. 'Is something wrong?' Her eyes narrowed as the car in front came to a sudden stop, and she uttered an unladylike curse as she stamped her foot hard on the brakes.

'Hell, Cassandra,' he muttered. 'Watch it!'

'Tell that to the guy in front.' Her voice held unaccustomed vehemence. Choosing silence for the remaining time it took to reach her apartment seemed a wise option. The last thing she coveted was an argument.

'Park in the visitors' bay,' Cameron instructed as she swept the car into the bricked apron adjacent to the main entrance.

'You're coming up?'

'It's either that, or we talk in the car.'

He didn't seem to be giving her a choice as he unbuckled his seat belt and slid out from the passenger seat.

She followed, inserted her personalised card into the security slot to gain entry into the foyer, and used it again to summon a lift.

'I hope this won't take long,' she cautioned as she preceded him into her apartment, then she turned to face him. 'OK, shoot.'

He closed his eyes, then opened them again and ran a hand through his hair. 'This isn't easy.'

The tension of the evening began to manifest itself into tiredness, and she rolled her shoulders. 'Just spit it out.'

'The firm is in trouble. Major financial trouble,' he elaborated. 'If Dad found out just how hopeless everything is, it would kill him.'

Ice crept towards the region of her heart. 'What in hell are you talking about?'

'Preston-Villers is on a roller-coaster ride to insolvency.'

'What?' She found it difficult to comprehend. *'How?'*

He was ready to crumple, and it wasn't a good look.

'Bad management, bad deals, unfulfilled contracts. Staff problems. You name it, it happened.'

She adored her brother, but he wasn't the son her father wanted. Cameron didn't possess the steel backbone, the unflagging determination to take over directorship of Preston-Villers. Their father had thought it would be the making of his son. Now it appeared certain to be his ruination.

'Just how bad is it?'

Cameron grimaced, and shot her a desperate look. 'The worst.' He held up a hand. 'Yes, I've done the round of banks, financiers, sought independent advice.' He drew in a deep breath and released it slowly. 'It narrows down to two choices. Liquidate, or take a conditional offer.'

Hope was uppermost, and she ran with it. 'The offer is legitimate?'

'Yes.' He rubbed a weary hand along his jaw. 'An investor is prepared to inject the necessary funds, I get to retain an advisory position, he brings in his professional team, shares joint directorship, and takes a half-share of all profits.'

It sounded like salvation, but there was need for caution. 'Presumably you've taken legal advice on all this?'

'It's the only deal in town,' he assured soberly. 'There's just a matter of the remaining condition.'

'Which is?'

He hesitated, then took a deep breath and expelled it. 'You.'

Genuine puzzlement brought forth a frown. 'The deal has nothing to do with me.'

'Yes, it does.'

Like pieces of a puzzle, they began clicking into place, forming a picture she didn't want to see. 'Who made the offer?' Dear God, no. It couldn't be…

'Diego del Santo.'

Cassandra felt the blood drain from her face. Shock, disbelief, anger followed in quick succession. 'You can't be serious?' The words held a hushed quality, and for a few seconds she wondered if she'd actually uttered them.

Cameron drew in a deep breath, then released it slowly. 'Deadly.' To his credit, Cameron looked wretched.

'Let me get this straight.' Her eyes assumed an icy gleam. 'Diego del Santo intends making this personal?' His image conjured itself in front of her, filling her vision, blinding her with it.

'Without your involvement, the deal won't go ahead.'

She tried for *calm,* when inside she was a seething mass of anger. 'My *involvement* being?'

'He'll discuss it with you over dinner tomorrow evening.'

'The *hell* he will!'

'Cassandra—' Cameron's features assumed a

grey tinge. 'You want Alexander to have another heart attack?'

The words stopped her cold. The medics had warned a further attack could be his last. 'How can you even say that?'

She wanted to rail against him, demand why he'd let things progress beyond the point of no return. Yet recrimination wouldn't solve a thing, except provide a vehicle to vent her feelings.

'I want proof.' The words were cool, controlled. 'Facts,' she elaborated, and glimpsed Cameron's obvious discomfiture. 'The how and why of it, and just how bad it is.'

'You don't believe me?'

'I need to be aware of all the angles,' she elaborated. 'Before I confront Diego del Santo.'

Cameron went a paler shade of pale. 'Confront?'

She fired him a look that quelled him into silence. 'If he thinks I'll meekly comply with whatever he has in mind, then he can think again!'

His mouth worked as he searched for the appropriate words. 'Cass—'

'Don't *Cass* me.' It was an endearing nickname that belonged to their childhood.

'Do you have any idea who you're dealing with?'

She drew in a deep breath and released it slowly. 'I think it's about time Diego del Santo discovered who *he* is dealing with!' She pressed fingers to her throbbing temples in order to ease the ache there.

'Cassandra—'

'Can we leave this until tomorrow?' She needed to *think*. Most of all, she wanted to be alone. 'I'll organise lunch, and we'll go through the paperwork together.'

'It's Sunday.'

'What does that have to do with it?'

Cameron lifted both hands in a gesture of conciliation. 'Midday?'

'Fine.'

She saw him out the door, locked up, then she removed her make-up, undressed, then slid into bed to stare at the darkened ceiling for what seemed an age, sure hours later when she woke that she hadn't slept at all.

A session in the gym, followed by several laps of the pool eased some of her tension, and she re-entered her apartment, showered and dressed in jeans and a loose top, then crossed into the kitchen to prepare lunch.

Cameron arrived at twelve, and presented her with a chilled bottle of champagne.

'A little premature, don't you think?' she offered wryly as she prepared garlic bread and popped it into the oven to heat.

'Something smells good,' he complimented, and she wrinkled her nose at him.

'Flattery won't get you anywhere.' Lunch was a seafood pasta dish she whipped up without any fuss, and accompanied by a fresh garden salad it was an adequate meal.

'Let's eat first, then we'll deal with business. OK?'

He didn't look much better than she felt, and she wondered if he'd slept any more than she had.

'Dad is expecting us for dinner.'

It was a weekly family tradition, and one they observed almost without fail. Although the thought of presenting a false façade didn't sit well. Her father might suffer ill-health, but he wasn't an easy man to fool.

'This pasta is superb,' Cameron declared minutes later, and she inclined her head in silent acknowledgement.

By tacit agreement they discussed everything except Preston-Villers, and it was only when the dishes were dealt with that Cassandra indicated Cameron's briefcase.

'Let's begin, shall we?'

It was worse, much worse than she had envisaged as she perused the paperwork tabling Preston-Villers slide into irretrievable insolvency. The accountant's overview of the current situation was damning, and equally indisputable.

She'd wanted proof. Now she had it.

'I can think of several questions,' she began, but only one stood out. 'Why did you let things get this bad?'

Cameron raked fingers through his hair. 'I kept hoping the contracts would come in and everything would improve.'

Instead, they'd gone from bad to worse.

Cassandra damned Diego del Santo to hell and back, and barely drew short of including Cameron with him.

'Business doesn't succeed on *hope*.' It needed a hard, competent hand holding the reins, taking control, making the right decisions.

A man like Diego del Santo, a quiet voice insisted. Someone who could inject essential funds, and ensure everything ran like well-oiled clockwork.

There was sense in the amalgamation, and as Cameron rightly described, it was the only deal in town if Preston-Villers was to survive.

'Shall I contact Diego and confirm you've reconsidered his dinner invitation?'

'No.'

Disbelief and consternation were clearly evident.

'No?'

'My ball. My play.' Something she intended to take care of tomorrow. She stood to her feet. 'I need to put in an hour or two on the laptop before leaving to have dinner with Dad.' She led the way to the door of her apartment. 'I'll see you there.'

'OK.' Cameron offered an awkward smile. 'Thanks.'

'For what?' She couldn't help herself. 'Lunch?'

'That, too.'

It was after five when Cassandra entered the electronic gates guarding Alexander Preston-Villers' splendid home. Renovations accommodated wheelchair usage, and a lift had been installed for easy access between upper and lower floors. There was a resident housekeeper, as well as Sylvie, the live-in nurse.

Cassandra rang the bell, then used her key to enter the marble-tiled lobby.

It tore at Cassandra's heart each time she visited, seeing the man who had once been strong reduced to frail health.

Tonight he appeared more frail than usual, his lack of motor-skills more pronounced than they had been a week ago, and his appetite seemed less.

She looked at him, and wanted to weep. Cameron seemed similarly affected, and attempting to maintain a normal façade took considerable effort.

There was no way she'd allow *anyone* to upset Alexander. Not Cameron, nor Diego del Santo.

She made the silent vow as she drove back to her apartment. The determined bid haunted her sleep, providing dreams that assumed nightmarish proportions, ensuring she woke late and had to scramble in order to get to work on time.

Confronting Diego del Santo was a priority, and given a choice she'd prefer to beard him in his office than meet socially over a shared meal.

Which meant she'd need to work through her lunch hour in order to leave an hour early.

Cassandra found it difficult to focus on the intricate attention to detail involved with the creative-design project for an influential client.

Diego del Santo's image intruded, wreaking havoc with her concentration, and consequently it was something of a relief to pack up her work and consign it to the security safe before freshening her make-up prior to leaving for the day.

Del Santo Corporation was situated on a high floor of an inner-city office tower, and Cassandra felt a sense of angry determination as she vacated the lift and walked through automatic sliding glass doors to Reception.

'Diego del Santo.' Her voice was firm, clipped and, she hoped, authoritative.

'Mr del Santo is in conference, and has no appointments available this afternoon.'

She made a point of checking her watch. 'Put a call through and tell him Cassandra Preston-Villers is waiting to see him.'

'I have instructions to hold all calls.'

Efficiency. She could only admire it. 'Call his secretary.'

A minute...Cassandra counted off the seconds...a woman who could easily win secretary-of-the-year award appeared in Reception. 'Is there a problem?'

You betcha, Cassandra accorded silently, and I'm it. 'Please inform Diego del Santo I need to see him.'

A flicker of doubt. That's all she needed. Yet none appeared. Was his secretary so familiar with Diego's paramours, she knew categorically that Cassandra wasn't one of them?

'I have instructions to serve drinks and canapés at five,' his secretary informed. 'I'll mention your presence to him then.'

It was a small victory, but a victory none the less. 'Thank you.'

Half an hour spent leafing through a variety of glossy magazines did little to help her nervous tension.

Staff began their end-of-day exodus, and she felt her stomach execute a painful somersault as Diego's secretary moved purposely into Reception.

'Please come with me.'

Minutes later she was shown into a luxurious suite. 'Take a seat. Mr del Santo will be with you soon.'

How soon was *soon?*

Five, ten, thirty minutes passed. Was he playing a diabolical game with her?

Nervous tension combined with anger, and she was almost on the point of walking out. The only thing that stopped her was the sure knowledge she'd only have to go through this again tomorrow.

Five more minutes, she vowed, then she'd go in search of him...conference be damned!

The door swung open and Diego walked into the room with one minute to spare.

'Cassandra.'

She rose to her feet, unwilling to appear at a disadvantage by having him loom over her.

'My apologies for keeping you waiting.' He

crossed to the floor-to-ceiling plate-glass window, turned his back on the magnificent harbour view, and thrust one hand into his trouser pocket.

Her expression was coolly aloof, although her eyes held the darkness of anger. 'Really? I imagine keeping me waiting is part of the game-play.'

Sassy, he mused, and mad. It made a change from simpering companions who held a diploma in superficial artificiality.

'If you had telephoned, my secretary could have arranged a suitable time,' Diego inferred mildly.

'Next week?' she parried with deliberate facetiousness, and incurred a cynical smile.

'The very reason I suggested we share dinner.'

'I have no desire to share anything with you.' She paused, then drew in a deep breath. 'Let's get down to business, shall we?' She indicated the sheaf of papers tabled together in a thick folder. 'I have the requisite proof, and a copy of your offer. Everything appears to be in order.'

'You sound surprised.'

Cassandra swept him a dark glance. 'I doubt there's anything you could do that would surprise me.'

'I imagine Cameron has relayed the deal is subject to a condition?'

Her eyes glittered with barely repressed anger. 'He said it was personal. *How* personal?'

'Two separate nights and one weekend with you.'

She felt as if some elusive force had picked her

up and flung her against the nearest wall. 'That's barbaric,' she managed at last.

'Call it what you will.'

It took her a few seconds to find her voice. 'Why?'

'Because it amuses me?'

Was this payback? For all the invitations he'd offered and she'd refused...because she could. Now, her refusal would have far-reaching implications. Did she have the strength of will to ruin her father, the firm he'd spent his life taking from strength to strength?

'An investment of twenty-three million dollars against all sage advice, allows for—' he paused deliberately '—a bonus, wouldn't you say?'

She didn't think, or pause to consider the consequences of her actions. She simply picked up the nearest thing to hand and threw it at him. The fact he fielded it neatly and replaced it down onto his desk merely infuriated her further.

'Who do you think you are?' Her voice was low, and held a quality even she didn't recognise.

Stupid question, she dismissed. He knew precisely who he was, what he wanted, and how to get it.

'I'd advise you to think carefully before you consider another foolish move,' Diego cautioned silkily.

Her eyes sparked brilliant blue fire. 'What did you expect?' Her voice rose a fraction. 'For me to fall into your arms expressing my undying gratitude?'

She didn't see the humour lurking in those dark

depths. If she had, she'd probably throw something else at him.

'I imagined a token resistance.'

Oh, he did, did he? 'You realise I could lay charges against you for coercion?'

'You could try.'

'Only to have your team of lawyers counter with misinterpretation, whereupon you withdraw your financial rescue package?'

'Yes.'

'Emotional blackmail is a detestable ploy.'

'It's a negotiable tool,' Diego corrected, and in that moment she hated him more than she thought it possible to hate anyone.

'No.' Dear God, had she actually said the verbal negation?

'No, you don't agree it's a negotiable tool?'

'I won't have sex with you.'

'You're not in any position to bargain.'

'I'm not for sale,' Cassandra evinced with dignity.

'Everything has its price.'

'That's your credo in life?'

He waited a beat. 'Do you doubt it?'

She'd had enough. 'We're about done, don't you think?' She tried for calm, and didn't quite make it as she hitched the strap of her shoulder bag as she turned towards the door.

Damn Cameron. Damn the whole sorry mess.

'There's just one more thing.'

She registered Diego's silky drawl, recognised the

underlying threat, and paused, turning to look at him.

'Cameron's homosexuality.'

Two words. Yet they had the power to stop the breath in her throat.

Diego del Santo couldn't possibly know. No one knew. At least, only Cameron, his partner, and herself.

Anxiety meshed with panic at the thought her father might catch so much as a whisper...

Dear God, *no*.

Alexander Preston-Villers might find it difficult to accept Cameron had steadily sent Preston-Villers to the financial wall. But he'd never condone or forgive his son's sexual proclivity.

An appalling sense of anguish permeated her bones, her soul. Who had Diego del Santo employed to discover something she imagined so well-hidden, it was virtually impossible to uncover?

How deep had he dug?

No stone unturned. The axiom echoed and re-echoed inside her brain.

It said much of the man standing before her, the lengths he was prepared to go to to achieve his objective.

'I hate you.' The words fell from her lips in a voice shaky with anger. She felt cold, so cold she was willing to swear her blood had turned to ice in her veins.

Diego inclined his head, his eyes darkly still as

he observed her pale features, the starkness of defeat clearly evident in her expression. 'At this moment, I believe you do.'

He'd won. They both knew it. There was only one thing she could hope for…his silence.

'Yes.' His voice was quiet. 'You have my word.'

'For which I should be grateful?' she queried bitterly.

He didn't answer. Instead, he indicated the chair she'd previously occupied. 'Why don't you sit down?'

He crossed to the credenza, extracted a glass, filled it with iced water from the bar fridge, then placed the glass in her hand.

Cassandra didn't want to sit. She preferred to be on her feet, poised for flight.

Diego moved towards his desk and leaned one hip against its edge. 'Shall we begin again?'

Dear heaven, how did she get through this? With as much dignity as possible, an inner voice prompted.

'The ball's in your court.'

Did she have any idea how vulnerable she looked? The slightly haunted quality evident in those stunning blue eyes, the translucence of her skin.

He remembered the taste of her, her fragrance, the soft, tentative response… He'd sought to imprint her with his touch, unclear of his motivation. A desire to shock, to punish? A lesson to be wary of men whose prime need was sex?

Instead, it had been she who'd left a lingering memory, unexpectedly stirring his soul…as well as another pertinent part of his anatomy. A pubescent temptress, unaware of her feminine power, he mused, wondering at the time how she'd react if he took advantage of her youth.

Sixteen-year-old girls were out of bounds. Especially when this particular sixteen-year-old was the cherished daughter of one of the city's industrial scions. Her brother, the elder by two years, should have known better than to bring her to a party where drinks were spiked and drugs were in plentiful supply. A fact he'd cursorily relayed before bundling brother and sister out of the host's house, then following in their wake.

Relationships, he'd had a few. Women he'd enjoyed, taking what was so willingly offered without much thought to permanence. As to commitment…there hadn't been any woman he'd wanted to make his own, exclusively. Happy-ever-after was a fallacy. Undying love, a myth.

For the past year one woman had teased his senses, yet she'd held herself aloof from every attempt he made to date her, and he'd had to content himself with a polite greeting whenever their social paths crossed.

Until now.

'As soon as our personal arrangement has satisfactorily concluded,' Diego drawled, 'I'll attach my signature to the relevant paperwork and organise for funds to be released.'

Cassandra registered his words, and felt her stomach contract in tangible pain. 'And when do you envisage our *personal arrangement* will begin?'

'Anyone would think you view sex with me as a penance.'

'Your ego must be enormous if you imagine I could possibly regard it as a pleasure.'

'Brave words,' Diego drawled, 'when you have no knowledge what manner of lover I am.'

The mere thought of that tall, muscular body engaged intimately with hers was enough to send heat spiralling from deep inside.

Instinct warned he was a practised lover, aware of all the pleasure pulses in a woman's body, and how to coax each and every one of them to vibrant life with the skilled touch of his mouth, his hands.

It was there, in the darkness of his gaze…the sensual confidence of a man well-versed in the desires of women.

A tiny shiver started at the base of her spine, and feathered its way to her nape, settled there, so she had to make a conscious effort to prevent it from appearing visible.

'Wednesday evening I'm attending a dinner party. I'll collect you at six-thirty. Pack whatever you need for the night.'

The day after tomorrow?

An hysterical laugh rose and died in her throat. So soon? Oh, God, why not? At least then the first night would be over. One down, one and a weekend to go.

'The remaining nights?' Dear heaven, how could she sound so calm?

'Saturday.'

She felt as if she were dying. 'And the last?'

'The following weekend.' His gaze never left hers. 'One million dollars will be deposited into the Preston-Villers business account following each of the three occasions you spend with me. Monday week, Preston-Villers' creditors will be paid off.'

'A *condition*, tenuously alluded to in the documentation as "being met to Diego del Santo's satisfaction", doesn't even begin to offer me any protection. What guarantee do I have you won't declare the offer documented as null and void on the grounds the *condition* hasn't been met to your satisfaction?'

'My word.'

She had to force her voice to remain steady, otherwise it would betray her by shattering into a hundred pieces. 'Sorry, but that won't cut it.'

'Do you know how close you walk to the edge of my tolerance?'

'Don't insult my intelligence by detailing a *condition* that has so many holes in it, even Blind Freddie could see through them!'

'You don't trust me?'

'No.'

He could walk away from the deal. It was what he *should* do. Twenty-three million dollars was no small amount of money, even if in the scheme of things it represented only a very small percentage of his investments.

He enjoyed the adrenalin charge in taking a worn-down company, injecting the necessary funds and making it work again.

'What is it you want?'

It was no time to lose her bravado. 'Something in writing detailing those nights, each comprising no more than twelve hours spent in your company, represents my sexual obligation to you, as covered by the term *condition*, and said obligation shall not be judged by my sexual performance.' She took a deep breath, and released it slowly. 'The original copy will be destroyed when you release funds in full into the Preston-Villers business account.'

She watched as he set up a laptop, keyed in data, activated the printer, proofread the printed copy, then attached his signature and handed her the page.

Cassandra read it, then she neatly folded the page and thrust it into her shoulder bag. Un-notarised, it wouldn't have much value in a court of law. But it was better than nothing.

The melodic burr of his cellphone provided the impetus she needed to escape.

Diego spared a glance at the illuminated dial, and cut the call. He moved to the door, opened it, then he led the way out to the main foyer and summoned the lift.

'Six-thirty, Wednesday evening,' he reminded as the electronic doors slid open.

It nearly killed her to act with apparent unconcern, when inside she was a quivering mess. 'I won't say it's been a pleasure,' Cassandra managed coolly as she depressed the appropriate button to take her down to ground level.

As a parting shot it lacked the impact she would have liked, but she took a degree of satisfaction in having the last word.

Two weeks from now she would have fulfilled Diego del Santo's *condition*.

Three, no, four nights in his bed. She could do it...couldn't she, and emerge emotionally unscathed?

CHAPTER THREE

Two evenings later Cassandra stood sipping excellent champagne in the lounge of a stunning Rose Bay mansion.

Guests mingled, some of whom she knew, and the conversation flowed. However, the evening, the venue, the fellow guests…none had as much impact on her as the man at her side.

Diego del Santo exuded practised charm, solicitous interest, and far too much sexual chemistry for any woman's peace of mind. Especially hers.

Worse, she was all too aware of the way her nervous tension escalated by the minute.

She didn't want to be here. More particularly, she didn't want to be linked to Diego del Santo in any way.

Yet she was bound to him, caught in an invisible trap, and the clock was ticking down towards the moment they were alone.

Even the thought of that large, lithe frame, naked, was enough to send her heartbeat into overdrive.

'More champagne?'

His voice was an inflected drawl as he indicated her empty flute, and he was close, too close for comfort, for she was supremely conscious of him, his fine tailoring, the exclusive cologne, and the man beneath the sophisticated exterior.

'No,' she managed politely. 'Thank you.' There was some merit in having one drink too many in order to endure the night. However, the evening was young, dinner would soon be served, and she valued her social reputation too much as well as her self-esteem to pass the next few hours in an alcoholic haze.

Choosing what to wear had seen her selecting one outfit after another and discarding most. In the end she'd opted for a bias-cut red silk dress with a soft, draped neckline and ribbon straps. Subtle make-up with emphasis on her eyes, and she'd swept her hair into a careless knot atop her head. Jewellery was an intricately linked neck chain with matching ear-studs.

Packing an overnight bag had been simple...she'd simply tossed in a change of clothes and a few necessities. A bag Diego had retrieved from her hand as she emerged from the foyer and deposited in the trunk of his car.

Quite what she expected she wasn't sure. There had been nothing overt in his greeting, and he made no attempt to touch her as he saw her seated in his stylish Aston Martin.

During the brief drive to their hosts' home he'd

kept conversation to a minimum…presumably influenced by her monosyllabic replies.

What did he expect? For her to smile and laugh? Act as if this was a *date*, for heaven's sake?

He'd made her part of a deal, and she hated him for it. Almost as much as she hated being thrust among a coterie of guests for several hours.

Guests who were undoubtedly curious at Diego's choice of partner for the evening. Or should that be curiosity at *her* choice of partner?

Had whispers of Preston-Villers' financial straits begun to circulate? And if they had, what context was placed on Cassandra Preston-Villers appearing at Diego's side? Would gossip allude the amalgamation had moved from the boardroom to the bedroom?

Cassandra told herself she didn't care…and knew she lied.

Dinner. Dear heaven, how could she *eat*? Her stomach felt as if it were tied in knots, and primed to reject any food she sent its way.

'Relax.'

Diego's voice was a quiet drawl as they took their seats at the elegantly set table, and she offered a stunning smile. 'I'm perfectly relaxed.'

There were numerous courses, each a perfect complement served with the artistry and flair of a professional chef.

Compliments were accorded, and Cassandra

added her own, painfully aware her tastebuds had gone on strike.

She conversed with fellow guests, almost on autopilot, playing the social game with the ease of long practice. Although afterwards she held little recollection of any discussion.

Diego was *there*, a constant entity, and the build-up of tension accelerated as the evening progressed. The light brush of his hand on hers succeeded in sending her pulse into overdrive, and she almost forgot to breathe when he leaned close to refill her water glass.

She began to pray for the evening to end, to be free from the constraints of polite society. At least when they were alone she could discard the façade and fence verbal swords with him!

Somehow she made it through the seemingly endless meal, and it was a relief to retreat to the lounge to linger over coffee.

Diego seemed in no hurry to leave, and it was almost eleven when he indicated they bid their hosts goodnight.

The short drive to nearby suburban Point Piper was achieved in silence, and Cassandra felt her body stiffen as he activated the electronic gates guarding the entrance to a curved driveway illuminated by strategically placed lights leading to a large home whose architecturally designed exterior and interior had featured in one of the glossy magazines soon after its completion.

The Aston Martin eased beneath electronic garage doors and slid to a halt as the doors closed behind them with an imperceptible click.

Trapped.

Take me home. The words rose as a silent cry, only to die unuttered in her throat.

You have to go through with this, a silent voice prompted pitilessly. Think of Alexander, Cameron.

But what about *me*?

Diego popped the trunk, then emerged from behind the wheel and retrieved her bag as she slipped out of the passenger seat.

In silence she preceded him indoors, then walked at his side as he moved into the main foyer.

With a sense of increasing desperation she focused on the generous dimensions, the gently curving staircase with its intricately designed balustrade leading to the upper floor. A crystal chandelier hung suspended from the high ceiling, and solid mahogany cabinets added to the Spanish influence. Art graced the walls, providing an ambience of wealth.

Had he personally chosen all this, or consulted with an interior decorator?

Diego deposited her bag at the foot of the staircase, then he indicated a door on his right. 'A nightcap?'

Cassandra watched as he crossed the foyer and

revealed a spacious lounge. The thought of exchanging polite conversation and playing *pretend* was almost more than she could bear.

The entire evening had been a preliminary to the moment she'd need to share his bed. Drawing it out any further seemed pointless.

'If you don't mind, I'd prefer to get on with it.'

She was nervous. He could sense it in her voice, see the way her pulse jumped at the base of her throat, and he took pleasure from it.

'Cut to the chase?'

His query was a silky drawl that sent an icy feather sliding down her spine. 'Yes.'

Diego gave an imperceptible shrug as he closed the door and indicated the staircase. 'By all means.'

Was she *mad*? Oh, for heaven's sake, she chided silently. He's only a man, like any other.

They'd have sex, she'd sleep, he'd wake her at dawn for more sex, then she'd shower, dress, and get a cab to work.

How big a deal could it be?

The way the blood fizzed through her veins, heating her body was incidental. The rapid thudding of her heart was merely due to nervous tension. Stress, anxiety…take your pick. A direct result of the sexual price she'd agreed to pay with a man she told herself she didn't like.

Together they ascended the curved staircase, then

turned left, traversing the balustraded gallery to a
lavishly furnished master suite.

Cassandra entered the room, only to falter to a
halt as uncertainty froze her limbs. *Think,* she silently cajoled. Slip off your stiletto-heeled pumps,
remove your jewellery…

The ear-studs were easy, but her fingers shook as
she reached for the clasp at her nape.

'Let me do that,' Diego said quietly, and moved
in close.

Far too close. She could sense him behind her,
almost *feel* the touch of that powerful body against
her own. How much space separated them? An
inch? If she leant back, her shoulders would brush
his chest.

Oh, hell, *should* she, and make it easy for herself?
Play the seductress and melt into his arms?

His fingers touched her nape and she unconsciously held her breath as he dealt with the clasp.
Then it was done, and she took a step away from
him as he dropped the jewellery into her hand.

Cassandra crossed to where Diego had placed her
bag and tucked the jewellery into a pouch. When
she turned he was close, and her stomach clenched
as he reached for the pins in her hair.

His fingers grazed the graceful curve of her neck,
and sensation shivered the length of her spine.

'Beautiful.'

His silky murmur did strange things to her equilibrium, and she fought against the almost mesmeric fascination threatening to undermine her defences.

It would be so easy to sway towards him, angle her head, fasten her mouth on his and simply sink in.

Yet to meekly comply meant she condoned his actions, and there wasn't a hope in hell she'd ever forgive his manipulation.

'Let's not pretend this is anything other than what it is.'

Cassandra reached for the zip fastener on her dress, and managed to slide it down a few inches before his hand halted its progress.

'Highly priced sex?' Diego queried in a faintly accented drawl.

'You got it in one.'

She was nervous, and that intrigued him. Any other woman would have played the coquette, and provocatively stripped for his pleasure. Teasing, before undressing *him*, then moving in to begin a practised seduction before he took control.

'If you want to unwrap the package...' Cassandra managed what she hoped was a negligent shrug '...then go ahead.'

Diego's eyes narrowed, and his voice was a husky drawl. 'How could a man resist the temptation?'

He slid the zip fastener all the way down, then lifted his hands to the shoestring straps, slipping them over each shoulder so the gown slithered to a heap on the carpeted floor.

The only garment that saved her from total nudity was a silk thong brief, and she forced herself to stand still beneath his studied appraisal.

Her eyes blazed blue fire as his gaze lingered on her breasts, skimmed low, then lifted to meet the defiant outrage apparent.

With slow, deliberate movements he removed his shoes and socks, shed his jacket, loosened his tie and removed it, then he freed his trousers before tending to the buttons on his shirt.

He was something else. Broad shoulders, lean hips, a washboard stomach, olive-toned skin sheathed an enviable abundance of hardened sinew and muscle. Fit, not pumped, with a sleekness that denoted undeniable strength.

Black silk briefs did little to hide his arousal, and she hated the warm tinge that coloured her cheeks as he swept back the bedcovers.

With unhurried steps he closed the distance between them, and her eyes widened fractionally as he touched a gentle finger to her lips and traced the lower curve. Warmth flooded her body and became pulsing heat as he cupped her face, and a soundless groan rose and died in her throat as he lowered his head down to hers.

Whatever she'd expected, it wasn't the slow, evocative touch of his mouth on her own, or the way his tongue slid between her lips as his hands cupped her face.

She felt his thumbs brush each cheek, and the breath caught in her throat as he angled his mouth and went in deep.

He tugged at her senses and tore them to shreds, destroying the protective barrier she'd built up against him.

Her hands lifted to his shoulders in a bid to hang on, only to rest briefly, hesitantly there as he slid a hand to capture her nape while the other skimmed the length of her spine to curve over her bottom and pull her close.

In one fluid movement he dispensed with the scrap of silk, and she gasped as he sought the warm heat at the apex of her thighs.

There was little she could do to prevent his skilled fingers wreaking havoc there. He knew where to touch and how...light strokes that almost drove her wild, and just when she thought she couldn't stand any more he eased off, only to have her gasp as the oral stimulation intensified to another level.

'Let go,' Diego instructed huskily, and absorbed her despairing groan.

Her body might be tempted, but her mind wasn't in sync. Had it ever been? she registered cynically, aware that for her intimacy, while pleasurable, was hardly a mind-blowing experience. Why should it be any different this time?

Fake it, a silent imp prompted. Just…get it over with, then it'll be done. For tonight.

His hands shifted to cup her face. 'Don't.'

Cassandra stilled at his softly voiced admonition, and cast him a startled glance. 'I don't know what you mean.'

He traced the lower curve of her mouth with the pad of his thumb, and saw her eyes flare. 'Yes, you do.'

She could feel the warmth colour her cheeks. What was it with this man that he could lay bare her secrets?

Her previous partners had been so consumed with their own pleasure they hadn't cared about her own.

A strangled laugh rose and died in her throat. It wasn't as if she'd had numerous partners…only two, each of whom had declared undying devotion while fixing an eye on her father's wealth.

'I don't want to be here with you.'

'Perhaps not.' He waited a beat. 'Yet.'

'Are you sure there's enough space in this room for both you and your ego?'

His husky laugh was almost her undoing. 'You doubt I can make you want me?'

'It would be a first.' The words were out before she thought to stop them, and she saw his eyes narrow.

He was silent for what seemed an age, then he released her. In one fluid movement he reached for the bedcovers, restored them to their former position, then he indicated the bed. 'Get in.'

Uncertainty momentarily showed in her features. 'You prefer the bed?'

'It's more comfortable.'

Comfort. It beat tumbling to the carpeted floor. Although somehow she doubted Diego was prone to awkward moves.

'To sleep,' Diego added, watching confusion cloud her eyes.

'Sleep?' She felt as if she was repeating everything he said.

His gaze speared hers. 'For now,' he qualified evenly. 'Does that bother you?'

A stay of execution? She wasn't sure whether to be pleased or peeved. 'A reprieve? Should I thank you?'

'Don't push it, *querida.*' His voice held the softness of silk, but the warning was pure steel.

Capitulation would be a wise choice, she perceived, and crossed to her bag, extracted a large cotton T-shirt and pulled it on, then after a moment's hesitation she joined him in the large bed, settling as far away from him as possible.

Diego pressed a remote module and doused the lights, and Cassandra felt her body tense in the darkness as she waited for the moment he might reach for her.

Except he didn't, and she lay still, aware of the moment his breathing slowed to a steady pace.

Dammit, he was asleep! As easily and quickly as that, he'd been able to relax sufficiently to sleep.

Leaving her to lie awake to seethe in silence. The temptation to fist her hand and *punch* him was paramount! How dared he simply switch off? How *could* he?

She still had the imprint of his hands on her body, and her mouth felt slightly swollen from the touch of his.

Unfulfilled anticipation. Dear heaven, she couldn't be disappointed, surely?

Diego del Santo was someone she intensely disliked, *hated,* she amended. Just because there was an exigent chemistry between them didn't alter a thing.

How could she *sleep*, for heaven's sake? He was *there*, his large, powerfully muscled body within touching distance.

Was it imagination, or could she feel his warmth? Sense the heat of his sex, even in repose?

It was madness. Insane. She closed her eyes and summoned sleep, only to stifle the groan that rose and died in her throat.

Her limbs, her whole body seemed stiff, and she'd have given anything to roll over and punch her pillow, then resettle into a more comfortable position.

Yet if she moved, she might disturb Diego, and that wasn't a favoured option.

Cassandra counted sheep…to no avail. She concentrated on an intricate jewellery design she was working on, visualised the finished item and made a few minor adjustments.

How long had she been lying in the dark? Ten, twenty minutes? Thirty? How long until the dawn? Four, five hours?

There was a faint movement, then the room was bathed in soft light, and Diego loomed close, his upper body supported on one elbow.

'Can't sleep?' His voice was a husky drawl that curled round her nerve-ends and tugged a little.

Her eyes were large, and far too dark, her features pale.

'I didn't know you were awake.' He must sleep like a cat, attuned to the slightest movement, the faintest sound.

'Headache?'

It would be so easy to acquiesce, but she wasn't into fabrication. 'No.'

He lifted a hand and trailed gentle fingers across her cheek. 'Waging an inner battle?'

There was nothing like the witching midnight hour to heighten vulnerability. 'Yes.'

His mouth curved into a musing smile. 'Honesty is a quality so rarely found in women.'

'You obviously haven't met the right woman.'

Was that her voice? It sounded impossibly husky. *Sexy,* she amended, slightly shocked, and flinched as his fingers traced a path to her temple and tucked a swathe of hair behind her ear.

There was a sense of unreality in the conversation. She was conscious of the room, the bed...then the man, only the man became her total focus.

The pad of his thumb traced her lower lip, depressed its centre, then slid to her chin, holding it fast as he fastened his mouth on hers, coaxing in a prelude to the deliberate seduction of her senses.

The subtle exploration became an evocative sensual possession that took hold of her inhibitions and dispensed with them...far too easily for her peace of mind.

She should withdraw and retreat, protest a little. Except his touch held a magic she couldn't resist, and she groaned as his hands caressed her breasts, shaped the sensitive flesh, then tantalised the burgeoning peaks.

Heat flooded her veins, filling her body with sensual warmth as she arched against the path of his hand, and he absorbed her soft cry as he caught hold of her T-shirt and tugged it free.

For several long seconds she bore his silent appraisal, glimpsed the vital, almost electric energy apparent, and knew instinctively that intimacy would surely take place.

The intention, the driven need was there, clearly

evident, and sensation spiralled through her body at the thought of his possession.

All her skin-cells came achingly alive, acutely sensitive to his touch as he lowered his head over her breast and suckled its tender peak. Then she cried out as he used his teeth to take her to the brink between pain and pleasure.

Cassandra slid her fingers through his hair and tugged, willing him to cease, only to gasp as he trailed a path to her waist, paused to circle her navel with his tongue before edging slowly towards the apex of her thighs.

He couldn't, wouldn't...surely?

But he did, with brazen disregard for her plea to desist. The level of intimacy shocked her, and she fought against the skilled stroking, the heat and thrust of his tongue as he sent her high. So high, the acute sensory spiral tore a startled cry from her throat.

Just as she thought the sensation couldn't become more intense, it came again, so acutely piercing it arrowed through her body, an all-consuming flame soaring from deep within.

Dear heaven. The fervent whisper fell from her lips as an irreverent prayer as Diego shifted slightly and trailed his lips over her sensitised flesh to possess her mouth in a kiss that took her deep, so deep she simply gave herself over to it and shared the sensual feast.

Somewhere in the deep recesses of her mind an alarm bell sounded, and she stilled. 'Protection?'

'Taken care of.'

Cassandra felt him nudge her thighs apart, the probe of his arousal as he eased into her, and her shocked gasp at his size died in her throat.

His slick heat magnetised her, and she felt her muscles tense around him, then relax in a rhythm that gradually accepted his length. He stilled, his mouth a persuasive instrument as he plundered at will, sweeping her high until all rational thought vanished.

Then he began to move, slowly at first, so slowly she felt the passage inch by inch, and just as she began to think he intended to disengage, he slid in to the hilt in one excruciatingly sensual thrust, repeating the movement as he increased the pace. Until the rhythm became an hypnotic entity she had no power to resist.

Mesmeric, urgent, libidinous...it became something she'd never experienced before. An intoxicating captivation of her senses as he swept them high to a point of magical ecstasy.

She had no memory of the scream torn from her throat, the way her nails raked his ribs, or how she sought his flesh with her teeth. She was a wild wanton, driven beyond mere desire to a primitive place where passion became an incandescent entity.

Diego brought her down slowly, gently, soothing her quivering body until she stilled in his arms.

There were tears trickling down each cheek, and he felt his heart constrict at her vulnerability.

She felt exposed. As if this man had somehow managed to see into her heart, her soul, and that everything she was, all her secrets were laid bare.

There was little she could gain from his expression, and her mouth shook as he carefully rolled onto his back, taking her with him.

His gaze held hers in the soft light, and she couldn't look away. There were no words, nothing she could say, and the breath hitched in her throat as he lifted both hands to her breasts.

With the utmost care he tested their weight, then traced the gentle swell, using his thumb pad to caress the swollen peaks.

Her skin felt sensitive to his touch as he cupped her waist, then slid to her hips.

Cassandra felt her eyes widen as he began to swell inside her, and a soundless gasp parted her lips as he began a slow, undulating movement.

Again? He was ready for more?

She caught the rhythm and matched it, enjoying the dominant position, and what followed became the ride of her life…and his, for there was no doubting his passion, or the moment of his climax as it joined with her own.

Afterwards he drew her down against him and

cradled her close until her breathing, his own, returned to normal.

She could have slept right there, her cheek cushioned against his chest, and she began to protest as he disengaged and eased her to lie beside him.

Then she did voice a protest as he slid from the bed and swept her into his arms.

'What are you doing?' Her faintly scandalised query held an edge of panic as he crossed to the *en suite* and entered the spacious shower cubicle.

'We can't share a shower,' Cassandra protested, and earned a husky laugh.

'We just shared the ultimate in intimacy,' Diego drawled as he picked up the soap and began smoothing it over her skin.

So they had, but this…this was something else, and she put a hand to his chest in silent remonstrance.

'No.'

He didn't stop. 'Afterwards we sleep.'

She pushed him. Or at least she tried, but he was an immovable force. 'I can take care of myself.'

'Indulge me.'

'Diego—'

'I like the sound of my name on your lips.'

'Please!' His touch was a little too up close and personal, and he was invading her private space in a way no man had done before.

'You get to have your turn any minute soon,' he

drawled with amusement, then had the audacity to chuckle as she took a well-aimed swipe at his shoulder.

'If you want to play, *querida*, I'm only too willing to oblige.'

'I'm all played out.' It was the truth, for exhaustion was beginning to overpower her, combined with the soporific spray of hot water, heated steam and lateness of the hour. Plus she hurt in places she'd never hurt before.

He finished her ablutions, then set about completing his own. Within minutes he turned off the water, snagged a bath towel and towelled her dry before applying the towel to his own torso.

Seconds later he led her into the bedroom and pulled her down onto the bed, settled the covers, then doused the light.

With one fluid movement her gathered her in against him and held her there, aware of the moment tiredness overcame her reluctance and she slept.

CHAPTER FOUR

CASSANDRA woke slowly, aware within seconds this wasn't her bed, her room, or her apartment. Realisation dawned, and she turned her head cautiously...only to see she was the sole occupant of the large bed.

Of Diego there was no sign, and she checked the time, gasped in exasperated dismay, then she slid to her feet, gathered fresh underwear and day clothes from her bag and made for the *en suite*.

Fifteen minutes later she gathered up her bag and moved down to the lower floor. She could smell fresh coffee, toast...and felt her stomach rumble in growling protest as she made her way towards the kitchen.

Diego stood at the servery, dressed in dark trousers, a business shirt unbuttoned at the neck, and a matching dark jacket rested over the back of a chair with a tie carelessly tossed on top of it.

He looked far too alive for a man who'd spent the greater part of the night engaged in physical activity, and just the sight of him was enough to shred her nerves.

'I was going to give you another five minutes,'

he drawled. 'Then come fetch you.' He indicated the carafe. 'Coffee?'

'Please.' She felt awkward, and incredibly vulnerable. 'Then I'll call a cab.'

Diego extracted a plate of eggs and toast from a warming tray. 'I'll drive you home. Sit down and eat.'

'I'm not hungry.'

He subjected her to a raking appraisal, saw the darkened shadows beneath her eyes, the faint edge of tiredness. 'Eat,' he insisted. 'Then we'll leave.'

Any further protest would be fruitless, and besides, the eggs looked good. She took a seat and did justice to the food, sipped the strong, hot black coffee, and felt more ready to face the day.

As soon as she finished he pulled on his tie and adjusted it, then shrugged into his jacket.

She began clearing the table with the intention of doing the dishes.

'Leave them.'

'It'll only take a few minutes.'

'I have a cleaning lady. Leave them.'

Without a word she picked up her bag and followed him through to the garage.

The distance between Point Piper and Double Bay amounted to a few kilometres, and Cassandra slid open the door within seconds of Diego drawing the car to a halt outside the entrance of her apartment building.

There wasn't an adequate word that came to

mind, and she didn't offer one as she walked away from him.

The cat gave an indignant miaow as she unlocked her door, and she dropped her bag, put down fresh food, then took the lift down to the basement car park.

Minutes later she eased her vintage Porsche onto the road and battled morning peak-hour traffic to reach her place of work.

Concentration on the job in hand proved difficult as she attempted to dispel Diego's powerful image.

Far too often she was reminded of his possession. Dear heaven, she could still *feel* him. Tender internal tissues provided a telling evidence, and just the thought of her reaction to their shared intimacy was enough to bring her to the point of climax.

As if last night wasn't enough, he'd reached for her in the early dawn hours, employing what she reflected was considerable stealth to arouse her before she was fully awake and therefore conscious of his intention.

Worse, he had stilled any protest she might have voiced with a skilled touch, inflaming her senses and attacking the fragile tenure of her control.

How could she react with such electrifying passion to a man she professed to hate? To transcend the physical and unleash myriad emotions to become a willing wanton in his arms. Accepting a degree of intimacy she'd never imagined being sufficiently comfortable with to condone.

Yet she had. Swept away beyond reason or rational thought by sexual chemistry at its zenith.

Her cellphone buzzed, signalling an incoming text message, and she checked it during her lunch break, then responded by keying in Cameron's number.

'Just checking in,' her brother reassured.

'Enquiring how I survived Act One of the three-act night play?'

'Cynicism, Cassandra?'

'I'm entitled, don't you think?'

'Act Two takes place…when?'

'Saturday night.'

'I appreciate—'

'Don't,' she said fiercely, 'go there.' She cut the connection, automatically reached for the Caesar salad she'd ordered, only to take one mouthful and push the plate aside. Instead, she ate the accompanying Turkish bread and sipped the latte before returning to the workshop.

Mid-afternoon she gave in to a throbbing headache and took a painkiller to ease it, then she fixed the binocular microscope, adjusted the light, and set to work.

Cassandra was relieved when the day came to an end, and she stopped off at a supermarket *en route* to her apartment and collected groceries, cat food and fresh fruit.

Essential provisions, she mused as she carried the sack indoors, unpacked it, then she fed the cat, prepared fish and salad for herself. Television interested her for an hour, then she opened her laptop, double-checked design measurements and made some minor adjustments, then she closed everything down and went to bed.

Within minutes she felt the familiar pad of the cat's tread as it joined her and settled against her legs. Companionship and unconditional love, she mused with affection as she sought solace in sleep.

Difficult, when the one man she resented invaded her thoughts, filling her mind, and invaded her dreams.

Diego del Santo had a lot to answer for, Cassandra swore as the next day proved no less stressful. Her stomach executed a downward dive every time her cellphone rang as she waited for him to confirm arrangements for Saturday night.

By Friday evening she was a bundle of nerves, cursing him volubly…which did no good at all and startled the cat.

Consequently when she picked up the phone Saturday morning and heard his voice, it was all she could do to remain civil.

'I'll collect you at six-thirty. Dinner first, then we're due to attend a gallery exhibition.'

'If you'll advise an approximate time you expect to return home,' Cassandra managed stiffly, 'I'll meet you there.'

'No.'

Her fingers tightened on the cellphone casing. 'What do you mean…*no*?' She felt the anger begin a slow simmer, and took a deep breath to control it. 'You can take someone else to dinner and the gallery.'

'Go from one woman to another?'

He sounded amused, damn him. 'Socialising with you doesn't form part of the arrangement.'

'It does, however, entitle me to twelve hours of your time on two of our three legally binding occasions. If you'd prefer not to socialise, I'm more than willing to have you spend those twelve hours in my bed.'

She wanted to kill him. At the very least, she'd do him an injury. 'Minimising sex with you is my main priority.' Trying to remain calm took considerable effort. 'As I'll need my car for the morning, I'll drive to your place.'

'Six-thirty, Cassandra.' He cut the connection before she could say another word.

Choosing what to wear didn't pose a problem, for she led a reasonably active social life and possessed the wardrobe to support it.

For a brief moment she considered something entirely inappropriate, only to dismiss it and go with *stunning*.

Soft and feminine was the *in* style, and she had just the gown in jade silk georgette. Spaghetti straps, a deep V-neckline, and a handkerchief hemline. Guaranteed *wow* factor, she perceived as she swept her hair into a careless knot and added the finishing touches to her make-up.

It was six-twenty-five when she drew her car to a halt outside the gates guarding the entrance to Diego's home. Almost on cue they were electronically released, and she wondered whether it was by advance courtesy on his part or due to a sophisticated alarm system.

The Aston Martin was parked outside the main entrance, and Diego opened the front door as she slid out from her car.

Cassandra inclined her head in silent greeting and crossed to the Aston Martin.

'A punctual woman,' Diego drawled, and incurred a piercing glance.

'You said six-thirty.' She subjected him to a deliberate appraisal, taking in the dark dinner suit, the crisp white shirt, black bow-tie...and endeavoured to control the sudden leap of her pulse. 'Shall we leave?'

Polite, cool. She could do both. For now.

'No overnight bag?'

'I'll get it.' She did, and he placed it indoors before tending to the alarm.

'You've dressed to impress,' Diego complimented, subjecting her to a raking appraisal that had male appreciation at its base, and something else she didn't care to define.

There was an edge of mockery apparent, and she offered a practised smile. 'That should be...to *kill*,' she amended as he unlocked the car door, saw her seated, then crossed round the front to slide in behind the wheel.

'Should I be on guard for hidden weapons?'

Cassandra shot him a considering glance. 'Not my style.'

'But making a fashion statement is?'

'It's a woman's prerogative,' she responded with a certain wryness. 'Armour for all the visual feminine daggers that'll be aimed at my back tonight.'

'In deference to my so-called reputation?'

'Got it in one.'

The sound of his husky laughter became lost as he ignited the engine, and she remained silent for the relatively short drive to Double Bay, electing to attempt civility as the *maître d'* seated them at a reserved table.

'Australia must appeal to you,' she broached in an attempt at conversation. 'You've been based in Sydney for the past year.'

They'd progressed through the starter and were waiting for the main.

Diego settled back in his chair and regarded her with thoughtful speculation. 'I have business interests in several countries.' He regarded her with musing indolence. 'And homes in many.'

'Therefore one assumes your time of residence here is fairly transitory.'

'Possibly.'

Cassandra picked up her wine glass and took an

appreciative sip. 'Hearsay accords you a devious past.'

'Do you believe that?'

She considered him carefully. 'Social rumour can be misleading.'

'Invariably.'

There was a hardness apparent, something dangerous, almost lethal lurking deep beneath the surface. He bore the look of a man who'd seen much, weathered more…and survived.

'I think you enjoy the mystery of purported supposition.' She waited a beat. 'And you're too streetwise to have skated over the edge of the law.'

'Gracias.' His voice held wry cynicism.

The waiter presented their main, topped up their wine glasses, then retreated.

Cassandra picked up her cutlery and speared a succulent morsel. 'Do you have family in New York?'

'A brother.' The sole survivor of a drive-by shooting that had killed both their parents. A shocking event that happened within months of his initial sojourn in Sydney, the reason he'd taken the next flight home…and stayed to build his fortune.

It was almost nine when they entered the gallery. Guests stood in segregated groups. The men deep in discussion on subjects which would vary from the state of the country's economy to the latest business acquisition, and whether the current wife was aware of the latest mistress.

The women, on the other hand, discussed the latest fashion showing, which cosmetic surgeon was currently in vogue, speculated who was conducting a clandestine affair, and what the husband would need to part with in order to soothe the wife and retain the mistress.

The names changed, Cassandra accorded wryly, but the topics remained the same.

Tonight's exhibition was more about being seen than the purchase of a sculpture or painting. Yet the evening would be a success, due to the fact only those with buying power and social status received invitations.

Should nothing appeal, it was considered *de rigueur* to donate a sizeable cheque to a nominated charity.

Uniformed waitresses were circulating proffering trays with canapés, while waiters offered champagne and orange juice.

'Feel free to mix and mingle.'

Their presence had been duly noted, their coupling providing speculation which would, Cassandra deduced, run rife.

Had news already spread about the financial state of Preston-Villers? It was too much to hope it would be kept under wraps for long.

'Let's take a look at the exhibits,' Diego suggested smoothly, and led her towards the nearest section of paintings.

Modern impressionists held little appeal, and she

found herself explaining why as they moved on to examine some metal sculptures, one of which appeared so bizarre it held her attention only from the viewpoint of discovering what it was supposed to represent.

'Diego. I didn't expect to see you here.'

The silky feminine purr held a faint accent, and Cassandra turned to see Alicia move close to Diego.

Much too close.

'Cassandra,' the model acknowledged. 'I haven't seen Cameron here tonight.'

A barbed indication she should get a life, a lover...and not resort to accompanying her brother to most social events? Cameron relied on her presence as a cover, while she was content to provide it. A comfort zone that suited them both. Two previous relationships hadn't encouraged her to have much faith in the male of the species. One man had regarded her as a free ride in life on her father's money; the other had wanted marriage in order to gain eventual chairmanship of Preston-Villers.

'Cameron was unable to attend,' she answered smoothly. It was a deviation from the truth, and one she had no intention of revealing.

Alicia looked incredible, buffed to perfection from the tip of her Italian-shod feet to the elegantly casual hairstyle. Gowned in black silk which clung to her curves in a manner which belied the use of underwear, she was a magnet for every man in the room.

Alicia's eyes narrowed fractionally as a fellow guest commandeered Diego's attention, drawing him into a discussion with two other men.

'You're here tonight with Diego?' The query held incredulous disbelief. 'Darling, isn't he a little out of your league?'

Cassandra kept her voice light. 'The implication being…?'

'He's rich, primitive, and dangerous.' Alicia spared her a sweeping glance. 'You'd never handle him.'

This was getting bitchy. 'And you can?'

The model cast her a sweeping glance, then uttered a deprecatory laugh. 'Oh, *please*, darling.'

Well, that certainly said it all!

She resisted the temptation to tell the model the joke was on her. *Handling* Diego was the last thing she wanted to do!

'In that case,' Cassandra managed sweetly, 'why did Diego invite me along when you're so—' she paused fractionally '—obviously available?'

Anger blazed briefly in those beautiful dark blue eyes, then assumed icy scorn. 'The novelty factor?'

If you only knew! 'You think so?' She manufactured a faint smile. 'Maybe he simply tired of having women fall over themselves to gain his attention.'

Alicia placed a hand on Cassandra's arm. 'Playing hard to get is an ill-advised game. You'll end up being hurt.'

'And you care?'

'Don't kid yourself, darling.'

'Are you done?' She offered a practised smile, and barely restrained an audible gasp as Alicia dug hard, lacquered fingernails into her arm.

'Oh, I think so. For now.'

Anything was better than fencing verbal swords with the glamour queen, and Cassandra began threading her way towards the remaining exhibits, pausing now and then to converse with a fellow guest.

There was a display of bronze sculptures, and one in particular caught her eye. It was smaller than the others, and lovingly crafted to portray an elderly couple seated together on a garden stool. The man's arm enclosed the woman's shoulders as she leaned into him. Their expressive features captured a look that touched her heart. Everlasting love.

'Quite something, isn't it?' a male voice queried at her side.

Cassandra turned and offered a smile. 'Yes,' she agreed simply.

'Gregor Stanislau.' He inclined his head. 'And you are?'

'Cassandra.'

His grin was infectious. 'You have an interest in bronze?' He indicated the remaining sculptures and led her past each of them. He was knowledgeable, explaining techniques, discussing what he perceived as indiscernible flaws detracting from what could have been perfection.

'The elderly couple seated on the stool. It's your work, isn't it?'

He spread his hands in an expressive gesture. 'Guilty.'

'It's beautiful,' she complimented. 'Is it the only piece you have displayed here?'

He inclined his head. 'The couple were modelled on my grandparents. It was to be a gift to them, but I was unable to complete it in time.'

She didn't need to ask. 'Would you consider selling it?'

'To you?' He named a price she considered exorbitant, and she shook her head.

He looked genuinely regretful. 'I'm reasonably negotiable. Make me an offer.'

'Forty per cent of your original figure, plus the gallery's commission,' Diego drawled from behind her, and she turned in surprise as he moved to her side. How long had he been standing there? She hadn't even sensed his presence.

Gregor looked severely offended. 'That's an outrage.'

Diego's smile was superficially pleasant, but the hardness apparent in his eyes was not. 'Would you prefer me to insist on a professional appraisal?'

'Seventy-five per cent, and I'll consider it sold.'

'The original offer stands.'

'Your loss.' The sculptor effected a negligible shrug and retreated among the guests.

'You had no need to negotiate on my behalf,'

Cassandra declared, annoyed at his intervention. 'I was more than capable of handling him.'

Diego shot her a mocking glance, which proved a further irritation. Did he think *blonde* and *naïve* automatically went hand-in-hand?

Wrong. 'He saw me admiring it, figured I was an easy mark, so he spun a sentimental tale with the aim to double his profit margin.' She lifted one eyebrow and deliberately allowed her mouth to curve in a winsome smile. 'How am I doing so far?'

His lips twitched a little. 'Just fine.'

Cassandra inclined her head. 'Thank you.'

'I can't wait to see your follow-up action.'

'Watch and learn.'

'At a guess,' he inclined indolently, 'you'll file a complaint with the gallery owner, who'll then offer to sell you the sculpture at a figure less than its purported value, as a conscience salve for the sculptor's misrepresentation.'

A slow smile curved her mouth, and her eyes sparkled with musing humour. 'You're good.'

Cassandra was discreet. No doubt it helped her father was a known patron of the arts, and the name Preston-Villers instantly recognisable. Apologies were forthcoming, she arranged payment and organised collection, then she turned to find Alicia deep in conversation with Diego.

Nothing prepared her for the momentary shaft of pain that shot through her body. It was ridiculous, and she hated her reaction almost as much as she hated *him*.

Diego del Santo was merely an aberration. A man who'd callously manipulated a set of circumstances to his personal advantage. So what if he was a highly skilled lover, sensitive to a woman's needs? There were other men equally as skilled... Men with blue-blood birth lines, educated in the finest private schools, graduating with honours from university to enter the fields of commerce, medicine, law.

She'd met them, socialised with them...and never found the spark to ignite her emotions. Until Diego.

It was insane.

Was Alicia his current companion? Certainly she'd seen them together at a few functions over the past month or so. There could be no doubt Alicia was hell-bent on digging her claws into him.

'Cassandra—*darling*. I was hoping to find you here. How *are* you?'

There were any number of society matrons in the city, but Annouska Pendelton presided at the top of their élite heap.

The air-kiss routine, the firm grasp of Annouska's manicured fingers on her own formed an integral part of the greeting process.

Annouska working the room, Cassandra accorded silently, very aware of the matron's charity work and the excessively large sums of money she managed to persuade the rich and famous to donate to the current worthy cause.

'How is dear Alexander?' There was a click of the tongue. 'So very sad his health is declining.' There was a second's pause. 'I see you're with Diego del Santo this evening. An interesting and influential man.'

'Yes,' Cassandra agreed sweetly. 'Isn't he?'

Annouska's gaze shifted. 'Ah, Diego.' Her smile held charm. 'We were just talking about you.'

He stood close, much too close. If she moved a fraction of an inch her arm would come into contact with him. The scent of his cologne teased her nostrils, subtle, expensive, and mingled with the clean smell of freshly laundered linen.

'Indeed?' His voice was a lazy honeyed drawl that sent all her fine body hairs on alert.

'You must both come to next month's soirée.' The matron relayed details with her customary unfailing enthusiasm. 'Invitations will be in the mail early in the week.' She pressed Cassandra's fingers, then transferred them to Diego's forearm. 'Enjoy the evening.'

'Would you like coffee?' Diego queried as Annouska moved on to her next quarry.

What I'd like is to go home to my own apartment and sleep in my own bed...alone. However, that wasn't going to happen.

Already her nerves were playing havoc at the thought of what the night would bring.

'No?' He took hold of her hand and threaded his fingers through her own. 'In that case we'll leave.'

She attempted to pull free from his grasp, and failed miserably. 'Alicia will be disappointed.'

'You expect me to qualify that?'

Cassandra didn't answer, and made another furtive effort to remove her hand. '*Must* you?'

It took several long minutes to ease their way towards the exit, and she caught Alicia's venomous glare as they left the gallery.

'Do you mind?' This time she dug her nails into the back of his hand. 'I'm not going to escape and run screaming onto the street.'

'You wouldn't get far.'

'I don't need to be reminded I owe you.'

The Aston Martin was parked adjacent to the gallery and only a short-distance walk. Yet he didn't release his grasp until he'd unlocked the car.

She didn't offer so much as a word during the drive to Point Piper, and she slid from the seat the instant Diego brought the car to a halt inside the garage.

It wasn't late by social standards, but she'd been in a state of nervous tension all day anticipating the evening and how it would end.

Dear heaven, she *knew* what to expect. There was even a part of her that *wanted* his possession. What woman wouldn't want to experience sensual heaven? she queried silently.

So why did she feel so angry? Diego del Santo wasn't hers. She had no tags on him whatsoever. He was free to date anyone, and Alicia Vandernoot was undoubtedly a tigress in bed.

Wasn't that what men wanted in a woman? A whore in the bedroom?

A hollow laugh rose and died in her throat as she preceded Diego into the house.

'Would you like something to drink?' He undid his tie and unbuttoned his jacket.

Cassandra continued towards the stairs. 'Play *pretend*?' She reached the elegantly curved balustrade and began ascending the stairs. 'In order to put a different context on the reason I'm here?'

'A man and a woman well-matched in bed?' Diego countered silkily, and she paused to turn and face him.

'It's just…sex.' And knew she lied.

Without a further word she moved towards the upper floor, aware of the sensual anticipation building with every step she took.

The warmth, the heat and the passion of his possession became a palpable entity, and she hated herself for wanting what he could gift her, for there was a part of her that wanted it to be real. The whole emotional package, not just physical sex.

Yet sex was all it could be. And she should be glad. To become emotionally involved with Diego would be akin to leaping from a plane without a parachute.

Death-defying, exhilarating…madness.

Cassandra made her way along the gallery to the

main bedroom, and once there she stepped out of her stiletto-heeled pumps, removed her jewellery, then reached for the zip fastener of her gown.

She was aware of Diego's presence in the room, and the fact he'd retrieved her overnight bag. Her fingers shook a little as she took it from him and retreated into the *en suite*.

Minutes later she removed her make-up, then she unpinned her hair and deliberately avoided checking her mirrored image.

Showtime.

Diego was reclining in bed, his upper body propped up on one elbow, looking, she perceived wryly, exactly what he was...one very sexy and dangerous man.

She was suddenly supremely conscious of the large T-shirt whose hemline fell to mid-thigh, her tumbled hair and freshly scrubbed face.

The antithesis of glamour. Alicia, or any one of the many women who had shared his bed, would have elected to wear something barely-there, probably transparent, in black or scarlet. Provocative, titillating, and guaranteed to raise a certain part of the male anatomy.

Except she wasn't here to provoke or titillate, and she slid beneath the covers, settled them in place, then turned her head to look at him.

He lifted a hand and trailed fingers across her cheek, then threaded his fingers through her hair.

He traced the delicate skin beneath her ear, then

circled the hollow at the base of her neck as he fastened his mouth over hers.

She told herself she was in control, that this was just physical pleasure without any emotional involvement.

Only to stifle a groan in despair as his hand slid down her body to rest on her thigh.

How could she succumb so easily? It galled her to think she'd been on tenterhooks all evening, waiting for this moment, *wanting* it.

His tongue tangled with hers in an erotic dance as she began to respond. Her T-shirt no longer provided a barrier, and she exulted in the glide of his hands as he moulded her body close to his.

Diego rolled onto his back, carrying her with him, and he eased her against the cradle of his thighs, then shaped her breasts, weighing them gently as he caressed the sensitive skin.

Their peaks hardened beneath his touch, and the breath hissed between her teeth as he rolled each nub between thumb and forefinger, creating a friction that sent sensation soaring through her body.

With care he eased her forward to savour each peak in turn, and she cried out as he took her to the edge between pleasure and pain.

His arousal was a potent force, and he settled her against its thickened length, creating a movement that had the breath hitching in her throat.

Cassandra felt as if she was on fire, caught up in the passion he was able to evoke, rendering everything to a primitive level as he positioned her to accept him in a long, slow slide that filled her to the hilt.

Then he began to move, gently at first, governing her body to create a timeless rhythm that started slow and increased in depth and pace until she became lost, totally. Unaware of the sounds she uttered as she became caught up in the eroticism of scaling the heights, only to be held at the edge…and caught as she fell.

CHAPTER FIVE

IT WAS early when Cassandra stirred into wakefulness, the dawn providing a dull light filtering through the drapes, and she lay there quietly for a while before slipping from the bed.

With slow, careful movements she collected her bag and trod quietly from the room, choosing to dress at the end of the hallway before descending the stairs to the kitchen, where she spooned ground coffee into the coffee maker, filled the carafe with water, then switched it on.

When it filtered, she took down a mug and filled it, added sugar, and carried it out onto the terrace.

A new day, she mused, noting the glistening dew. The sun was just lifting above the horizon, lightening the sky to a pale azure, and there was the faint chirping of birds in nearby trees.

It was peaceful at this hour of the morning. Nothing much stirred. There wasn't so much as a breeze, and no craft moved in the harbour.

'You're awake early,' Diego drawled from the open doorway, and she turned to look at him.

He was something else. Tousled dark hair, hastily donned jeans barely snapped, bare-chested, nothing on his feet...gone was the sophisticated image, instead there was something primitive about his stance.

'I didn't mean to disturb you.'

Diego effected a faint shrug. 'I woke as you left the room.'

The memory of what they'd shared through the night was hauntingly vivid, and she swallowed the faint lump that rose in her throat. 'I'd like to leave soon. I have a few things to do, and I need to spend time with my father.'

'I'll start breakfast.'

'No. Please don't on my account. I'll just finish my coffee, then I'll get my bag.'

Suiting words to action, she drained the mug, then she moved through the house to the front door, collected her bag, and turned to say goodbye.

He was close, and she was unprepared for the brief hard kiss he pressed against her mouth.

Cassandra wasn't capable of uttering a word as he opened the door, and she moved quickly down to her car, slipped in behind the wheel, fired the engine, then she eased the Porsche down the driveway.

There were the usual household chores, and she spent time checking her electronic mail before leaving to visit her father.

His increasing frailty concerned her, and she didn't stay long. He needed to rest, and she conferred with Cameron as to who would contact Alexander's cardiologist.

An early night was on the agenda, and she slept well, waking at the sound of the alarm to rise and face the day.

An early-morning meeting to review the week's agenda, assess supplies and prioritise work took place within minutes of her arrival, then she took position at her workspace and adjusted the binocular microscope to her satisfaction.

It was almost midday when her cellphone buzzed, signalling an incoming text message, and she retrieved it to smile with delight at the printed text. 'home, dinner when, news. Siobhan'

For those with minimum spare time and a tight schedule, text messaging provided easy communication. Brief, Cassandra grinned as she keyed in a response, but efficient.

Within minutes they'd organised a time and place to meet that evening.

Suddenly the day seemed brighter, and she found herself humming lightly beneath her breath as she adjusted a magnification instrument, then transferred to a correction loupe. Using a calliper, she focused on the intricate work in hand.

It was almost seven when Cassandra stepped into the trendy café. Superb food, excellent service, it was so popular bookings needed to be made in advance.

A waiter showed her to a table, and she ordered mineral water, then perused the menu while she waited for Siobhan to arrive.

She was able to tell the moment Siobhan entered the café. Almost in unison every male head turned towards the door, and everything seemed to stop for a few seconds.

Cassandra sank back in her chair and watched the effect, offering a quizzical smile as Siobhan extended an affectionate greeting.

'Cassy, sorry I'm late. Parking was a bitch.'

Very few people shortened her name, except Siobhan who used it as an endearment and fiercely corrected anyone who thought to follow her example.

The clothes, the long blonde flowing hair, exquisite but minimum make-up, the perfume. Genes, Siobhan blithely accorded, whenever anyone enviously queried how she managed to look the way she did. One of the top modelling agencies had snapped her up at fifteen, and she was treading the international catwalks in Rome, Milan and Paris two years later.

Yet for all the fame and fortune, none of it had gone to her head. On occasion she played the expected part, acquiring as she termed it, the *model* persona.

Together, they'd shared private schools and formed a friendship bond that was as true now as it had been then.

Siobhan barely had time to slip into a seat before a waiter appeared at her side, and she gave him her order.

'Mineral water. Still.'

The poor fellow was so enraptured he could hardly speak, and barely refrained from genuflecting before he began to retreat.

Cassandra bit back a smile as she sank back in her seat. 'How was Italy?'

'The catwalk, behind-the-scene diva contretemps, or the most divine piece of jewellery I acquired?'

'Jewellery,' she said promptly, and gave an appreciative murmur of approval as Siobhan indicated the diamond tennis bracelet at her wrist. Top-grade stones, bezel setting…exquisite. 'Beautiful. A gift?'

'From me to me.' Siobhan grinned. 'Otherwise known as retail therapy.'

Cassandra gave a delighted laugh. 'Moving on…tell me about the Italian count.'

'Sustenance first, Cassy, darling. I'm famished.'

It wasn't fair that Siobhan could eat a healthy serving of almost anything and still retain the fabulous svelte form required by the world's top designers to model their clothes.

Cassandra made a selection, while Siobhan did likewise, and another waiter appeared to take their order the instant Siobhan lowered the menu.

'Dining with you is an incredible experience,' Cassandra said with an impish grin. 'The waiters fall over themselves just for the pleasure of fulfilling your slightest whim.'

Siobhan's eyes twinkled with devilish humour. 'Helpful when things are hectic, and I have like—'

she gestured with her glass '—five minutes to take a food break.' Her cellphone rang, and she ignored it.

'Shouldn't you get that?'

'No.'

'O-K,' she drew out slowly. 'You're not taking phone calls in general, or not from one person in particular?'

'The latter.'

Their chicken Caesar salads arrived and were placed before them with a stylish flourish.

'Problems?' Cassandra ventured.

'Some,' Siobhan admitted, and sipped from her glass.

'The Italian count?'

'The Italian count's ex-wife.'

Oh, my. 'She doesn't want you to have him?'

'Got it in one.' Siobhan picked up her cutlery and speared a piece of chicken.

'You're not going to fill in the gaps?'

'She wants to retain her title by marriage.' Siobhan's eyes rolled. 'Lack of social face, and all that crap.'

'You don't care a fig about the title.' It was a statement, not a query.

'They share joint custody of their daughter. The ex is threatening to change the custody arrangements.'

'Can she do that?'

'By questioning my ability to provide reasonable

care and attention while the child is in the paternal home due to my occupation and lifestyle.'

'Ouch,' she managed in sympathy.

'Aside from that, Rome was wonderful. The fashion showing went well...out front,' she qualified. 'Out back one of the models threw a hissy fit, and was soothed down only seconds before she was due to hit the catwalk.' She leaned forward, and made an expressive gesture with her fork. 'Your turn.'

Where did she begin? Best not to even start, for how could she justify complex and very personal circumstances?

'The usual.' She effected a light shrug. 'Nothing much changes.'

'Word has it you and Diego del Santo are an item.'

Ah, the speed of the social grapevine! 'We were guests at a dinner party, and attended the same gallery exhibition.'

'Cassy, this is *me*, remember? Being fellow guests at the same event is something you've done for the past year. It's a step up to arrive and leave with him.'

'A step up, huh?'

'So,' Siobhan honed in with a quizzical smile. *'Tell.'*

'It seemed a good idea at the time,' she responded lightly. It was part truth, and the model's gaze narrowed.

'You're hooked.'

'Not in this lifetime.'

'Uh-huh.'

'You're wrong,' Cassandra denied. 'He's—'

'One hell of a man,' Siobhan finished, and her expressive features softened. 'Well, I'll be damned.'

A delighted laugh escaped her lips as she lifted her glass and touched its rim to the one Cassandra held. 'Good luck, Cassy, darling.'

Luck? All she wanted was for the next week to be over and done with!

They finished their meal and lingered over coffee, parting well after ten with the promise to catch up again soon.

Thursday morning Cassandra woke when the cat began to miaow in protest at not being fed, and she rolled over to check the time, saw the digital blinking, and muttered an unladylike oath. A power failure during the night had wiped out her alarm, and she scrambled for her wrist-watch to check the time...only to curse again and leap from the bed.

It didn't make a good start to the day.

Minutes later she heard the dull burr of the phone from the *en suite* and opted to let the machine pick up, rather than dash dripping wet from the shower.

Towelled dry, she quickly dressed, collected a cereal bar and a banana to eat as she drove to work, caught up her briefcase, and was almost to the door before she remembered to run the machine.

Cameron's recorded voice relayed he had tickets

to a gala film première that evening, and asked her to return his call.

She'd planned a quiet night at home, but her brother enjoyed the social scene and she rarely refused any of his invitations. Besides, an evening out would help her forget Diego for a few hours.

As if.

His image intruded into every waking thought, intensifying as each day went by. As to the nights...they were worse, much worse. He'd begun to invade her dreams, and she'd wake mid-sequence to discover the touch of his mouth, his hands, was only a figment of an over-active imagination.

She cursed beneath her breath as she waited for the lift to take her down to the basement car park. Whatever gave her the idea she could enter into Diego's conditional arrangement and escape emotionally unscathed?

Fighting peak-hour traffic merely added to her overall sense of disquiet, and it was mid-morning before she managed to return Cameron's call.

The workshop prided itself on producing quality work, and there was satisfaction in achieving an outstanding piece. Especially a commissioned item where the designer had worked with the client in the selection of gems and setting.

Software made it possible to assemble a digital diagram, enhance and produce an example of the finished piece.

There was real challenge in producing something

strikingly unusual, even unique, where price was no object. Occasionally frustration played a part when the client insisted on a design the jeweller knew wouldn't display the gems to their best advantage.

It was almost six when she let herself into the apartment, and she fed the cat, watered her plants, then showered and dressed for the evening ahead.

On a whim she selected an elegant black trouser suit, added a red pashmina, and slid her feet into stiletto-heeled sandals. Upswept hair, skilful use of make-up, and she was ready just as Cameron buzzed through his arrival on the intercom.

The venue was Fox Studios, the film's lead actors had jetted in from the States, and Australian actors of note would attend as guests of honour, Cameron informed as they approached the studios.

Together they made their way into the crowded foyer, where guests mingled as waiters offered champagne and orange juice.

The film was predicted to be a box-office success, with special effects advertised as surpassing anything previously seen on screen.

There was the usual marketing pizzazz, the buzz of conversation, and Cassandra recognised a few fellow guests as she stood sipping champagne.

'I imagine Diego will be here tonight.'

'Possibly,' she conceded with deliberate unconcern, aware that if he did attend it was unlikely to be alone.

'Does that bother you?'

'Why should it? He's a free agent.' The truth shouldn't hurt so much. 'I'm just a transitory issue he decided to amuse himself with.'

She didn't want to see him here...or anywhere else for that matter. It would merely accentuate the difference between their public lives and the diabolical arrangement Diego had made in forcing her to be part of a deal.

'He's just arrived,' Cameron indicated quietly.

'Really?' Pretending indifference was a practised art, and she did it well. She told herself she wouldn't indulge in an idle glance of the foyer's occupants, only to have her attention drawn as if by a powerful magnet to where Diego stood.

Attired in an immaculate evening suit, he looked every inch the powerful magnate. Blatant masculinity and elemental ruthlessness made for a dangerous combination in any arena.

Cassandra's gaze fused with his, and in that moment she was prepared to swear everything stood still.

Sensation swirled through her body, tuning it to a fine pitch as she fought to retain a measure of composure.

Almost as if he knew, he inclined his head in acknowledgement and proffered a faintly mocking smile before returning his attention to the man at his side.

It was then Cassandra saw Alicia move into his

circle, and she felt sickened by Alicia's effusive greeting.

With deliberate movements she positioned herself so Diego was no longer in her line of vision, and she initiated an animated conversation with Cameron about the merits of German and Italian motor engineering.

Cars numbered high on his list of personal obsessions, and he launched into a spiel of detailed data that went right over her head.

He was in his element, and she allowed her mind to drift as she tuned out his voice.

Diego didn't owe her any loyalty. If he'd issued her with an invitation to partner him here tonight, she would have refused. So why did she care?

Logic and rationale were fine, but they did nothing to ease the pain in the vicinity of her heart.

Are you crazy? she demanded silently. You don't even *like* him. Why let him get to you? Except it was too late…way too late. He was already there.

'…and given a choice, I'd opt for Ferrari,' Cameron concluded, only to quizzically ask, 'Have you heard a word I said?'

'It was an interesting comparison,' Cassandra inclined with a faint smile.

'Darling, don't kid yourself. You were miles away.' He paused for a few seconds, then said gently, 'Alicia isn't *with* him. She's just trying to make out she is.'

'I really don't care.'

'Yes, you do. And that worries me.'

'Don't,' she advised with soft vehemence. 'I went into this with my eyes open.'

'There's only the weekend, then it's over.'

Now, why did that send her into a state of mild despair?

It was a relief when the auditorium doors opened and the guests moved forward to await direction to their seats.

'Cassandra. Cameron.'

She'd have recognised that faintly accented drawl anywhere, and she summoned a polite smile as she turned towards the man who'd joined them.

'Diego,' she acknowledged, and watched as he shifted his gaze to Cameron.

'If I had known you were attending I could have arranged a seating reallocation.'

'I was gifted the tickets last night,' Cameron relayed with regret.

'Pity.'

Alicia appeared at Diego's side, and curved her arm sinuously through his own. 'Diego, we're waiting for you.' She made a pretence of summoning charm. 'Cassandra, Cameron. I'm sure you'll excuse us?'

Diego deliberately released her arm from his, and Cassandra wondered if she was the only one who caught the dangerous glitter in Alicia's eyes.

To compound the situation, Diego ushered Cassandra and Cameron ahead, and Cassandra felt

Alicia's directed venom like hot knives piercing her back.

'That was interesting,' Cameron accorded quietly as they slid into their seats. 'Alicia is a first-class bitch.'

'They deserve each other,' Cassandra declared with dulcet cynicism, and incurred a musing glance.

'Darling, Diego is light-years ahead of her.'

'Is that meant as a compliment or a condemnation?'

Cameron laughed out loud. 'I'll opt for the former. I'm sure you prefer the latter.'

Wasn't that the truth!

The film proved to be a riveting example of superb technical expertise with hand-to-the-throat suspense that had the audience gasping in their seats.

Eventually the credits rolled, the lights came on, and guests began vacating the theatre.

Cassandra sent up a silent prayer she'd manage to escape without encountering Diego. Except the deity wasn't listening, and the nerves inside her stomach accelerated as he drew level with them in the foyer.

His gaze locked with hers, and she could read nothing from his expression. 'We're going on for coffee, if you'd care to join us.'

Are you kidding? You expect me to sit opposite you, calmly sipping a latte, while Alicia plays the vamp?

'Thank you, no,' she got in quickly before

Cameron had a chance to accept. 'I have an early start in the morning.' She didn't, but he wasn't to know that, and she offered a sweet smile as he inclined his head.

'I'll be in touch.'

Alicia's mouth tightened, and Cassandra glimpsed something vicious in those ice-blue eyes for a timeless second, then it was gone.

Cassandra wasn't conscious of holding her breath until Diego moved ahead of them, then she released it slowly, conscious of Cameron's soft exclamation as she did so.

'Watch your back with that one, darling,' he cautioned. 'Alicia has it in for you.'

She met her brother's wry look with equanimity. 'Tell me something I don't know.'

They reached the exit and began walking towards where Cameron had parked the car. 'If she discovers Diego is sleeping with you...' He left the sentence unfinished.

'I can look after myself.'

He caught hold of her hand and squeezed it in silent reassurance. 'Just take care, OK?'

CHAPTER SIX

'CASSANDRA, phone.'

Diego, it had to be.

Cassandra took the call, and tried to control the way her pulse leapt at the sound of his voice.

'We're taking the mid-morning flight. I'll collect you at nine tomorrow.'

'I can meet you at the airport.' That way her car would be there when they returned.

'Nine, Cassandra,' he reiterated in a quiet drawl that brooked little argument, then he cut the connection.

He was insufferable, she fumed as she returned to her workspace.

The resentment didn't diminish much as day became night, and she rose early, packed, put out sufficient dry food and water for the cat, then a few minutes before nine she took the lift down to Reception.

The Gold Coast appeared at its sparkling best. Clear azure sky, late-spring warm temperatures, and sunshine.

Diego picked up a hire car and within half an hour they reached the luxurious Palazzo Versace hotel complex.

It was more than a year since Cassandra had last visited the Coast, and she adored the holiday atmosphere, the canal estates, the trendy sidewalk café's and casual lifestyle.

The hotel offered six-star accommodation, plus privately owned condominiums and several penthouse apartments.

Why should she be surprised to discover Diego owned a penthouse here? Or that he'd elected to take the extra total designer furnishing package including bed coverings and cushions, towels, china, glassware and cutlery?

The total look, she mused in admiration. Striking, expensive, and incredibly luxurious.

There was a million-dollar view from the floor-to-ceiling glass walls, and she took a deep breath of fresh sea air as Diego slid open an external glass door.

Delightful. But let's not forget the reason he's brought you here, an imp taunted silently.

Bedroom duties. The thought should have filled her with antipathy, but instead there was a sense of anticipation at a raw primitive level to experience again the magical, mesmeric excitement he was able to evoke.

Was it so wrong to want his touch, his possession without any emotional involvement other than the pleasure of the moment?

Don't kid yourself, she chided inwardly. Like it

or not, you're involved right up to your slender neck!

After this weekend her life would return to normal...*whatever* normal meant. Work, she mused as Diego took their overnight bags through to the bedroom. The usual social activities...which would never be quite the same again as she encountered Diego partnering Alicia, or any one of several other women all too willing to share his evening. Dammit, his *bed*.

How would she cope, imagining that muscular male body engaged in the exchange of sexual body fluids? The entanglement of limbs, the erotic pleasure of his mouth savouring warm feminine skin as he sought each sensual hollow, every intimate crevice?

It would be killing, she admitted silently. Perhaps she could retreat into living the life of a social recluse, and simply bury herself in work.

Except that would be accepting defeat, and she refused to contemplate a slide into negativity.

For now, there was the day, and she intended to make the most of it. With or without him. The night he would claim as his, but meantime...

Cassandra heard him re-enter the spacious lounge, and she lifted a hand and gestured to the view out over the Broadwater. 'It's beautiful here.'

Diego moved to stand behind her, and she was supremely conscious of him. Her skin tingled in reaction to his body warmth, and the temptation to lean back against him was almost irresistible.

'Do you spend much time here?' It seemed almost a sacrilege to leave the apartment empty for long periods of time.

'The occasional weekend,' he drawled.

But not often, she concluded, and wondered if and when he took a break to enjoy the fruits of his success. He possessed other homes, in other countries...perhaps he chose somewhere more exotic where he could relax and unwind.

'Lunch,' Diego indicated. 'We can eat in the restaurant here, cross the road to the Sheraton Hotel, or explore nearby Tedder Avenue.'

She turned towards him and saw he'd exchanged tailored trousers for shorts, and joggers replaced hand-tooled leather shoes.

'You're allowing me to choose?'

'Don't be facetious,' he chided gently.

'Tedder Avenue,' Cassandra said without hesitation. 'We can walk there.' Half a kilometre was no distance at all.

One eyebrow rose in quizzical humour. 'You want exercise, I can think of something more athletic.'

'Ah, but my sexual duties don't begin until dark...remember?'

He pressed an idle finger to the lower curve of her lip. 'A sassy mouth could get you into trouble.'

'In that case, I'll freshen up and we can leave.'

His husky laugh curled around her nerve-ends, pulled a little, then she stepped around him and walked through to the master bedroom.

She took a few minutes to change into tailored shorts and blouse, then she snagged a cap, her shoulder bag, and re-entered the lounge.

'Let's hit the road.'

It was a pleasant walk, the warmth of the sun tempered by a light breeze, and they settled on one of several pavement cafés, ordered, then ate with evident enjoyment.

They were almost ready to leave when Diego's cellphone buzzed, and she looked askance when he merely checked the screen and didn't pick up.

'It'll go to message-bank.'

'Perhaps you should take that,' Cassandra said when it buzzed again a few minutes later.

Diego merely shrugged and ignored a further insistent summons.

Within a few minutes Cassandra's cellphone buzzed from inside her bag, and she retrieved it, saw the unfamiliar number displayed, then engaged the call.

'You're with Diego.' The feminine voice was tight with anger. 'Aren't you?'

Oh, lord. 'Alicia?'

'He's taken you to the Coast for the weekend, hasn't he?'

'What makes you think that?'

'Fundamental mathematics.'

'No chance you might be wrong?'

'Darling, I've already checked. Diego picked you up from your apartment this morning.'

Counting to ten wouldn't do it. Hell, even *twenty* wouldn't come close. 'You have a problem,' Cassandra managed evenly.

'*You* in Diego's life is the problem.'

'I suggest you discuss it with him.'

'Oh, I intend to.'

She cut the connection and met Diego's steady gaze with equanimity. 'You owe Alicia an explanation.'

'No,' he said quietly. 'I don't.'

'She seems to think you do.'

The waitress presented the bill, which he paid, adding a tip, then when she left he sank back in his chair and subjected Cassandra to an unwavering appraisal.

'Whatever Alicia and I shared ended several months ago.'

She raised an eyebrow and offered him a cynical smile. 'Yet you continue to date her?'

'We have mutual friends, we receive the same invitations.' He lifted his shoulders in a negligible shrug. 'Alicia likes to give the impression we retain a friendship.'

She couldn't help herself. 'Something she manages to do very well.'

Diego's eyes hardened. 'That bothers you?'

'Why should it?'

Did she think he was oblivious to the way her pulse quickened whenever he moved close? Or feel the thud of her heart? The soft warmth colouring her skin, or the way her eyes went dark an instant before his mouth found hers?

'It's over, and Alicia needs to move on.'

A chill slithered down her spine. As she would have to move on come Monday? What was she *thinking*, for heaven's sake? She couldn't wait for the weekend to be over so she could get on with her life.

A life in which Diego didn't figure at all.

Now, why did that thought leave her feeling strangely bereft?

'Let's walk along the beach,' Cassandra suggested as they stood to their feet. She had the sudden need to feel the golden sand beneath her feet, the sun on her skin, and the peace and tranquillity offered by a lazy outgoing tide.

The ocean lay a block distant, and within minutes she slid off her sandals and padded down to the damp, packed sand at the water's edge.

They wandered in companionable silence, admiring the long, gentle curve stretching down towards Kirra. Tall, high-rise apartment buildings in varying height and colour dotted the foreshore, and there was a fine haze permeating the air.

Children played in the shallows while parents stood guard, and in the distance seagulls hovered, seemingly weightless, before drifting slowly down onto the sand to dig their beaks in in search of a tasty morsel.

It was a peaceful scene which changed and grew more crowded as they neared Surfer's Paradise.

'Feel like exploring the shops?' Diego ventured, and Cassandra inclined her head.

'Brave of you. That's tantamount to giving a woman *carte blanche*.'

'Perhaps I feel in an indulgent mood.'

'Who would refuse?' she queried lightly, and changed direction, pausing as they reached the board-walk to brush sand from her feet before slipping on her sandals.

It became a delightful afternoon as they strolled along an avenue housing several designer boutiques before venturing down another where Cassandra paused to examine some fun T-shirts.

She selected one and took it to the salesgirl, whereupon Diego extracted his wallet and passed over a bill.

'No.' Cassandra waved his hand aside, and shot him an angry glance as he insisted, to the amusement of the salesgirl, who doubtless thought Cassandra a graceless fool. 'Thank you, but no,' she reiterated firmly as she forcibly placed her own bill into the salesgirl's hand.

She was the first woman who'd knocked back his offer to pay, and her fierce independence amused him. There had been a time when he'd had to watch every cent and look to handouts for clothing and food. Nor was he particularly proud he'd resorted to sleight-of-hand on occasion. Very few knew he now donated large sums of money each year to shelters for the homeless, and funded activity centres for underprivileged children.

'Let's take a break and linger over a latte,' Diego suggested as they emerged from the shop.

'Can't hack the pace, huh?' Cassandra teased as she tucked her fingers through the plastic carry-bag containing her purchase.

There wasn't an ounce of spare flesh on that powerful body, and she wondered what he did to keep fit.

A gym? Perhaps a personal trainer?

They took a cab back to the Palazzo as dusk began to fall, and on entering the penthouse Cassandra headed for the bedroom, where she gathered up a change of clothes and made for the *en suite*.

There was a necessity to shampoo the salt-mist from her hair, and she combined it with a leisurely shower, then she emerged from the glass stall, grabbed a bath-towel and she had just secured it sarong-style when Diego walked naked into the *en suite*.

Oh, my, was all that came immediately to mind. Superb musculature, olive skin, a light smattering of dark, curly hair on his chest. Broad shoulders, a tapered waist, slim hips...

She forced her appraisal to halt there, unable to

let it travel lower for fear of how it would affect her composure.

It was difficult to meet his gaze, and she didn't even try. Instead she moved past him and entered the bedroom, sure of his faint husky chuckle as she closed the door behind her.

There was a certain degree of satisfaction in witnessing her discomfort. In truth, it delighted him to know she wasn't entirely comfortable with him, and there was pleasure in the knowledge her experience with men was limited.

His body reacted at the thought of the night ahead. Her scent, the taste of her skin...*por Dios,* how it felt to be inside her.

He hadn't felt quite this sense of anticipation for a woman since his early teens when raging hormones made little distinction between one girl or another.

Now there was desire and passion for one woman, only one. Cassandra.

If he had his way, he'd towel himself dry, go into the bedroom and initiate a night-long seduction she'd never forget.

Soon, he promised himself as he turned the water dial from hot to cold. But first, they'd dine at the restaurant downstairs overlooking the pool. Fine wine, good food.

Cassandra put the finishing touches to her makeup, then she caught up an evening purse and preceded Diego from the apartment.

The classic black gown with its lace overlay was suitable for any occasion. The very reason she'd packed it, together with black stiletto-heeled pumps. A long black lace scarf wound loosely at her neck was a stunning complement, and she wore minimum jewellery, diamond ear-studs and a diamond tennis bracelet.

With her hair twisted into an elegant knot atop her head, she looked the cool, confident young woman. Who was to know inside she was a mass of nerves?

Act, a tiny voice prompted. You can do it, you're good at it. Practised social graces. Taught in the very best of private schools.

The restaurant was well-patronised, and the *maître d'* presided with friendly formality as he saw them seated.

Wine? One glass, which she sipped throughout the meal, and, although they conversed, she had little recollection of the discussion.

For there was only the man, and the sexual aura he projected. It was a powerful aphrodisiac...primitive, *lethal*.

She had only to look at his hands to recall the magic they created as they stroked her skin. And his mouth...the passion it evoked in her was to die for, almost literally.

For she did die a little with each orgasm as he led her towards a tumultuous climax and joined her at the peak, held her there, before toppling them both in glorious free-fall.

The mere thought sent the blood racing through her veins, the quickened thud of her heartbeat audible to her ears as she waited for the moment Diego would settle the bill.

How long had the meal lasted? Two hours, three? She had little recollection of the passage of time.

The apartment was dark when they returned, and Cassandra crossed to the wall of glass to admire the night-scape.

The water resembled a dark mass, dappled by threads of reflected light. Bright neon flashed on buildings across the Broadwater, and there were distant stars dotting an indigo sky.

She sensed rather than heard Diego stand behind her, and she made no protest as he cupped each shoulder and drew her back against him.

His lips caressed the delicate hollows at the edge of her neck, and sensation curled deep within, radiating in a sweet, heated circle through her body until she felt achingly alive.

Diego slid a hand down to grasp hers, and he led her down to the bedroom. He dimmed the lights down low, then slowly removed each article of her clothing until she stood naked before him. With care he lifted both hands to her hair and slowly removed the pins, so its length cascaded down onto her shoulders.

He traced a pattern over her breasts, then drew a

line down to her belly before seeking the moist heart of her.

'You're wearing too many clothes,' she managed shakily, and watched as he divested each one of them.

Then he lowered his head and kissed her, arousing such passion she soon lost a sense of time or place as she became lost in the man, a wanton willing to gift and take sensual pleasure until there could be only one end.

It was then Diego pulled her down onto the bed and ravished her with such exquisite slowness she cried out in demand he assuage the ache deep within.

Afterwards they slept, to wake at dawn to indulge in the slow, sweet loving of two people in perfect sexual accord.

It was an idyllic place, Cassandra bestowed wistfully as they sat eating breakfast out by the pool, and wondered how it would feel to fall asleep in Diego's arms every night, knowing he was *there*. To gift him pleasure, as he pleasured her.

Whoa…wait a minute here. So the sex is great. Hell, let's go with fantastic. But it stops with tonight.

Early tomorrow morning they'd take the dawn flight back to Sydney and go their separate ways.

She should be happy it was nearly over. Instead she felt incredibly bereft.

Given the option of how to spend the day,

Cassandra chose the theme park. Lots of people, plenty of entertainment, and it meant she didn't have much opportunity to dwell on the coming night.

Tigers, baby cubs, the Imax theatre were only a few of the features available, and the hours slipped by with gratifying ease.

'Want to dine out, or order in?' Diego queried as they returned to the penthouse.

'Order in.' It would be nice to sit out on the balcony beneath dimmed lighting, sip chilled wine, and sample food while taking in the night scene out over the marina, where large cruisers lay at berth and people wandered along the adjacent board-walk.

He moved to where she stood and trailed light fingers down her cheek. 'Simple pleasures, hmm?'

Sensation began to unfurl deep inside, increasing her pulse-beat. It was crazy. Think with your head, she bade silently. If you go with what your heart dictates, you'll be in big trouble. Somehow she had the feeling it was way too late for rationale.

'I'll go freshen up.' If she didn't move away from him, she'd be lost.

A refreshing shower did much to restore a sense of normalcy, and she donned jeans and a cotton-knit top, tied her hair back, then added a touch of lipgloss.

Diego was standing in the lounge talking on his cellphone, and he concluded the call as she entered the room.

'Check the menu while I shower and change.'

Seafood, Cassandra decided as she viewed the selection offered, and chose prawn risotto with bruschetta. Diego, when he re-emerged in black jeans and polo shirt, endorsed her suggestion and added lobster tail and salad.

Diego opened a bottle of chilled sauvignon blanc while they waited for the food to be delivered, and they moved out on the balcony as the night sky began to deepen.

Lights became visible in a number of luxury cabin cruisers berthed close by, and Cassandra stilled, mesmerised, as Diego leant out a hand and freed the ribbon from her hair.

'All day I've resisted the temptation.' He threaded his fingers through its length so it curved down over her shoulders.

The breeze stirred the fine strands, tumbling them into a state of disarray. A warm smile curved his mouth as he leaned in close and took possession of her mouth in an exploratory open-mouthed kiss that teased and tantalised as he evoked her response.

He tasted of cool wine, and she placed a steadying hand to his shoulders and leaned in for a few brief moments until the electronic peal of the doorbell broke them apart.

Diego collected the restaurant food while Cassandra set the small balcony table with fine china and cutlery, and they shared a leisurely meal, offering each other forked morsels of food to sample in a gourmet feast.

The moon shone brightly, and there were myriad tiny stars sprinkling the night sky. Magical, she accorded silently.

They lingered over the wine, and when a fresh breeze started up they carried everything indoors, dealt with the few dishes, dispensed the food containers, and contemplated coffee.

It wasn't late, yet all it took was the drift of his fingers tracing the line of her slender neck, the touch of his lips at her temple, and she became lost.

With one fluid movement he swept her into his arms and carried her down to the bedroom, where dispensing with her clothes, his, became almost an art form.

She wanted to savour every moment, each kiss, the touch of his hands, his mouth, and exult in his possession. To gift him pleasure and hear the breath hiss between his teeth, his husky groan as she drove him to the end of his endurance.

When he reached it, she drew him in, the long, deep thrust plunging to the hilt, and he felt her warm, slick heat, revelled in the way she enclosed him, urging a hard, driving rhythm that scaled the heights with a shattering climax that left them both exhausted.

Afterwards they slept for a few hours, and Cassandra stirred as he carried her into the *en suite* and stepped into the spa-bath.

Dreamlike, she allowed his ministrations, and stood like an obedient child as he blotted the moisture from her body before tending to his own, then he took her back to bed to savour her body in a long, sweet loving that almost made her weep.

All too soon it was time to shower and dress, pack, drink strong black coffee, then drive down to Coolangatta Airport. Check-in time was disgustingly early, the flight south smooth and uneventful.

It was just after eight when they disembarked at Sydney Airport, and it took scant minutes to traverse the concourse to ground level.

'I'll take a cab,' Cassandra indicated as they emerged from the terminal.

Diego shot her a dark look that spoke volumes. 'Don't be ridiculous.'

'I need to get to work.'

One eyebrow slanted. 'So I'll drop you there.'

'It's out of your way.'

'What's that got to do with anything?'

She heaved an eloquent sigh. 'Diego—'

'Cool it, Cassandra. You're coming with me.'

Like a marionette when the puppeteer pulls the string? She opened her mouth to protest, only to close it again as the Aston Martin swept into the parking bay with an attendant at the wheel.

She remained silent during the drive into the city, and she had her seat belt undone with her hand on the door-clasp when he eased the car to a halt adjacent to the jewellery workshop.

'Thank you for a pleasant weekend.' The words sounded incredibly inadequate as she slid from the passenger seat. 'If you pop the trunk I'll collect my bag, then you won't need to get out of the car.'

Except her words fell on deaf ears as he emerged from behind the wheel, collected her bag and handed it to her.

Then he lowered his head and took possession of her mouth in a brief, hard kiss that left her gasping for breath. Then he released her and slid into the car as she walked away without so much as a backward glance.

Could anyone see her heart was breaking? Somehow she doubted it as she got on with the day. She checked with Sylvie, Alexander's nurse, and arranged to share dinner that evening with her father.

At four Cameron rang, jubilant with the news Diego had released the balance of funds.

Mission accomplished, she perceived grimly as she took a cab to her apartment, changed and freshened up, then she drove to Alexander's home.

He looked incredibly frail, and she felt her spirits plummet at the knowledge he'd deteriorated in the short time since she'd seen him last.

His appetite seemed to have vanished, and she coaxed him to eat, amusing him with anecdotes that brought forth a smile.

Cassandra stayed a while, sitting with him until Sylvie declared it was time for him to retire. Then she kissed his cheek and held him close for a few long minutes before taking her leave.

Meeting Diego's demands had been worth it.

Alexander remained ignorant of Cameron's business inadequacies, together with details surrounding his private life.

What about *you*? a tiny voice demanded a few hours later as she tossed and turned in her bed in search of sleep.

CHAPTER SEVEN

THURSDAY morning Cassandra woke with an uneasy feeling in the pit of her stomach. A premonition of some kind?

She slid out of bed, fed the cat, made a cup of tea and checked her emails, then she showered, dressed, and left for work.

There was nothing to indicate the day would be different from any other. Traffic was at its peak-hour worst, and an isolated road-rage incident, while momentarily disconcerting, didn't rattle her nerves overmuch.

Work progression proved normal, with nothing untoward occurring. Cameron rang, jubilant the Preston-Villers deal with Diego was a *fait accompli*, suggesting she join him for a celebration dinner.

So why couldn't she shake this sense of foreboding that hung around like a grey cloud?

It was almost six when she entered the apartment, and she greeted the cat, fed her, and was about to fix something to eat for herself when her cellphone buzzed.

'Cassandra.' Sylvie's voice sounded calm and unhurried. 'Alexander is being transported to hospital by ambulance. I'm about to follow. I've spoken to

Cameron, and he's already on his way.' She named the city's main cardiac unit. 'I'll see you there.'

Cassandra's stomach plummeted as she caught up her bag, her keys, and raced from the apartment. The cardiologist's warning returned to haunt her as she took the lift down to basement level, slid into her car to drive as quickly as traffic and the speed limit would allow.

Hospital parking was at a premium, and she brought her car to a screeching halt in a reserved space, hastily scrawled *emergency* onto a scrap of paper and slid it beneath the windscreen wiper, then she ran into the building.

What followed numbered among the worst hours of her life. Sylvie was there, waiting, and Cameron. The cardiac team were working to stabilise Alexander, but the prognosis wasn't good.

At midnight they sent Sylvie home, and Cassandra and Cameron kept vigil as the long night crept slowly towards dawn.

'Go home, get some sleep,' Cameron bade gently, and she shook her head.

At nine they each made calls, detailing the reason neither would be reporting for work, and took alternate one-hour shifts at Alexander's bedside.

It was there Diego found her, looking pale, wan and so utterly saddened it was all he could do not to sweep her into his arms and hold her close.

Not that she'd thank him for it, he perceived, aware he had no place here. Strict *family only* regulations applied, but he'd managed to circumvent them in order to gain a few minutes to express regret and ask if there was anything he could do.

'No,' Cassandra said quietly. 'Thank you.'

Diego cupped her shoulder, allowed his hand to linger there before letting it fall to his side.

A hovering nurse cast him a telling look, indicated the time, and he inclined his head in silent acquiescence.

'I'll keep in touch.'

'How did he get in here?' Cassandra asked quietly minutes later, and Cameron responded wearily,

'By sheer strength of will, I imagine. It happens to be one of his characteristics, or hadn't you noticed?'

In spades, she acknowledged, then jerked to startled attention as the machines monitoring her father's vital signs began an insistent beeping.

From then on it was all downhill, and Alexander slipped away from them late that evening.

Cassandra lapsed into a numbed state, and both she and Cameron shared a few silent tears in mutual consolation.

'Maybe you should spend the night at my place.'

She pulled away from him and searched for a handkerchief. 'I'll be fine. I just want to have a shower and fall into bed.'

'That goes for me, too.'

They walked down the corridor to the lift and took it down to ground level, then emerged into the late-night air. Cameron saw her to the car, waited until she was seated, then leaned in. 'I'll follow and make sure you get home OK.'

At this hour the streets carried minimal traffic, and as she reached Double Bay a light shower of rain began to fall. She saw the headlights of Cameron's car at her rear, and as she turned in to her apartment building he sounded his horn, then executed a semicircle and disappeared from sight.

Weariness hit her as she stepped out of the lift, and she was so caught up in reflected thought she didn't see the tall male figure leaning against the wall beside her apartment door.

'Diego? What—?'

He reached out and extricated the keys from her fingers, unlocked the door and gently pushed her inside.

'—are you doing?' she finished tiredly. 'You shouldn't be here.'

'No?' He removed her shoulder bag, put it down on the side-table, then led her towards the kitchen. He made tea, invaded her fridge and put a sandwich together.

'Eat.'

Food? 'I don't feel like anything.'

'A few mouthfuls will do.'

It was easier to capitulate than argue, and she obediently took a bite, sipped the tea, then she pushed the plate away. Any more and she'd be physically ill.

'Shower and bed,' Cassandra relayed wearily as she stood to her feet. 'You can let yourself out.' She didn't bother to wait for him to answer. Didn't care to see if he stayed. It was all too much, and more than anything she needed to sleep.

Diego fed the cat, washed the few dishes, checked his cellphone, made one call, then he doused the lights and entered her bedroom.

She was already asleep, and he undressed, then carefully slid beneath the covers. The thought she might wake and weep with grief alone was a haunting possibility he refused to condone.

Cassandra was dreaming. Strong arms held her close, and she felt a hand smoothing her hair. Lips brushed her temple, and she sank deeper into the dreamlike embrace, savouring the warmth of muscle and sinew beneath her cheek, the steady beat of a human heart.

It was comforting, reassuring, and she was content to remain there, cushioned in security, and loath to emerge and face the day's reality.

Except dreams didn't last, and she surfaced slowly through the veils of sleep to discover it was no dream.

'Diego?'

'I hope to hell you didn't think it could be anyone else,' he growled huskily, and met her startled gaze.

'I didn't want you to be alone.'

She tried to digest the implication, and found it too hard at this hour of the morning.

He watched as comprehension dawned on her pale features, saw the pain and glimpsed her attempt to deal with it.

'Want to talk?'

Cassandra shook her head, and held back the tears, hating the thought of breaking down in front of him.

'I'll go make coffee.' It would give him something to do with his hands, otherwise he would use them to haul her close, and while his libido was high, he was determined the next time they made love it would be without redress.

He slid from the bed, pulled on trousers and a shirt, then he entered the *en suite*, only to re-emerge minutes later, wryly aware a woman's razor was no substitute for a man's electric shaver.

In the kitchen he ground fresh coffee beans, replaced a filter, and switched on the coffee maker.

It was after eight, and breakfast was a viable option. Eggs, ham, cheese…ingredients he used to make two fluffy omelettes, then he slid bread into the toaster.

Cassandra dressed in jeans, added a blouse, then tended to her hair. She felt better after cleansing her face, and following her usual morning routine.

Not great, she assured her mirrored image, but OK. Sufficient to face the day and all it would involve.

The smell of fresh coffee, toast and something cooking teased her nostrils, and she entered the kitchen to find Diego dishing food onto two plates.

Her appetite didn't amount to much, but she ate half the omelette, some toast, and sipped her way through two cups of coffee.

'Shouldn't you be wherever it is you need to be at this hour of the morning?'

'Later,' Diego drawled, leaning back in his chair, satisfied she looked less fragile. 'When Cameron arrives, I'll leave.'

Her eyes clouded a little. 'I'm OK.'

One eyebrow slanted. 'I wasn't aware I implied you weren't.'

The cat hopped up onto her lap, padded a little, then settled.

She owed him thanks. 'It was thoughtful of you to stay.'

'I had Cameron's word he'd contact me if you insisted on returning home.'

Diego had done that out of concern? For her?

At that moment the phone rang, and she answered it. Cameron was on his way over.

Cassandra began clearing the table, and they dealt with the dishes together. There was an exigent awareness she was loath to explore, and she concentrated on the job in hand.

When it was done, she used the pretext of tidying the bedroom to escape, and the intercom buzzed as she finished up.

Cameron didn't look as if he'd slept well, and she made fresh coffee, served it, and was unsure whether to be relieved or regretful when Diego indicated he would leave.

The days leading up to Alexander's funeral were almost as bleak as the funeral itself, and Cassandra took an extra day before returning to the jewellery workshop.

Sylvie stayed on at Alexander's home, Cameron flew to Melbourne on business, and Cassandra directed all her energy into work.

Diego rang, but she kept the conversations short for one reason or another and declined any invitation he chose to extend.

A pendant commissioned by Alicia would normally have had all the fine hairs on Cassandra's nape standing on end. As it was, she took extra care with the design, ensuring its perfection.

The ensuing days ran into a week, and Cameron returned to Sydney briefly before taking a flight interstate within days.

'Cassandra, you're wanted at the shop.'

She disengaged from the binocular microscope, ran a hand over the knot atop her head, then made her way towards the retail shop.

A client wanting advice on a design? Soliciting suggestions for a particular gem? Or someone who had admired one of her personal designs and wanted something similar?

Security was tight, and she went through the entry procedure, passed through the ante-room and entered the shop, where gems sparkled against dark velvet in various glass cabinets.

Two perfectly groomed assistants stood positioned behind glass counters, their facial expressions a polite mask as they regarded a tall young woman whose back and stance seemed vaguely familiar.

Then the woman swung round, and Cassandra saw why.

Alicia. Beautifully dressed, exquisitely made-up, and looking very much the international model.

Trouble was the word that immediately came to mind.

'Miss Vandernoot would like to discuss the pendant she commissioned.'

'Yes, of course,' Cassandra said politely and crossed to where Alicia stood. 'Perhaps you'd care to show it to me.' She reached for a length of jeweller's velvet and laid it on the glass counter top.

'This,' Alicia hissed as she all but tossed the pendant down.

It was a beautiful piece, rectangular in shape with five graduated diamonds set in gold. The attached chain, exquisite.

'There are scratches. And the diamonds are not the size and quality I originally settled on.'

It was exactly as Alicia had commissioned. The diamonds perfectly cut and set.

Cassandra extracted her loupe, and saw the

scratches at once. Several. None of which were there when Alicia inspected and took delivery of the pendant. Inflicted in a deliberate attempt to denigrate her expertise?

'My notes are on file,' she began politely, and she turned towards the senior assistant. 'Beverly, would you mind retrieving them? I need to check the original details with Miss Vandernoot.'

It took a while. Cassandra went through the design notations and instructions with painstaking thoroughness, taking time to clarify each point in turn, witnessed and checked with Beverly. By the time she finished, Alicia had nowhere to go.

'There's still the matter of the scratching.'

Cassandra could have wept at the desecration to what had been perfection. 'They can be removed,' she advised quietly.

Alicia drew herself up to her full height, which, aided by five-inch stiletto-heeled sandals, was more than impressive.

'I refuse to accept substandard workmanship.' She swept Cassandra's slender frame with a scathing look.

'If you care to leave the item, we'll assess the damage and repair it at no cost to you.'

'Restitution is the only acceptable solution,' Alicia demanded with haughty insolence. 'I want a full credit, and I get to keep the item.'

Cassandra had had enough. This wasn't about

jewellery. 'That's outrageous and against company policy,' she said quietly.

'If you don't comply, I'll report this to the jewellers' association and ensure it receives media attention.'

'Do that. Meanwhile we'll arrange an expert evaluation of the scratches by an independent jeweller, and his report will be run concurrently.'

She'd called Alicia's bluff, and left the model with no recourse whatsoever. Alicia knew it, and her expression wasn't pretty as she scooped up the pendant and chain and flung both into her bag.

With deceptive calm Cassandra turned towards Beverly. 'I'll see Miss Vandernoot out, shall I?'

It was a minor victory, but one that lasted only until they reached the street.

'Don't think you've won,' Alicia vented viciously. 'I want Diego, and I mean to have him.'

'Really?' Cassandra watched as the model's gaze narrowed measurably. 'Good luck.'

'Keep your hands off him. I've spent a lot of time and energy cultivating the relationship.'

For one wild moment, Cassandra thought Alicia was going to hit her, and she braced herself to deal with it, only to hear the model utter a few vehement oaths and walk away.

Settling back to work took effort, and she was glad when the day ended and she could go home.

Grief sat uneasily on her shoulders, and Alicia's hissy fit only served to exacerbate her emotions. It would be all too easy to rage against fate or sink into a well of tears.

What a choice, she decided as she let herself into her apartment. The cat ran up to her, and she crouched down to caress the velvet ears. A feline head butted her hand, then smooched appealingly before curling over onto its back in silent invitation for a tummy rub.

'Unconditional devotion,' she murmured as she obligingly rubbed the cat's fur, and heard the appreciative purr in response.

She was all alone with no one close to call.

Cameron was in Melbourne, Siobhan had returned to Italy, and she couldn't, *wouldn't* ring Diego.

OK, so she'd feed the cat, fix herself something to eat, then she'd clean the apartment. An activity that would take a few hours, after which she'd shower and fall into bed.

CHAPTER EIGHT

WORK provided a welcome panacea, and Cassandra applied herself diligently the following morning as she adjusted the binocular microscope and focused on the delicate setting. Its intricate design provided a challenge, professionally and personally.

She wanted the best, insisted on it, aware such attention to minuscule detail brought the desired result...perfection.

If achieving it meant working through a lunchhour, or staying late at the workshop, nothing mattered except the quality of the work.

Yet there were safety precautions in place. Loose stones were easy to fence, and therefore provided a target for robbery. Priceless gems, expensive equipment. Security was tight, the vault one of the finest. Bulletproof glass shielded those who worked inside, and a high-priced security system took care of the rest.

It all added up to a heightened sense of caution. Something she had become accustomed to over the years, and one she never took for granted.

The cast-in-stone rule ensured two people, never one alone, occupied the workshop on the premise that if by chance something untoward happened to one, the other was able to raise the alarm.

In the three years she'd worked for this firm, no one had attempted to breach the security system in daylight.

Oh, for heaven's sake! Why were such thoughts chasing through her mind? Instinct, premonition? Or was it due to an acute vulnerability?

No matter how hard she tried, she was unable to dismiss Diego from her mind. He was an intrusive force, every waking minute of each day.

She could sense his touch without any trouble at all. *Feel* the way his mouth moved on her own. As to the rest of it…

Don't go there. The memories were too vivid, too intoxicating.

Great while it lasted, she admitted. A fleeting, transitory fling orchestrated for all the wrong reasons. Manipulation at its worst.

So why was she aching for him?

The deal was done. Preston-Villers would flourish beneath Diego's management. Cameron retained anonymity in his private life. As to her? She'd fulfilled all obligations and was off the hook.

A hollow laugh sounded low in her throat. Sure she was! She'd never been so tied up in her life!

She barely ate, she rarely slept. Some of it could be attributed to grieving for her father. The rest fell squarely on Diego's shoulders.

The electronic buzzer sounded loud above background music from wall-speakers, and Cassandra glanced up from her work to see a familiar figure holding twin food bags on the other side of the door.

Sally from the café near by with their lunch order.

'Want to take those sandwiches, or shall I?' Cassandra queried, only to see Glen in the throes of heating fine metal. 'OK, I'll get them.'

She laid down her tools, then moved towards the door, released the security lock and reached for the latch.

At that moment all hell let loose.

She had a fleeting glimpse of Sally's terrified expression, caught a blur of sudden movement as Sally catapulted into the workroom, followed by a man whose facial features were obscured by a woollen ski-mask.

A nightmare began to unfold as he whipped out a vicious-looking knife and brandished it.

The drill in such circumstances was clear. Do what you're told…and don't play the hero.

A knife wasn't a gun. She had self-defence training. Could she risk attempting to disarm him?

'Don't even think about it.' The harsh directive chilled her blood as he pulled out a hand gun and brandished it. In one swift movement he hooked an arm round her shoulders and hauled her back against him, then he pressed the tip of the knife to her throat.

Calm, she had to remain calm. Not easy with a

gun in close proximity, not to mention the threat of a knife.

At the edge of her peripheral vision she glimpsed Glen making a surreptitious move with his foot to the panic button at floor level. An action that would send an electronic alert to the supervisor's pager, the security firm and the local police station.

Had the intruder seen it? She could only pray not.

'Empty the vault.' The demand held a guttural quality, and she saw Glen lift his hands in a helpless gesture.

'I don't know the combination.'

He was buying time, and the intruder knew it.

'You think I'm a fool?' the intruder demanded viciously, tightening his hold on Cassandra's shoulders. 'Open it *now*, or I'll use this knife.'

She felt the tip of it slide across the base of her throat, the sting of her flesh accompanied by the warm trickle of blood.

Glen didn't hesitate. He crossed to the vault, keyed in a series of digits, then pulled open the door.

'Put everything into a bag. *Go!*'

Glen complied, moving as slowly as he dared.

'You want me to hurt her bad?'

The knife pressed hard, and Cassandra gasped at the pain.

'I'm being as quick as I can.' And he was, withdrawing trays, tossing the contents into a bag. 'That's all of it.'

'Give it to me!' He released her, and backed towards the workshop door.

She saw what he could not, and she deliberately kept her expression blank as two armed security guards positioned themselves each side of the outer door.

One well-aimed kick, the element of surprise, that was all it would take to disarm the intruder and provide the essential few seconds' confusion to give the guards their opportunity to burst in and take him down.

She went into calculated action, so fast it was over in seconds as her foot connected with his wrist and the gun went flying.

A stream of obscenities rent the air as he lunged for her, and she barely registered the door crashing open, or the security guards' presence as he swung her in against him.

Oh, God. The pressure against her ribs was excruciating, and she had difficulty breathing.

Sally began to cry quietly.

'Let her go.' One of the security guards made it a statement, not a plea, and earned a scathing glare.

'Are you crazy? She's going to be my ticket out of here!'

'Put down the knife.'

'Not in this lifetime, pal.' His snarl was low, primal, and frightening.

What began as a robbery had now become a hostage situation.

Then Cassandra heard it…the distant sound of a siren, the noise increasing in velocity, followed by the diminishing sonorous wail as the engine cut.

Seconds later the phone rang.

'Pick it up!'

The guard's movements were careful as he obeyed, listened, spoke, then he held out the receiver to her captor. 'It's for you.'

'Tell the man I want clear passage out of here and a fifteen-minute start. That's the deal.'

They wouldn't buy it. At least, not without resorting to any one of several psychological ploys in an attempt at negotiation.

The scene was too close to a movie script. Worse, the man holding her was desperate and wouldn't hesitate to hurt her.

Did your life flash before your eyes in a moment of extreme crisis? Cassandra pictured her mother, father. Cameron was there. *Diego.* Oh, hell, why Diego?

She didn't have a future with Diego. Dammit, she might not have a future at all!

'I want all of you out. *Now!*' He was incandescent with rage, and she consciously held her breath.

The guards, Sally and Glen filed out quietly, the door closed, leaving only Cassandra and the madman in the workshop.

'We're going to take a ride together, you and me.' His voice was close to her ear. 'If you're very good,

I just might let you go when we've put in some distance from here.'

Sure. And the sun shone bright at midnight in the Alaskan winter-time.

His hand closed over her breast, and squeezed. 'Or maybe you and me could shack up together awhile, have some fun.'

'In your dreams.'

He pinched her, hard, then thrust her roughly against a work-bench. 'Pick up that damned phone, and tell those bastards to get their act together.'

She could hardly believe they'd let him walk out of here alone. The gems in the vault were worth a small fortune. And there was the matter of her life.

Her hand stung, and she saw blood seeping from a deep cut as she lifted the receiver.

'Stay calm. Do what he says. We've set up road blocks. He can't get far.' The masculine voice was quiet, steady. As if he controlled a hostage situation on a weekly basis. Maybe he did, she thought wildly.

'They make a wrong move, and you're history, y'hear?'

What happened next was a nightmare of action, noise, fear in a kaleidoscope of motion as she was forced to carry the bag of gems, then used as a human shield as her captor hustled her towards his waiting car.

Would they try to take him out? Shoot, or hold their fire?

In those few terrifying seconds out in the open she consciously prepared herself for anything, and it wasn't until he shoved her across the driver's seat and climbed in almost on top of her that she realised he was about to make good his escape.

Taking her with him.

He fired the ignition and surged forward, wheels screeching as he took off at a frightening speed.

Cassandra automatically reached for the dashboard, not that it afforded her any purchase, and heard his maniacal laughter as he swerved in and out of traffic, then he took a hard turn left, only to scream with rage as he saw the road block up front.

She barely had a second to gauge his next move when he swung the car round and roared back down the road to crash through a hastily set-up road block.

The car bounced off another vehicle with a sickening thud of grinding metal before careening off down the road. Car horns blasted, brakes screamed.

Cassandra saw impending disaster a few seconds ahead of contact, and she acted entirely on impulse, throwing open the passenger door and leaping out an instant before the car hit.

There was a moment of searing pain as her body hit the asphalt, a conscious feeling of movement, then nothing.

Cassandra was dreaming. Her body felt strangely weightless, and at some stage she seemed to drift towards consciousness, only to retreat into a non-intrusive comfort zone.

There were voices, indistinguishable at first, then invasive as she came fully awake.

White walls, bustling movement, the faint smell of antiseptic...and a uniformed nurse hovering close checking her vital signs.

Hospital.

She became aware of an intravenous drip, bandages on one arm...and the dull ache of medicated pain. Her head, shoulder, hip.

'Good. You're awake.'

And alive. Somehow that fact held significance!

The nurse spared Cassandra a steady look. 'Multiple contusions, grazed skin, superficial knife wounds. Concussion.'

No fractures, no broken bones. That had to be a plus!

'We have you on pain relief. Doctor will be in soon. Meantime, you have a visitor.' Someone who had descended on the hospital within minutes of the patient being admitted, the nurse acknowledged silently. Insistently demanding the best specialists be summoned, and the patient allocated a private suite. Each attempt to compromise had been met with a steely glare.

'A visitor?'

'If you don't feel up to it, I can have him wait.' It wouldn't hurt to have him cool his heels a little longer. And if he dared upset the patient, she'd have his guts for garters.

Who knew she was here? It was probably a police officer needing her statement.

'It's OK.'

'Five minutes,' the nurse stipulated, and left the suite.

No sooner had she swept through the door, than it swung back and Diego entered. A tall, dark force whose presence seemed to fill the room.

Her surprised expression brought a faint smile to his lips, one that didn't reach his eyes as he advanced towards the bed.

'No *hello*?' He lowered his head and brushed his lips to her cheek.

Not even being pumped up with painkillers stilled the fluttering inside her stomach, nor did it prevent her quickening pulse. 'I'm temporarily speechless.'

'That I should come visit?' He kept his voice light, and wondered if she had any idea what he'd been through in the past few hours. Anger…hell, no, *rage* on being informed what had happened. And fear. Unadulterated fear he could have lost her.

He was still fighting both emotions, controlling them by sheer force of will. Her captor would pay…and pay dearly for putting this woman's life at risk.

'No one could stop me,' Diego drawled, his voice a mix of steel and silk.

Cassandra looked at him with unblinking solemnity. 'Who would dare?' His power was a given. His use of it, unequivocal.

His expression softened, and his eyes warmed a little. 'How are you, *querida*?'

The quietly voiced endearment almost brought her undone. 'As comfortable as can be expected.'

He lifted a hand and trailed gentle fingers along the edge of her jaw. 'Is there anything you need?'

You. Except he wasn't hers to have. 'When can I get out of here?'

The pad of his thumb traced the lower curve of her mouth. 'A day or two.'

She had to ask. 'My abductor?'

Diego's features became a hard mask. 'Arrested and behind bars.'

So there was justice, after all.

The door opened and the nurse returned. 'I must ask you to leave. The patient needs to rest.'

For a moment Cassandra thought he was going to refuse, then he moved in close, lowered his head and covered her mouth with his own.

It was a gentle kiss, and his tongue slid in to tangle briefly with hers. Electrifying seconds that sent a rush of blood to her head. Then he straightened, touched a light finger to her cheek, and vacated the suite.

Flowers arrived late afternoon. A bouquet from the workshop staff, and three dozen red roses with *'Diego'* scrawled in black ink on the attached card, together with a special-delivery package from one of the élite lingerie boutiques.

'Definitely *ah-hh* time,' an attentive nurse declared as Cassandra revealed two exquisite nightgowns and a matching robe. There were also essential toiletries—Chanel. He was nothing if not observant.

Cassandra ate little, endured a short visit from the police, gave a detailed account covering events during and after the robbery.

Then she slept, and she was unaware of Diego's presence in the room as he stood observing her features in repose.

So small, such a petite frame. Porcelain skin, and a mouth to die for.

He wanted to gather her up and take her home. To share his bed and hold her through the night. Just so he could. To protect, and ensure no one ever got close enough to hurt her again.

He, Diego del Santo, who'd bedded any number of women in his lifetime, now only wanted to bed one.

A slip of a thing, whose beautiful blue eyes had captivated him from the start. Without any effort at all she'd slipped beneath his skin and stolen his heart.

Was she aware of the effect she had on him?

The question was what he intended to do about it.

*   *   *

Cassandra woke early, accepted the nursing ritual and took a supervised shower. This morning the intravenous drip would be removed, and she wanted out of here.

The specialist was less than enthusiastic. 'I'd prefer you remained under observation for another twenty-four hours.'

'Prefer, but it's not essential?'

'Do you live alone?'

Tricky. 'Not exactly.' A resident cat didn't count. But she had the phone, her cellphone, and a caring neighbour.

He checked her vital signs, perused her chart. 'Let's effect a compromise. I'll check on you this afternoon with a view to possible release.' He gave her a piercing look. 'You have someone to collect and drive you home?'

She'd take a cab.

Which she did, arriving at her apartment just after six that evening. The manager produced a spare key and there was a sense of relief in being *home*.

The cat greeted her with a plaintive protest, and she fed her, put down fresh water, then made herself a cup of tea.

The *ouch* factor was very much in evidence, and she swallowed another two painkillers.

A nice quiet evening viewing television followed by an early night. By Monday she should be able to return to work.

Cassandra settled comfortably on the sofa, and

smiled as the cat jumped onto her lap. She surfed the television channels, selected a half-hour comedy and prepared to relax.

The insistent ring of the intercom buzzer was an unwelcome intrusion, and she transferred the cat, then moved to check the security screen.

Diego.

She picked up the in-house phone. 'I'm fine, and I'm about to go to bed.'

'Release the door.' His voice was deceptively mild.

'I'm too tired for visitors.'

'You want for me to get the manager and explain you left hospital under false pretences?'

'I already spoke to him. He gave me a spare key.'

'Cassandra—'

'Leave me alone. Please,' she added, then she replaced the receiver and moved back to take up her position on the sofa.

The cat had just re-settled itself on her lap when her doorbell rang. Her neighbour?

The manager, she determined through the peephole, with Diego at his side.

She unlocked and opened the door. The manager looked almost contrite. 'Your—er—friend expressed concern about your welfare.'

'As you can see, I'm fine.' If she discounted the pain factor.

Diego turned towards the man at his side. 'I'll take it from here.'

He looked momentarily nonplussed. 'Cassandra?'

What could she say? 'It's OK.'

Seconds later she closed the door and turned to face the man who'd managed to turn her life upside-down. 'Just what do you think you're doing?'

He was silent for a fraction too long, and there was something very controlled in his manner. 'You want me to pack a bag, or will you?'

'I beg your pardon?'

'You heard,' Diego said calmly. 'You get to come with me, or I sleep here.' His gaze lanced hers, and there was no mercy in the silkiness of his voice. 'Choose, Cassandra.'

'I don't want you here.' It was a cry from the heart, and her breath hitched at the pain from her ribs.

Diego's eyes went dark, and a muscle bunched at his jaw. Without a word he turned and made for her bedroom.

'You can't do this!' Dammit, he was several steps ahead of her.

'Watch me.'

'Diego…' She faltered to a halt at the sight of him opening drawers and tossing contents into a holdall before crossing to her walk-in wardrobe, where he chose clothes at random. From there he moved into the *en suite* and swept items into a toiletry pouch.

'OK, let's go.'

'I'm not going anywhere with you!'

'Yes, you are. On your feet, or I get to carry you.'

He waited a beat. 'On your feet is the better option.'

Cassandra wanted to hit him...*hard*. 'Just who in hell do you think you are?' she demanded furiously.

Diego sought control, and found it. 'You need to rest, recuperate. I intend to see that you do.'

'I can look after myself.'

'Sure you can.' He closed the zip fastener on the holdall and caught the straps in one hand. 'Next week.'

His gaze seared hers in open challenge. 'Until then, I get to call the shots.'

'And if I refuse?'

'I carry you out of here.'

There was no doubt he meant every word. Dignity was the key, and she observed it in silence as she followed him out into the lobby, then rode the lift down to the entrance foyer.

The Aston Martin was parked immediately outside, and she slid into the passenger seat, then watched as he crossed round to the driver's side.

Minutes later they joined the flow of traffic, traversing the relatively short distance to his Point Piper home.

Cassandra barely held her temper. He was the most impossible man she'd ever had the misfortune to meet. Dictatorial, indomitable, omnipotent.

She could think of several more descriptions, none of which were ladylike.

Diego swept the car along the driveway, activated the modem controlling the garage doors, then eased to a halt and switched off the engine.

Cassandra heard the dull click as the doors closed and made no attempt to exit the car.

'How long do you intend to sulk?'

She threw him a fulminating glare. 'I don't *sulk*.' She drew in a deep breath, and winced. 'I simply have nothing to say to you.'

Whereas he had a lot to say to her about taking risks and being a hero. Dammit, did she have any idea what the outcome could have been?

His blood ran cold just thinking about it.

However, it would have to wait. If she felt anywhere near as fragile as she looked, the only thing she needed right now was some tender loving care.

Diego slid out from behind the wheel and reached for her holdall, then he crossed round to open the passenger door. 'Let's take this inside.' He reached in and released her safety belt.

'I'd prefer to go home.'

'We've already done this.'

So they had, but she was in a perverse mood and uninclined to comply.

'Stubborn.' He slid one arm beneath her knees and lifted her out from the car, then he bent down, caught up the holdall, used one hip to close the car door, and strode through to the foyer.

'I hate you,' Cassandra said fiercely.

'It's a healthy emotion.'

'Put me down.'

He began ascending the stairs. 'Soon.'

'If you intend taking me to bed, I'll *hit* you.'

They gained the gallery, and reached the master suite seconds later, where he lowered her gently down onto her feet. With deft movements he turned back the covers and built up a nest of pillows.

'Get into bed. I'll bring you a cup of tea.'

'I don't need you to play nursemaid.'

Diego loosened his tie and discarded his jacket, and threw both over a nearby chair. 'It's here with me, or the hospital.'

'You're giving me a choice?'

He undid the top few buttons of his shirt. 'I made the choice for you.' He walked to the door, then paused as he turned to face her. 'If you're not in bed when I come back, I'll put you there.'

'Fat chance.' Empty retaliatory words that gave her a degree of satisfaction.

She spared a glance at the bed, and the comfort it offered was sufficient for her to snag a nightshirt and toiletries from her holdall, then retreat with them into the *en suite*.

Every movement hurt, her body ached, and she began to wonder at her wisdom in leaving hospital too soon.

Minutes later she emerged into the bedroom and slid carefully beneath the covers. It would be so easy just to close her eyes and drift off to sleep.

Diego re-entered the room, tray in hand, and quietly closed the door behind him. The snack and hot tea could wait. He could wait.

Just the sight of her lying in repose against the nest of pillows was enough to stop the breath in his throat and send his heart thudding to a faster beat.

He should dim the lights, exit the room quietly and let her sleep.

He did the first, laid down the tray, then settled his lengthy frame into a chair. There was a sense of satisfaction in watching over her.

Here was where she belonged. Where he wanted her to stay.

Diego sat there for a long time, alert to her faintest move, the slightest murmur of pain. In the depth of night he extracted two painkillers, part-filled a glass with water, then had her swallow both.

Only when she slipped effortlessly back to sleep did he discard his clothes and slide carefully in beneath the bedcovers to lay awake until the early pre-dawn hours.

CHAPTER NINE

CASSANDRA drifted through the veils of sleep into wakefulness, aware from the room's shadowed light that night had become morning. Early morning, unless she was mistaken.

Her body tuned into numerous bruises and made her painfully aware that any sudden movement on her part was not going to be a good idea.

The bed, this room...they weren't her own. Then she remembered...and wished she hadn't.

She turned her head slowly and encountered Diego's dark gaze. He lay on his side, facing her, his body indolently at ease as he appraised her features.

An improvement on last night, he perceived, lifting a hand to brush a swathe of hair back from her cheek.

His eyes narrowed at the thin line inches long at the base of her throat. It would heal, and after a while the scar would fade.

'Want to talk about it?'

'A verbal post-mortem?' She tried for flippancy, and failed miserably. 'The facts are in the official report.'

Facts he'd read, assimilated, and dealt with. 'You

didn't follow the book.' He still went cold at the thought of what could have happened.

'Concern for my welfare, Diego?'

'That surprises you?'

It seeded a germ of hope. She attempted a light shrug, and didn't quite pull it off. 'Banking, gem merchants and jewellers are high-risk industries for robbery.'

So they were. But employees were drilled to respond passively, not attack or act with aggression.

'You scared the hell out of me.' He traced the outline of her mouth with a gentle finger. 'Next time don't be a hero, hmm?'

Cassandra didn't answer. No one in their right mind wanted a *next time*.

'What would you have done in a similar situation?'

Diego's eyes narrowed. He'd known the streets in his teens, lived on them for a while, worked them. Taken risks that brought him too close to the law, but never close enough to be caught. He'd carried a knife, but never a gun, studied and practised oriental techniques of combat and self-defence. Techniques that could kill a man with a well-aimed blow from the hand or foot.

In answer to her question, he would have judged the odds and taken a calculated risk. As she had done.

'If you dare tell me it's OK for a man, but not a

woman,' Cassandra said with quiet vehemence, 'I'll have to hit you.'

His eyes darkened and assumed a musing gleam. 'Now, that could prove interesting.'

She could only win if he allowed her to, she perceived, aware there were few, if any, capable of besting him in any arena.

There was much more beneath the surface than he permitted anyone to see. No one, not even the most diligent member of the media, had uncovered much of his past. It made her wonder if the shadows shielded something that didn't bear close scrutiny...and what there had been to mould him into the person he'd become.

'Hungry?'

For food or you? *Both*, she could have said and almost did. Except the former had priority, and was a much safer option than the latter.

Besides, she retained too vivid a memory of what they'd shared together in this bed.

'Shower, then breakfast.' Decisive words followed by smooth action as she slipped out of bed and crossed to the *en suite*.

Cassandra set the water temperature to warm, then she stepped into the glass and marble stall, caught up the shampoo and began with her hair.

There was a need to thoroughly cleanse her skin of her abductor's touch. She hated the memory of his hands, his almost manic expression, and the sound of his voice. It could have been worse, much

worse, and she trembled at the thought. Delayed reaction, she determined, and vigorously massaged
shampoo into her scalp.

'Let me help you with that.'

She stilled, locked into speechless immobility for
a few electric-filled seconds, then she released the
pent-up breath she'd unconsciously held. 'I can
manage.'

'I don't doubt it,' Diego drawled, as he began a
series of slow, soothing, circular movements.

His gaze narrowed as he took in her bruised ribcage, the deep bluish marks on her arms. He wanted
to touch his mouth to each one, and he would...
soon. But for now he was content to simply care for
her.

Dear heaven, Cassandra breathed silently. To
stand here like this was sheer bliss...magical. She
closed her eyes and let the strength of his fingers
ease the tension from her scalp, the base of her neck,
then work out the kinks at her shoulders.

He had the touch, the skill to render her body
boneless, and an appreciative sound sighed from her
lips as he caught up the soap and began smoothing
it gently over the surface of her skin.

When he was done, he caught her close and cradled her slender frame against his own, then nuzzled
the curve at her neck.

Diego felt her body tremble, and he trailed his
mouth to hers in a gentle exploration that brought
warm tears to her eyes.

Did he see them, taste them? she wondered, wanting only to wrap her arms round him and sink in. The temptation was so great, it took all her strength to resist deepening the kiss.

With considerable reluctance she dragged her mouth from his and rested her cheek against his chest.

It felt good, so good to be here with him like this. To take the comfort he offered, savour it and feel secure.

Cassandra felt him shift slightly, and the cascading water stilled.

'Food, hmm?' He slid open the door, snatched a towel and began rubbing the moisture from her body before tending to his own.

It took scant minutes to utilise toiletries and clean her teeth before she escaped into the bedroom, where she retrieved jeans and a loose shirt from her bag, then, dressed, she caught up a brush and restored order to her hair.

Diego emerged as she applied pins to secure its length, and her gaze strayed to his reflected image, mesmerised by the smooth flex of sinew and muscle as he donned black jeans and a polo shirt.

She tamped down the warmth flooding her veins, the core of need spiralling deep inside. Crazy, she acknowledged. She was merely susceptible to circumstance...and knew she lied.

He turned slightly and his gaze locked with hers. For a brief moment everything else faded from the periphery of her vision, and there was only the man and a heightened degree of electric tension in the room.

It felt as if her soul was being fused with his, like twin halves accepting recognition and magnetically drawn to become one entity.

Mesmeric, primitive, incandescent.

She forgot to breathe, and she stood still, like an image caught frozen in time and captured on celluloid.

Then the spell broke, and she was the first to move, thrusting her hands into the pockets of her jeans as she turned towards the door.

Had Diego felt it, too? Or was she merely being fanciful?

Coffee. She needed it hot, strong, black and sweet.

Cassandra took the stairs and made her way towards the kitchen, aware Diego followed only a step behind her.

'Go sit down on the terrace. I'll fix breakfast.'

Soon the aroma of freshly made coffee permeated the air, the contents in the skillet sizzled, and minutes later he placed two plates onto the table.

The morning sun held the promise of warmth, the air was still, and the view out over the infinity pool to the harbour provided a sense of tranquillity.

Cassandra ate well, much to her surprise. She hadn't expected to do the meal justice, and she pushed her empty plate to one side with a sense of disbelief.

'More coffee?' It was a token query as Diego refilled her cup, then his own.

She felt at peace, calm after the previous afternoon's excitement.

'I'll call a cab.'

His expression remained unchanged, but there was a sense of something dangerous hovering beneath the surface. 'To go where?'

His tone was deceptively mild…too mild, she perceived. 'My apartment.' Where else?

He replaced his empty cup down onto its saucer with care. 'No.'

'What do you mean…*no*?'

'It's a simple word,' Diego drawled. 'One not difficult to understand.'

She looked at him carefully. 'I don't want to fight with you.'

'Wise choice.'

'But—'

'There has to be a *but*?'

It was time to take a deep breath…except her ribs hurt too much, and she had to be content with *shallow*. 'Thank you for—' She paused fractionally. For what? Taking care of her, bringing her here…caring. Oh, hell, she had to keep it together! 'Looking after me,' she concluded. 'It was very kind.'

He was silent for a few measurable seconds, and his eyes narrowed, masking a hardness that was at variance with the softness of his voice. 'Are you done?'

'Yes.' She waited a beat. 'For now.'

'I'm relieved to hear it.'

He was something else. All hard, muscular planes, and leashed strength as he leaned back in his chair, looking as if he owned the world...and her.

Total power, she accorded silently, and was determined not to be swayed by his sense of purpose.

Cassandra discarded her coffee and rose to her feet, then began stacking empty plates onto a tray, only to have it taken from her hands.

Without a further word she moved from the room and made her way upstairs.

It didn't take much to scoop her belongings into the holdall Diego had thrust them in the previous evening, and minutes later she picked up the bedroom extension, punched in the digits for a cab company, and was in the process of giving instructions when Diego entered the room.

Without a word he crossed to where she stood and cut the connection.

An action which sparked indignant anger as she turned to face him. 'How *dare* you?'

'Easily.'

'You have no right—'

He held up a hand. 'Last night you discharged yourself from hospital against medical advice. Your brother is in Melbourne, and unless I'm mistaken he's unaware of yesterday's escapade. You live alone.' His eyes were dark and held a latent anger that most would shrink from. 'Want me to go on?'

'I don't need a self-appointed guardian.'

'Like it or not, you've got one…for another twenty-four hours at least.'

Her chin tilted. 'You can't force me to stay.'

'It's here, or hospital readmission,' Diego said succinctly. 'Choose.'

She considered punching him, then discarded the idea on the grounds it would inevitably hurt her more than it would him. 'You're a dictatorial tyrant,' she said at last.

'I've been called worse.'

He wasn't going to budge. She could see it in his stance, the muscle bunching at his jaw.

'Who said you get to make the rules?' It was a cry from the heart, rendered in anger.

He didn't answer. He didn't need to.

'I need to feed my cat.' She threw one hand in the air to emphasise the point, then winced as pain shot through her body. 'Dammit.'

Diego swung between an inclination to shake or kiss her, considered the former followed by the latter, then went with rationale. 'So, we'll go feed him.'

'She,' Cassandra corrected. 'The cat's a *she*.'

He collected his keys and moved towards the door, then paused, turning slightly to look at her when she hadn't shifted position. 'You need to think about it?'

She wanted to throw something at him, and would have if there had been something close at hand. Instead she opted for capitulation…reluctantly.

Silence won over recrimination during the short drive to her apartment building, and she cast Diego a hard glance as he slid from behind the wheel.

'You don't have to come up with me.' What did he think she might do? Lock herself in? A speculative gleam lit her eyes…now, there was a thought!

He didn't answer as he joined her at the security area immediately adjacent to the entrance, and she restrained from uttering an audible sigh as he walked at her side to the bank of lifts.

A deeply wounded *miaow* greeted her the moment she unlocked her apartment door, and the cat butted its head against her leg in welcome.

Bite him, Cassandra silently instructed as Diego leant down and fondled the cat's ears.

The cat purred in affectionate response, and ignored her.

Great. Three years of food, a bed to sleep on and unconditional love…for all that I get ignored? There was no accounting for feline taste.

It took only minutes to put down food and fresh water, and Cassandra spared Diego a level look. 'I'm fine. Really.'

One eyebrow rose. 'So…go now and leave me alone?' He examined her features, assessing the pale cheeks, the dark blue eyes. 'We've done this already.'

So they had, but she felt akin to a runaway train that couldn't stop. 'I'm sure you have a social engagement lined up for this evening.' It was, after all, Saturday. 'I'd hate to be the reason you cancelled. Or cause problems with your latest—' she paused momentarily '—date.'

'Are you through?'

'I don't want to be with you.'

He didn't move, but she had the impression he shifted stance. How did he do that? Go from apparent relaxation mode to menacing alert?

'Afraid, Cassandra?'

Yes, she wanted to cry out. Not of you. Myself. For every resolve I make away from you disintegrates into nothing whenever you're near. And I can't, *won't* allow myself to fall to pieces over you.

Too late, a silent imp taunted. You're already an emotional wreck.

Every reason for her to walk away *now.* If only he would leave.

'Of yourself…or me?' Diego queried quietly.

Her chin tilted. 'Both.'

His mouth curved into a soft smile. 'Ah, honesty.' His gaze swept the room. 'If there's nothing else you need to do, we'll leave.'

Her lips parted in protest, only to close again as he pressed a finger against them.

'No argument, hmm?'

On reflection it was a restful day.

Within minutes of returning to Point Piper, Diego

excused himself on the pretext of work and entered the study, leaving Cassandra to amuse herself as she pleased.

She made a few calls from her cellphone, then she browsed through a few glossy magazines. Lunch was a light meal of chicken and salad eaten alfresco, and afterwards she slotted a DVD into the player and watched a movie.

Work took Diego's attention, leaving her with little option but to spend time alone. Restless, she ventured outdoors and wandered the grounds, admiring the garden.

Flowers were in bud, providing a colourful array in sculpted beds. Topiary clipped with expert precision, and a jacaranda tree in bloom, its fallen petals providing a carpet of lavender beneath spreading branches.

She reached the pool area, and she ascended the few terracotta-tiled steps to the terrace, crossed to a comfortable lounge setting beneath a shaded umbrella and sank into a seat.

The pool sparkled and shimmered beneath the sun's warmth, its infinity design providing the illusion its surface melded with the harbour beyond. Subtle shades of blue...pool, harbour, sky.

A sense of peace reigned as she took in the magnificent panoramic view. The city with its tall buildings of concrete and glass, the distinctive lines of the Opera House, the harbour bridge. Not to mention various craft skimming the waters and numerous mansions dotting the numerous coves.

Beautiful position, magnificent home.

And the man who owned it?

Cassandra closed her eyes against his powerful image. Four weeks ago he'd been a man she politely avoided.

Now... Dear heaven, she didn't want to think about *now*. Or what she was going to do about it. Hell, what *could* she do about it?

Loving someone didn't always end with happy-ever-after. And she wasn't the type to flit from one partner to another, enjoying the ride for however long it happened to last.

Tomorrow she'd return to her apartment, and her life as she knew it to be. Whenever her path crossed socially with Diego's, she'd greet him politely and move on. As she had during the past year.

Chance would be a fine thing, she alluded with unaccustomed cynicism. How could she do *polite* with a man with whom she'd shared every intimacy?

And fallen in love.

The to-the-ends-of-the-earth, the depth-of-the-soul kind.

Maybe she should take a leave of absence from the jewellery workshop and book a trip somewhere. A change of place, new faces.

Cassandra must have dozed, for she came awake at the sound of her name and a light touch on her shoulder.

'You fell asleep.' Diego didn't add that he'd kept watch over her for the past hour, reluctant to disturb her until the air cooled and the sun's warmth began to fade.

He was close, much too close. She could sense the clean smell of his clothes, the faint musky tones of his cologne. For a wild moment she had the overwhelming urge to reach up and pull his head down to hers, then angle her mouth in against his in a kiss that would rock them both.

Except such an action would lead to something she doubted she could handle...and walk away from.

His eyes darkened, almost as if he could read her thoughts, then he touched gentle fingers to her mouth and traced its curve.

'There's steak to go with salad. Go freshen up and we'll eat, hmm?'

Ten minutes later she sat opposite him, sampling succulent, melt-in-your-mouth beef fillet, together with crisp fresh salad and crunchy bread rolls.

'You can cook,' she complimented, and met his musing smile.

'That's an advantage?'

'For a man, definitely,' Cassandra conceded.

'Why, in this era when women maintain careers equal to those of men?'

'Do men think hearth and home, *food,* in quite the same way a woman does?' she countered.

'The man works to provide, while the woman nurtures?' He took a sip of wine. 'A delineation defining the sexes?'

'Equality in the workplace,' she broached with a tinge of humour. 'But outside of it, men and women are from two different planets.'

'And not meant to cohabit?'

'Physically,' she agreed. 'The emotional aspect needs work.'

'*Vive la difference,* hmm?'

It proved to be a leisurely meal, and afterwards they viewed a movie on DVD. When the credits rolled she rose to her feet and bade him a polite goodnight.

She couldn't, wouldn't slip into the bed she'd shared with him last night, she determined as she ascended the stairs to the upper level.

It took only minutes to collect her nightwear and toiletries and enter another bedroom. There were fresh sheets and blankets in the linen box at the foot of the bed, and she quickly made up the bed, undressed, then slid beneath the covers.

She was about to snap off the bedside light when the door opened and Diego entered the room.

'What are you doing here?'

'My question, I think,' he drawled as he crossed to the bed and threw back the covers. 'You want to walk, or do I get to carry you?'

'I'm not sleeping in your bed.'

'It's where you'll spend the night.'

Cassandra could feel the anger simmer beneath

the surface of her control. Soon, it would threaten to erupt. 'Sex as payment for you taking on the role of nursemaid?' She regretted the words the instant they left her lips.

'Would you care to run that by me again?' His voice sent icy shivers scudding down the length of her spine.

'Not really.'

Without a further word Diego turned and walked from the room, quietly closing the door behind him. An action that was far more effective than if he'd slammed it.

Dammit, what was the matter with her?

Subconsciously she knew the answer. Fear...on every level.

Ultimately, for losing something she'd never had...the love of a man. Not just any man. Diego del Santo.

Cassandra lay in the softly lit room, staring at the walls surrounding her, and faced the knowledge that life without him would amount to no life at all.

Her eyes ached with unshed tears, and she cursed herself for allowing her emotions free rein.

She had no idea how long it was before she fell into an uneasy sleep where dark figures chased her fleeing form.

At some stage she came sharply awake, immensely relieved to have escaped from a nightmarish dream. Until memory returned, and with it the knowledge she was alone in a bed in Diego's home...and why.

She closed her eyes in an effort to dispel his image, and failed miserably as she accorded herself all kinds of fool.

The admission didn't sit well, and after several long minutes she slid from the bed and crossed to the *en suite*.

There was a glass on the vanity top, and she part-filled it with water, then lifted the glass to her lips, only to have it slip from her fingers, hit the vanity top and fall to the tiled floor, where it shattered into countless shards.

It was an accident, and she cursed the stupid tears welling in her eyes as she sank down onto her haunches and collected the largest pieces of glass.

There was a box of tissues on the vanity top, and she reached for them, tore out several sheets and began gathering up the mess.

It became the catalyst that unleashed her withheld emotions, and the tears overflowed to run in warm rivulets down each cheek, clouding her vision.

'What the hell—?'

Cassandra was so intent on the task at hand she didn't hear Diego enter the room, and her fingers shook at the sound of his voice.

'I dropped a glass.' As if it wasn't self-explanatory.

He took one look at her attempt to gather the shards together, and the breath locked in his throat.

'Don't move.' The instruction was terse. 'I'll be back in a minute.'

He made it in three, and that was only because he had to discard one broom cupboard and search in another for a brush and pan.

In one fluid movement he lifted her high and lowered her down onto the bedroom carpet, then he completed the clean-up with deft efficiency.

Cassandra could only stand and watch, mesmerised by the sight of him in hastily pulled-on jeans, the breadth of his shoulders and the flex of muscle and sinew.

He made her ache in places where she had little or no control, and she turned away, wanting only for him to leave before she lost what was left of her composure.

'Use one of the other bathrooms until morning just in case there are any splinters I might have missed.'

She had difficulty summoning her voice. 'Thanks.' She made a helpless gesture with one hand. 'I'm sorry the noise disturbed you.'

Did she have any idea how appealing she looked? Bare legs, a cotton nightshirt with a hem that reached mid-thigh, and her hair loose and tousled?

No other woman had affected him quite the way she did. He wanted to reach beneath the nightshirt, fasten his hands on warm flesh and skim them over her skin. Touch, and be touched in return in a prelude that could only have one end.

'Are you OK?'

How did she answer that? She'd never be *OK* where he was concerned. 'I'm fine.' An automatic response, and one that took first prize in the fabrication stakes.

'I'll get rid of this.'

The pan, brush and broken glass. She nodded, aware he crossed to the door, and she registered the moment he left the room.

She should get into bed, douse the light and try to get some sleep. Instead she sank down onto the edge of the mattress and buried her head in her hands.

Reaction could be a fickle thing, and she let the tears fall. Silently, wondering if their release would ease the heartache made worse by having crossed verbal swords with the one man who'd come to mean so much to her in such a short time.

It was crazy to swing like a pendulum between one emotion and another. The sooner she returned to her apartment and moved on with her life, the better.

She wanted what she had before Diego del Santo tore her equilibrium to shreds and scattered her emotional heart every which way.

Oh, *dammit*, why did love have to hurt so much?

With a sense of frustration she rubbed her cheeks and smoothed the hair back from her face. It was then she saw Diego's tall frame in the open doorway.

If there was anything that undid a man, Diego acknowledged, it was a woman's tears. He'd witnessed many in his time. Some reflecting genuine grief; others merely a manipulative act.

None had the effect on him to quite the degree as evidence of this woman's distress did.

There were occasions when words healed, but now wasn't the time.

In silence he crossed the room and gathered her into his arms, stilling her protest by the simple expediency of placing the palm of one hand over her mouth.

It took a matter of seconds to reach the master suite, and he released her carefully down onto her feet.

Without a word he skimmed the nightshirt over her head and tossed it onto the carpet, then followed it with his jeans.

'What do you think you're doing?' As a protest it failed, utterly.

His eyes were dark, so dark she thought she might drown in them, as he captured her arms and slid his hands up to cup her face.

'This is the one place where everything between us makes sense,' he drawled as his head lowered down to hers.

She felt the warmth of his breath a second before his mouth took possession of hers in a kiss that liquefied her bones.

A faint moan rose and died in her throat as he

took her deep, so deep she lost track of where and who she was as emotion ruled, transcending anything they'd previously shared.

Somehow they were no longer standing, and she gasped as Diego's mouth left hers and began a slow descent, savouring the sensitive hollow at the edge of her neck before trailing a path over the line at the base of her throat where her captor had pierced her skin with the tip of his knife.

With the utmost care Diego caressed each bruise, as if to erase the uncaring brutality of the man who'd inflicted them.

The surface of her skin became highly sensitised, and her pulse raced to a quickened beat, thudding in unison with his own. She could feel it beneath her touch, the slide of her fingers.

What followed became a leisurely, sweet loving, so incredibly tender Cassandra was unable to prevent the warm trickle of tears, and when at last he entered her she cried out, exulting in the feel of him as warm, moist tissues expanded to accept his length.

Sensation spiralled to new heights, and she wrapped her legs around his waist, urging him deep, thrilling to each thrust as he slowly withdrew, only to plunge again and again in the rhythm of two lovers in perfect unison in their ascent to the brink of ecstasy.

Diego held her there, teetering on the edge, before

tipping them both over in a sensual free-fall that left them slick with sweat and gasping for breath.

The aftermath became a gentle play of the senses, with the soft trail of fingertips, the light touch of lips.

CHAPTER TEN

CASSANDRA stirred, and gradually became aware she wasn't alone in the bed. For her head lay pillowed against Diego's chest, a male leg rested across her own, and his arms loosely circled her body as he held her close.

Diego sensed the quickened heartbeat, the change in her breathing, and brushed his lips to her hair. Tousled silk, he mused, inhaling its fresh, clean smell. A man could take immense pleasure from waking each morning with a warm, willing woman in his arms.

Not just any woman...*this* woman.

'You're awake.'

She heard his quiet drawl, *felt* the sound of it against her cheek, and offered a lazily voiced affirmative.

He trailed the tips of his fingers down the length of her spine, shaped the firm globe of her buttock, then he traced a path over her hip, settled briefly in the curve of her waist before shifting to her breast.

There was a part of her that knew she should protest. To slip so easily into intimacy meant she accepted the current situation...and she didn't.

Dear heaven. She bit back a gasp as he eased her

gently onto her back, then lowered his mouth to suckle at one tender peak.

Seconds later the breath hissed between her teeth as his hand trailed to the soft curls at the apex of her thighs and began a teasing exploration.

She went up and over, then groaned out loud as another orgasmic wave chased the first with an intensity that took hold of her emotions and spun them out of control.

His arousal was a potent force, and just as she thought she'd scaled the heights he nudged her thighs apart, slid in, and took her higher than she'd ever been before, matching her climax with his own in a tumultuous fusion of the senses.

It took a while for their breathing to settle into its former rhythm, and they lay entwined together, spent as only two people could be in the aftermath of very good sex.

Make that incredible, off-the-planet sex, Cassandra amended as she closed her eyes and indulged her mind and body in an emotional replay.

It had, she mused indolently, been all about her pleasure. Soon, she'd seek to even the scales a little.

And she did, later, taking delight in testing his control…and breaking it.

Enjoy, Cassandra bade silently. For within a few hours she'd return to her apartment and a life from which Diego would fade.

Later, much later they rose from the bed, shared a shower, then, dressed, they descended the stairs to the kitchen for a meal that was neither breakfast nor lunch but a combination of both.

Diego's cellphone buzzed as they lingered over coffee, and he checked the caller ID, then rose to his feet.

'I'll have to take this.'

Cassandra lifted a hand, silently indicating he should do so, and she watched as he crossed the terrace.

French, she registered, barely discerning a word or two...and wondered how many languages he spoke.

Business, she determined, and let her gaze drift across the pool to the harbour beyond.

'I have to meet with two business colleagues. Their scheduled stopover was cancelled and they took an earlier flight,' Diego relayed as he returned to the table. 'I'll be an hour or two.' He drained the rest of his coffee, then leant down and took brief, hard possession of her mouth. 'We need to talk.' His lips caressed hers with a soothing touch.

She wasn't capable of saying a word, and he uttered a husky imprecation.

'Cassandra—'

The insistent sound of his cellphone brought forth a harsh expletive, and she saw the flex of muscle at his jaw as he sought civility. 'Dammit.' He raked fingers through his hair.

'It's OK.'

His eyes darkened. It was far from OK. Yet delegation was out of the question. There were only two associates capable of handling the current negotiations, and neither were in the same state.

'I should be able to tie this up within an hour or two.'

'Go,' she managed quietly. 'They,' whoever *they* were, 'will be waiting for you.'

He shot her a piercing look, then turned and made his way through the house, collected his briefcase and keys and entered the garage.

Minutes later Cassandra stood to her feet, cleared the table, then dealt with dishes and tidied the kitchen.

Stay, or leave.

If she stayed, she'd be condoning an affair. And while she could live with that if mutual *love* was at its base, she found it untenable when the emotion was one-sided.

She wasn't an 'it's OK as long as it lasts' girl. Nor could she view hitching up with a man for whatever she'd gain from the relationship.

No contest, she decided sadly as she made her way upstairs.

It didn't take long to pack, or to pen a note which she propped against the side-table in the foyer. Then she crossed to the phone and called for a cab.

The cat greeted her with an indignant sound and a swishing tail. The message light on her answering machine blinked, and she organised priorities by feeding the cat, then she tossed clothes into the washing machine, fetched a cool drink, then she ran the machine.

Siobhan… 'Tying the knot in Rome next week-end. Need you there, darling, to hold my hand.'

Cameron… 'Flying home Tuesday. Let's do din-ner Wednesday, OK?'

Alicia… 'Hope you're enjoying the ride. It won't last.'

Cassandra didn't know whether to laugh or cry at the latter. The ride, as Alicia called it, was over.

Keeping busy would help, and when the washing-machine cycle finished she put the clean clothes into the drier.

The contents of the refrigerator looked pathetic, and she caught up her car keys. Milk, bread, fresh fruit and salad headed her mental list, and she took the lift down to the basement car park, then drove to the nearest store.

There was a trendy café close by, and she ordered a latte, picked up a magazine, and leafed through the pages while she sipped her coffee.

It was almost five when she swept the car into the bricked apron adjacent to the apartment building's main entrance, automatically veering left to take the descending slope into the basement car park.

It was then she saw a familiar car parked in the visitors' area. As if there was any doubt, Diego's tall frame leaning indolently against the Aston Martin's rear panel merely confirmed it.

For a few heart-stopping seconds she forgot to

breathe, then she eased her car towards the security gate, retrieved her ID card and inserted it with shaking fingers and drove down to her allotted space, killed the engine, then reached for the door-clasp...only to have the door swing open before she had a chance to release it.

She tilted her head to look at him, and almost wished she hadn't, for his features appeared carved from stone.

'What are you doing here?'

'Did you think I wouldn't come after you?'

She felt at a distinct disadvantage seated in the car. By comparison he seemed to tower over her, and if they were going to get into a heated argument she needed to even the stakes a little.

With careful movements she slid from behind the wheel, then closed and locked the door before turning to face him. 'I don't know what you're talking about.'

'Yes, you do.' His voice resembled pure silk, and she swallowed the sudden lump that rose in her throat.

'Why didn't you stay?'

'There was no reason to,' she managed. 'We don't owe each other a thing.'

'All obligations fulfilled,' Diego accorded with dangerous softness.

It almost killed her to say it. 'Yes.'

'No emotional involvement. Just good sex?'

She was breaking up, ready to shatter. 'What do

you want from me?' It was a cry from the heart that held a degree of angry desperation.

'I want you in my life.'

'For how long, Diego?' she demanded. 'Until either one of us wants it to end?' As it would. 'Nothing lasts forever, and lust is a poor bedfellow for love.'

A car swept close by and slid into an adjacent space. She recognised the driver as a fellow tenant, and she met his concerned glance.

'Everything OK, Cassandra?'

Diego hardly presented a complacent figure. She managed a reassuring smile. 'Yes.'

The tenant cast Diego a doubtful look, glimpsed a sense of purpose in those dark eyes, and chose to move on.

'Let's take this upstairs.'

If he touched her, she'd be lost. One thing would lead to another…

It was better to end it now. 'No.'

Diego barely resisted the temptation to shake her. 'Tell me what we share means nothing to you.'

She couldn't do it. Her eyes clouded, then darkened as she struggled to find something to say that wouldn't sound inane.

Some of the tension eased in his gut as he reached for her. He cupped her nape with one hand and drew her in against him with the other, then his mouth was on hers, moving like warm silk as he took possession.

When he lifted his head she could only look at him.

'You're a piece of work,' he accorded quietly. 'No woman has driven me as crazy as you have.' His lips curved into a warm smile. 'A year of being held at a distance, when you've politely declined every invitation I extended. I've had to be content with brief, well-bred conversations whenever we attended the same social functions.'

Cassandra recalled each and every one of those occasions. The edgy onset of nerves the instant his familiar frame came into view; a recognition on some deep emotional level she was afraid to explore, fearing if she entered his space she'd never survive leaving it.

'Marry me.'

Cassandra opened her mouth, then closed it again. 'What did you say?'

'Marry me.'

She could only look at him in shocked silence.

'Do you really want our children to learn their father proposed to their mother in a basement car park?' Diego queried gently.

This was a bad joke. 'You can't be serious.'

'As serious as it gets.'

'Diego—'

'I want to share the rest of your life,' he said gently. 'I want to be the father of your children and grow old with you.'

There could be no doubt he meant every word. It

was there in the depth of his dark eyes, the heartfelt warmth of his voice, his touch.

Joy began a radiating spiral as it sang through her veins, piercingly sweet and gloriously sensual.

A faint smile lifted the edges of his mouth as he gave the concrete cavern a sweeping glance. 'I'd planned on different surroundings from these.'

Cassandra's lips parted in a tremulously soft smile. 'I don't need soft music, dimmed lights, fine food or wine.'

Diego brushed his fingers along the edge of her jaw, tilting her chin a little as he caressed the curve of her lower lip with his thumb. 'Just the words, *querida*?'

She felt as if she was teetering on the edge of something wonderful. 'Only if you mean them.'

'You're the love I thought I'd never find,' he said gently. 'I want, *need* you. *You*,' he emphasised gently. 'For the rest of my life.'

For a moment she didn't seem capable of finding her voice. It overwhelmed her. *He* overwhelmed her. In an instinctive gesture she pressed her mouth against his palm.

'I didn't want to like you,' Cassandra said shakily. 'I especially didn't want to fall in love with you.' She'd fought him every inch of the way, hating him for forcing recognition their souls were twin halves of a whole.

'Because of my so-called dangerous past?' he queried with teasing amusement.

'It shaped and made you the man you've become.' Providing the tenacity, strength of will and integrity lacking in many men his equal.

He fastened his mouth on hers in a kiss that was so evocatively tender it melted her bones.

Minutes later Diego caught hold of her hand and began leading her towards the lift. 'We need to get out of here.' His smile held the heat of passion overlayed with a tinge of humour. 'Your place or mine?'

'You're letting me make the decision?'

He paused to take a brief, hard kiss, tangled his tongue with hers, and felt the breath catch in her throat. 'You have a sassy mouth.'

'That's a compliment?'

Seconds later the lift doors opened and they entered the cubicle. 'Foyer?' Diego queried as he indicated the panel. 'Or your apartment?'

'There's the cat—'

'Not the foyer.'

The lift began its ascent towards her floor. 'I need clothes,' Cassandra continued.

'The cat will adjust.'

'To what?'

'Her new home.'

She looked at him, and melted. 'I love you.'

'Love me, love my cat?' he quizzed with amusement.

'Uh-huh. She's with me.' The lift slid to a stop, and she preceded him into the lobby.

He took the keys from her hand and unlocked and entered the apartment, then he closed the door behind them.

'I take it that's a *yes*?'

Her expression sobered as she looked at him. The love was there, for her, only her. She doubted anyone had ever seen him so vulnerable, and it moved her more than anything he could have said.

'Yes,' she said simply.

He needed to show her just how much she meant to him…and he did, with such thoroughness the end of the day faded into night, and it was after midnight when they raided the fridge, made an omelette, toast, and washed them both down with coffee.

'Groceries!' Cassandra exclaimed in despair. 'I left them in my car.' She thought of spoiled milk and other comestibles, and shook her head.

'Do you have any specific plans over the next few weeks?' Diego queried idly. She looked adorable, sparkling eyes, warm skin, and gloriously tumbled hair. He reached out a hand and pushed an errant swathe back behind her ear.

'Any particular reason?'

His smile assumed musing indulgence. 'A wedding. Ours.'

There would come a day when nothing he did or said would surprise her…but she had a way to go before that happened.

'Something low-key, in deference to your father. Just family, a few close friends. If you have your heart set on a traditional ceremony, we can reaffirm our vows in a few months.'

'Weeks?' Cassandra reiterated with a sense of stunned amusement. 'I'm due in Rome this weekend for Siobhan's wedding—'

'Perfect. We'll fly in together, spend some time there—'

She put up a hand. 'Whoa! You're going too fast.'

'And arrive back in time to meet our marriage-application requirements,' he concluded.

'The honeymoon before the wedding?' She tried for humour, and didn't quite make it.

'You object?'

How could she, when all she wanted to do was be with him? 'You take my breath away,' she admitted shakily in an attempt to get her head around organising a wedding, travel plans for Rome. Then there was work...

He witnessed her emotional struggle, and sought to ease it. 'All it involves is a series of phone calls. Let me take care of it.'

CHAPTER ELEVEN

ROME was magical, with Siobhan's wedding to her Italian count a glamorous event with much love and rejoicing.

The week that followed became a special time as Diego indulged Cassandra in a tour of the city's galleries, the exclusive jewellery boutiques, with leisurely lunches in one trendy trattoria or another. At night they visited a theatre, or lingered over dinner.

And made love with a passion that was both evocatively sensual and intensely primitive.

They flew in to Sydney three days before their own wedding was scheduled to take place. Days which merged one into the other as Cassandra ran a final check with the dressmaker, the florist, caught up with Cameron, and organised the last remaining items from her apartment to Diego's home.

Sunday dawned bright and clear, and within hours the last-minute touches were being made by various people employed to ensure every detail represented perfection.

Gardeners put finishing touches to the grounds, and florists lined the gazebo with white orchids. An altar was set ready for the marriage celebrant, and the caterers moved into the kitchen.

Cameron arrived ahead of the guests, and Cassandra accepted his careful hug minutes before they were due to emerge onto the red-carpeted aisle that led to the gazebo.

'Nervous?'

'Just a little.'

'Don't be,' he reassured, and she offered a shaky smile as the music began.

Diego stood waiting for her at the altar, and Cassandra's heart skipped a beat as he turned to watch her walk towards him.

Everything faded, and there was only the man.

Tall, dark and attractive, resplendent in a superbly tailored suit. But it was his expression that held her entranced. There was warmth, caring...and passion evident. Qualities she knew he'd gift her for the rest of his life.

In an unprecedented gesture he moved forward and took her hand in his, raised it to his lips, then he led her the remaining few yards to the gazebo.

It was a simple ceremony, with a mix of conventional and personal vows. By mutual consent, they'd agreed to choose each other's wedding ring.

Jewellery design was her craft, and Cassandra had selected a wide gold band studded with a spaced line of diamonds. It was masculine, different, and one of her personal designs.

There had been a degree of subterfuge in Diego's choice, for the ring he slipped onto her finger was a feminine match of his.

'For what we've already shared, what we have now,' Diego said gently, adding a magnificent solitaire diamond ring together with a circle of diamonds representing eternity. 'The future.'

She wanted to cry and smile at the same time, and she did both, one after the other, then gave a choking laugh as Diego angled his mouth over hers in a kiss that held such a degree of sensual promise it was all she could do to hold back the tears.

It was later, much later when they were alone, that she took the time to thank him.

Instead of booking a hotel suite, they'd opted to remain at home. It seemed appropriate, somehow, to spend their wedding night in the bed where they'd first made love.

'You're welcome,' Diego said gently as she slid her arms high and pulled his head down to hers.

'I love you.' Emotion reduced her voice to a husky sound. 'I always will.'

He brushed his lips across her forehead, then trailed a path to the edge of her mouth, angled in and took his time. *'Mi amante, mi mujer,* my life.'

A deliciously wicked smile curved her lips. *'Gracias, mi esposo.'*

Diego gave a husky laugh, and uttered something incomprehensible to her in Spanish.

'Translate.'

He offered a devilish grin. 'I'll show you.'

And he did.

On the edge of sleep he curled her close and held her…aware one lifetime would not be enough.

THE MARTINEZ
MARRIAGE REVENGE
HELEN BIANCHIN

CHAPTER ONE

'CAN WE HAVE another turn? Please.'

The noise and colour of the carnival was all around them. Loud music, laughter, childish shrieks in wonderment of the merry-go-round, the Ferris wheel...so many sideshows to capture the attention of a young child.

There were striped tents providing exciting adventure for children, booths selling candyfloss, hot dogs, and stands offering a variety of stuffed toys as prizes for knock-em-down revolving ducks.

Beauty in miniature, Nicki's smile was to die for, her sunny nature a blessing, and Shannay caught her young daughter close in a loving, laughing hug.

Small arms wound round her neck. 'We're having fun, aren't we?'

Shannay felt the familiar pull on her heartstrings for the gift of an unconditional trusting love of a child, in all its innocence.

'One more time,' she agreed, and paid for another ride. 'Then we really need to leave.'

'I know,' Nicki capitulated sunnily. 'You have to go to work.'

'And you need a good night's sleep so you can be bright-eyed at kindergarten tomorrow.'

'So I can grow up and be clever like you.'

The music grew loud, the merry-go-round began to move, and Nicki clutched the reins attached to the brightly painted horse.

OK, so she'd graduated from university with a degree. But not so clever, Shannay mused reflectively, when it came to her personal life.

A broken marriage less than two years after vowing to love and cherish for a lifetime couldn't exactly be viewed as a *plus*, despite mitigating circumstances.

Water under the bridge and no regrets, she assured herself silently as the merry-go-round slowed and drew to an easy halt.

'All done.'

Shannay stepped down and lifted her daughter from the colourful horse.

Beautiful dark eyes sparkled with delicious laughter as she giggled and planted a smacking kiss on her mother's cheek.

Nicki's father's eyes, Shannay reflected, and tamped down the slight tension curling her stomach at the thought of the man she'd married in haste five years ago in another country.

Marcello Martinez, born in France to Spanish parents, raised and educated in Paris, and attended university in Madrid.

Multi-lingual, attractive, sensual, charming…he'd swept her off her feet and into a life far different from her own.

She had told herself she would adjust…and she did, successfully. Or so she'd thought. But not according to his family, who had made it plain she didn't match their élite social status.

An added complication had been the family's favoured choice of a suitable Martinez bride…Estella de Cordova. The stunning raven-haired, dark-eyed socialite possessed impeccable credentials, stellar lineage and obscene wealth.

Something the Martinez family and Estella never permitted Shannay to forget. Or the fact that Marcello and Estella had been lovers…a situation which continued soon after their marriage, if persistent rumour could be believed. Rumour actively fostered by some members of the Martinez family in a bid to diminish Shannay's defences.

Seemingly irrefutable proof of Marcello's infidelity just twenty months after their marriage was the ultimate betrayal, and following an explosive argument Shannay had moved into a hotel and taken the first available flight back to Australia.

Within a matter of weeks she'd obtained a good job in a local pharmacy in suburban Perth, leased an apartment, purchased a car…and become determinedly resolved to dispense Marcello where he belonged.

In her past.

Difficult, when his image had intruded during her daylight hours and haunted her dreams each night.

Impossible, when a persistent stomach upset had necessitated medical examination resulting in the discovery that she was several weeks pregnant.

It seemed incredibly ironic, given how desperately she'd hoped to gift Marcello a child, that confirmation of conception should occur when the marriage was already shattered, with legal dissolution a distinct probability.

The decision not to inform Marcello about his impending fatherhood continued through pregnancy, initially due to fear of a possible miscarriage, and afterwards Shannay had become so fiercely maternal, enlightening him just hadn't been a considered option.

As a precaution, she'd covered her tracks successfully, resorting to her late mother's maiden name and ensuring any mail directed to her arrived via a circuitous route.

Now, almost four years after fleeing Madrid, life was good.

Ordered, she elaborated mentally. She owned an apartment in a modern, upscale building in suburban Applecross, and she worked the five-to-midnight shift as a registered pharmacist not far from her home. Ideal, for it enabled her to spend the days with Nicki, and for her to also pay Anna, a kindly widow in a neighbouring apartment, to sit with Nicki each evening.

'Can I take some candyfloss home to share with Anna?' Nicki's earnest expression was pleadingly angelic.

'I promise I'll brush my teeth afterwards.'

Shannay opened her mouth to offer the diced organic cantaloupe melon she'd stored in a small container as a snack in her backpack, only to change her mind. 'OK.' And refrained from adding any caution. What was a visit to a carnival without sampling candyfloss?

Nicki's face lit up with delighted pleasure. 'Love you, Mummy. You're the best.'

Shannay hugged her daughter close. 'Love you, too, imp.' She laughed and bent low to kiss Nicki's cheek. 'Candyfloss it is. Then we hit the road for home.'

She lifted her head…and froze with shock as her gaze locked on two people she'd thought never to see again. *Hoping* no member of the Martinez family would ever cross her path.

What were the chances, when they resided on opposite sides of the world?

And why *here,* at a carnival camped on council park grounds in suburban Perth?

Did a heart stop beating? She was willing to swear hers did before it accelerated again into a maddened tattoo.

Recognition was clearly apparent, and with it the indisputable knowledge there could be no escape.

'Shannay.' There was an imperceptible pause as Sandro Martinez marshalled his expression into polite civility.

Her chin lifted as she held Marcello's younger brother's intently speculative gaze as it shifted to Nicki and lingered over-long, before returning to fix on her own.

'Sandro.' Cool, *polite*...she could do both. 'Luisa,' she acknowledged the young woman at his side.

She had to get away. *Now.*

'Mummy?'

No. From the mouth of an innocent child came the one word which removed any element of doubt as to whom Nicki belonged.

Shannay saw Sandro's mouth tighten into an uncompromising line. 'Your daughter?'

Before she could offer a word, Nicki offered a solemnly voiced— 'My name is Nicki, and I'm three.'

Oh, sweetheart, she almost groaned aloud. Do you have any idea what you've just done?

The silent accusation in Sandro's dark eyes alarmed her, and she had no doubt had she been alone he'd have delivered a blistering no-holds-barred denunciation.

The Martinez familial ties were so strong Shannay knew there wasn't a snowflake's chance in hell that Sandro would remain silent.

She barely resisted the urge to gather Nicki into her arms and run, test the speed limit to the place she called home...and pack. Take a flight to the east coast and lose herself in another city.

'If you'll excuse me?' she managed coolly. 'We're already late.'

Shannay tightened her hold on Nicki's hand, then she turned away and forced herself to walk with controlled ease toward the exit, her back straight and her head held high.

Pride. She had it in spades. And she refused to take a backward glance as they were swallowed up by the crowd.

Could a stomach twist into a painful ball? It felt as if hers did, and the blood in her veins turned to ice as she clipped Nicki into her booster seat in the rear of her compact sedan.

'We forgot the candyfloss.'

Oh, hell. 'We'll get some on the way home.' The supermarket sold it in packets. She fired the engine and put the car in drive.

'It won't be the same,' Nicki offered without rancour.

No, it wouldn't. Oh, damn. *Dammit,* she cursed beneath her breath. If they hadn't taken another turn on the merry-go-round...

But they had done. And it was too late for recriminations now.

Shannay headed towards her suburban apartment and went into automatic pilot as she bathed and changed Nicki, readied herself for work, then she handed her daughter into Anna's care and drove to the pharmacy.

Somehow she managed to get through the evening, dispensing medications and offering advice to customers who sought it.

Concern, fear, dread...the palpable mix heightened her tension to almost breaking point, and by closing time she'd developed a doozy of a headache.

It was a relief to reach the sanctuary of her apartment, thank Anna, check on Nicki, then undress and slip into bed.

But not to sleep.

Estimating her estranged husband's reaction on discovering she had a child...*his* child, didn't bear thinking about.

Could she insist *he* wasn't Nicki's father?

A hollow laugh rose and died in her throat.

All Marcello had to do was insist on a DNA paternity test to shoot that one out of the water.

And afterwards?

A slight shiver shook her slender form.

Marcello was a ruthless strategist, possessed of sufficient power and wealth to dispense with anyone or anything that might stand in his path.

Shannay was the exception.

She'd make sure of it.

No one would be permitted to come between her and Nicki. *No one.*

A resolve which remained uppermost when she woke next morning, and strengthened with each passing hour. Together with an increasing degree of nervous tension.

It wasn't a matter of *if,* but *when* Marcello would make contact. Either in person, or via legal representation.

Marcello Martinez might not care about *her.* But a child, indisputably *his* child, would be another matter entirely.

Given Sandro could pinpoint her location, just how difficult would it be for someone of Marcello's calibre to discover where she lived and worked?

A piece of cake, a silent voice assured in taunting response.

Knowledge which didn't sit well. She barely ate and every waking hour was spent attempting to predict any possible scenario Marcello might choose to present.

The necessity to ensure Anna take every precaution while Nicki was in her care resulted in only one query.

'Are you in trouble with the law?'

Oh, dear God. 'No...*no,* of course not,' Shannay reiterated.

'That's all I need to know.'

An apparently single mother and child... How difficult was it to do the maths and reach the conclusion of a looming custody battle?

'Thanks,' she expressed with genuine gratitude.

How long would it take Marcello to plan his strategy and put it into action?

A few days? A week?

Meantime, she needed to consult a lawyer to spell out her legal rights in fine detail. She was aware of the basics, and sufficiently astute to realise what appeared logical and rational didn't always hold true.

She also intended to file for divorce.

Given she could prove a separation of more than the legal requirement, it should only be a matter of time before she gained a dissolution of the marriage.

Whereupon the only issue that could arise would be *custody*.

An icy chill invaded her body and settled in her bones.

Marcello couldn't enforce custody of Nicki…surely?

What rights would he possibly have?

Shannay wrapped her arms tightly over her midriff, and barely prevented her body from shaking with very real fear.

Her soon-to-be ex-husband possessed the wealth and the power to surmount any objective he set out to achieve.

A silent scream echoed inside her brain.

If he decided he wanted Nicki, then he'd move heaven and earth to get her.

Over my dead body, Shannay resolved.

CHAPTER TWO

MARCELLO MARTINEZ moved through the international-terminal lounge with Carlo, his personal assistant and trusted bodyguard, at his side, seemingly unaware of the speculative interest in his tall, broad frame.

The Martinez legacy had gifted him the compelling well-defined features of his forefathers, arresting, wide-set dark, almost black eyes which projected the hardness of a man well-versed in the frailty of human nature.

There was an aura of power and intense masculinity apparent, together with a dangerous ruthlessness that boded ill for any adversary.

He was linked to Spanish nobility, with a personal wealth that placed him high on a list of the European rich.

And it showed…as he meant it to do, from the Armani tailoring, hand-stitched Italian shoes, to the fine Rolex at his wrist.

The long flight had done little to ease the anger simmering beneath his control. The luxuriously fitted Gulf Stream privately owned jet offered every comfort, geared with the latest technology enabling him to have an essential office in the sky.

* * *

Although he'd worked, studying print-outs, graphs and data, checked his BlackBerry and kept in touch with Sandro...he hadn't been able to switch off and sleep.

Something he usually achieved at will, given the comfortable bed situated with its own *en suite* at the rear of the jet.

Instead he was plagued by a young woman's image, startlingly vivid and recently taken via camera phone.

Shannay Martinez...née Robbins.

And his daughter.

The *before* and *after* shots.

The first serene, happy and loving. Mother and child, laughing.

In the second image, the child's expression remained the same. His estranged wife's features, however, mirrored shock and something else...

The innate knowledge *life* as she'd known it since leaving Spain was about to change?

Without doubt.

A muscle bunched at the edge of his jaw as he exited the terminal's automatic glass doors and stepped into a limousine waiting at the kerb.

The chauffeur stowed his bags in the boot and moved up front to slide in behind the wheel.

Marcello barely noticed the passing scene beyond the tinted windows as the limousine left the airport and began picking up speed *en route* to the city.

A child.

Anger, barely held in control since Sandro's enlightening phone call, rose to the surface.

How *dared* Shannay keep him in ignorance of the child's existence?

His initial reaction had been to instruct his pilot to ready the Gulf Stream jet for an immediate flight to Australia.

Instead, he'd delegated with icy calm, consulted his legal team and planned his strategy.

Tomorrow he intended to bring it into play.

Marcello's suite in the inner-city hotel offered first-class luxury, and with practised ease he shrugged off his jacket, discarded his tie, organised his unpacking and settled down to peruse the report handed to him on check-in.

The private-investigation resource he'd utilised had done a good job. The document revealed a detailed listing of Shannay's movements over the past few days, her address, unlisted telephone number, the make, model and registration of her car, place of work, Nicki's kindergarten facility.

Details which filled in some of the blanks, and revealed she hadn't touched so much as a cent of the money he'd initially deposited into a bank account bearing her name. Or the amount he'd contributed each month since.

He wanted to *shake* her, and would have if she'd been within reach.

What was she trying to prove?

Something he already knew.

His family connections, his wealth and social status had never impressed her.

She'd fallen into his life, literally, he mused, recalling the moment the fine heel of one of her stilettos had become caught in a metal grating and had pitched her against him on a busy city street in the heart of Madrid.

He'd been unprepared for the instantaneous physical chemistry…and an instinctive need to lengthen contact with her.

They'd shared coffee in a nearby upmarket café, exchanged cellphone numbers…and the rest was history. Marcello closed the report and crossed to the wide expanse of double-glazed glass offering a brilliant view of the Swan river.

The sky provided an azure backdrop to tall city buildings, selected greenery…a colourful panoramic pictorial, he noted absently, reminding him of a similar visit a few brief years ago when his ring on Shannay's finger had claimed her as his wife.

A time when they couldn't get enough of each other, and had rarely spent a moment apart.

Marcello felt his body tighten at the memory of all that they'd shared. Her uninhibited enthusiasm, her laughter, her passion.

His own libidinous response and loss of control.

Something he'd never experienced with another woman to the same degree.

Or in any other area of his life.

He held a reputation in the business arena for icy calm in any volatile situation. A trait which earned him the respect of his contemporaries.

With a slow roll of his shoulders he turned away from the plate-glass window and checked his watch.

It had been a long flight, crossing countries, entering another time zone and the need to adjust to it.

Stroking several punishing laps in the hotel pool, followed by a session in the gym, would help iron out any kinks and ease the tension.

With that in mind he keyed a text message to Carlo, then he shed his clothes, donned swimming trunks, shrugged on a complimentary robe, caught up a towel, essentials, and took the lift to the appropriate floor.

An hour and a half later, showered and dressed in a formal business suit, he walked out into the late-afternoon sunshine, stepped into his chauffeured limousine and instructed the driver to deliver him to a mid-town address.

The highly qualified Perth-based lawyer engaged by Marcello's legal team to represent his Australian interests confirmed certain legalities, offered assurances and advice on procedure, and the consultation concluded at the close of the business day.

On his return to the hotel he shed his jacket and tie, ordered a meal from Room Service, connected his laptop to the internet and engaged a link to his Madrid office.

Shannay crouched down to Nicki's eye level and caught her close, whispered "Love you", and heard her daughter's "Love you back", then she rose fluidly to her full height and smoothed a gentle hand over Nicki's head.

'Have a fun day.'

Kindergarten was carefully structured, mostly fun and, importantly, Nicki loved spending time with the other children as they moved from play-dough to finger-painting, played games and listened to stories read by one of the carers.

'You, too.'

Nicki happily moved to her place on the mat and Shannay hid a soft smile as Nicki engaged in animated chatter with one of her friends.

Time to leave, get into her car and head home. There were phone calls and household chores to complete before returning to collect her daughter.

A short while later she exchanged fitted jeans and tailored shirt for shorts and a cropped top, then she set to work.

Dusting, mopping and polishing helped Shannay expend some nervous energy, and she wielded the vacuum cleaner with zealous speed.

Another five minutes and she'd be done, then she'd hit the

shower, dress, make the few calls and head off to Nicki's kindergarten facility.

The ring of the in-house phone was barely audible above the sound of the vacuum cleaner, and she shut it down, then she crossed the room and tamped down a strange prickling sense of foreboding…which was crazy.

For several days she'd been on tenterhooks waiting for Marcello to make his move, agonising when it would happen and what it might entail.

Oh, for heaven's sake, she railed in silent self-castigation. It could be anyone buzzing her apartment…so take a deep breath and go check the security-video screen.

The tight security features employed here were some of the main reasons she'd purchased the apartment.

Protection and safety were an issue in any large city, and she rested more easily knowing she'd taken every available precaution.

The insistent ring of the buzzer impelled her to cross the room…and her breath hitched painfully in her throat the moment she recognised the male figure revealed on-screen.

Marcello Martinez…in person.

His monochrome image did little to detract from his forceful features…the strong facial bone structure, piercing gaze and well-shaped mouth.

Shannay felt her stomach muscles clench in unbidden reaction, for it took only one look at him for all the memories to flood back.

The good ones where his care and passion ignited something wild deep within her soul…and the not-so good when the arguments began to escalate into varying degrees of anger.

Pick up, why don't you?

Delaying the inevitable wouldn't achieve a thing.

Her fingers shook a little as she caught hold of the receiver, intoned a brief acknowledgment and saw his features harden.

'Buzz me in, Shannay. We need to talk.'

She bit back an angry retort. 'I have nothing to say to you.'

For a moment his gaze became faintly hooded, and his voice assumed a dangerous silkiness. 'I intend to see my daughter.'

'You have no proof she's yours,' she was goaded into stating.

His dark eyes seemed to pierce her own via the video link. 'You want to do this the hard way?'

'We lost the art of polite dialogue a long time ago.'

Marcello's expression hardened, and she had the uncanny sensation he could *see* her…which was, of course, impossible.

Yet that fact did little to aid reassurance, or prevent the shivery finger of fear feathering the length of her spine.

It was easy to close down the video screen. Not so easy to cast him out of her mind, and his forceful image refused to subside despite every effort she made to conquer it as she quickly showered, pulled on black dress jeans, added a singlet top, some *faux* bling, swept her hair into a casual twist and applied minimum make-up.

Then she caught up her bag, collected keys, locked the apartment and took the lift down to the basement car park. Nervous tension rose up a notch as the doors slid open, and she stepped out and began walking towards her sedan…only to falter fractionally as she caught sight of a tall male figure leaning against the passenger door.

CHAPTER THREE

MARCELLO.

With one hand resting in his trouser pocket, the casual stance portrayed studied indolence...a look she knew to be misleading, for it bore the stamp of a predator awaiting the opportunity to strike.

For a wild second she considered turning back towards the lift. Except she refused to give him the satisfaction.

Besides, it was paramount she collect Nicki from kindergarten.

He wanted a confrontation? She'd darned well give him one!

Shannay lifted her chin and fixed him with a determined look...which presumably had little or no effect, for his position remained unchanged as she drew close.

Her shoulders lifted, she straightened her back and she fearlessly met his dark, almost black eyes.

OK, so she'd start out being civil. 'Marcello.'

'Shannay.'

The timbre of his faintly accented voice curled round her nerve-ends and tugged...much to her dismay. She didn't want to be affected by him, nor did she want any reminder of what they'd shared.

Which was a travesty, given the fact that they had Nicki's existence as living proof!

'This is a private car park.'

One eyebrow slanted in open mockery. 'Next, you'll ask how I accessed entry.'

'I don't have time for idle conversation.' She made a point of checking her watch.

'Then we should get straight to the point.'

His drawled response rankled, and she determinedly ignored the icy chill scudding the length of her spine.

'Which is?' As if she didn't know!

Eyes as dark as sin became hard and implacable. 'My daughter.'

His raking appraisal was unsettling, and she made a concentrated effort to strengthen her resolve.

'The father is not listed on her birth certificate.'

A protective choice at the time, and, she had to admit, motivated by an act of defiance.

'I've accessed hospital records,' Marcello enlightened with deadly softness. 'Nicki was born full-term. Which narrows down the time of her conception to around six weeks before you left Madrid.'

She knew what was coming, and she closed her eyes as if the action would prevent the damning words he would inevitably relay.

'I've authorised a DNA paternity test through a private biolab.' He waited a beat. 'They have my sample, and require one from Nicki, preferably within the next twenty-four hours.' A muscle bunched at his jaw. 'I have the requisite paperwork for you to sign.'

She wanted to hit him...*hard,* preferably where it would hurt the most.

'No.' Her voice was terse as she battled with her anger, and his eyes hardened.

'You refuse permission?'

'Yes, damn you!'

'Then I file for custody, and it gets ugly.'

The chilling finality in his voice succeeded in sending a wave of fear washing through Shannay's body.

He could command the finest legal brains in the country to present a case in his favour.

No surprise there. It was a measure of the man to ensure every detail was in place before he struck.

'You bastard.'

One eyebrow lifted in a gesture of deliberate cynicism. 'No descriptive adjectives, Shannay?'

'Too many,' she owned grimly, hating him more than she'd hated anyone in her life.

'Your call. You have twenty-four hours to provide me with your decision.'

Her eyes sparked dark fire. 'Go to hell, Marcello.'

He extracted a card and held it out to her. 'My cellphone number. Call me.'

'Not in this millennium.'

The atmosphere between them became so highly charged it threatened to ignite.

Marcello's eyebrow slanted in visible mockery. 'Perhaps you should reconsider, given I'm aware of your address, Nicki's kindergarten, the park you both frequently visit.' His expression didn't change. 'Shall I go on?'

Consternation filled her at the thought he might appear un-announced at any of those places…the effect he would have without suitable introduction and explanation.

'You'd do that?' Shannay demanded, stricken at the mere thought. 'Frighten, even *abduct* her?'

'*Mierda.*' His voice was husky with anger, his features a hard mask. 'What kind of man do you think I am?'

She thought she knew *once*. Now too much was at stake for her to even hazard a guess.

'I intend to meet her, spend some time in her company.' Chilling bleak eyes trapped hers. 'Accept it's going to happen, Shannay.' His pause was imperceptible. 'One way or another.'

He was giving her a choice, that much was clear…The easy way, or via a legal minefield.

She momentarily closed her eyes against the sight of him, hating the position he was placing her in.

It was on the tip of her tongue to tell him to go to hell, and be damned.

For herself, she didn't care. But she was fiercely protective of her daughter, and she'd tread over hot coals before she'd willingly expose Nicki to anything that would upset or destroy her trust.

'You're a ruthless son-of-a-bitch.' Her voice was filled with bitterness, and he merely inclined his head.

'So what else is new?'

'Nicki is *mine*. *I* chose to carry her, give birth to her.' Her eyes blazed with pent-up emotion. 'I was the one to nurture and love her.'

A muscle tensed close to his jaw. 'You denied me the opportunity to be there.'

'We were *through!*'

'You opted out.'

The correction hurt. 'Instead of staying to fight for you?' She offered a dismissive gesture and her voice became husky.

'*Please.* I hit my head against a figurative brick wall at every turn. In the end, your mistress and your family won.'

His eyes narrowed. 'You were my wife.'

The *'were'* did it, and her chin tilted as she flung him a look of blazing defiance. 'Fat lot of difference that made.'

'I gave my vow of fidelity,' he reminded with pitiless disregard, watching the conflicting emotions chase fleetingly across her expressive features.

Shannay didn't want to think of their wedding day, or the days and weeks that had followed when everything in their world had seemed perfect. Until reality intervened, insidiously at first, until she was forced to recognise the manipulative calculation of planned destruction.

'Empty words, Marcello?'

'This is old ground, is it not? Now there is a more pressing matter to be resolved.'

Nicki.

Shannay felt pain shaft through her body, and her features became strained.

'Where would you prefer to meet?' he pursued hardily. 'The kindergarten or your apartment?'

Dear heaven, *no.* 'Not the kindergarten.' Her mind scrambled for a compromise.

Nor the apartment. She couldn't bear to have him invade her sanctuary, her space, where he'd assume control and she'd have to sacrifice her own in Nicki's presence…or risk a situation which would alarm her daughter.

Lunch. She could do lunch. Somewhere child-friendly that Nicki was familiar with, and they'd keep it short and sweet…the shorter the better.

She named a venue and stated a time. 'Tomorrow,' she added, and saw his mouth tighten.

'Today.'

'No,' she said firmly. She needed to assume some form of control in the situation.

His gaze seemed to bore into hers. '*Today,* Shannay. Twelve-thirty.' He paused imperceptibly, and his voice became deadly quiet. 'Be there.'

Today. Tomorrow. What was the difference? How would twenty-four hours change anything?

Marcello was *here.* And now she had no recourse but to deal with the situation.

'If—*if,*' she stressed, 'I agree, there would need to be conditions.'

'Such as?'

A pulse beat fast at the base of her throat, a visible sign of her inner turmoil.

Marcello regarded her steadily, noting the darkness of her eyes, the faint shadows beneath, and her pale features.

It would seem she hadn't slept any better than he, and there was a certain satisfaction to be had in that.

'As far as Nicki is concerned, you're just—' she hesitated, aware *friend* wasn't the word she wanted to use '—someone I know.'

Marcello felt like shaking her, and barely controlled the need. 'And when the paternity test reveals otherwise?'

Shannay's features whitened dramatically. She really didn't want to go there…at least, not until she had to. She checked her watch, and felt her stomach curl with apprehension. 'I have to leave now, Marcello.' Even if the traffic lights were in her favour, she was going to be late picking Nicki up.

Marcello straightened and extracted a set of keys. 'I'll follow at a discreet distance.'

Her eyes flared. 'Because you don't trust me?'

'It's a more simple process than consulting a map.'

Without a further word he crossed to a sleek sedan and slid in behind the wheel.

The sound of the car's engine igniting galvanised Shannay into action, and she quickly copied him as she sent her car onto street level.

Dammit, she silently fumed. Who did he think he was?

A man who made his own rules and expected others to abide by them, she conceded grimly.

Nicki was waiting with a carer when Shannay entered the kindergarten, and she offered an apology, gave Nicki a reassuring hug, then she elicited a brief update on the morning before catching hold of her daughter's hand as she led the way out towards the car.

She deliberately didn't glance towards the street to check if Marcello's sedan was parked in the vicinity.

'We're going out for a while.' She kept her voice light, bright, as she attempted to still the nervous tension spiralling through her body.

'To the park?' Nicki queried hopefully. 'Can we feed the ducks?'

Shannay fervently wished such a simple pleasure as eating a packed lunch in the park formed part of the day as she lifted Nicki into her booster seat and secured the safety fastenings.

She leaned in close and dropped a light kiss on her daughter's nose. 'After lunch, on the way home,' she promised, aware there was no better time than now to impart whom they were meeting and why.

'A friend of mine is visiting from Spain, and he's invited us to share lunch with him.' She smoothed a hand over Nicki's hair and summoned a smile. 'Won't that be fun?'

Oh, sure, and little pink pigs should sprout wings and fly!

How could she state *this man is your father?*

Worse, voice her deepest fear…

Traffic was light, and she fought the temptation to take the route back to her apartment. Only the knowledge Marcello would seek her out and make the situation incredibly more difficult than it already was ensured she drove to the restaurant.

Taking a circuitous route was a minor act of defiance.

Did he know? Possibly. Although he gave no indication as she effected an introduction…and watched dry-mouthed as Marcello hunkered down to Nicki's eye level.

Shannay stood tense and incredibly protective…anxious to the point of paranoia over her daughter's reaction to the man who posed such a potent threat to their existence.

Quite what she expected, she wasn't sure.

She was intently aware of Marcello, but it was Nicki who held her undivided attention.

Outgoing, polite and friendly, Nicki regarded Marcello with wide-eyed unblinking solemnity. Weighing him up with the innocence of youth, reserving judgement until instinct dismissed an initial wariness and a smile curved her mouth.

'Hello. I'm Nicki.' Unbidden, a small hand extended in formal greeting, and with great care Marcello enfolded it within his own.

Hearts didn't melt, stomachs didn't really perform somersaults…but it sure felt like hers did both as conflicting emotions took hold with unsettling reality.

Father and child.

There was a part of her that wanted to encapsulate the moment for safe-keeping…for Nicki, she assured herself silently.

The venue proved eminently suitable, the food pleasantly presented and palatable. Not, Shannay mused, what her estranged husband was used to, but perfect for a young child.

It was difficult to summon light laughter and appear relaxed and at ease, when inside she'd have given anything for Marcello to be anywhere but *here*.

Maintaining the pretence of friendship proved to be a strain, and she battled emotional turmoil at the developing rapport between father and child.

Why shouldn't Nicki be entranced by the man her mother had introduced as *friend?* The mere appellation sanctioned approval, and heaven knew Marcello possessed innate charm when he chose to employ it.

And he did, with an ease Shannay could only reluctantly admire, whilst silently hating him for capturing her daughter's innocent heart.

'We're going to stop and feed the ducks on the way home,' Nicki announced as Marcello took care of the bill.

Shannay's offer to contribute her share merely incurred a telling glance, and she accepted his refusal with grace.

'That sounds like fun,' Marcello said gently, and Nicki laughed with delight.

'You can come, too, if you like.'

Please don't, Shannay silently begged. Lunch was enough. If she had to spend any more time in his company, it would be way too much.

He pocketed his wallet and gave Nicki his whole attention. 'I have another appointment this afternoon. But I'd like to watch you feed the ducks another day.'

'Tomorrow?'

Marcello spared Shannay a glance. 'If it's all right with your mother?'

Thanks for putting me in such an invidious position! A refusal would be petty, and disappoint her daughter. Besides, she was damned if she'd give Marcello the satisfaction.

She summoned a smiling assent. 'Tomorrow's fine.' A short sojourn, then she'd plead the need to take Nicki home.

'Perhaps we could share a picnic lunch.'

Nicki clapped her hands together in delight. 'I love picnics.'

If looks could kill, Marcello mused, he'd be dead. Although he had to concede Shannay covered it well. As to his daughter—*his,* without a shred of doubt—he was hard-pressed not to scoop her into his arms.

He'd expected to feel a connection, even a degree of affection. But this deep encompassing bond surprised him completely.

Marcello copied Shannay's actions and rose to his feet. His gaze skimmed her averted features and settled on bright, innocent brown eyes. 'We have a date.'

'A date,' Nicki repeated as she reached for her mother's hand, unaware of the tension simmering between the two adults.

OK, so you're in the minority here, Shannay conceded silently, and wanted to cry *foul.* It wasn't fair of Marcello to manipulate a child.

But then Marcello was ruthless when in pursuit of what he wanted…and he wanted Nicki.

They exited the restaurant and crossed to the adjoining car park.

'Thank you for lunch.' She could do polite, as an essential example in good manners. She caught the faint gleam apparent in his eyes, and determinedly ignored it.

He extracted a slim envelope from his suit-jacket pocket and handed it to her. 'The permission form. Sign and return it to me tomorrow.'

The DNA paternity test.

She could stall him.

How long? A few days…a week?

If she refused and he was forced to travel the legal route…

'Don't,' Marcello cautioned quietly.

How was it possible for one small word to hold such a wealth of meaning?

Supremely conscious of Nicki's interested attention, she slid the envelope into her bag, proffered a superficial smile and led Nicki to the car, aware of his presence as she settled her daughter safely in the rear seat.

'See you tomorrow,' Nicki bade as Marcello opened the door to allow Shannay to slide in behind the wheel.

His mouth parted in a warm smile that skimmed lightly over Nicki's trusting features and settled briefly on her own.

For a few interminable seconds she was caught in the thrall of remembered chemistry. Jolted by the sensuality that coursed through her veins, unbidden, electric…and definitely unwanted.

It had been *there,* simmering beneath the surface from the moment she'd heard his voice. Seeing him, sharing his company only made it worse.

For she was forced to recall memories, evocative, spellbinding in their intensity.

Even now, her body seemed to recognise his, and she attempted to control the curl of sensual emotion stirring deep within.

She didn't want to remember the all-consuming passion, the feel of his hands, his mouth…how she'd lost herself so completely in him.

Go, a silent voice urged.

Ignite the engine and leave.

Now.

Somehow she managed to get through the remainder of the day, and she bore Nicki's excited chatter about "Mummy's friend" and the proposed picnic as she bathed and fed Nicki, then readied herself for work.

'I have lots to tell Anna.'

Shannay leant down and kissed her daughter's cheek as the doorbell rang. 'Be good, hmm?'

'Always,' Nicki responded solemnly.

A light chuckle emerged from her throat. 'Imp.'

'A nice imp.'

Shannay gathered her in for a hug, then smoothed a hand over dark curls. 'Extra-specially nice,' she agreed, and crossed to let Anna into the apartment.

CHAPTER FOUR

MARCELLO'S IMAGE haunted Shannay's subconscious and provided scattered dreams which seemed to reach nightmarish proportion throughout the night.

Consequently she woke to the insistent sound of the alarm clock feeling as if she hadn't slept at all.

Not good.

She had a responsible job, she worked nights, and right now she'd give anything to bury her head in the pillow, snatch an hour's dreamless sleep, and face an untroubled day.

Not possible.

'Are you awake, Mummy?'

Bright eyes, tousled hair, a smile to die for…the light of her life.

Shannay reached for her daughter, gathered her close and pressed a light kiss to Nicki's forehead.

'Morning, sweetheart.'

'We're going to the park for a picnic today.'

'Uh-huh.' She playfully tickled Nicki's ribs and the action brought forth a series of giggles. 'Time to rise and shine, dress, have breakfast and—'

'Be on the road by nine,' Nicki completed a familiar mantra as she slid from the bed.

The picnic, the ducks, Marcello.

Not necessarily in that order, although combined they were the sole topic of Nicki's conversation that morning.

Shannay gritted her teeth as she headed home after delivering her daughter to kindergarten.

If she heard his name mentioned again, she'd…do or say something regrettable!

One hour in his company, and he held Nicki in his thrall.

It was so not fair. And so typical of the man's effect on the female species.

Traffic lights up ahead changed and she eased the car to a halt.

Figuratively speaking she was between a rock and a hard place. Signing or not signing the DNA paternity form only presented a relatively minor issue compared to the big picture.

The demons of the night returned tenfold, and the sudden strident sound of a car horn thrust her back into the present.

The insistent burr of her cellphone within minutes of clearing the intersection resulted in a juggling action as she changed lanes and pulled over to take the call.

'Shannay.'

The familiar faintly accented male voice upped her nervous tension by several notches, and it took effort to summon a cool acknowledgement.

'What do you want?'

'We need to talk. There's a café not far from your apartment. Meet me there in ten minutes.'

'I have things to do, Marcello.'

'This morning,' Marcello elaborated, 'in Nicki's presence, or during your evening work hours, we will talk.'

'You can't—' The words spilled, only to stop mid-sentence. He had no scruples whatsoever when it came to achieving his objective.

'Choose.'

She could feel the anger surging through her body, and at that moment she truly hated him. 'There is no choice.'

'I'll order a latte for you.'

Damn him to hell. It was on the tip of her tongue to tell him exactly what he could do with the latte, except in some instances silence was golden, and she simply cut the connection.

Shannay reached her apartment block and eased the car down into the underground car park, locked it, then took the lift to ground level and walked out into the morning sunshine.

The café was close by, upmarket with outdoor tables and boutique sun umbrellas. A meeting place where friends assembled over designer coffee and sumptuous food to talk business, chat and watch the world go by.

There, seated outdoors, was Marcello.

Absent was the designer business suit, for today he'd chosen casual dark chinos and a white shirt unbuttoned at the neck.

It lent him a relaxed façade…one she knew to be misleading. Despite appearances to the contrary, Marcello rarely lowered his guard. It was what he'd become, who he was…and it showed.

There was something exigent that wrought a second look, a curiosity, sometimes fleeting, to check the level of power he emanated. A hint of the primitive, which unleashed could cause untold sensual havoc to a woman's equilibrium.

A quality other men admired and coveted, but few possessed.

Marcello glanced up as she approached, and she felt the full impact of those dark eyes as they seared her own, witnessing for one moment the naked vulnerability apparent before she successfully masked it.

He signalled the waitress as Shannay slid into a seat opposite him.

Make-up free, except for a touch of gloss to her mouth, her hair caught together with a decorative clip, and dressed in jeans and a singlet top she looked scarcely more than a teenager.

Except looks could be deceptive, he mused, all too aware of the latent passion that lurked beneath that cool façade.

He remembered too well the sensual delight of her body, the persuasive touch and her eagerness to share…everything.

Heat unfurled and ran hot as he felt his own unbidden response, the need to render her willing and wanton. *His*, as she had been…and would be again.

No other woman came close, and he'd wanted what he once had.

Worse, he wanted her to pay for attempting to deny him any knowledge of his daughter.

'Shannay.'

The waitress delivered her latte, and she selected two sugar tubes, broke them open and stirred in the contents.

Shannay took a deliberate sip of the frothy, milky liquid, then she carefully replaced the glass onto its saucer and met Marcello's studied gaze.

'Let's get this over with, shall we?' she suggested coolly.

'Put our cards on the table, so to speak?' Marcello drawled.

He was a superb strategist who played the game according to his own rules…and inevitably saved the sting for a *coup de grâce*.

Estimating precisely what that would encompass had kept her awake many nights and had haunted her dreams for a long time.

'Yes.' Delay wouldn't achieve a thing, and wasn't discovering the enemy's game-plan half the battle?

'The initial step is establishing legal evidence of my paternity.'

'Something I won't consent to without being fully aware of your intentions.' Her voice was even, polite. 'Immediate and long term.'

His eyes narrowed fractionally. 'Whatever is decided will be primarily in Nicki's best interests,' he assured with hateful ease.

'How can that be so?' Shannay demanded, glaring at him. 'Establishing custody rights will provide a total disruption to her life. Schooling, friends, family. Any hope of *stability*.' She could feel herself winding up. 'I'm her mother, *dammit*.'

He looked at her for what seemed an age, noting the fine edge of her anger, the restrained need to fight him…regardless of common-sense.

'Nicki hasn't displayed any curiosity about the absence of a father in her life?'

She ignored the silkiness in his voice, the latent anger held in tight control, and her eyes sharpened beneath the dark inflexibility evident in his.

'Inevitably, soon after she began attending kindergarten,' she revealed.

'And?'

Her gaze didn't waver. 'I told her the very basic truth.'

An eyebrow lifted. 'Enlighten me.'

'I left her father before she was born.' She lifted a hand and smoothed it over her hair in an unconscious gesture. 'A number of children have single parents nowadays.'

Marcello leaned back in his chair and regarded her thoughtfully. 'Except you're still married, Shannay. To me.'

'Not for much longer.'

His smile was a faint facsimile. 'In four years you have only considered filing for divorce now?'

'I'm not part of one of your business deals, Marcello. So quit playing psychological games.' Shannay buttoned down her frustrated anger. 'Spell out exactly what you intend.'

For a moment she imagined she glimpsed a fleeting shadow in the depth of his eyes, only to dismiss it.

'With Nicki?'

'Of course, with Nicki!'

'Initially, I want to gift a sick elderly man the opportunity to meet his only great-grandchild.'

It wasn't the answer she expected, nor was the mixture of emotions that tore at her heart. 'Ramon is ill?'

The one person who had attempted to smooth over the family discord at Marcello's choice of a wife. Someone who saw more than anyone intended, and became her ally. 'How ill?'

'The medical professionals predict he has only a matter of months. Maybe less.'

The implications assumed vivid reality. Achieving his objective would involve taking Nicki to Spain.

Pain escalated as it raced through her body, consuming her mind with turmoil. 'I won't allow you to take her overseas.' Rationality went out the window. 'She doesn't have a passport. Hell, she doesn't even *know* you!'

What if he didn't bring Nicki back?

What if Nicki became distressed, distraught…?

'Naturally, you would accompany her.'

Revisit a place where she had spent the worst twenty months of her life?

Mix with a family who hid their disapproval of Marcello's choice of a wife beneath a thin veneer of politeness? A former lover, touted not to be so *former,* who delighted in causing mischief and mayhem?

'You have to be kidding!'

'A few weeks,' Marcello elaborated. 'That's all.'

Shannay closed her eyes, then opened them again. 'No.'

'I gave Ramon my word.'

Something which only made the situation worse. 'Ramon knows about Nicki?'

'My grandfather was—' he paused fractionally '—inadvertently appraised of Nicki's existence.'

It wasn't difficult to do the maths. 'Penè.' Marcello's widowed aunt, a disgruntled woman who took delight in running interference.

She had no difficulty envisaging Sandro informing Marcello of his chance encounter a week ago, or the manner in which Penè came to hear of it.

Happy families. *Not.*

There was more. Ramon's illness was only a part of it.

Her eyes narrowed. 'And?'

One eyebrow slanted in silent query.

She took a deliberate sip of coffee, then another, before replacing the glass onto its saucer as she speared him with a direct look.

'I don't doubt the validity of your request. But don't attempt to use it as a smokescreen.' Did he think she was a naive fool?

'Why would I do that?'

Shannay had positioned the figurative nail, now she chose to hammer it home. 'To gain my sympathy, and dilute the major issue here.' She waited a beat. 'Your plans to gain custody.' Her expression hardened a little. 'Or is that not to form part of this *discussion,* and you'll instruct your legal representative to inform mine of your intention?'

She was fearless when it came to protecting her child. He admired her strength and determination…and pondered if she was fully aware it was no match for his.

'It will take time to work out a mutually amicable custody agreement,' Marcello offered with deceptive indolence. 'We need to consult and compare our individual schedules, and above all, ensure the arrangements we propose suit Nicki's best interests. Her emotional welfare is the priority, is it not?'

Defensive assurance rose to the fore. 'My daughter's emotional status is just fine as it is.'

'But circumstances have changed,' he posed with deliberate calm. 'Nicki is no longer the child of one parent. She has two. The legal system is purported to be fair. If we're unable to reach an amicable agreement, a court judge will review our respective cases and award custody.' He paused deliberately, his gaze intent on her expressive features. 'Given the facts, do you doubt any judge will deny me reasonable access to my daughter?'

No, she conceded the hollow knowledge. But she was confident she could insist such access be confined within Australia.

'Why do I get the feeling there's an underlying reason behind all this?' she demanded with increasing vexation.

'One you obviously haven't considered,' Marcello ventured, then elaborated with faint emphasis. 'Nicki's rightful inheritance as a legitimate member of the Martinez dynasty.'

Her chin tilted, and her eyes became dark, gold-flecked obsidian. 'For this, you require proof of paternity?'

'A considerable fortune is involved.'

Sufficient to put Nicki on a spoilt-little-rich-girl list and all that entailed.

'No.'

'It is her right as a Martinez heir.'

'Never sure of being liked for herself, or for who she is and what she can do for them? Living in a gilded cage, guarded and protected? Unable to enjoy the freedom of a normal childhood?'

Marcello drained his coffee and signalled the waitress for another, indicating only one when Shannay shook her head.

'Wealth brings risks. Bodyguards are discreet. It's something one learns to live with.'

She made a sweeping glance of the area, then returned her attention to him. 'Next, you'll tell me *yours* is seated near by.' It was a comment veiled with deliberate cynicism, and she caught the slight twist at the edge of his mouth.

'Three tables to your right. Tall, dark hair, shades, dressed in jeans and polo shirt. Carlo doubles as my personal assistant.'

So much for flippancy.

She hadn't sensed anyone's presence, or felt that inexplicable prickling at the back of her neck…and she definitely hadn't *seen* anything to arouse suspicion.

But then, the possibility hadn't occurred to her. She was here in Perth, Australia. A woman and her young daughter living a normal life.

Far, far removed from Madrid and the Martinez lifestyle where protection of its family members formed an integral part of their existence.

She was all too aware of Marcello's veiled scrutiny, the watching quality as he gauged her mood, divined it, then closed in for the kill.

'Sign the permission form, Shannay. Apply for Nicki's passport, and request urgency on the grounds overseas travel is imminent.'

A chill shiver slithered its way down her spine. Without a passport Nicki was confined within Australia.

Once a passport was issued, her daughter would be able to travel…anywhere, independent of her mother.

The mere thought escalated her nervous tension and sent her mind spiralling with very real fear of abduction…by Marcello, if he was so inclined to take Nicki to Madrid, with or without Shannay's permission.

Something she'd fight to guard against, at any cost.

'Or else you'll drag me through the courts, Marcello?'

'Why not view a sojourn in Madrid as an opportunity for Nicki to become accustomed to my home, my family, and to enjoy aspects of the city in the security of your company?'

She knew what would follow, and he didn't disappoint.

'Ramon will have time with his great-grand-daughter. Is that too much to ask of you?'

'And how is this *holiday* to be explained to Nicki? She's intelligent for her age. She'll ask questions, expect answers.'

'Why not lead her into the truth a step at a time?'

Shannay viewed him with scepticism. 'A suggestion from a man who has no experience with children?'

'Is it so difficult to accept such a suggestion might have some merit?'

'I'm all ears,' she evinced with deliberate mockery.

'Not to mention doubtful and prejudiced.'

Her eyes flashed chips of gold fire. 'With good reason.'

'Let's focus on the current issue, shall we?'

'Oh, by all means.'

He wanted to take hold of her fire and change it to passion, to still the anger and have her sigh beneath the touch of his mouth, his hands. To come alive and move with him, savour the anticipation, the slow emotive path to sensual ecstasy they had once enjoyed.

And would again. He intended to make certain of it.

For the challenge…and for revenge.

'Allow Nicki to know I'm a relative of Ramon. It will explain why I am escorting you both to visit him in Madrid.'

'You think Ramon will go along with that?'

'I know so.'

'And Penè?' Shannay gave a laugh of cynical disbelief.

'Penè will conform,' Marcello declared hardily.

'Sure, and cows jump over the moon!'

'Your analogy amuses me.'

'But…*apt*.'

'You seem to forget I control the Martinez finances, from which Penè is allocated a very generous contribution to suit her preferred lifestyle.'

She got it. And knew he was sufficiently ruthless to enforce the threat should his aunt choose to ignore his wishes.

'Perhaps you'll explain when you intend Nicki should know—'

'I'm her father?' Marcello intervened. 'When the right moment occurs.'

Which possibly might not be during their few weeks in Madrid. It even seemed feasible, for she and Nicki would obviously be staying in hotel accommodation, and making daily calls to see Ramon…whose illness would preclude lengthy visits.

There would be time to show Nicki some of the cultural aspects of her paternal heritage, to explore and have fun. It would be so easy to give in. And she almost did. Except there were still matters needing clarification.

'What's the catch, Marcello?'

'Why should you think there is one?'

His voice was too mild, too neutral. 'I have reason to be wary of your motives.'

'While I have been nothing but honest with you.'

Shannay regarded him carefully, seeing the latent power apparent, and chose to play a few cards of her own.

'Before I'll agree to anything,' she voiced with quiet determination, 'you need to furnish notarised documentation stating a custody schedule for the next two years, subject to my approval and renewable at my discretion.'

His expression didn't change. 'Perhaps you'll offer some indication what arrangements you find acceptable?'

'Nicki can spend two weeks with you, twice a year.' It was so small a concession it was almost pathetic. 'While you, of course, are welcome to visit her in Perth as frequently as your business interests permit.'

'Those are your terms?' His query was silk-smooth and almost deadly.

'There's one more thing. Return airline tickets in Nicki's and my names, and accommodation for two weeks.'

'Three.'

'Excuse me?'

'Three weeks. Airline tickets are unnecessary. We'll travel in my private jet.'

She barely managed to hold back a choked laugh. How could she have neglected to remember the private jet? 'In that case, one-way tickets from Madrid to Perth.'

'Specify a date, and I'll ensure the jet is available for your return.'

Shannay rose to her feet, retrieved a note to cover the cost of her latte, and slid it beneath the saucer.

A gesture of independence, she assured silently as she caught up her wallet. 'I'll print up a copy of everything we've discussed and give it to you when we meet at the park.' She cast her watch a quick glance, and was surprised at the passage of time.

Without a further word she turned and retraced her steps to the apartment building, aware of the strange feeling in the pit of her stomach.

She'd expected Marcello to argue her terms, even dismiss them out of hand.

Why hadn't he?

Because he'd achieved his objective…her permission for Nicki to meet Ramon Martinez, patriarch of the Martinez dynasty.

Yet *she* had set the boundaries.

What was more, she'd insisted on a number of specific conditions to be set down in notarised legalese. Plus Nicki's passport would remain in Shannay's possession for the entire sojourn, she'd make sure of that.

All contingencies taken care of, she decided with satisfaction as she printed out two copies, closed down the laptop, then she collected a cool-pack filled with fresh fruit and drinks, caught up her bag and took the lift down to basement level.

Nicki's excitement was palpable as Shannay collected her from kindergarten and drove towards the park.

Yes, she assured, they were on time.

Yes, she'd remembered to bring a packet of sliced bread to feed the ducks.

And yes, she was sure Marcello knew where to meet them.

The park was a popular spot, and there were several couples and families relaxing on the grassy banks overlooking the water.

It was a beautiful early summer's day, with the whisper of a breeze teasing the heavily leaf-laden trees as Shannay selected a pleasant spot and spread a picnic rug on the ground.

'I think he's here,' Nicki announced breathlessly minutes later. 'Yes, it's him.' She raised her arms and waved to attract his attention.

Smile, Shannay bade silently as Marcello joined them, and she buried the faint resentment at just how easily her daughter appeared to be falling beneath his spell.

As picnics went, it was a tremendous success...from Nicki's perspective.

The *best,* Nicki accorded with enthusiasm as she recounted every high point...and there were many, mostly centred around Marcello.

There was no doubt about the mutual attraction developing between father and child. Nicki's giggles and unaffected laughter testified to it. So too did the unguarded affection Marcello displayed for his daughter.

He was a natural, Shannay had to admit, unsure how she felt about their burgeoning bond.

Dammit, it had to be a good thing, she allowed as she drove to work later that afternoon.

If she repeated the words often enough, maybe she'd begin to believe them.

The signed notarised document was already in her possession, courtesy of express courier delivery. Perusal clarified it duplicated the print-out she'd handed Marcello during lunch.

Attached had been a contact name and number to expedite the issue of Nicki's passport.

By week's end, they should be able to leave for Madrid.

Providing she adhered to their agreement, countersigned the notarised document, signed the DNA paternity permission form, lodged the necessary passport documentation and arranged leave of absence from her place of work.

An exceedingly efficient set of suggestions offered to hasten their departure.

Instructions, Shannay corrected, under no illusion they

were anything other than Marcello's ability to use his wealth and influence to achieve his objective.

There was a part of her that understood his motives, together with a degree of sympathy for an ailing elderly man wanting to see his only great-grandchild.

She'd covered all her bases…hadn't she?

And three weeks was hardly a lifetime.

So why did she feel this faint niggle of apprehension?

It stayed with her as she worked, although she deliberately consigned it to the back of her mind as she gave her full attention to dispensing prescriptions, greeting and conversing with patients and customers frequenting the pharmacy.

There was the usual early-evening rush, followed by a lull, during which she had the opportunity to request a leave of absence.

John Bennett, the owner of the pharmacy who was both employer and friend, paused from his task of checking stock and gave Shannay his full attention.

'This is a bit sudden. Care to provide the reason?'

Shannay offered the bare minimum, aware he filled in the blanks himself.

'You consider this a wise move, Shannay?'

John was a nice man, caring and pleasant to work with. He also wanted to date her…something she refused to do. She liked him, but…and it was the *but* that mattered.

Friendship was fine, but not a relationship. With John, it could only be the latter and she wouldn't contemplate taking that step.

'It's an amicable one.' At least I'm being led to believe it is, she added silently. 'And I've taken precautionary protective measures.'

'Such as?'

Shannay crossed to her bag, extracted the notarised agreement and handed it to him, watchful of his expression as he read the contents.

'You want my honest opinion?'

'Of course.'

John folded the paperwork and passed it back to her.

'My main concern is whether, if contested, it would stand up in a court of law.' He paused. 'Do you trust him?'

Trust encompassed much. 'With Nicki's welfare. Yes.'

'And with yours?' he persisted quietly.

I don't know. 'It's only three weeks, John.'

'If you're sure.'

Sure? How could she be sure of anything that involved Marcello? They had a chequered history, one of extreme highs and lows.

A roller-coaster ride, she added silently, and stilled the sensual curl threatening to unfurl deep within her memory of what they'd shared…during the good times.

The evening followed its usual pattern, with a busy period as the nearby cinema-plex emptied and the occasional parent desperate for nursery supplies made a hurried trip to the dispensary.

It was almost closing time when the electronic door buzzer announced a last-minute arrival. Shannay checked the security-cam, and felt the breath catch in her throat as she saw Marcello moving towards the counter.

Gone were the chinos and collarless shirt he'd worn during the day. Tailored trousers, an open-necked shirt and jacket adorned his strong masculine body.

'I'll close up.'

Shannay heard John's words, and quickly turned towards

him, then she gathered herself together sufficiently to effect an introduction.

'What are you doing here, and why now?' she asked quietly as John moved towards the front entrance.

'Whatever happened to *hello?*' Marcello drawled, watching as she efficiently checked data on the computer, then closed down.

'You were in the area and thought you'd call in?' She lifted an eyebrow. 'Or primarily to collect paperwork which I have yet to sign?'

'Both,' he concurred smoothly. 'I'm sure John won't object to witnessing your signature.'

Shannay was tempted to provide further delaying tactics, just for the hell of it. Except such an action would be retaliatory and pointless.

It didn't take long, and Marcello slid the paperwork into his jacket pocket, then waited while she pulled on a jacket and caught up her bag.

She didn't particularly want him to accompany her out into the cool night air.

He…affected her, and she wasn't comfortable with it. Any more than she felt at ease witnessing John's silent reticence in Marcello's presence.

There shouldn't *be* this faintly breathless sense of sexual energy attacking the fragile tenure of her control.

It made her feel slightly off-balance, aware of him at some tenuous level that threatened to shift the foundations she'd fought so hard to cement during the past few years.

Crazy, she dismissed. She was tired, that was all, and tense. Worse, she was allowing her imagination to run riot.

She shot him a cursory look as they reached the front of the pharmacy. 'I have my own car.'

'You object to me ensuring you reach it safely?'

His mild query elicited a faintly derisive dismissal. 'You're being ridiculous.'

They walked out into darkness where illumination was provided by distant streetlights and a sickle moon.

He was too close. Within touching distance, and the faint aroma of his cologne teased her senses, together with the male scent that was his alone.

Her car was parked in full view, and she deactivated the alarm, paused as Marcello opened the door, then she quickly slid in behind the wheel.

He held the door and leaned down towards her. 'I'll be in touch.'

Shannay inclined her head, fired the engine and sent the sedan out onto the road in the direction of home.

CHAPTER FIVE

THE LUXURIOUSLY FITTED Gulf Stream jet cruised at a diminishing altitude as it began its descent to Barajas Airport.

A long flight, during which Shannay had plenty of time to reflect…and wonder for the umpteenth time *why* she'd agreed to leave the relative security of her own territory for a city in a country which held so many conflicting memories for her, not all of them good.

Carlo's presence helped ease the intimacy of so few passengers sharing the cabin, and he was a pleasant man in his early forties, tall, whipcord-lean and alert in a way that behoved his position.

It will be fine, she silently reassured.

She was in control, she'd covered every contingency, and this was only a very temporary visit to Madrid.

Nicki travelled well, in awe of her surroundings, the flight, and was almost heartbreakingly willing to please.

Marcello had become Nicki's new best friend during the week it had taken to confirm his paternity and complete travel documentation.

There had been only one awkward moment when Nicki had asked Marcello in childish innocence, 'Are you my uncle?'

'I'm related to the Spanish side of your family,' he'd re-

sponded gently, and solemn young eyes viewed him with unblinking regard.

'Do you know my daddy?'

'Yes, I do.'

'Will I meet him?'

Oh, dear heaven, *don't*. Not now, not yet, Shannay
silently beseeched.

'I can promise you will.'

The undisguised rapport they shared had to be a good thing,
Shannay constantly reminded herself as she bit down her
reaction to the gentle patience he displayed with their daughter.

It made her think of other times when *she* had delighted in
the touch of his hand, his warm smile…and his love.

For it had been *love* in all its various facets, when she'd
believed nothing could rend it asunder.

Yet it had, and being in his company, returning to Madrid,
brought everything back into vivid focus.

She could deal with it. She had to, for Nicki's sake.

Her daughter's happiness, contentment and security
were paramount.

So…get over it.

The jet touched down smoothly, completed the allotted
runway, then slid into a designated bay where they disembarked, Marcello dealt with their baggage and formalities
before directing them to a waiting limousine bearing the
discreet but influential Martinez emblem.

Madrid temperatures in October were not too dissimilar to
the early-summer temperatures in Perth. A pleasant time of
year in both cities, neither too hot nor too cold.

Shannay saw Nicki seated in the centre of the rear seat,
then slid in beside her, aware Marcello gained access on
Nicki's right.

He'd showered, shaved and changed clothes during the flight, so too had she, and, while she'd lain down with Nicki in the bedroom compartment, sleep had come only in brief snatches.

The drive into the city's heart would take slightly less than half an hour. She had little concern about Marcello's choice of hotel accommodation…only an impending sense of relief that their arrival would provide escape from his company at least until the next day.

He might be accustomed to changing time zones on a regular basis, but both she and Nicki were not.

Madrid, a city of splendid architecture, combining a fascinating mix of the old and modern, the cacophony of sounds, traffic, voices in a language she hadn't heard spoken in almost four years.

Shannay felt the light press of Nicki's fingers curled within her own, and examined her daughter's features as she took intent interest in the passing scene beyond the lightly tinted windows.

'It's different,' Nicki said tentatively.

'The traffic travels in the opposite way from where you live. Soon it will become familiar,' he assured, and met Shannay's faintly lifted eyebrow.

In a three-week time-frame? I don't think so.

A faint smile tugged the edges of his mouth as he transferred his attention to Nicki. 'Not much longer, *pequena,* and we will be there.'

Nicki regarded him solemnly. 'What did you call me?'

'Pequena,' he said gently. 'It's an affectionate name for a little girl.'

She tried it out, copying his intonation, and his smile broadened with gentle warmth as he complimented her, resulting in a beam of childish delight.

They were bonding well…and that had to be a good thing, Shannay accepted. So why did it hurt so much?

She met his gaze, attempted to read his expression, failed miserably, and transferred her attention to the scene beyond the limousine window.

Marcello did *enigmatic* very well.

What did she expect? For his expressed warmth towards her in Nicki's presence to contain a grain of genuine emotion?

Please.

She didn't feel a thing for him. *Did she?*

Whatever was causing her heart to quicken its beat, or the butterflies having a ball in her stomach, was merely tension. The stress of ensuring Nicki's emotional welfare remained on an even keel.

Nearly four years' absence had wrought few changes, and a slight frown creased her forehead when the limousine branched off the main arterial route leading into the city.

It took a few kilometres for her tension to escalate as suspicion finally dawned.

No. Please, *please* let me be wrong.

Shannay kept her voice light, when inwardly she was beginning to silently seethe. 'Where are you taking us, Marcello?'

'My home in La Moraleja.'

She shot him a look that inaudibly expressed *you have to be joking.* 'A hotel suite would be more convenient.'

'Ensuring difficulty in enforcing necessary security measures.'

His voice held a degree of steely purpose she couldn't fail to recognise…as he had meant her to.

Her eyes sparked anger as they clashed with his, and if she could have hit him, she'd have lashed out and to hell with the consequences.

Except Nicki was closeted between them, blissfully unaware of her mother's rapidly mounting anger.

But wait, just *wait,* her scathing look silently promised, until I get you alone, behind closed doors and well out of Nicki's hearing.

It was difficult to maintain a sense of calm during the time it took to reach La Moraleja, one of Madrid's exclusive and luxurious suburbs.

Marcello's home was a testament to his wealth and position. Set in beautiful grounds, behind high walls and guarded by electronic gates, the mansion stood as a craftsmen's masterpiece of rambling structural design combining two levels in cream stucco, a cream and terracotta-tiled roof and large curved windows with folding doors, most of which opened out onto a wide terracotta-tiled forecourt.

The entrance was amazing with huge double wood-panelled doors studded in polished brass, reached from a *porte cochère* whose floor featured an exquisite detailed design in marble, accented in polished brass.

She told herself she didn't want to be here. Didn't want to be reminded of the painful memories…or the good ones.

It was too personal, too painful, and *too much.*

Marcello had to know how being here would impact on her.

A house with rooms where they'd argued, fought, made love…

Yet it would become Nicki's temporary home for designated periods of time throughout the year.

Years, she corrected mentally. A place her daughter needed to familiarise herself with, feel welcome in, comfortable.

Being here *now* made sense…for Nicki.

For Shannay, it represented a torture that would stretch her nerves to breaking point over the next three weeks.

He knew it, had planned it, and had deliberately kept her in the dark.

For that he would pay…big time, she vowed as she stepped from the limousine and accompanied Nicki into the large formal foyer where they were greeted by Maria and Emilio, trusted staff of Marcello's who lived in and took care of the house and grounds.

Marble floors, a sweeping staircase, which curved elegantly to the upper floor, a glittering crystal chandelier against a backdrop of coloured patterned glass.

Antique furniture rested against cream walls on which hung original works of art, interspersed with decoratively corniced mini-alcoves displaying an eclectic mix of exquisite vases, bowls and Venetian glassware.

The mansion bore two wings separated by a wide oval balustraded gallery…one designed for formal entertaining with a large dining room, lounge, gourmet kitchen on the first level, while the upper floor held a large study, adjoining library, entertainment room and informal lounge. The west wing comprised three formal guest suites separated by an informal lounge on the first level, with five private suites reposing on the upper level.

The grounds held an infinity pool, a cabana, a well-equipped gym and a tennis court. There were separate self-contained staff quarters built above a large six-car garage.

A large home for one man, Shannay reflected…aware he used it as his main base in between frequent flights to various major cities in various European countries, wheeling and dealing as head of the Martinez corporation.

Marcello's personal portfolio was enviable, providing him with billionaire status in a business world frequented by the ruthless drive for power.

Shannay wondered if he continued to entertain on a regular basis, whether he was active on the social scene and continued to support a few selected charities.

In four years there had to have been at least a few women in his life. Imagining Marcello as a celibate was beyond the bounds of credibility.

Which inevitably led to Marcello's former lover…and Shannay's nemesis. Estella de Cordova.

Was the *über* socialite still on the scene?

And if so, did Marcello intend to marry Estella after they divorced?

A cold hand clutched her heart and squeezed mercilessly *hard*.

Please, dear God, *no*.

The thought Estella might have any part in Nicki's welfare was enough to make Shannay want to throw up.

'You've had a long flight,' Maria began quietly. 'I have tea and some light food prepared. Afterwards, perhaps you would like to rest.'

Carlo brought in their bags and took them upstairs.

'Tea would be lovely. Perhaps a glass of milk for Nicki,' Shannay suggested as Marcello indicated the staircase.

'First, I'll show you to your rooms.'

A personal escort? Somehow she expected him to disappear into his home office.

'It's a big house,' Nicki voiced quietly as they reached the upper level. 'Do other people live here?'

'Sometimes there are guests,' Marcello said gently, meeting her dark, solemn gaze.

'Like Mummy and me.'

'Yes.'

Shannay felt her stomach execute a slow somersault as he

turned away from the wing containing the guest suites and moved down the opposite passage.

She knew the family wing well. Elegant suites, beautifully furbished and furnished.

Did Marcello sleep alone in the master suite, or had he chosen another?

Whoa. Where had that come from?

As if she cared where he slept…as long as it was in a suite far from the one Maria had prepared for herself and Nicki.

The master suite rose vividly in her mind. Positioned at the far end of the family wing, it comprised a large bedroom, two *en suites,* two walk-in wardrobes and an adjoining room containing comfortable deep-seated chairs, a sofa, reading lamps.

Had he had the suite redecorated?

'No.'

Shannay heard his soft drawl and refused to look at him, hating that he still retained the ability to read her mind.

He paused at an open door. 'I think you'll be comfortable here.'

Here was two bedrooms separated by an *en suite,* with one of the bedrooms decorated especially for a young girl. Different shades of pink, from the palest shade to watermelon. Prints hung on the walls, toys in abundance, and the bed was fit for a princess.

Nicki's room.

Shannay got it.

A room that was Nicki's alone, for whenever she visited. A suite she would become familiar with, feel comfortable in and look forward to occupying.

Not too far in distance from where Marcello slept while she was young, so she would feel secure, knowing he was within calling distance.

There was a part of her that hated him for deliberately setting the scene for Nicki's future.

Yet there was also a feeling of gratitude that she didn't want to acknowledge. Together with a mounting anxiety that played havoc with her emotions.

'Is this where I'll sleep?'

Nicki's voice held a degree of wondrous awe.

'Yes.' Marcello moved towards the *en suite,* opened the connecting door and crossed to the opposite door which led into an adjoining bedroom. 'Your mother will sleep here.'

'Can the doors stay open?' Nicki queried tentatively, and he offered a reassuring smile.

'Of course.'

Nicki caught hold of her mother's hand. 'Aren't we lucky?' she said simply, to which Shannay could only answer in the affirmative.

'Marcello is kind to let us stay here.'

She could think of numerous descriptive adjectives…not one of them remotely resembled *kind,* given he had his own agenda.

Their luggage stood at the end of the bed, and Marcello indicated both suitcases. 'Maria will unpack for you. Freshen up, then come downstairs.'

He gave Nicki a warm smile, extended it towards Shannay, then he turned and left the room.

Unpacking would take only a matter of minutes, and Shannay tended to her own, then she transferred Nicki's clothes into the connecting bedroom.

A short while later she accompanied Nicki downstairs to the informal lounge, where Maria served tea, delicate sandwiches and a bowl of freshly cut fruit.

Dinner would be served late…way past Nicki's usual

bedtime, and Shannay decided sandwiches and a glass of milk would suffice as an evening meal on this occasion.

Marcello's presence was unexpected. For some reason she had imagined he'd disappear into his home office and remain there until dinner. A meal she intended to skip on the pretext of bathing Nicki and settling her to sleep.

The flight had been long, his company a constant, and she desperately needed a break from him.

Nicki ate little, drank her milk and began to visibly droop.

'If you'll excuse us?' Shannay took hold of her daughter's hand. 'Say goodnight, darling.'

Nicki politely obliged, and Marcello surprised them both by lifting the young child into his arms.

'I can take her.' She reached out, expecting Nicki to lean towards her…except her daughter remained where she was.

She told herself she wasn't hurt. Silently assured herself it didn't matter. But it did.

Nicki's head had tucked in against the curve of his throat as they reached the bedroom, and he gently lowered her down onto the bed.

'Thanks.' It was a polite, perfunctory gesture that didn't fool him in the slightest.

His eyes seared her own. 'I'll see you at dinner.'

'I'd prefer to remain close to Nicki in case she wakes.'

He regarded her steadily. 'There's a monitor in her room, and auditory receptive devices in every room in the house.' His gaze didn't waver. 'Dinner will be served in two hours. Plenty of time for you to bathe and settle her to sleep before you join me.'

Shannay longed to tell him to go jump. She was on edge, angry, and feeling the effects of jet lag. The thought of sharing a meal with him held no appeal whatsoever.

Yet it would provide the opportunity to vent…and she so badly needed to vent!

He leant down and brushed his lips to Nicki's temple.

'Sleep well, *pequena*.' He straightened, sent Shannay a piercing look, then he turned and left the room.

She had the childish desire to pull a face behind his back, except she restrained herself and tended to her daughter.

Two hours and five minutes later she descended the stairs and made her way towards the informal dining room.

Five minutes over time was acceptable, and in her case deliberate, for she refused to conform to every one of Marcello's dictates.

She'd chosen to wear a black singlet top over which she wore a fine lace black blouse tied at her waist, pencil-slim black skirt, black stilettos, hair pulled back into a French twist secured by a jewelled comb, a slim gold bracelet, understated make-up and lipgloss.

Dressed to kill was an adequate description.

Ready for battle was more apt!

Marcello was waiting for her as she entered the dining room, and one look at him was enough to set the pulse at her throat thrum to a faster beat.

Attired in black tailored trousers, a white chambray shirt, his casual appearance belied the almost barbaric handsomeness of the man.

Strength and power, a degree of ruthlessness made for a dangerous mix she had every reason to view with caution.

Yet there was so much banked-up resentment and anger towards him, it took leashed control to avoid launching into attack mode.

Play nice…for now, she reminded herself silently.

Appear to enjoy a few sips of excellent vintage wine, be

polite through the starter, aim for neutrality as they sampled the main course, then open the verbal discourse over coffee.

That was the plan.

'Shannay.' His voice was a lazy, faintly accented drawl, and she unconsciously lifted her chin.

'Marcello.'

'Can I get you something to drink?'

Civility. She could do that. 'A light medium white, thank you.'

He crossed to a storage cabinet, extracted the appropriate bottle, opened it, poured a quantity into a crystal goblet and extended it towards her.

'Nicki settled well?'

She was careful to avoid his fingers as she took the goblet from his hand. 'Yes. Thank you.'

'So polite, Shannay?'

Her eyes sparked shards of golden fire. 'I thought we'd feign peace and leave war until after dinner.' Her chin lifted a little. 'I have respect for my digestion.'

His soft laughter was almost her undoing as he indicated the table set with fine china, silver flatware and no less than three crystal goblets. 'Let's eat, shall we?'

Maria had surpassed herself with a delicate starter, followed by a seafood paella steaming aromatically beneath a covered serving dish.

'Ramon is anxious to meet Nicki,' Marcello informed as he touched the rim of his goblet to her own in a silent salute. 'How do you feel about tomorrow?'

'Perhaps it could be delayed by a day?' Shannay countered. 'Nicki has had to absorb a lot in the past week, followed by a long flight.' She made a sweeping gesture with her hand to indicate his home. 'All of this.'

'I'll make arrangements.'

It was happening, the increase in Marcello's control to the detriment of her own.

Ramon she could cope with…even look forward to reconnecting with the generous elderly man.

Ramon's daughter, Penè, however, was a different matter.

Ramon's son, Marcello and Sandro's father, had been killed instantly in a car crash when Marcello had been in his late teens.

Nicki was the bonus…the one bright star in the Martinez firmament. No one, not even Penè, would be permitted to say a word out of place in Nicki's hearing.

Shannay sampled the starter, and insisted on a small portion of paella. She'd grown unused to eating so late, and she merely sipped her wine, choosing instead to drink chilled water, and declined dessert or coffee.

'Finish your wine.'

She met his faintly hooded gaze with equanimity. 'I prefer to have a clear head.'

Marcello sank back in his chair and regarded her with interest. 'To indulge in verbal warfare?'

'You doubt it?' She barely hid an edge of bitterness in her voice. 'I specifically requested our own accommodation.'

'Yet I have provided accommodation, have I not?' he offered reasonably.

Far more luxurious than the most expensive hotel. 'That isn't the point.'

'What *is* the point?'

'You could have asked for my approval.'

One eyebrow lifted in silent mockery. 'And your answer would have been?'

'Not in this lifetime!'

He spread his hands wide. 'Precisely.'

She wanted to throw something at him. Anything to disrupt his chilling air of calm. 'Doesn't it matter that I don't want to be here?'

'In Madrid? This house? Or with me?'

'All of that…and more!' The words tumbled out with vehement ire.

'*Querida.*' His faintly accented drawl curled round her heart and tugged a little. 'Perhaps you should have given thought to informing me of Nicki's existence from the beginning, instead of hoping fate and distance would continue to keep me in ignorance.'

'Don't…call me that.'

'Darling? Lover?' He offered a faint smile. 'But you are both, yes?'

'Not any more. And never again,' Shannay added with angry intent, and attempted to tamp down the vivid images that immediately flooded her mind.

In his bed, *theirs,* she corrected. Naked, beneath him, her thighs wrapped around his waist, urging him on, pleading, begging for the release only he could give…the heat and the passion. Loving him with her heart and her soul. *His…only his.*

'Careful, *amada.* I could view that as a challenge.'

'In a pig's eye,' she managed fiercely, hating his silky indolence. Not to mention the instinctive feeling he was deliberately toying with her.

He regarded her carefully. 'Had I known you were pregnant, I'd have taken the next flight to Perth and dragged you back here.'

As he had done *now,* she perceived. 'It wouldn't have changed my decision to file for divorce.'

His pause was deliberately significant. 'Yet you failed to do so until very recently.'

'It was my choice to avoid all contact with you,' Shannay offered coolly. 'Even via legal channels.' She waited a beat, and aimed the figurative dart. 'Reciprocal, obviously.'

'Yet circumstances have changed.'

Suspicion clouded her eyes. 'What are you implying?'

'There will be no divorce.'

'The hell there won't!'

He shrugged in an expressive negligent gesture. 'Why bother with legalities?'

'It might suit you to conveniently have a wife in another country, but I don't want a husband!'

'Not even the faithful John waiting patiently in the background?'

'He's my boss and a friend. Nothing more.'

'No?' Marcello arched silkily, and watched her temper flare into vibrant life.

'Damn you, *no.*'

His eyes narrowed slightly. 'Almost four years, Shannay, and you haven't welcomed another man into your bed?'

She wanted to pick something up and throw it at him.

'Don't,' Marcello warned softly. 'I might seek retribution.'

'Bite me.'

'What an interesting concept.' His lazy drawl held amusement…and something else.

'Go to hell.' She hated the faint shakiness in her voice.

She wanted to leave…the room, this house, *him.*

Yet leaving would amount to an admission of sorts, and she refused to give Marcello the satisfaction.

Besides, there was Nicki. And for her daughter, she'd lay down her life. Without askance, or question.

'Not a very comfortable place to be, wouldn't you agree?'

Shannay closed her eyes, then opened them again as she

flashed him a look of gold-flecked enmity. 'Let's balance the scales, shall we?' Her voice held a darkness she didn't know she possessed. 'Or is the list of willing women anxious to share your bed too extensive to recall?'

'You have a vivid imagination, *mi mujer.*'

My wife. She didn't need or want the reminder. 'With just cause.'

'Something, if you remember,' he drawled, 'I refuted at the time.'

Her gaze remained steady. 'You were very credible, Marcello, in light of the facts.'

One eyebrow rose in a gesture of distaste. 'The fabrication of a disturbed woman?'

'We've been there, done that,' Shannay said in a dismissive tone. 'It's old ground.'

'Consign it to the *too hard* basket, and not seek a resolution?'

'There's nothing to resolve.'

'Yet it had a drastic effect on our lives and eroded what we once shared.'

Destroyed it, she wanted to fling at him…and knew she lied. The sensual pull was as strong now as it had ever been. Almost as if her soul reached out to his in a pagan call as old as time.

She could feel it, sense it deep inside, stirring to life in damning recognition.

Why? she demanded silently. And why now?

Tension. Stress. Jet lag.

A lethal combination which attacked her vulnerability, she justified without conviction.

'I'm over it.' It took tremendous effort to say the words, but she achieved them…barely.

She'd had enough, and her nerves were stretched to breaking

point. With a careful movement she rose to her feet and held the dark, gleaming gaze of the inimical man seated opposite.

'I'm going to bed.'

She turned, and had taken only a few steps when she heard the quiet silky timbre of his voice.

'For the record…we're not done.'

Her stomach jolted at the thinly veiled threat, and it was only through sheer strength of will she didn't falter.

Seconds later she reached the wide arched doorway, and she sensed the faint mockery as he bade,

'Sleep well.'

CHAPTER SIX

SHANNAY CAME AWAKE slowly, stretched a little, reached for her watch to check the time and gave a gasp of dismay.

Nicki.

She flung back the covers, caught up her robe and hurried through the *en suite* to the adjoining bedroom, felt her heart leap to her throat at the sight of Nicki's bed neatly made and no sign of her daughter.

Where…?

It was then she caught sight of the note propped against the pillow, and she hurriedly snatched it up, read the brief script in bold black ink, "Nicki downstairs in Maria's care," and felt the panic begin to subside.

All it took was ten minutes to shower, pull on dress jeans and a casual top over bra and briefs, slide her feet into heeled sandals, then she made her way down to the informal dining room to greet a glowing Nicki being fussed over by the benevolent Maria.

'Marcello said not to wake you,' the housekeeper relayed as she poured steaming aromatic coffee into a cup, offered a wide choice of food for breakfast and shook her head slightly when Shannay chose fresh fruit and yoghurt.

'It's mid-morning,' Shannay reminded with a wry smile. 'My body clock needs time to adjust.'

'Marcello said we can go to a park after lunch,' Nicki informed as Shannay took a seat at the table.

'That's nice.' What else could she say? Any hope Marcello might absent himself in his city office each day seemed doomed. Which meant any form of freedom wasn't going to happen.

Goodbye to checking out theme parks as carefree tourists. No spur-of-the-moment shopping excursions.

This was Madrid. Here she was affiliated to the Martinez family, where extreme wealth necessitated due care with a bodyguard in attendance beyond the safety of home.

She hadn't liked it then. Any more than she did now. Except there was Nicki, with little or no conception of her true identity…yet. A vulnerable child who hadn't been groomed almost from birth to always be aware of possible danger, to unquestionably obey the people in charge of her welfare, or having been taught simple but vital diversionary survival tactics.

It was a heavy load for such a young child, and not something instantly learned.

Although she was loath to admit Marcello had been right in bringing them into his home, it made perfect sense to utilise their three-week sojourn as a learning curve.

It was no use wishing fate hadn't had a hand in bringing Nicki's existence to Sandro and Luisa's attention.

Life was filled with coincidence, occasionally against all the odds…and she had to deal with it.

Shannay finished her breakfast, drained the rest of her coffee and extended a hand towards her daughter.

'Shall we go explore?'

The house first, then the grounds…with Carlo in attendance at a reasonable distance when they ventured outdoors.

High walls, electronic gates, sophisticated security monitoring the grounds.

Together she and Nicki trod the neat paths as they viewed the immaculate lawns, the gardens with their beautiful flowerbeds providing brilliant colour, carefully tended shrubbery precision-clipped to landscaped perfection.

'It's pretty,' Nicki announced, then pointed in excitement. 'There's a swimming pool. Are we allowed to swim in it?'

'Only when I'm with you,' she cautioned firmly.

'Or Marcello?'

Shannay inclined an agreement, and felt a degree of maternal alarm at the thought of Nicki being left unsupervised when she wasn't around. Then she calmed down a little. For the next two years, Nicki's sojourns here would be restricted to a few...except how could she ever learn to let go?

She'd be a nervous wreck from the time her daughter boarded the jet until she returned to Australian soil.

'It's a very big house,' Nicki declared, visibly awed by the luxurious interior as they moved through the various rooms.

Shannay provided a running explanation as they completed the first level and trod the stairs to the upper level.

'I like our wing best,' Nicki clutched a tighter hold of Shannay's hand, ''specially my room.'

Who wouldn't?

Marcello joined them for lunch, and from his casual attire he'd obviously conducted the morning's work in his home office.

Black jeans, a white shirt unbuttoned at the neck and the long sleeves rolled back at the cuffs, he resembled a dark angel, rugged with his hair less smoothly groomed than usual...almost as if he'd thrust fingers through its thickness in exasperation. And if so, why?

In the early days of their marriage she would have walked up to him, cupped his broad facial features between both hands and leaned in to savour the touch of his mouth. Feel his arms close round her slim body as he deepened the kiss, and exult in his arousal.

A time when she'd thought nothing could damage their love. How naive had she been?

'Must I have a nap?'

Shannay caught the subdued excitement bubbling beneath the surface as Nicki silently pleaded with her.

'Uh-huh.' She tempered it with a smile, hating the disappointment clouding her daughter's expressive features. 'Everyone has a siesta after lunch.'

Nicki's eyes grew round with surprise. 'Even grown-ups?' She looked at Marcello. 'You, too?'

'Sometimes, if I'm home and not too busy.' His smile transformed his features, and Shannay felt the familiar sensation curl deep within in memory of how they'd shared the afternoon siesta when *sleep* hadn't been a factor.

Marcello's sanction made it OK, and Nicki obediently caught hold of Shannay's hand as she led her daughter upstairs to her room.

With outer clothes removed and tucked beneath light covers, Nicki fell asleep within minutes, and Shannay moved through to her own room, too restless to do other than flick through a magazine.

No matter how hard she tried, she couldn't shake an instinctively inexplicable feeling of impending…*what?*

She shook her head in exasperation, then dispensed with the magazine. It was crazy. *She* was crazy.

It was mid-afternoon when Carlo brought the expensive Porsche four-wheel-drive to the front door, and with Nicki happily ensconced in the rear seat between Shannay and Marcello they headed for the nearest park.

Her daughter's enthusiasm for everything new appeared boundless, and she watched as Nicki explored, frequently calling for Marcello to come look at a butterfly, a bee, a pretty flower.

By day's end, fed and bathed, Nicki contentedly settled in bed as Marcello read her a bedtime story, then when he reached the end he brushed a light kiss to his daughter's forehead, bade her goodnight and left the room.

Shannay adjusted the night-light, checked the internal monitor, and when she turned Nicki was already breathing evenly in sleep.

If she could, she'd request a tray in her room in lieu of dinner. Except it would be seen as a cop-out, and she refused to allow Marcello to witness so much as a chink in her feminine armour.

Instead, she showered and dressed in an elegant trouser suit, left her hair loose, applied minimum make-up and went down to join Marcello.

A familiar sensation knotted her stomach as she caught sight of his tall, compelling frame, only to tighten considerably as he turned to face her.

There was a degree of lazy arrogance apparent in those dark eyes…a knowledge that probed deep beyond the surface and saw too much.

In the full blush of love, she'd thought it incredibly romantic. Now she viewed it as an aberration.

Once again she declined wine in favour of chilled water, and sought to set the record straight.

'There's no need for you to ignore your social life while Nicki and I are here.'

'Once our daughter is settled for the night I should feel

under no obligation to entertain her mother?' Marcello's voice held a tinge of something she didn't care to define.

'You got it in one.'

'Why would you imagine I'd choose to ignore a guest in my home?'

'Cut the polite verbal word play,' Shannay advised. 'There's no need to insult my intelligence by pretending we're anything other than opposing forces in all areas of our lives.'

'Nicki being the one exception?'

'The *only* exception.'

'But a very important factor, wouldn't you agree?'

He was doing it again, and she glared at him as she took a seat at the table.

'I concede the need to maintain a friendly relationship in Nicki's presence. But rest assured, the less I see of you, the better.'

'Afraid, Shannay?'

'Of you? No.'

'Perhaps you should be,' Marcello warned silkily as he indicated she should help herself to the chicken stew gently steaming in the serving dish.

'Oh, please.' She transferred a small portion of stew onto her plate, replaced the ladle and speared him a glittering look. 'Cut me a break, why don't you?'

He served himself a generous portion, then he selected a fork from the flatware displayed.

'Almost four years,' he drawled. 'Yet the pulse at the base of your throat betrays you with a faster beat.'

'Your ego astounds me.'

'Have you not wondered how our lives would be now had you remained here?'

'Not at all,' she managed coolly, and knew she lied, aware

of the nights she had lain awake imagining that very thing. How their pursuit of happiness had faltered, then fallen apart. Perhaps Nicki wouldn't be the only child she'd bear...because for the life of her she couldn't think of sharing her body with another man or having his child.

'Interesting.'

Shannay carefully folded her linen napkin and placed it on the table, then she rose to her feet and shot him a killing look. 'Go to hell, Marcello.'

'Sit down, Shannay.'

'Only to be picked apart and analysed merely for your amusement? Forget it.'

She turned away from the table and had only taken a few steps when firm hands closed over her shoulders.

In a strictly reactive movement she lifted her head and glared at him. 'What next? Strong-arm tactics?'

'No. Just this.'

He lowered his head down to hers and captured her mouth with his own in a hard kiss that took her by surprise and plundered at will.

The faint cry of distress rose and died in her throat, and almost as if he sensed it his touch gentled a little and became frankly sensual, seeking the sensitive tissues before stroking the edge of her tongue with the tip of his own in a flagrant dance that stirred at the latent passion simmering beneath the surface of her control.

She felt his hands shift as one slid to cup the back of her head, while the other smoothed down her back and brought her close against him.

Her eyelids shuttered down as she fought against capitulation. The temptation to return his kiss was unbearable, and she groaned as he eased back and began a sensual tasting, teasing the soft fullness of her lower lip, nipping a little with the edges of his teeth, until she succumbed to the sweet sorcery he bestowed.

Dear heaven. It was like coming home as he shaped her mouth with his own, encouraging her response, taking her with him in an evocative tasting that became *more*...and promised much.

Her breasts firmed against his chest, their sensitive peaks hardening in need...for the touch of his hand, his mouth, and she whimpered, totally lost in the moment.

The hardness of his erection was a potent force, and warmth raced through her veins, activating each pleasure pulse until she felt so incredibly sensually *alive,* it was almost impossible not to beg.

It was the slide of his hand over the curve of her breast, the way he shaped it, then slid to loosen the buttons that gave her a moment's pause for thought.

It would be so very easy to link her hands behind his neck and silently invite him to rekindle the flame.

And she almost did. *Almost.*

Except sanity and the dawning horror of where this was going provided the impetus to pull away.

What was she doing?

Was she out of her mind?

'I hate you.' The words came out as a tortured whisper as she dropped her arms and attempted to move back a pace.

For what seemed an age Marcello examined her features, the dilated eyes so dark, almost bruised, with passion. The soft, swollen mouth trembling from his possession.

The shocked dismay.

'Perhaps you hate yourself more,' he offered quietly.

For losing control? *Enjoying* his touch?

And, dear lord…wanting it all.

He watched as she straightened her shoulders, tilted her chin and summoned a fiery glare.

'I'm done. And *that*,' she flung recklessly, 'was a ridiculous experiment.'

Marcello let her go, watching as she moved towards the door and exited the room.

Experiment? Far from it.

A mark of intent.

And he was far from done.

The photograph had been taken with a telephoto lens. Had to be, for Shannay couldn't recall seeing a photographer anywhere as they'd disembarked from Marcello's private jet.

Marcello Martinez with a woman and child in tow had sent the news-hounds into a frenzy. How long would it have taken to filch out archival data and discover the woman was Marcello's estranged wife…and determine the child was his own?

Not long.

The caption, even in Spanish, was unmistakable.

How difficult was it to interpret *reconciliacón?*

Or resurrect her knowledge of the language sufficiently to comprehend Señor Martinez' remark, upon being requested to comment?

Anything is possible.

Really?

Anger suffused her body, coalescing into one great tide of fury, taxing her control to the limit.

With care she tore out the offending page, then folded it a few times and slid it into the pocket of her jeans, determined to initiate a confrontation.

He was home…but *where?*

His home office would be the best place to begin.

She sought out Maria, who took one look at the clenched jaw, the blazing eyes, and immediately caught hold of Nicki's hand.

'Come, *pequena,* we will go into the kitchen and bake some biscuits, *si?*'

Shannay even achieved a tense smile. 'Thank you.' She smoothed a hand over Nicki's hair. 'Be good for Maria. I'll check with you soon. OK?'

'OK.'

Marcello's home office was situated in the far corner of the first level, overlooking the gardens and pool area. Two adjoining rooms whose dividing wall had been removed and refurbished to hold a large executive desk, hi-tech computers, a laptop and the requisite office equipment in one half of the room, while floor-to-ceiling bookcases lined the walls of the remaining half, together with a few comfortable leather chairs, lamps and side-tables.

A very male domain, and one she entered with barely an accompanying knock to announce her presence.

Marcello glanced up from a computer screen, caught the gleaming anger apparent in her dark eyes and settled back in his chair to regard her with thoughtful speculation.

Attired in black jeans and a watermelon-pink top, her hair pulled back into a careless pony-tail and no make-up he could discern, she looked little more than a teenager. Harbouring self-righteous anger he was tempted to stir into something more.

Her honest emotions had always intrigued him, for she rarely held back…a quality lacking in many women of his acquaintance. Sophisticated women who played a false seductive game with both eyes on the main chance.

Shannay had been different. She hadn't known who he was, and didn't appear to care when she did.

Four years ago he hadn't been able to prevent her leaving. Hadn't fought for her as he should have done, erroneously supposing all he needed to do to soothe some of the hurt and pain inflicted by Estella and his widowed aunt was provide evidence of his love by gifting sex.

Exceptional lovemaking, he reflected, and felt his body tighten in remembered passion.

'There's something you want to discuss?'

He looked so damned laid-back, controlled. Even, she decided furiously, faintly amused.

With studied calm she extracted the folded newsprint from her pocket, opened it out and tossed it down onto his desk.

'Perhaps you'd care to explain?'

He merely gave it a glance. 'I'm sure your knowledge of the Spanish language is sufficient to provide a reasonably accurate translation.'

The fact he was right didn't sit well. 'That isn't the issue here.'

His eyes never left her face. 'What is the issue, Shannay?'

'A reconciliation was *never* on the cards.' Her eyes flashed gold sparks, and her fingers curled into her palm in frustrated anger. 'There's no way in hell it's going to happen.'

'You think not?'

'I demand you order a retraction.'

'No.' His voice was dangerously soft, his expression an unyielding mask. 'You deny it would be advantageous for Nicki to have two parents, a stable family life, and thus negate custody arrangements in two countries on the opposite sides of the world?'

'With a mother and father constantly at war? *Please.*'

'Would there necessarily need to be dissension?' He made an encompassing gesture with one hand. 'You would enjoy every social advantage and as my wife, be gifted anything you want.'

Marcello watched the fleeting expressions, divined each and every one of them, and moved in for the kill.

'Not even to please a very ill old man with only a short time to live?'

Conflicting emotions tore at her emotional heart and lent shadows to her eyes.

'Ramon has a very progressive form of cancer,' he relayed quietly. 'Various surgical procedures have delayed the inevitable. However, the brain tumour is inoperable, and the medical professionals predict it will only be a matter of weeks before he lapses into a coma.'

Shannay was unable to hide the shock, or her genuine regret. 'I'm so sorry. Why didn't you warn me?'

'I thought I had.'

She searched for the precise words he'd used. 'You said he was ill,' she recalled. 'You didn't say he is dying.'

She was conscious of his scrutiny, the studied ease with which he regarded her as the impact of his words sank in.

'Given the circumstances, is it too much to ask?'

Her eyes held his. 'What about Nicki? Ramon wants to meet her, but have you given a thought to how Ramon's rapidly deteriorating health will affect her? She's only a child, and she's much too young to assimilate and cope with illness of this magnitude.'

'I've agonised over it,' Marcello assured quietly. 'At the moment Ramon spends a short time sitting in a comfortable chair in the *sala*. He looks old, a little tired and fragile, but he's remarkably lucid.' He regarded her thoughtfully. 'You will be able to judge for yourself.' An entire gamut of conflicting emotions vied for supremacy, including doubt. In the end, compassion won out.

'You give me your word you'll allow me to decide when Nicki's visits should cease?'

'Without question.' He sank further back in his chair and raised his hands to cup his nape. 'The purported reconciliation? You'll agree to the pretence for Ramon's sake?'

Why did she harbour the feeling she was being led deeper into deception with every passing day?

She wanted no part of it.

Yet it seemed so little to do to ease an elderly man's mind. To let him believe...what? That his beloved eldest grandson had reconciled with his wife? Spend time with his only great-grandchild?

Couldn't she gift Ramon that much?

'Aren't you forgetting something? *Someone?*' Shannay asked at last.

Marcello didn't pretend to misunderstand.

'Nicki will be told precisely who I am before we visit Ramon.'

'Which will be *when?*'

He checked his watch. 'At eleven.'

Just over an hour? 'Excuse me?'

'You heard.'

Without thought she reached for a paperweight and threw it at him.

Only to miss, as he fielded it in one hand.

For a moment the air was electric, stark and momentous in its silence, and her eyes darkened with horrified disbelief as Marcello placed the glass weight onto the desk, then rose slowly to his feet.

She couldn't move, her feet seemingly cemented to the floor as he crossed to her side.

There wasn't a word she could utter, for her voice couldn't

pierce the lump that had risen in her throat, and she stood powerless as he captured her chin.

His eyes were dark, almost black with forbidding anger, and his voice emerged in husky warning.

'Play with fire, *querida,* and you risk getting burned.'

He ran a finger along the edge of her jaw, almost caressing its shape, and a shiver slithered through her body.

'So much emotion,' Marcello opined silkily. 'Why is that, do you suppose?'

'Because I hate you.'

'Better hate than indifference.'

His fingers curled over her chin as he stroked a thumb over her lower lip…felt it tremble beneath his touch, and offered a faint smile.

'Shall I put it to the test?' He traced the column of her throat with the tip of one finger, rested briefly in the hollow between her breasts, then slid to cup one soft mound and brush its peak with a provocative sweep of his thumb.

She felt it swell and harden beneath his touch, and hated her traitorous reaction.

'Let me go.'

His voice lowered to an indolent purr. 'But we're not yet done.'

His mouth brushed hers in a teasing tracery that almost made her sway, and she stifled a faint groan as he pulled her lower lip between his teeth.

She was hardly aware of the fingers of one hand working the snap at her waist, or the subtle slide of the zip fastening…until she felt his palm against the bare skin of her stomach.

Then it was too late and her startled protest became lost in the way he filled her mouth, and she felt her body jerk spasmodically as his fingers slid through the soft curling hair at the junction of her thighs, then sought and found the moist warmth at her feminine core.

With unerring accuracy he stroked the swollen clitoris and watched the way her eyes glazed as sensation arced through her in an encompassing wave. One which swelled again and again with every tantalising stroke, and he absorbed her cry as he used his fingers in a simulated thrust that sent her high.

He wanted more, much more, and the temptation to take her here, now, was an almost unbearable hunger.

On the desk, the floor, straddling him on the chair, pushed against the wall.

The fact he could acted as a deterrent, and he simply held her, softening the touch of his mouth against her own until the shudders raking her slender form slowed and subsided.

With care he withdrew his hand, closed the zip fastening on her jeans and pressed the snap.

The action brought her back to her senses, and she pushed away from him, unable to believe she'd allowed what had just happened…to *happen*.

How could she have relaxed her guard and become so seduced by his touch…dear heaven, his intrusion?

She didn't want to look at him. Couldn't bear to see the satisfaction evident in his eyes, or his pleasure at her downfall.

For an age neither of them spoke, and the only audible sound in the room was the slightly uneven sound of her breathing.

'That was despicable,' Shannay managed, hating him so much she almost shook with it. She lifted a hand and wiped the back of it across her mouth in an attempt to dispense the taste of him.

And glimpsed the compelling sensuality apparent before he masked his expression.

'But…enlightening, wouldn't you agree?'

'You're keeping score?' she countered with a tinge of bitterness, and saw his expression harden.

'Where is Nicki?'

She took a deep breath and released it slowly. 'In the kitchen with Maria making biscuits.'

'Then let's go get her.'

She looked at him sharply. 'Now?'

Get a grip, why don't you?

How, when her emotions were in turmoil and her body had yet to recover? Even thinking about his touch was enough to cause tiny spasms in the most sensitive part of her anatomy.

'We'll tell her together.'

With an effort she pulled herself together. 'I should be the one—'

'She deserves to have both her parents present.'

Apprehension didn't cover it as they collected Nicki and took her upstairs, and as they neared her room Shannay began doing deals with the deity.

This was major. *Major,* she reiterated silently as Marcello placed Nicki on her bed, and hunkered down to her eye level.

He kept the telling simple. So very simple, it was easy to follow his lead. And Nicki's reaction became a timeless moment, one that caught the heartstrings and plucked the emotional depths as she stood and unhesitatingly wrapped her arms around Marcello's neck.

His eyes burned fiercely over Nicki's head as he hugged her close, and Shannay had to blink hard to prevent the shimmer of tears spilling down her cheeks.

Father and child together.

Nicki's delight and wholehearted acceptance, whose childish words said it all. 'You're my daddy.'

It was a beginning, Shannay acknowledged, for Nicki

was a perceptive child for her age and eventually there would be questions.

But for now, one of the most important hurdles had been conquered.

Marcello pressed a light kiss to his daughter's temple. 'Now we will all get ready to go visit with your *bisabuelo,* Ramon.'

He rested a hand briefly on Shannay's shoulder. 'Fifteen minutes. I'll wait for you downstairs.'

Together they chose Nicki's prettiest dress, and with her hair neatly caught together she followed Shannay into her room as Shannay selected a slim-fitting dress in jade linen, attached a belt, then tended to her hair and make-up beneath her daughter's interested gaze.

Marcello was standing in the foyer as they descended the stairs, and he smiled at Nicki's childish beam when she placed her small hand in his on reaching his side.

Carlo drove through the suburban avenues to Ramon's mansion, parking it in the forecourt immediately adjacent to the main entrance.

Shannay was unprepared for the physical changes in the elderly man, who'd been one of the few Martinez family members to view her kindly before and during her brief marriage to his eldest grandson.

She remembered him as a strong man, despite his advancing years. Vibrant and powerful, yet compassionate to the young woman who'd captured Marcello's heart.

Ramon had encouraged her struggle to learn the Spanish language, to come to terms with the Martinez wealth and life-style, and to accept the things she couldn't change.

In a way, he'd been her mentor, and to now discover the shell of the man she'd once adored was heartbreaking.

At first she was tentative, unsure whether the affection they'd shared still existed. After all, it had been she who'd left under cover of night, leaving only a brief note for Marcello to find on his return home, and no word for anyone else.

'*Holà.*' It wasn't so much the greeting, but the husky-voiced delivery accompanied by a gentle smile that filled her eyes with unshed tears.

'Ramon.' She didn't hesitate in crossing to the cushioned chair where he sat. Nor did she pause in brushing her lips to his cheek. 'How are you?'

The dark eyes twinkled with humour. 'How do I look?'

She tilted her head slightly to one side. 'A little less the Martinez lion than I remember.'

'How beautifully you lie.' His soft laughter almost undid her. 'But I forgive you for indulging an old man.' He caught hold of her hand and held it within his own. 'Now introduce me to my great-granddaughter.'

Marcello moved forward with Nicki held in his arms.

'Nicki,' he said gently, 'this is Ramon.'

Ramon's features softened dramatically, and his eyes misted. 'Bring her closer.'

For a moment Nicki looked hesitant, then she nodded as Marcello offered a few soft, reassuring words.

'*Holà, Bisabuelo.*'

Shannay's eyes widened in startled surprise. The pronunciation was good. Who? Marcello...of course, possibly coached by Maria.

For a moment she had mixed feelings, then they were overcome by Ramon's obvious delight.

'Nicki. A beautiful name for a beautiful little girl,' he said gently.

'Marcello—my daddy—sometimes calls me *pequena*,' Nicki said solemnly. 'That means little.'

His smile melted Shannay's heart. 'Indeed it does. You must visit often, and I will teach you some Spanish.'

'I'll have to ask Mummy if it's OK.'

'Of course,' Ramon agreed with equal solemnity, and cast Shannay an enquiring glance.

'It will be a pleasure.' How could she say anything else?

'Marcello shall bring you.'

Nicki looked momentarily unsure. 'Mummy, too?'

'Naturally. We shall make it mornings, then you will have the rest of the day to explore.' He glanced up at the slight sound of a door opening. 'Ah, here is Sophia with our tea.'

Tea with delicious bite-size sandwiches and pastries, some pleasant conversation, after which Marcello indicated they should leave.

'Hasta mañana.'

Until tomorrow.

Carlo drove them past the Warner Bros Park, a visit to which Marcello promised as a treat in store.

'You're a busy man,' Shannay protested lightly.

'Impossible I have learnt to delegate?'

'Improbable.'

'You are wrong.'

She looked at him carefully. 'We don't expect you to give up your time.'

Dark eyes travelled to her mouth and lingered there a moment too long. 'It is my pleasure to do so.'

Pleasure being the operative word, and unmistakable.

Shannay could feel colour tinge her cheeks, and she shot him a dark glance before becoming seemingly engrossed in the scene beyond the car window.

It was during dinner that evening that she brought up his social life, and a firm reiteration she didn't require to be entertained…especially by him.

'Won't your—er—' she paused with deliberate delicacy '—current lover,' she lightly stressed, 'become impatient at your absence?'

One eyebrow slanted in silent mockery. 'From her bed?' And noted with interest the increased thud of a pulse at the base of her throat. 'Possibly,' he drawled, and took his time in adding, 'If I had one.'

She refused to rise to the bait. 'Estella has become the consummate mistress?'

'Something you would need to ask of her husband.'

Estella had married? 'I find it difficult to believe she gave up on you.'

His smile was a mere facsimile. 'It takes two, *amada,* and I was never a contender.'

It wasn't easy to feign indifference, but she managed it. 'Could we change the subject?'

'Yet you brought it up,' he reminded with hateful simplicity.

'Is Ramon in much pain?' She kept the faintly desperate edge from her voice, and had the impression it didn't fool him at all.

Marcello's gaze didn't shift from her own as he inclined his head. 'He has ongoing medical attention with a doctor and nurse in residence. It is his wish to remain at home.'

Shannay knew his condition, and the odds. There was little to be done, except keep him comfortable.

'I would ask that you and Nicki remain here until Ramon slips into a coma.'

She should have seen it coming, and she cursed herself for not foreseeing just this eventuality.

'I have a job,' she reminded. 'We have an agreement. After three weeks Nicki and I return to Perth.'

'I'm sure your leave can be extended on compassionate grounds.'

It could. If she wanted it extended.

The truth being she didn't trust herself to stay in Marcello's company any longer than she had to.

They shared a history, a potent chemistry she didn't dare stir into vibrant life.

He was dangerous, primitive, and intently focused.

A surge of helpless anger rose to the fore at his manipulation, and her gaze hardened as she sought a measure of control.

'You believe I brought you here with an ulterior motive in mind?'

How could she doubt it? *'Yes.'*

'Perhaps you'd care to elaborate?'

His voice was a silky drawl as his eyes pierced her own, silently daring her to avoid his gaze.

'I think you'll do whatever it takes to ensure you get what you want,' she retaliated heatedly.

'And what is it you imagine I want?'

'Nicki.'

His expression didn't change. 'Of course. What else?'

She couldn't bear to be in his presence a moment longer, and she stood to her feet, tossed aside her napkin and turned away from him.

'One day you won't run.'

Shannay swivelled and sent him a venomous glare. 'You *think?*'

He had the strong desire to haul her over his shoulder and carry her kicking and protesting to his bed.

As he had done once in the past, when mere words had

become an impossible means of communication. Kisses tempered by anger assumed reluctant passion, then became more, so much more, until there was no denial of need, or a mutual sensual recognition that overcame all else...until reality in the light of day intruded.

Was her memory of what they'd shared as hauntingly vivid as his own?

Did it keep her awake nights?

He was counting on it.

CHAPTER SEVEN

SHANNAY CHECKED her appearance, and wondered how she could look so calm, when her nerves were shot to pieces and it seemed as if a dozen butterflies were beating their wings madly inside her stomach.

She really didn't want to do this.

Re-entering the Madrid social scene had never been part of the plan.

Hell, *nothing* that had happened in the past few weeks formed part of any plan she could have envisaged in her worst nightmare!

Yet the evening represented a fundraiser for a worthy charity, one of a few supported by the Martinez corporation.

Marcello's attendance was a given and, as his purported newly reconciled wife, she was expected to appear by his side.

Something suitable to wear had been dealt with with remarkable ease. All it had taken was a phone call to a prominent boutique with her measurements to have a selection of gowns delivered to Marcello's home.

Now she viewed the *café-au-lait* gown in silk organza with its elegant, finely pleated bodice, thin spaghetti straps and full-length soft, flowing skirt, the stiletto-heeled evening shoes…and felt reasonably confident her choice was the right one.

Understated make-up with emphasis on her eyes, a faint

tinge of blush at her cheeks and lipgloss…with her hair in a smooth twist.

'You look like a princess.'

Shannay turned towards Nicki and blew her a kiss. 'Thank you.'

'*Gracias,*' her daughter corrected with a grin. 'Me and Maria are going to watch *Shrek.*'

'Just for a little while. When Maria says it's time for bed, you won't fuss. OK?'

''Kay.'

Time to go downstairs, join Marcello, then step into a Martinez chauffeured limousine…secure in the knowledge Nicki would be well looked after in Maria's care, with Carlo in charge, and a direct private line on speed-dial to both her and Marcello's cellphone.

Shannay collected the matching evening bag, then held out her hand. 'Come on, imp. Party-time.'

A faint knock on Nicki's bedroom door accompanied by the sound of a familiar male voice had the little girl racing through the connecting *en suite.*

'Daddy's here!'

Large as life and far too stunningly attractive in dark evening wear, Shannay perceived as she attempted without success to still the warmth flooding through her veins at the mere sight of him.

Fine white shirt linen provided a stark contrast with his olive skin and dark, well-groomed hair, his tailored suit displaying an impeccable fit as it moulded his superbly muscled frame.

It was little wonder women of all ages felt emboldened to flex their flirting skills in his presence, for he possessed a raw sexuality combined with the hint of something forbidden, almost verging on the savagely primitive.

A modern-day warrior who fought daily with powerful brokers in numerous countries around the world, constantly seeking an essential edge…and always watching his back.

Dark inscrutable eyes took in her slim form, the child regarding him with dancing anticipation, and he leant down and scooped Nicki into his arms.

'Isn't Mummy beautiful?' his daughter confided, and his mouth curved into a generous smile.

'Beautiful,' Marcello agreed. 'Just like you.'

A compliment that earned him an enthusiastic kiss to his cheek.

Ten minutes later Shannay sat in the rear seat of the limousine as it cleared the gates and traversed the avenue leading towards the main arterial route into the city.

'There's something missing,' Marcello drawled and reached into his jacket pocket, extracted a small velvet case and snapped it open.

'Give me your hand.'

He sensed her hesitation and simply caught hold of her left hand, and slid the exquisite baguette-style diamond ring onto the appropriate finger.

Her wedding ring. The one she'd left behind the night she'd fled his home, his country.

'I don't—'

'Want to wear it?' His dark eyes met hers and held them. 'But you will.'

'Why?'

'I would have thought it obvious.'

'The orchestrated reconciliation,' she acknowledged drily, and saw his cynical smile.

'Need I remind you the marriage remains intact?'

'For the time being.' She'd play the game for the duration of her stay, for Ramon's sake. An extra week or two was little to gift him from her lifetime.

The wide platinum diamond-encrusted band shot prisms of brilliantly coloured fire as the light caught the numerous facets, and its unaccustomed weight felt strange.

'There's also these.'

He revealed a pear-shaped diamond pendant and matching earrings he'd gifted her on their first wedding anniversary.

Without a word he leant towards her and attached the delicate platinum chain in place and fastened the clasp at her nape.

It took only seconds, but it felt like an age as his warm breath feathered her cheek, and the touch of his fingers at her nape wrought an intimacy in the close confines of the limousine.

How easy would it be to move her head a little and have her cheek brush his own? To turn into him and seek his mouth, feel the sensuous slide of his tongue in an erotic tasting that could never be enough…merely a tantalising preliminary to how the evening would end. As it had in the early days of their marriage.

A time when she had dared and teased, and exulted in every moment.

Now she sat still, waiting with indrawn breath for him to move away so her heartbeat could return to its normal rhythm.

She made a slightly strangled protest as he lifted his fingers to her ear and carefully attached the hooked pin of one ear-stud before tending to her other earlobe.

Shannay couldn't fault his touch, or accuse it lingered a little too long. But the action felt incredibly personal, intimate…and she had to fight against the way it affected her wayward emotions.

As he meant it to do?

And if so, to what purpose?

Physically, Marcello could do nothing to prevent her leaving the country.

So why this persistent niggle of doubt?

The hotel was one of the city's finest, and Shannay cursed Marcello afresh as she pinned a smile on her face and prepared to play an expected part.

Numerous photographers' cameras flashed as they alighted from the limousine and trod the red carpet into the foyer.

Marcello's hand was warm as it rested at the back of her waist, and the bodyguard who'd ridden up front in the limousine now flanked her as they moved towards the gracious staircase leading to the mezzanine level.

A well-remembered scene, Shannay perceived, with the beautiful people who mostly came to be seen. Women who chose to showcase designer gowns and expensive jewellery, gifted by husbands and lovers who presided as captains of industry.

Socialites, fashionistas, models…she caught a glimpse of a few familiar faces, smiled and kept her head high.

Waiters and waitresses dutifully presented trays of drinks, from which Marcello selected two flutes of champagne and placed one in her hand.

Alcohol on an empty stomach wasn't such a good idea, and she merely took a sip of the chilled bubbly liquid, then regarded the flute as a prop.

'Marcello!'

'Miguel and Shantal Rodriguez,' Marcello intoned quietly as a man and woman greeted them, followed by voluble Spanish…which Marcello immediately explained was not his wife's first language.

Shannay was supremely conscious of him at her side, the occasional touch of his hand at the edge of her waist, his attentive manner, and suppressed the wayward desire it was real, instead of the expected portrayal of a husband with his wife.

It was a relief when the large ballroom doors opened and guests were instructed to begin making their way to reserved seats at designated tables.

There was one face in the crowd Shannay subconsciously searched for, and failed to notice.

Estella de Cordova.

A woman whose presence at the evening's prestigious event would be obligatory.

Then there she was, tall, impossibly elegant in Versace only someone with a superb figure and an overdose of panache could wear.

Dark, thick, curling hair framed her perfect features, and an abundance of diamonds sparkled with every move she made.

The centre of attention as always, and actively seeking to make an impression.

Shannay's gaze shifted slightly to the man at her side. Distinguished, and at least fifteen years Estella's senior.

Estella de Cordova was known to scope out a room, hone in on her quarry, then patiently wait for the opportune moment to strike.

Somehow Shannay doubted anything had changed.

Impossible the news of Marcello's reconciliation with his Australian wife hadn't reached Estella's notice. Or the knowledge Shannay's attendance tonight at his side wouldn't garner speculation.

It wasn't so much a matter of if Estella would make her move, only when.

Not, she perceived, before the guests were all seated.

Those who had been aware of the purported affair between Estella de Cordova and Marcello Martinez would

To many...or just Estella?

Shannay waited a few minutes, then she leaned towards him. 'You're verging on overkill, *querido,*' she warned in a softly taunting voice.

Marcello lowered his head to hers. 'There's the need to set a precedent.'

She took the opportunity to surreptitiously check her cell-phone, saw an SMS message alerting Nicki had gone to sleep at eight-thirty, and felt a sense of relief.

There were speeches in between numerous courses, some discourses brief and amusing...others long as the charity was lauded, together with the efforts of the tireless volunteers without whose help the fundraiser would not have been as successful.

Or at least that was the overall drift, and she joined in the applause, aware Marcello had placed his arm across the back of her chair.

An action which brought him close, and heightened her level of awareness.

As he meant it to do?

Did he know the effect he had on her?

She assured herself she didn't like or condone what he was doing. Or his manipulation. For at almost every turn she was caught in a trap, bound by love for her daughter, her affection for an elderly ill man, and now the subterfuge of deception.

Only for a certain length of time, she reminded, for her sojourn in Madrid would reach an end and she'd return with Nicki to resume their life in Perth.

Custody arrangements involving travel would be minimal for the next two years, and Marcello's visits brief, if relatively frequent.

She could cope. So too would Nicki.

So what if she played the game according to Marcello's dictum in the presence of others?

It was only temporary.

At that moment there was an entertainment announcement, and a female singer offered a rousing rendition in Spanish while colourfully attired back-up dancers performed an energetic routine.

Coffee was served, and Shannay declined the strong espresso in favour of tea.

It was the time of evening when guests were no longer restricted to their seats, and several rose to seek out friends, to linger, share coffee and conversation.

Would Estella make her move now? Or engineer a staged encounter as Marcello rose to leave?

She told herself she didn't care. But she did, and a tension headache took hold behind her eyes.

Presenting a sparkling façade had taken its toll. So too had attempting to correlate much of a language she hadn't practised in a few years.

Consequently it was a relief when Marcello withdrew his cellphone and summoned their driver to wait out front.

There was the opportunity for a few brief words with Sandro and Luisa before their attention was diverted.

They were about to exit the ballroom minutes later when a familiar sultry feminine voice purred a greeting, and a sinking feeling manifested itself in the pit of her stomach.

'Estella.' She could do polite. It really was the only way to go.

Was it chance or design the man at Estella's side drew Marcello into conversation, conveniently allowing Estella an opportunity to deliver a verbal barb or three?

'I see Marcello was able to persuade you to return.' There

was a very subtle pause. 'Not very clever of you to deny him the child.' Her smile failed to reach the coolness in her eyes. 'I doubt he'll forgive you for that.'

If the figurative knives were out, it was time to dispense with the niceties. 'You don't read the media news?'

'The reconciliation announcement?' A soft, humourless laugh escaped her lips. 'A mere ploy to soothe Ramon's rapidly ailing health.'

'And this concerns you…because?'

Something shifted in the woman's eyes. 'He's a very—' Estella paused, weighting the momentary silence with innuendo '—special man.'

'Yes, he is.' Shannay aimed for a secretive smile, and saw Estella's mouth tighten a little.

'If you'll excuse us?' Marcello's voice held a silky quality Estella chose to heed.

'Of course.'

It could have been worse, Shannay accorded as the limousine eased its way clear of the hotel's entrance and joined the flow of traffic.

She let her eyelids drift down in an attempt to shut out the neon lights and the frequent stab of headlights as the headache moved towards migraine territory.

'You don't have your medication with you?'

He knew? 'If I did, I'd have taken some by now.'

There was the faint whisper of sound, followed by another as he released both safety belts, then firm hands positioned her to rest against him. A male arm curved down her back and settled over her thigh, holding her there as she began to protest.

'Just close your eyes and relax.'

Relax? With her body curled into the contours of his, her

head cradled against the curve of his shoulder? Her face mere inches from his own?

He had to be joking!

Warmth heated her veins, tantalising her senses as the perceived intimacy invaded pleasure places they had no right to be.

It wasn't what she wanted. And knew her mind to be at odds with the dictates of her body.

How easy would it be to slip free a few buttons on his shirt and slide her hand to rest against the strong beat of his heart. To feel it kick into a quickened beat as she caressed a male nipple.

Hear his husky murmur as she lowered her hand and traced the hardened outline of his arousal held in tight restraint within the confines of his evening trousers.

To tease a little, then lift her mouth and savour the touch of his in a preliminary to what they'd soon share in the privacy of their bedroom.

A slow, teasing discovery, or a quick shedding of clothes as desire and need meshed and became electrifying passion.

A time when they'd been in perfect sync, two halves of a whole…and she'd innocently believed nothing and no one could touch them.

How wrong had she been.

It almost made her wish it were possible to turn back the clock, and possess the power to change actions and words.

Except it was done, and the past couldn't be altered.

Did Marcello have any regrets?

How could he?

He hadn't followed her to Perth.

Hadn't sought to make contact.

As far as he was concerned, she could have vanished from the face of the earth.

Until a chance encounter had brought her beneath his radar.

Because of Nicki.

Let's not be fooled in thinking otherwise.

So what in hell was she doing resting against him like this? Savouring a little self-indulgence?

It would be simple to push against him and straighten into a sitting position...except his arms tightened and held her in place.

'Stay there. We're almost home.'

All the more reason for her to move.

This time he didn't try to stop her.

Nor did he attempt to touch her as they alighted from the limousine and moved indoors.

He merely acknowledged her "goodnight" with a brief nod, and watched as she ascended the stairs.

CHAPTER EIGHT

'Is RAMON GOING to die?'

The plaintive query from so young a child was heart-rending, and Shannay went down on one knee and gathered her daughter close.

'He's very sick,' she said gently.

'Like Fred.'

Fred had been a pet white mouse who'd developed a tumour, and been replaced, after due ceremony, by a goldfish.

'Like Fred,' she agreed solemnly.

'It'll be sad,' Nicki ventured, and Shannay inclined her head, then sought to offer a distraction by suggesting a swim in the pool.

It was a warm day, with no breeze to riffle the tree-leaves, and together they donned swimsuits, lathered on sunscreen cream, then gathered up towels, alerted Carlo as to their whereabouts, and wandered down to the pool.

Nicki was like a fish in water, diving, floating, and showing her swimming prowess with a credible crawl...for a young child.

It was fun to play, to splash, laugh a little and temporarily relax her guard.

'Daddy!'

Shannay turned slowly in the direction Nicki indicated, and

saw Marcello's tall masculine figure walking the path through the grounds towards the few marble steps leading to the pool and its surrounds.

Attired as he was in a short black towelling robe with a towel slung over one shoulder, his intention to join them was obvious, and she tried to ignore the unbidden convulsing sensation deep inside.

She didn't want to feel like this, and hated her body's traitorous reaction. It wasn't fair to be constantly reminded of the sensual heat that coursed through her veins in remembered passion.

With every passing day it became more intense, the memories disruptive. The nights were worse when she lay alone in her bed, so aware of his presence as he slept in a suite not far from her own.

Did he sleep easily, or did he lie awake as she did, caught up in emotional hunger?

Enough, a silent voice taunted.

Yet being here, in his home and his constant company, attacked her defences and seriously eroded them.

There was a part of her that wished he absented himself in the city each day, instead of utilising the benefits of modern technology to keep in touch with the business world from home.

Although she had to accept he had reason enough to rearrange his life in order to spend as much time as possible with his daughter.

Now here he was, about to shrug off a robe and join them in the water.

Wearing, Shannay noted with a quick glance, a very respectable pair of black boxer swim shorts.

Her heart rate accelerated at the sight of his powerful frame with its fluid flex of muscle and sinew, and his eyes caught hers for a few timeless seconds before she deliberately shifted her attention to Nicki.

'Daddy, watch me swim.'

He did, slipping into the water and applauding his daughter's efforts as Nicki went through her paces.

Shannay was conscious of the brevity of her *maillot,* cut high at the hip and a halter-neck plunging to a deep V between breasts a little fuller since Nicki's birth.

Had he noticed?

Oh, for heaven's sake…*stop,* she cautioned in silent castigation. What are you *thinking?*

Yet the warmth of his touch as he'd cradled her close in the limousine had stirred something deep inside, reminding her too vividly of everything they'd shared…and never would again.

So get over it.

'Nicki is a beautiful child,' Marcello opined quietly. 'Obedient and unspoilt. You've done well with her.'

She looked at him carefully. 'A compliment, Marcello?'

'Is it so difficult to accept I might offer you one?'

He was close, within touching distance, and she stilled the almost irresistible urge to move away.

'In the circumstances, yes,' she stated coolly, and heard a faint drawling quality enter his voice.

'Perhaps it is wise to ignore circumstances.' His pause held a weight of meaning she chose not to explore. 'And attempt to move on.'

'I was doing fine,' Shannay offered sweetly. 'Until you dragged me here under threat.' With that, she used breaststroke to glide effortlessly away and did her best to ignore him.

Difficult, when Nicki sought his attention at every turn, laughing with delight as he splashed her, then allowed her to catch him.

He was good with her. Kind, playful and clearly her idol.

Daddy peppered her conversation with tremendous regularity, and she squealed as he lifted her onto his shoulders and ascended the tiled steps leading out from the pool.

Maria served tea in the *sala,* together with a nutritious evening meal for Nicki, whose bedtime was gradually being extended to conform with local custom.

Where Shannay predicted difficulties, none appeared to exist. Nicki had slipped happily into her new lifestyle, accepting the changes with surprising ease.

Instead *she* was the one having problems as ambivalent emotions invaded her being, causing increasing turmoil with every passing day.

'Mummy's turn tonight,' Nicki declared as Shannay tucked her into bed and picked up a book of fairy tales, aware Marcello had taken a chair close by.

It was hard to shut him out as she endeavoured to focus on reading the story of the princess and the pea.

He was *there,* a physical entity impossible to ignore, and she was conscious of his hooded gaze, the sheer dynamic presence of the man.

Nicki listened with rapt attention, valiantly fighting sleep until her eyelids drifted down and her breathing settled into a slow even rhythm.

Shannay carefully closed the book, checked the bedcovers, the monitor and night-light, then she paused in the doorway before closing the door softly behind her.

Marcello followed, and she turned at the same time he did and brushed against him.

An automatic apology fell from her lips, and she moved quickly to widen the distance between them as they both traversed the gallery leading to the staircase.

'Nicki is fortunate to have you as a mother.'

A flippant response rose in her throat, and didn't find voice. Instead she uttered a quiet, 'I can't imagine my life without her.'

Dark eyes swept her features as they began descending the stairs. 'There is a solution.'

Something took hold of her emotions and turned them upside down. 'Such as?' She paused as they reached the spacious foyer.

'Stay.'

Shannay closed her eyes, then opened them again. 'With you? I don't think so.'

'It's a large house. You would have an enviable lifestyle. And never need to be parted from Nicki,' he added.

Shannay was suddenly icily calm. 'Define *enviable?*'

'An unlimited expense account. Jewellery. Any vehicle you care to name. A personal bodyguard. Everything the wife of a very wealthy man can provide.'

She wanted to hit him. 'You think I *care* about a collection of designer gowns, the Manolo Blahniks and Jimmy Choos, jewellery?' She paused for breath. 'Attending the opera, the theatre, charity fundraisers in all their various guises, glittering first nights, that parties are my ultimate choice in entertainment?' She was filled with pent-up anger, and unable to prevent it from spilling over. 'Live in this mansion, give my time to charity committees and become the exemplary wife in and out of the bedroom? You think any of that is important to me?'

Marcello regarded her with a degree of amusement. 'Not even the bedroom?'

'No.' And knew she lied.

His voice became dangerously soft. 'Then, perhaps you'd care to elaborate?'

She tilted her chin a little and seared his dark eyes with her own. If only it were possible to turn back the clock, to recapture the love they'd once shared. Except that didn't form part of any equation she could envisage.

'You think you can buy whatever you want. Everything has a price. Even me. You're so wrong!' Her eyes assumed a molten hue.

'As to your suggestion…' She was almost beyond words. 'Forget it!'

She took a deep breath to help control her rising disbelief. 'Not even for Nicki's sake will I be trapped in a loveless marriage,' she added with pent-up vehemence.

An eyebrow rose in mocking silence at her lack of hesitation.

'You broke my heart once.' Any hope it had healed went out the window the moment she heard his voice and saw his image on video camera as he stood in the entrance bay of her apartment building just a few weeks ago. 'No way will I give you the chance to do it again.'

'I see I didn't make myself clear,' Marcello drawled. 'We not only share the same roof, we occupy the same room, the same bed.'

'Let me get this right. You're offering sex as a bonus?'

A muscle bunched at the edge of his jaw. 'A normal marriage. The possibility of adding to our family.'

'Forgive me.' She was on a roll, and like a runaway train she couldn't stop. 'I've experienced your version of *normal*, and I hated the way it worked out.'

'And nothing I say will convince you otherwise?'

Shannay drew herself up to her full height and glared at him with a look that would have seared a lesser man to a crisp. 'No.' With that she turned on her heel and began retracing her steps.

The thought of sitting opposite him calmly forking food into her mouth didn't appeal. Besides, she wasn't hungry.

Instead, she'd retrieve a book, go settle somewhere and read.

It would have been a good plan if she'd been able to concentrate on the written word.

After a while she tossed the book aside and turned on the television, only to channel-hop in a bid to find something of interest.

A cooking programme looked good, although it only served to remind her that she'd deliberately missed dinner.

OK, so admit you're mad at him.

To think of agreeing to his so-called proposal is an insult.

It hadn't been his wealth and position that had attracted her to him in the first place. Dammit, she hadn't even known who he was!

The next few weeks couldn't pass quickly enough, then she'd return *home* with Nicki and resume an ordinary life.

She must have slept, for she came sharply awake at the sound of a child's cry, followed by a heart-wrenching sobbing.

Ohmigod…*Nicki.*

Shannay raced through the connecting *en suite* to find Nicki sitting up in bed drenched in tears, and she scooped her onto her lap and held her close.

'Sweetheart, what's wrong?'

The words had barely emerged from her mouth when Marcello entered the room, crossed to her side and queried quietly,

'A bad dream?'

Concern shadowed her features. 'She's never woken like this before.' She pressed a cheek to Nicki's temple. 'Tell Mummy, darling.'

Gradually the sobs reduced to intermittent hiccups, and Shannay was hardly aware of Marcello's absence until he pressed a damp face-washer into her hand, which she proceeded to use.

'There,' she murmured gently. 'That's better.'

Marcello hunkered down and took hold of his daughter's hand, only to mask his feelings as Nicki looked at him with large sorrow-filled eyes.

'I don't want Bisabuelo Ramon to die like Fred.'

He spared Shannay a quick, enquiring glance, then smoothed a hand over Nicki's head on hearing the brief explanation. 'Sometimes when people and animals are very very sick and medicine can no longer help them get better, they go to a special place where they're no longer in pain.'

'Like Fred.'

His smile held gentle warmth. 'Yes, just like Fred,' he agreed softly.

'I talked to Fred all the time when he was sick.'

'As you do when we visit Ramon, *si?*'

An earnest look entered her childish features and pierced his heart. 'Can we see him tomorrow?'

'Of course.'

'Every day?'

'Every day, I promise.'

'I like him a lot.'

'And he loves you very much.'

Nicki turned her head and looked at her mother. 'I think I'll go back to sleep now.'

The simplistic logic of children, Shannay perceived as she preceded Marcello out onto the gallery and quietly closed the door behind her.

He was close…too close, and she was conscious of the black T-shirt moulding his muscular frame, the jeans he'd quickly dragged on at the sound of Nicki's first cry.

Did he still sleep naked between the sheets?

Shannay tried to ignore the image that rose too readily to mind…and failed miserably.

How was it possible to crave the touch of a man she professed to hate?

It didn't make sense to be so *drawn,* to want to lean in against him, lift her mouth to his and savour all he chose to gift her.

Marcello caught the darkness in her eyes, the way her lower lip trembled a little…and lowered his head to her own, tasting the sweetness that was hers alone, heard the soft sigh whisper in her throat, and chose a gentle exploration that teased and tantalised, until she reached for him, holding his head fast as she angled her mouth into his own.

It felt good. *He* felt so good. The way his hands slid over her shoulders to rest at her waist as he drew her slender frame in against him, and she sensed his hunger, knew it met and matched her own.

His mouth became flagrantly sensual, deepening with devastating effect as he swept her steadily beyond rational thought to a place where nothing else mattered…except the need for more, so much *more.*

The long oversized T-shirt she wore proved no barrier to his questing hands as they sought the hemline and settled on silken flesh.

One hand cupped her bottom while the other slid to caress her breast, shaping the soft fullness as he brushed a thumb back and forth across the tender peak, feeling it swell and harden beneath his touch.

He eased his mouth free from her own and traced a path down the arched line of her throat to settle in the hollow at its base, before seeking the sensitive curve at the edge of her neck.

An open-mouthed kiss there sent a shivery sensation arching through her body, and her fingers sought and freed the snap fastening of his jeans in the need to explore warm muscle and sinew.

With one quick movement she tugged his T-shirt high and slid tactile fingers over the hard musculature beneath his ribcage, then slipped to trace his navel, before easing low over his arousal to cup his scrotum…and squeeze a little.

A husky growl sounded close to her ear, and strong hands slid beneath her knees as he carried her down to the master suite and used the heel of one foot to close the door before easing her down the hard length of his body to her feet.

Feverish hands rapidly dispensed with what clothes remained, and Shannay uttered a sharp cry as Marcello lifted her high and wrapped her thighs round his waist before lowering his mouth to her breast.

Sensation radiated from her central core, and she gasped out loud as he took the tender peak between his teeth and rolled it gently, taking her from intense pleasure almost to the edge of pain.

It was she who sought the curve at the edge of his neck…and suckled there, deliberately marking him before soothing the bite with the tip of her tongue.

He shifted slightly, and slowly lowered the most vulnerable and sensitive part of her anatomy over his swollen arousal, held her there, then gently rocked her until she groaned out loud in frustration.

'Now.' It was a muttered agonised plea he refused to heed, and she dug her fingers in his hair and tugged a little.

'Please.'

In one smooth movement he slid her down and onto him, then inch by tortuous inch until he filled her.

Oh, dear heaven, it felt so good. Joined with him, awash with coalescing sensation as passion escalated and demanded more.

It was then he moved to the bed and carefully eased her down onto the sheets, and she tossed her head in abject denial as he withdrew, then began a tracery of feather-light kisses over each breast in turn, pausing to savour there before moving lower over her abdomen.

She wanted his mouth on hers…except he had a different destination in mind, and she cried out as he sought the moist heat, laving the clitoris into vibrant, erotic life, sending her high with sensual spasms so intense she cried out as each wave consumed her body and reached right down to her soul.

Then, and only then did he enter her again, surging to the hilt in one powerful thrust, and she became boneless, so caught up with witching abandon she no longer knew who she was…only aware she never wanted this shameless rapture to end as she arched her body and took him again and again until they reached the brink, then soared together in glorious ecstasy.

It took a while for her rapid breathing to slow and return to something resembling normal, and she held on as he carefully rolled onto his back and took her with him, cradling her close, his lips buried against her temple.

It was then he felt the moistness on her cheek, and he smoothed a gentle hand over her hair, tucking some of it behind her ear as he searched her tear-filled eyes.

'I hurt you?'

She didn't trust herself to speak, and she simply shook her head.

He lifted a hand and brushed her cheek with his thumb, then he caressed her lips with his own, softly and with such tenderness fresh tears spilled and ran down each cheek in warm rivulets to pause at the edges of her mouth.

Light fingers traced her spine, soothing her as she buried her face into the curve of his neck.

She didn't want to move. Didn't feel as if she *could*.

Soon, she silently vowed, she'd disentangle herself from his arms, catch up her abandoned T-shirt, then quietly retreat to her room.

But for now she'd simply enjoy the aftermath of good sex. Very good sex, she amended silently, and felt the faint pull of unused muscles, the sheer euphoria of sensual fulfilment.

There was a part of her which yearned to be held through the night, to be comforted by the beat of Marcello's heart beneath her hand, her cheek. To move in the night and be gathered in close against him.

She must have dozed, for she drifted awake to the realisation of a warm body curved round her own, a steady heartbeat against her back…and memory surfaced in a slow, unfolding image.

No. It was a dream, surely? Like one of many which haunted her mind in the dark hours of night.

Yet this was no dream. The arms which held her were real. And she froze for a few interminable seconds, then carefully, slowly, she began to ease herself free. Only to feel those arms tighten as warm breath teased her hair.

'You're not going anywhere.'

'Please.' Her voice was a strangled whisper of sound, and she felt the press of his mouth against her nape.

'What if—?'

'Nicki?'

Ohmigod, *Nicki*. What was she thinking?

Be honest, a wicked voice taunted. You weren't *thinking* at all. 'If she wakes and I'm not there.' The words tumbled out in a rush, only to come to a halt as Marcello pressed a hand over her mouth.

'Don't,' he cautioned quietly as he cupped her face and

kissed her, slowly, lingeringly, as he felt his body harden with need and her own response.

With care he gathered her in, his persuasive touch wreaking havoc with her emotions as he branded her his own in a highly sensitised coupling that surpassed what they'd previously shared.

CHAPTER NINE

SHANNAY WOKE to the muted sound of the shower running, registered the large bed, the rumpled sheets…and closed her eyes in automatic reflex as memory provided a vivid image of what had transpired through the night and with whom.

If there was the slightest edge of doubt, her body bore numerous signs to disprove it. Not the least of which was the need to shower and retreat to her room to dress.

Nicki.

She reached out and checked her discarded watch, then let out her indrawn breath. Six. It was only six o'clock. Nicki rarely stirred before seven.

The shower ceased, and she hurriedly tossed back the covers and slid from the bed.

Where was her T-shirt? A hasty glance over the floor revealed nothing. Had Marcello picked it up?

Oh, hell, surely not Maria? At this early hour, the likelihood was so remote it was immediately dismissed.

So where the devil was it? She required *something* to cover her nudity, and she crossed to Marcello's walk-in wardrobe, selected the first shirt her fingers touched, slid an arm into each sleeve, then re-emerged into the bedroom at the same time Marcello emerged from the *en suite* with a towel hitched at his hips.

Broad shoulders, expanse of naked chest, the fluid flex of muscle as he towelled his hair dry, powerful thighs.

There was no chance she could escape before he saw her, and almost as if he sensed her presence he lowered his arms.

A slow smile curved his generous mouth as he caught her drinking in the sight of him, and his lips curved as her gaze slithered to a point near the vicinity of his left shoulder.

'Buenos dias.' His voice was a husky, intimate drawl as he crossed to stand within touching distance, and she was powerless to prevent the descent of his head as he covered her mouth with his own in a slow, evocative kiss.

Her eyes dilated with a conflicting mix of emotions as he lifted his mouth fractionally from her own, and he had no trouble determining each and every one of them.

'Marcello—'

He cut off the tumble of words by the simple expediency of brushing his lips over hers…and sensed rather than heard her soft moan in protest as it remained locked in her throat.

Her eyelids drifted down, only to spring open again seconds later as his hand cupped her breast and teased the tender peak before slipping down over her abdomen to the soft curls at the apex of her thighs.

His touch was incredibly gentle as he stroked the sensitive bud still acutely responsive from his attention, and he absorbed the slight hitch in her breath as he sent her spiralling to climax, then he held her until the spasms diminished.

For a moment the past didn't exist as he brushed his lips to each closed eyelid in turn before releasing her.

'Great fashion accessory, *mi mujer.*' He ran a finger down

the shirt's open edge, his gleaming gaze locking with hers. 'Although I prefer you without it.'

Shannay dragged the edges together in a delayed sense of modesty as she turned away from him.

He waited until she reached the door, then cautioned quietly, 'From now on you sleep here with me.'

She didn't answer, for she was unable to find the words in acquiescence or argument as she turned the door-handle and walked from the room.

It was a relief to discover Nicki still fast asleep, and she quickly showered, then dressed in a gypsy-style skirt in shades of brown and a fashionable top, dried her hair, caught it in a casual twist and anchored it with a wide hinged clip, added lipgloss, then heard her daughter begin to stir.

Breakfast was a convivial meal eaten out on the glass-enclosed terrace, and Shannay endeavoured to focus on Nicki's excited conversation with Marcello on learning they were to experience the Aquopolis theme park after their morning visit with Ramon.

Something she achieved with difficulty, given the distraction provided by Marcello's presence directly opposite.

If she looked at him, her eyes betrayed her as they settled briefly on his mouth, and recalled vividly its erotic tasting. How his hands had explored her body and gifted untold pleasure. And, ultimately, the sex.

Mind-blowing electrifying passion that liquefied her bones and made her *his* more thoroughly than any words he might offer.

It shouldn't have happened.

She should have done more than utter a weak-willed protest, then given in to the provocative power of his touch and its pagan promise to banish her restraint.

Worse, allow him to lead her through intoxicating desire to join him again and again in mesmeric primitive climax.

His possession had made her acutely aware of sensitive tissues, and she could still feel the slight throb deep within resulting from his sexual presence.

It was…entrancing, consuming, and made her supremely conscious of what they'd shared. And would again.

Unless she chose to deny him.

Except denying him meant also denying herself, and she hated the disruptive annihilating *need* he generated in her with such ease.

'Mummy, you're not listening.'

Shannay summoned a smile and avoided meeting Marcello's gaze as she gave Nicki her whole attention.

She knew what he would see, and she refused to allow him the benefit of reading her mind, for he managed to divine her innermost thoughts despite her efforts to the contrary.

'We need to pack swimming gear for the visit to Aquopolis?' She hazarded the guess, and heard his faint chuckle at Nicki's audible sigh.

'Daddy says we can take a picnic to another park. Not tomorrow, but the day after.'

'That sounds lovely, darling.' She noticed her daughter's empty cereal bowl. 'What would you like on your toast?'

A return to the prosaic might have fooled Nicki, but she doubted the man seated opposite was under any such illusion, and it was a relief to temporarily escape when the meal concluded.

Ramon appeared to have faded slightly, his air of fragility a little more pronounced, yet his smile was warm and his eyes displayed delight as Nicki greeted him with affection.

Their visit was brief, on medical advice, for he seemed to tire more easily with each passing day.

Aquopolis proved to be a wonderful attraction, with plenty of fun to keep Nicki enthralled for several hours, for there were slides and numerous water features. Add a picnic lunch, and their daughter pronounced it *heaven.*

It was late when they left, and Nicki barely made it through her bath and a light evening meal before falling asleep within seconds of her head touching the pillow.

Shannay retreated to her suite to shower and change for dinner…only to discover her clothes reposing in the capacious wardrobe were no longer there.

The few drawers into which she'd stowed some personal items were now empty, and when she examined the adjoining *en suite,* all of her toiletries and make-up had been removed.

Marcello?

Or Maria, acting on his instructions?

Whatever…transferring her and her belongings to the master suite wasn't going to happen.

One night's transgression was enough.

There wasn't going to be a repeat.

With that in mind, she walked the gallery to his suite and entered without bothering to knock.

The shower was running, and she quickly crossed to the second walk-in wardrobe, retrieved her clothing and tossed it onto the bed, then she gathered up her personal items and transferred them to her room further along the gallery before returning to clear what remained.

Drawers she'd utilised in the past held everything she needed, and she was in the process of scooping them out when a deep, drawling voice momentarily arrested the movement of her hands.

'Looking for something?'

She took a few seconds to draw a deep breath, then she turned to face him, hating the sudden traitorous curl unfurling deep inside at the sight of his near-naked frame.

'I'm not moving into your room.'

Marcello slanted an eyebrow. 'You'd prefer me to move into yours?'

Shannay wasn't deceived by his even tone. 'No.'

'Then we have a problem.'

'No, we don't.'

'You intend to slink in here in the dead of night and leave at dawn?'

She tilted her chin and sent him a steady look. 'Last night was—'

'An aberration? A mistake?' The dangerous silkiness in his voice took hold of her nerve-ends and tugged a little.

'We each became carried away and indulged ourselves with sex?'

A sudden lump rose in her throat, and she attempted to swallow it in order to speak. 'Yes.'

'Justify the night however you choose. It doesn't change where you'll sleep.'

He watched the colour leave her cheeks, and hardened his heart. 'The bed's large, and sex,' he gave the word a faint emphasis, 'won't be on the menu unless you choose for it to be.'

Share the same bed, lie within touching distance... 'You have to be joking!'

'No.' He turned and moved towards his walk-in wardrobe. 'I'm going to dress for dinner.' He paused fractionally.

'Transfer everything to your room, if that's what you want. But if you go to bed there, you'll wake up in mine.'

Shannay merely glared at him and marched into the *en suite,* where she stripped off her clothes and took a long, hot shower in the hope it might help diminish her anger.

OK, so it was war, she declared silently as she dried off with a towel, then she wound it sarong-style around her body, secured it above her breasts and re-entered the bedroom.

Marcello caught the heat of battle apparent, and veiled his eyes against a faint gleam of humour as he rolled back his shirt-cuffs, then slid his feet into comfortable leather loafers.

'Did anyone tell you you're *impossible?'*

He had the satisfaction of offering—*'Touché.'*

She bore the look of someone much younger than her years with unbrushed hair and features free of make-up.

He restrained the desire to cross the room, dispense with the towel and kiss her senseless.

The fact he *could* provided a degree of satisfaction.

'Maria has dinner waiting.'

Shannay almost told him precisely what he could do with dinner, except she didn't trust herself to speak. Instead she extracted fresh underwear from a drawer, caught up a dress, then disappeared into the *en suite* again.

In an act of defiance she took longer than necessary, and emerged to discover he was conversing in French on his cellphone.

She selected a pair of heeled sandals and secured the straps.

'Problems?' she queried sweetly as he closed the connection.

'Nothing I can't handle.'

'How…eminently satisfying to be the epitome of professionalism.'

He almost laughed, for she was unlike any woman he knew. 'Shall we adjourn downstairs?'

'Oh, by all means, let's adjourn.'

Sassy, definitely sassy. He wondered if she'd be quite so brave when they returned upstairs to retire for the night.

Maria had excelled herself, providing a rice pilaf to die for, a fresh salad, with a fruit flan for dessert.

'I'd like to take Nicki into the city tomorrow afternoon,' Shannay declared as she poured coffee, and made tea for herself.

'A shop-till-you-drop mission?'

She shook her head. 'Some small gifts to take home for a few of her friends. Something special for Anna.'

'On the condition both Carlo and I accompany you.'

'We could take the metro.'

'No.'

'A limousine and a bodyguard?' she queried with intentional mockery, and met his studied gaze.

'A necessary precaution.'

The Martinez billions were tied up in numerous corporations throughout the world. It was a given Marcello's personal fortune had escalated dramatically over the past four years.

So many assets. Yet only a few knew the extent of the Martinez benevolence to various charities, the hospitals they'd funded in third world countries.

It made the family a target. At risk from the insurgents who hated wealth and all it represented. The beautiful people who appeared to have everything while the less fortunate lived in tenements and fought for food.

During the two years of her marriage she'd given tirelessly of her time to help Penè organise events for charity, frequently suffering the older woman's acerbic tongue and endless criticism as they worked together.

Possibly Ramon's daughter saw it as a necessity to figuratively strengthen the spine of her nephew's wife, and her
manner had achieved that, not without some resentment and
restrained anger on Shannay's part at the time.

'If you insist,' Shannay conceded, aware that to argue with
him over the protection issue was a waste of time. 'On the condition you allow me to judge what purchases are bought. I
won't have Nicki acquire an inflated sense of her own importance and become a spoilt little madam.'

Marcello inclined his head. 'We'll drive into the city after
visiting with Ramon.'

'Thank you.'

She finished her tea, then she transferred everything from
the table onto a mobile trolley and wheeled it into the kitchen.
It took only minutes to stow food into the refrigerator and
stack the dishwasher.

'I need to make a few international calls, send some
emails,' Marcello informed as she returned to the dining room.

Good. With luck she'd be asleep in her room by the time
he came upstairs.

As a plan, it worked very well. Except she failed to take
into consideration he'd carry through with his threat.

For she came sharply awake as her room was flooded with
light, followed seconds later by firm hands lifting her effortlessly against a hard male chest as Marcello calmly carried
her along the gallery to the master suite.

'You fiend.' The accusation came out as a strangled whisper
as she clenched a fist and thumped it against his shoulder.

An action which had no effect whatsoever, and she angled
her head, then sank her teeth into hard muscle, heard his
indrawn breath and then yelped as he closed the door behind
him with one hand and released her to stand on the floor.

'Get into bed.' His voice was a silken drawl. 'And shut that sassy mouth, before I'm tempted to shut it for you.'

She cast him a furious look that should have withered him on the spot. 'Go to hell.'

Without a further word he hefted her over one shoulder and crossed to the bed, then he slid between the covers, placed her struggling body firmly to one side and curved his own around her.

A simple movement and the light was extinguished, and she lay there fuming, desperately wanting to fight, but aware precisely what it would lead to if she did.

'Go to sleep.'

Sure. That was likely!

Held close against him, absorbing his body heat, and attempting to ignore the intense sensuality apparent?

As if *sleep* was going to happen any time soon!

Yet the day's events coupled with the previous night finally caught up with her, and the last thing she remembered was feeling...safe.

Once again Shannay woke to find herself alone in the large bed, and she had a moment of displacement before realisation hit.

It was morning, she'd apparently slept through the night without waking, curled against the man she'd sworn not to be with...and the knowledge he'd won out raised her anger levels an extra notch or two.

Yet sleep was the operative word, for they hadn't...had they?

Of course not. Sex with Marcello wasn't something she had to think twice to recall!

The fact Marcello had kept his word rankled slightly. So too did the fact he'd held her close through the night and made no attempt to seduce her into awareness.

If he had, she would, she assured as she traversed the gallery to her room, have fought him tooth and nail.

So why this vague feeling of disappointment?

It didn't make sense.

She checked on Nicki, saw she was still asleep, and quickly tended to her usual early-morning routine, then she dressed in a skirt and knit-top. By which time Nicki was awake.

Marcello was nowhere in sight when they went downstairs to breakfast, and he joined them with an apology as she was in the process of helping Nicki peel back the shell of her boiled egg.

With childish happiness Nicki lifted her face to accept the brush of his lips to her cheek, and returned the favour.

Shannay felt her eyes widen as he crossed to her side and bestowed a similar salutation…unusual in their daughter's presence, and one which garnered her surprise.

What was he playing at?

A discussion regarding plans on the day's agenda saw them through breakfast, and there was time for Nicki to develop her swimming skills before drying off and retreating upstairs to change.

Lunch was a leisurely meal eaten out on the covered terrace, followed by a siesta.

There was a part of her that wanted to play tourist, to wander at will, pause at a café for refreshments and hunt for bargains.

Except with Marcello and Carlo in attendance, playing tourist wasn't going to happen.

They'd agreed to meet in the foyer at four, visit Ramon, then head into the city.

She chose a black tailored straight skirt and white blouse, added minimum make-up and twisted the length of her hair into a knot atop her head. Stilettos completed the outfit and she collected a shoulder-bag, caught Nicki's hand, then together they descended the stairs to the foyer.

She met Marcello's speculative gaze with equanimity, glimpsed the faint gleam apparent in those dark eyes and lifted her head fractionally.

'Ready?'

An innuendo? For battle, or the afternoon ahead. She decided to be generous and go with the latter.

Ramon appeared to be enjoying a reasonable day, and Nicki regaled him with her exploits at the Aquopolis, and her excitement at visiting Madrid city.

The elderly man's pleasure in his great-granddaughter's company was reciprocal, and despite the tremendous age difference their mutual rapport was something to see.

Even short visits tended to tire Ramon, and they took their leave when his attendant nurse indicated he should rest.

Once they were seated in the Porsche four-wheel-drive Marcello handed Shannay a leather folder.

'For your use.'

Inside the zipped compartment was a list of numbers, personal, business and emergency. A bank account and affiliated high-end credit card in the name of Shannay Martinez.

Definite overkill for a sojourn lasting a matter of weeks.

She looked at him carefully, and was unable to discern anything from his expression. 'Thank you,' she acknowledged quietly. 'But I have money of my own.'

His eyes speared hers, dark and impossibly enigmatic, and for a moment she thought he meant to insist. Instead he merely inclined his head.

'Your prerogative.'

She turned her attention to Nicki as Marcello pointed out places of interest.

Madrid city bore little change. Brilliant architecture vied with the old, and there was an air of timelessness, of great history.

Carlo dropped them off and moved on to find parking, while Marcello settled Nicki into the curve of one arm.

Exclusive boutiques were dotted along the Calle de Serrano and interconnecting avenues, bearing ruinously expensive designer labels so far beyond her budget there seemed little point engaging the vendeuse's attention.

Except what was a visit to Madrid city without viewing the superb leather-goods, the shoes and bags? Or window-shopping at Las Perlas, Loewe's and Prada?

Carlo met up with them, and together he and Marcello flanked her as they strolled and browsed.

It brought to mind the clothes Marcello had insisted on gifting her during the early years of her marriage...all of which she'd left behind. Had he consigned them to charity?

Nicki enjoyed the overall view from her vantage position held in the curve of her father's arm, and there were purchases Marcello insisted on making.

His prerogative, he insisted as he gifted his daughter a beautiful dress, cropped trousers, tops and shoes.

Shannay's protest was ignored, and she didn't have the heart to deny Nicki so much pleasure.

The shops closed their doors at eight, and Marcello selected a café and ordered a light evening meal for Nicki, while he and Carlo drank coffee and Shannay opted for tea.

It was after nine when they reached the La Moraleja mansion, and Marcello carried a visibly wilting Nicki upstairs to her room, where Shannay quickly bathed and tucked her into bed.

The thought of eating a meal comprising more than a light salad didn't appeal, and for a moment she looked longingly at her own bed, barely resisting the temptation to shed her own clothes, shower and slip beneath the bedcovers.

Except Marcello would come find her, and she didn't feel inclined to clash verbal swords with him tonight.

Spanish mealtimes were unusually late by Australian standards, and she picked at the succulent salad, refused a portion of excellent sirloin and selected a delectable peach in lieu of dessert.

'Thank you for gifting Nicki her new clothes.'

'My pleasure.' He doubted she realised just how much it meant to see the wonder in his daughter's eyes, her joy at receiving gifts, and the small arms that wound round his neck in childish gratitude.

It was beyond price, the unconditional love of a child. His child. A child he had no intention of giving up for months at a time while she resided with her mother on the other side of the world.

The meal came to its conclusion, and Marcello excused himself with the need to spend some time in his home office, and Shannay began transferring the table's contents into the kitchen.

Upstairs she checked on Nicki, then she crossed through to her own room and stripped down to her briefs, removed her make-up, then she slid between the sheets.

It was there Marcello found her two hours later, and he stood regarding her recumbent form with a degree of musing exasperation.

And need. Damnable need for the one woman who vowed she didn't want him. Only to have her come alive beneath his touch.

With care he reached down, lifted her into his arms and carried her to his bed, all too aware of her near-naked form, the soft silkiness of her skin and the desire hardening his body.

CHAPTER TEN

THE ENSUING FEW DAYS followed a similar pattern with morning visits with Ramon, followed by an outing for Nicki's benefit with Carlo in attendance.

Together they spent hours at the Warner Bros Park at San Martin de la Vega, and, perhaps the most exciting of all, the Parque de Atracciones.

A magical time for a child, Shannay accorded indulgently as Nicki fell asleep each night before the first page was turned of her bedtime story.

As to the nights… Attempting to sleep in her own suite, only to find herself waking in Marcello's bed, became an exercise in futility. Accepting she was no match for her husband irked unbearably.

Eventually she admitted defeat and slid into his bed at the end of another tiring day.

Where she stayed. Not, she assured herself, because she *wanted* to…merely to prove she could lie within touching distance and *sleep*…eventually.

She just wickedly hoped he *suffered*.

As she did, when he gathered her close…yet made no further move. A hand that slid to her breast…and remained still. Or rested on her hip, and stayed there.

Was he deliberately testing her?

Maybe she should respond in kind and test *him*.

Except such a move could be tricky. What if he divined it as an indicative sanction for sex?

Then she would not only lose the battle, she'd also lose the war.

And that would never do.

The weekend brought Marcello's obligatory attendance at a gala event lauded by the city's scions.

Invitation only, black tie, and Shannay was apprised of the need to wear something *stunning* by Penè, who had stopped by the mansion to visit Nicki.

The unspoken message was very clear, and racked up Shannay's nervous tension to unbelievable heights during a shopping expedition the day before with Marcello's aunt in attendance for *the* gown, stilettos and accessories.

It was an indisputable fact that Penè *knew* fashion as they progressed from one boutique to another, and they eventually settled on a dream of a gown by Armani in pale peach and apricot silk chiffon. Full-length, the skirt was cut on the bias and bore a clever bias-cut overlay in peach over apricot. A silk chiffon stole added an extra elegance, and Shannay could only applaud Penè's selection.

Exquisite evening sandals and matching evening bag were added to the growing collection Carlo stowed in the back of the Porsche.

Penè was in her element, clearly revelling in playing the *grande dame* with the various *vendeuses,* and enjoying their obsequious attention.

Shannay found it all a bit much as the evening closing hours drew near.

'Minimum jewellery,' Marcello's aunt stated. 'The gown requires little enhancement. Your hair should be confined in a sleek style, definitely not loose. Understated make-up with emphasis on the eyes and mouth.'

'I agree.'

'You look peaky.' Penè eyes were piercing above her patrician nose. 'Is my nephew keeping you awake nights?'

Oh, my. A *yes* or *no* would be an equally incriminating response.

The look sharpened. 'Are you pregnant?'

Now that was a definite negative. 'No.'

'You should have another child,' Penè said bluntly. 'Marcello needs a son to take the Martinez name into the next generation.'

She couldn't help herself. 'He already has a daughter.'

'A son,' Penè insisted imperiously. 'Named Ramon, in honour of my father.'

'What if I were to consider filing for divorce?' She chose not to reveal she'd already set the legalities in motion.

'Divorce for a Martinez isn't an option. Marcello would refuse to countenance such a thing.' She looked suitably astonished. 'Foolish girl. What are you thinking? He can give you everything you desire.'

Except the one thing I want.

His heart.

I gave him mine, unconditionally…only to discover he didn't value it.

'I think we're done,' Shannay said aloud. She even managed a faint smile as Carlo added another emblem-emblazoned designer bag to their mounting collection.

Carlo delivered Penè to Ramon's residence, then continued to La Moraleja.

Nicki was tucked in bed with Marcello seated on its edge as he read from a storybook when Shannay entered the bedroom.

Attired in black jeans and a black chambray shirt, he looked totally at ease, and she tamped down the emotional reaction stirring deep within at the mere sight of him.

Pheronomes, intense sexual awareness…it was attraction at its most dangerous, and need, basic and earthy, pulsed through her body.

She remembered only too well when she had only to look at him to witness the secret promise in those dark eyes, and know how the night would end…as it almost always did.

A time when they couldn't get enough of each other.

Until the doubts crept in, and everything began to change.

'Mummy!'

There was time out for a mutual kiss and a hug before Nicki settled back against the pillow.

'Daddy and me went swimming in the pool. And I've had dinner and a bath.' Brown eyes widened. 'And I cleaned my teeth.'

'Well done,' Shannay said with warmth, including both man and child, and incurred a studied appraisal. 'Thanks,' she added quietly.

'No problem.' He glimpsed the faint edge of pain, the aftermath of several hours in Penè's company. 'A productive afternoon?'

'I'm sure we maxed your credit card.'

A faint smile tugged the edges of his mouth. 'Doubtful.'

Yes, she supposed it was, and she added— 'Thank you. Penè's help was invaluable.'

But tiring, he deduced, all too aware of his aunt's incessant need to constantly verbalise with an opinion on everything in an often uncompromising manner.

'Can I see what you bought?'

Marcello leant forward and lightly touched Nicki's cheek. 'In the morning, *pequena*. Now let's find out what happens to Cinderella, shall we?'

'She goes to the ball and comes home in a pumpkin,' Nicki relayed solemnly, and Marcello smiled.

'I think you've heard this story before.'

'It's my favourite.'

One of many, Shannay reflected as she sat down on the opposite side of the bed while Marcello finished reading, by which time Nicki had fallen asleep, and Shannay turned down the light and preceded him from the room.

'I'll go change, then meet you downstairs.' The thought of food held little appeal. Given a choice she'd prefer to eat at the time of the late-afternoon *merienda,* as Nicki did.

A quick shower proved refreshing, and she slipped into dress jeans, pulled on a short-sleeved rib-knit top in a deep coral, twisted her hair into a loose knot, then added lipgloss.

Dinner comprised a light omelette with salad, followed by fresh fruit, during the eating of which they caught up on their individual afternoon activities.

'Penè was suitably restrained?'

Shannay took a careful sip of water and replaced the glass down onto the table before directing Marcello a pensive look.

'You want polite?'

He pushed his plate to one side and viewed her with speculative interest. 'I'm very familiar with my aunt's penchant for plain speaking.'

'In essence, I'm peaky…the cause of which must be you keeping me awake nights, or I'm pregnant. Preferably the latter, as it's my duty to provide you with another child. A son.'

Marcello sank back in his chair. 'I'm intrigued to hear your response.'

'Let's just say it invoked the reminder a Martinez would never countenance divorce.'

His eyes seared her own. 'You can have whatever you want, Shannay…with one exception. A divorce.'

A sudden lump rose in her throat, and she swallowed it carefully. 'I don't want gifts, haute couture or a high-profile social life. They mean nothing to me. They never did.'

'Yet we share the gift of a child.'

'The one thing I won't let you take away from me,' Shannay vowed with renewed fervour, and something flickered in the depths of his eyes before it was successfully masked.

'It was never my intention to do so.'

'Yet you'd consign us both to a convenient marriage where we maintain a façade in public?' Her eyes darkened, and pain curled deep inside. 'For what purpose, Marcello?' She drew in a slightly ragged breath. 'Revenge…because I didn't inform you of Nicki's existence?'

'Is that what you think?'

'I think you're playing a game,' she flung, sorely tried as she rose to her feet.

Dignity and pride. She possessed both, and she walked away from him without a further glance, uncaring whether he followed or not.

Sleep proved elusive, and she tossed and turned, only to slip out of bed and take something to ease a tension headache.

Eventually she must have slept, for she came awake aware she was no longer in her own bed, but held in strong masculine arms as Marcello traversed the dimly lit gallery *en route* to his own suite.

'Put me down!' Her voice was little more than a sibilant hiss as she struggled against him.

Without success, and she balled a fist and lashed out uncaring as to where it landed.

In a matter of seconds he entered the suite, closed the door behind him, then released her down to stand in front of him.

Shannay glared at him in open defiance, hating him in that instant as she ignored the darkness evident in his eyes and the bunched muscle at the edge of his jaw.

'This is ridiculous. You're *impossible!*' She released a growl of frustration.

'That's the best you can do?'

She ignored his indolent drawl, the waiting, watching quality in his stance…and launched into a barely restrained diatribe that used every emotive adjective she could recall.

One eyebrow slanted as she came to a halt, and he posed silkily, 'You're done?'

'*Yes,* dammit!'

'Good.'

He captured her shoulders and drew her in, then he closed his mouth over her own, took all the fiery heat and tamed it, ignoring her flailing fists as they faltered and fell to her sides.

He wanted her unbidden response, and deliberately sought it, sensing the low groan deep in her throat as she fought against capitulation. Followed soon after by the involuntary slide of her tongue against his own, the sudden hitch in her breath as she angled her head and allowed him free access.

One hand slid to her nape, while the other moved down her back, bunched the oversized T-shirt and slipped beneath the cotton fabric to cup and gently squeeze her bottom.

His body tightened unbearably and he lifted her, eased her thighs apart, then positioned her to accept his fully aroused length as he eased into the slick, welcoming heat, heard her faint sigh…and surged in to the hilt.

Then it was his turn to bite back a guttural sound as her vaginal muscles enclosed him, and he began to move, creating a rhythm that sent them both high until they reached the brink, then soared together in a shattering climax.

At some stage Marcello had dispensed with her T-shirt, although she had no recollection of *when,* only that she was naked in his arms and his lips were tantalising hers, nibbling and teasing until she held fast his head and kissed him with such exquisite eroticism he was hard-pressed not to take her again.

Instead he crossed to the bed, eased down onto his back with her sitting astride him.

Her mouth was softly swollen, and his eyes darkened as she lifted both hands and tucked her hair behind each ear. The movement lifted her breasts, and he traced their soft curves, teased the tender peaks…and watched her eyes glaze over.

They were both at each other's mercy, and she shifted deliberately, glimpsed the increasing darkness apparent in his gleaming gaze, then she gave a startled cry as he brought her down and took one tender peak into his mouth.

Intense pleasure spiralled through her body as he suckled, and a warning hiss escaped from her lips as he caught the swollen bud between his teeth and rolled it to the point beyond pleasure to the imminent edge of pain.

It made her acutely vulnerable, and she opened her mouth to plead with him, only for the pressure to ease as he soothed the tender peak.

Then he wrapped his arms around her slender frame and rolled until she lay beneath him. For a moment he drank in the sight of her, the wildness of her hair, the sensual glow warming her skin, and the magical passion they shared.

She moistened her lips, and he drove into her only to almost withdraw before repeating the action again and again, increasing the intensity of the rhythm until she joined him in a climax more shattering than the first.

Afterwards he gathered her close and rested his lips against her temple in the lazy afterglow of spent passion.

Shannay was close to sleep when he manoeuvred her onto her tummy and began a wonderfully soothing massage of her neck and shoulders, easing out the kinks there before slipping down to knead her calf muscles and finally her feet.

His lips pressed a trail of light kisses over her leg, bit gently into the globe of her bottom, then eased up to her nape.

She turned into him and rested her mouth into the curve at the base of his throat, murmured something indistinct, then drifted into deep sleep.

The gala event held in one of the city's splendid theatres appeared to be a sell-out, with numerous fashionistas vying for supremacy in designer gowns and exquisite jewellery.

The *crème de la crème* of Madrid society, patrons of the arts, who paid an exorbitant ticket price to attend the evening's classical production.

In pairs, small groups, they gathered in the large foyer, and Shannay stood at Marcello's side with a ready smile in place as guests mixed and mingled.

Tall, dark, impeccably groomed, his evening suit a perfect tailored fit, pristine white shirt and black bow-tie, he looked the epitome of the powerful, sophisticated male.

He stood out from the rest. Not so much for his attractive features or his clothing, but for the primitive aura he projected beneath the hard-muscled frame…a disruptive sensuality that threatened much and promised to deliver.

It drew women to him like bees to a honeypot, and there were those who simply adored to flirt, while a few made moves, subtle and not so subtle, to attract his attention.

In the early days of their marriage she'd hugged to her heart the knowledge he was *hers,* believing nothing and no one could harm what they shared.

How naive she had been!

'Ah, there you are.'

Shannay turned and met Penè's encompassing appraisal, caught the brief nod of approval and leant forward to bestow the obligatory air-kiss to each cheek.

'How is Ramon?'

'Fading. The physician expects him to lapse into a coma within the next few days. Sandro and Luisa are with him.'

Such an incredibly sad end for a man who had once headed the Martinez empire.

'I'm so sorry.' Shannay's empathy was genuine, and Marcello's aunt inclined her head in acknowledgment.

'Tonight may well be the last public engagement at which the family appear. The usual mourning period will understandably be observed.'

'Of course.'

'I must greet Pablo and Angelique Santanas,' Penè announced, and melted into the crowd.

Soon the massive doors swung open and the guests gradually drifted into the auditorium to take their seats.

The classical performance proved superb, with brilliant costumes and high-tempo music. Stirring, passionate, with a touch of pathos.

A break between Act I and II proved welcome, so too when the curtain came down after the second act.

'Can I get you something to drink?' Marcello asked as they entered the foyer.

'Anything chilled and non-alcoholic,' Shannay requested with a faint smile, and watched as he signalled a hovering waiter.

It was only a matter of minutes later when she turned slightly and saw Estella moving towards them.

Oh, *joy*.

The woman resembled a picture-perfect Latin doll attired in a Spanish-inspired chiffon gown in stunning red and white diagonal chiffon frills that moved with exquisite fluidity at every step she took.

Sexy, Shannay accorded silently. Very deliberately sexy, from the top of her gloriously coiffured head to the tip of her beautiful lacquered toenails in matching red.

'Shannay.' The greeting was polite, brief, then Estella gave Marcello her full attention.

'*Querido.*'

Could a woman's voice purr?

Definitely.

'Estella.'

Hmm, was that a tinge of warning beneath Marcello's pleasant tone?

Play polite, Shannay bade silently as she summoned a smile and offered an innocuous remark...which Estella totally ignored.

'We are thinking of going on to a nightclub afterwards. Perhaps you'd care to join us?'

'Thank you. No,' Marcello responded civilly, and the woman offered a convincing pout.

'Your wife—' she gave the word a faint emphasis and touched a lacquered nail to the lapel of his jacket '—accompanies you, and you become less fun.'

'Perhaps,' Marcello drawled, carefully removing her hand, 'my wife provides all the fun I need.'

Estella cast Shannay a look that contained thinly veiled mockery. 'Indeed?'

In some instances silence was golden, Shannay perceived. This wasn't one of them.

'Marcello is a superb tutor. Don't you agree?'

Estella's gaze shifted to Marcello as she ran the tip of her tongue over her upper lip and offered a knowing smile. 'The best, darling.'

It's an act, she qualified. A deliberate attempt to undermine.

Four years ago she would have taken the bait.

Now she simply offered quietly, 'Yet he chose not to marry you. Why was that, do you suppose?'

The faint disbelief evident before it was quickly masked should have brought a sense of satisfaction.

Except instinct warned Shannay that Estella would merely choose her moment for the next verbal strike.

'Possibly I decided he wasn't the best *marriage* material?' She waited a few seconds, then honed in sweetly, 'Isn't that why you left him?'

Bitch.

If she asserted Marcello hunted her down, she'd leave herself open for Estella to drag Nicki into the verbal equation, and she refused to allow that.

'No.'

The supercilious arched eyebrow did it.

Forget politeness. 'Go find your husband, Estella.' The silent implication "and leave mine alone" was clearly evident.

The mocking smile conceded nothing as the socialite turned with a slow, deliberately sensual movement and began weaving her way through the gathered patrons.

'Your support was gratifying,' Shannay noted quietly, unsure whether she was pleased or relieved, and bore his appraisal.

'You were doing so well on your own.'

'She's a—'

'Femme fatale,' Marcello drawled. 'Who thrives on playing games with the vulnerable.'

Her chin tilted and her eyes lanced his own. 'The term *vulnerable* no longer applies to me.'

Marcello cast her a musing glance as he caught hold of her hand and brushed a soothing thumb over the veins at her wrist, where the quickened beat of her pulse belied her contrived air of calm.

The intervening years had provided a level of maturity and independence he could only admire.

With every passing day his desire for revenge lessened, and it irked him, for he wanted to make her pay for denying him the experience of her pregnancy, the birth, and his daughter's infancy.

There was still a degree of anger beneath the surface vying with an overpowering physical need he fought hard to control.

As she did.

Two opposing forces caught up with events of the past, and fighting to reconcile their future.

A future he was determined to secure.

Shannay felt a sense of relief when it came time to be seated for the third and final act.

Marcello enclosed her hand in his throughout, and his fingers merely tightened whenever she tried to withdraw.

Once he lifted their joined hands to his lips, brushed hers lightly, then rested them on his lap, and her heart jumped and refused to settle for what seemed an age.

His arousal beneath the conventional clothing was a potent hidden force, and it took considerable effort to focus on the players on the stage as the act progressed towards its conclusion.

She didn't move, could barely bear to breathe, and she was never more glad of the theatre's darkened interior.

Dear heaven, did his aunt notice?

She sincerely hoped not, and refused to glance in Penè's direction.

It was a tremendous relief when the curtain came down, then rose again to applause, and the lights came on.

Exiting the auditorium became a slow process, noisy with audience chatter against muted background recorded music, and there was the obligatory pause or ten when they reached the foyer and moved towards the main entrance.

Penè bade them goodnight as her car and driver pulled into the kerb, followed minutes later as Carlo eased their own car to a halt.

They were scarcely seated when Marcello reached for her hand and threaded his fingers through her own.

Shannay attempted to free them without success, and she looked at him in silent askance.

What was he doing?

They had no audience, no one to impress with their pretended togetherness.

Twice she endeavoured to pull free during the drive to La Moraleja, and he refused to allow her to succeed.

When they reached the mansion he drew her indoors, then he simply lifted her over one shoulder and made for the stairs.

'What in hell are you playing at?'

'Taking you to bed.'

'I can walk,' she assured his back in scandalous tones, and heard his husky laughter.

'Humour me.'

'Aren't you in the least wary I might kick you where it hurts?'

'Don't try it, *querida*. You'll spoil the fun, and I can promise you won't like my retaliation.'

'Fun? You think it's *fun* being hauled around like a sack of potatoes?'

They reached the gallery and, at its end, the master suite, where he slid her down to her feet.

Without a word he caught her close and kissed her...gently at first, savouring the taste and texture of her lips, her mouth. Then with a sensual intensity that reached right down and took hold of her soul.

She was helpless, mindless, and barely aware of his fingers releasing the zip fastening on her dress...until it slithered to the floor in a silken heap. Her bra came next, followed by the satin briefs, and she gasped as he cupped her breast and lowered his mouth to suckle its peak.

A hand slid down over her stomach and sought the moist warmth at the apex of her thighs, and the breath hitched in her throat.

'Undress me.'

He helped her dispense with his clothes, his shoes, as she slid out of stilettos, then he lifted her onto the bed and moved down beside her.

The trail of his lips followed the same path as his fingers as he brought her to climax again and again, until she cried out, begging for the release only he could give.

It was then he sought the moist heat with his fully engorged penis and thrust in to the hilt in one forceful movement, waited until she caught her breath, and sought the familiar rhythm that sent them both soaring to unbelievable heights, held them there in a spectacular climax, then tipped them over the brink in a slow, sensual free-fall.

Later, much later, she gifted him a tasting that left the breath hissing through his clenched teeth, and tested his control to the limit.

It was her turn to cry out as he pulled her on top of him and took her for the ride of her life.

CHAPTER ELEVEN

TWO DAYS LATER Ramon slipped into a coma, from which he never recovered, and his funeral was a private family occasion, followed by a memorial service attended by close friends, family and captains of industry.

It was an infinitely sad time for them all, especially Penè who went into a decline and cancelled everything on her social calendar for an unspecified time.

Ramon's will distributed his considerable personal fortune equally between Penè, Marcello, Sandro…and Nicki.

Marcello and Shannay were named as Nicki's trustees, and the inheritance made their daughter a very rich little girl.

Marcello's presence was required in the city on frequent occasions during the ensuing week. Days when he left early and returned late, sometimes long after Nicki had fallen asleep.

To compensate he rang and spoke to his daughter through the day and again before she went to bed.

Shannay filled the days as best she could, supervising Nicki with her swimming, reading, finger-painting and constructing models with play-dough.

She also offered to assist Penè in any way possible, without success.

'Leave her grieve,' Marcello advised when she broached

it one evening after he arrived home late. 'She needs to come to terms with Ramon's death in her own time, in her own way.'

She looked at him carefully, noting the lines fanning out from the corners of his eyes seemed more pronounced, the grooves slashing his cheeks a little deeper.

'And you, Marcello?'

'Concerned for me, *querida?*'

'Perhaps. A little.'

He discarded his suit jacket, loosened his tie, toed off his shoes, then he reached for her, pulling her close to kiss her deeply, taking his time before he lifted his mouth from her own.

'Come share my shower.'

She tilted her head to one side and regarded him thoughtfully. 'That could be dangerous.'

His eyes gleamed and he gave a husky chuckle. 'So take the risk and live a little.'

'In the shower?'

His fingers slid to the hem of her singlet top and pulled it free from the waistband of her jeans, stripped her of it in one easy movement, then he undid the clip on her bra.

'Since when has that presented a problem?'

He reached for the snap on her jeans, slid the zip down and eased the denim over her hips.

It felt so good to have his hands shape her slender form, to drift his fingers over the highly sensitive curve at the base of her neck, the touch of his lips to her nape, the gentle tactile exploration that unfurled a capricious sexuality and became raw with hunger...for him, only him.

He branded her with his mouth, the edges of his teeth in a coupling that was explosive, primitive as he demanded her compliance and made her his own.

It said much as she lost herself in him and became greedy,

meeting him with each thrust as she urged him almost to a point of savagery, and she held on, soaring with him to unbelievable heights in a sexual climax more pagan than any they'd previously shared.

Afterwards he simply rested his cheek against her temple as their breathing slowed, and the water cascaded over their bodies slick with sexual sweat.

He said something in Spanish beneath his breath, then trailed his mouth down to capture hers in a kiss so incredibly gentle, her eyes shimmered with emotive tears.

With care, he took the soap and smoothed it over her body, his eyes dark and impossibly slumberous as he caught the faint pink smudges marking her tender flesh.

When he was done, she took the soap from his hand and returned the favour, exulting in the hard musculature, olive skin darker than her own, and the inherent masculinity that was intensely male and his alone.

It took a while before they pulled on towelling robes and emerged into the bedroom.

Her cellphone beeped intermittently, alerting a text message, and a slight frown creased her forehead as she read the text.

'Anything urgent?' Marcello queried as he discarded the robe and slid naked between the bedcovers.

'It's John,' she relayed slowly, meeting his gaze. 'He wants to know when he can expect me back.'

His eyes darkened, and he went completely still. 'You won't be returning to Perth.'

Shannay opened her mouth, then closed it again. 'Marcello, my job, my life, everything is there.'

'It was never *there* from the moment I discovered Nicki's existence.'

Oh, dear lord. 'You don't understand,' she protested, feeling sick and slightly stricken as she took in his hardened features.

'Make me understand,' Marcello began in a dangerously silky tone. 'How you can lose yourself in my arms night after night…and yet still want to leave.'

He had her there, and she felt suddenly bereft of words. Too ashamed to admit he held the power to render her wanton and solely his. To need him as a flower in the desert craved water in order to survive.

That without him, she simply existed.

'You asked me to stay longer for Ramon's sake, and I have.'

Say it, she begged silently. Say you care. Tell me I mean something to you.

'Leaving isn't an option.' The reiteration held an adamant non-negotiation hardness that chilled her to the bone.

There was only one thing she could do, and she tightened the belt on her robe and moved to the door.

'I'll sleep in another room.'

It killed her to walk through the door and close it quietly behind her.

Stupid tears gathered and rolled slowly down each cheek as she traversed the gallery to the suite she'd occupied during the initial few days after her arrival.

For some reason she needed to check on Nicki, to see her sweet face in sleep, and try to quantify her wayward emotions.

The dim night-light revealed a child at peace, silently trusting, and so much a part of her just the thought brought an ache to her throat.

Nicki was happy here…and hadn't that been the object of this excursion?

A visit, to help Nicki adjust to spending time with her father. Thinly disguised custody posing as holidays.

Preparation for what the future would involve.

Shannay had never in her wildest imagination expected the visit to be anything else.

Yet she hadn't counted on being so acutely vulnerable to the father of her child. Or to remember so vividly what they'd shared.

She'd been a fool. Incredibly naive not to foresee maintaining a formal relationship couldn't last long.

Had he knowingly plotted just this outcome? Planned to seduce her and force her to stay?

Even get her pregnant?

It was a long time before she fell into an uneasy sleep, and late next morning when she woke.

Nicki was happily ensconced in the kitchen beneath Maria's care, and relayed Marcello had left early for the city.

There was a need to do something constructive with the day, preferably away from the house.

Shopping held no appeal but, recalling how much Nicki had loved the children's section of the Parque de Attracciones, Shannay thought it would be great to enjoy a return visit.

With Carlo in attendance, of course.

It was relatively easy to arrange, and they set off with a delighted little girl whose excitement became infectious as the day progressed.

The rides, the people, the other children and the carnival-like atmosphere helped diminish Shannay rehashing the fallout from John's text message.

How could she remain in Madrid when there were unresolved issues?

Worse, how could she bear to stay in a marriage simply because of *convenience?* Even more disturbing…consider adding another child?

It wasn't enough to *pretend*. To attempt to believe the marriage was alive and healthy simply because the sex was good.

Oh, tell it like it is, why don't you? It's fantastic…off the Richter scale.

She'd been there, suffered, and thrown in the towel.

Why put herself through it again?

Except you're already in over your head.

Admit it.

Something…instinct, maternal or otherwise, alerted her attention.

Nicki. Where was *Nicki?*

Fear, panic, both meshed into something incredibly frightening as she consciously searched for the red top and cropped jeans Nicki was wearing, the bright red bow in her hair…felt her heart leap when she thought she caught a glimpse of red, only to have her hopes dashed seconds later.

Carlo? Where in hell was Carlo?

How could they *both* be missing?

'Please, have you seen a little girl…' She began frantically questioning one stranger after another, some of the children…in a mixture of English and Spanish as she described Nicki and her clothing…to which she received visual concern, the shake of a head, *nothing*.

Oh, dear God. She prayed, made deals with the deity, and in a moment of common sense extracted her cellphone and rang Marcello's private number on speed dial.

He picked up on the second tone, listened to her garbled explanation and issued an icily calm directive.

'Stay where you are. I'm on my way.'

He immediately excused himself from an important meeting, made a personal call to the chief of police, issued orders to various staff as he had his car brought kerb-side in front of the building's main entrance, and he attempted to make contact with Carlo.

By the time he arrived at the *parque*, he'd gathered an overview of the situation…and Carlo's cellphone had been switched off.

So too had the personal tracking device he carried at all times when leaving the house.

Two factors which sent alarm bells screaming inside Marcello's head.

Nicki's existence had been kept as low-profile as possible. Except it didn't take a mathematician to work out the value of a child with direct connections to the Martinez dynasty. Factor in Ramon's recent demise, and the value accelerated a thousandfold.

The abductors had to be professionals. Carlo was the best, and if they'd slipped beneath his alert surveillance it had to be a highly planned operation.

Shannay saw Marcello the instant he came into view, and she looked at him in silent desperation as he joined her.

There was little evident in his expression as he gathered her close, and one glance at her pale features was sufficient for him to reassure,

'Don't blame yourself.'

Then he began firing questions over the top of her head.

His presence did little to ease the panic pumping through her body. She was too stunned to cry, too inwardly frozen to do more than operate on some form of automatic pilot as police joined the *parque*'s security personnel.

The majority of their rapid Spanish went beyond her comprehension, and she stood at Marcello's side, endeavouring to dismiss numerous images too horrifying to contemplate.

How could Marcello deal with the situation with such apparent *calm?*

Shannay searched his features, caught the clenched muscle at the edge of his jaw, heard the tightness in his voice…and exchanged calm for control.

There would be a phone call.

Wasn't that how a kidnapping unfolded?

She was a total mess, mentally and emotionally, desperately wanting to rewind the clock, wishing she hadn't taken her eye off Nicki for a second.

For that was all it had taken.

'Carlo? Who are these men?' Nicki's small hand tightened within his own. 'Where are they taking us?'

Carlo was wired, he'd already activated the panic button, but any minute soon they'd pat him down…and any existing contact would be lost.

The important thing was to protect his charge. To minimise the impact of the kidnapping and to remain alert for any eventuality.

'Just a little ride, *pequena*,' he assured gently. 'It's OK.'

His training served him well, and no one, especially the child whose trust in him at this moment was unconditional, guessed beneath his calm persona there was a concealed Glock aimed right at his kidney.

They reached a nondescript dark-coloured van, the rear doors opened and Carlo lifted Nicki and deposited her on the metal floor.

'There aren't any seats to sit on,' Nicki whispered as he leaned in close.

He watched her eyes widen as he spread his arms and legs wide…hiding, he hoped, the fact he was being competently searched, his sports watch taken in case it contained an alert device.

A guttural oath sounded from behind as the taped wire was discovered, and he clenched his teeth as it was wrenched free. Then a hard metal object slammed into his kidneys, his hands were cuffed and he was pushed into the van, managing by reflex action to roll into an upright position without making a sound. Difficult when suffering excruciating pain.

'I don't like those men.'

Neither did he.

The doors slammed shut, he heard the lock catch, followed seconds later by the faint throb of the engine.

'We're going on an adventure,' Carlo offered gently. 'Shall I tell you a story?'

There was a tiny electronic device in his shoe. Virtually a panic button, which when activated provided a direct link to the police. As long as the device remained undetected, it would allow the police to track their whereabouts.

It wouldn't be too difficult to extract, but he couldn't risk Nicki asking what he was doing.

On the off-chance a listening device was planted inside the van, he lifted his cuffed hands to his face and pressed a finger to his lips.

Nicki copied his action and nodded.

Good. She'd remembered the few basic alerts he'd offered in explanation of why he always accompanied members of her family, instilling gently he would always win and she should never be frightened.

He began to intone a nursery rhyme as he quietly worked, controlling the slow slide as the van took a corner, the pause as it halted at a traffic intersection.

Their abductors were taking no chances, he perceived, for their speed was regulated, normal, and they were heading in a northerly direction.

There was a sense of satisfaction when he freed the electronic device, then once it was activated he replaced it carefully out of sight.

By now, Shannay would have alerted Marcello, notified the police…and it was only a matter of time.

He gave Nicki an indicative victory sign, and moved from one story to another. Heaven help him, he even sang a few songs, silently encouraging Nicki to join in…which, bless her brave little heart, she did.

It would take time to set up a roadblock, and his main objective was providing sufficient distraction to prevent Nicki from becoming too frightened.

Together they discussed her favourite stories, and *Shrek* the movie, Fiona, Puss in Boots and Donkey.

Once, she lifted hands and wiped tears from her cheek. 'When will I see my mummy?'

'Soon, *pequena*. Soon,' he promised, and prayed he was right. 'Your daddy will make sure of it.'

Every minute seemed like an hour, each one the worst and the longest in Shannay's life.

Nothing else came close.

Then two things happened almost simultaneously.

Marcello's cellphone rang…and seconds later he smiled.

Hope soared as she waited anxiously for him to relay news, and when he did it was all she could do not to subside in a heap.

Nicki was safe.

Carlo had her.

Their abductors had been forced to a halt at a police road-block on the northern outskirts.

Nicki was in Carlo's care, and their abductors were under arrest.

Reaction, immense relief…the emotional fall-out from a living nightmare began to have an effect, and tears welled up and spilled to run silently down each cheek.

Marcello took one look and cradled her face between his hands, easing the warm moisture with each thumb.

'Nicki is fine. They're on their way home in a police car. We'll meet them there.'

She wasn't capable of uttering so much as a word, and he lowered his head to hers and pressed his lips to each eyelid in turn.

A gesture which only increased the flow of tears, and his mouth closed over her own in a brief, evocative kiss before he lifted his head.

'Let's go home, hmm?'

Shannay was grateful for the arm he curved across the back of her waist as he led her to his car. Seated, he spared her a brief glance, glimpsed her still pale features and dark eyes fixed unseeing beyond the windscreen and he swore softly beneath his breath.

'Let it go, *querida,*' he advised gently, and she turned towards him with tear-drenched eyes.

'How can I?' Her mouth quivered with emotion. 'What if Carlo—?' She couldn't say the words. Didn't want to voice them.

'From tomorrow, Carlo will have a partner, and they'll both shadow your every move.'

If he meant to reassure, he failed miserably.

Two bodyguards.

The thought of always needing protection freaked her out. Never being able to make a spontaneous decision.

She didn't want Nicki to grow up always on the defensive, intensely cautious and wary.

Heaven knew what effect this afternoon's episode would have, or the long-term toll it might take.

'I'll ensure it will never happen again,' Marcello vowed quietly, and she shot him a disbelieving look.

'You can't promise that. We both know Nicki has become a target.'

There were choices.

And she knew which one she had to make.

Nicki appeared subdued and clung to each of them in turn the instant they entered the foyer.

Carlo was there, so too was Maria, as well as a plain-clothes policewoman who spent considerable time talking with Nicki. A psychology tool which undoubtedly helped, and afterwards Marcello took Carlo aside for an in-depth rundown of the abduction.

Shannay couldn't bear to let Nicki out of her sight, and she bathed her, then she picked at a salad while encouraging Nicki to eat.

Together with Marcello, they shared reading a bedtime story, and afterwards she remained at Nicki's bedside long after her daughter fell asleep.

It was late when Marcello returned to the room and hunkered down beside the chair.

'Come to bed,' he bade quietly. 'Nicki is perfectly safe.'

'I need to be here if she wakes.'

'The sensors monitor every sound. We'll hear the instant she stirs.'

She looked at him in the dimmed lighting and slowly shook her head. 'I can't.'

He remained silent for several telling seconds, then he rose to his full height and walked from the room.

She wanted to cry, but she was all teared out, and she sat staring into space, living and reliving the afternoon from the moment before Nicki disappeared, trying to pin down something…anything that would provide a visual clue so she could correlate it in her mind with the facts Carlo had relayed.

Shannay wasn't aware of falling asleep, only that she woke with a start, experienced a moment of disorientation before she recognised her whereabouts.

She checked Nicki, then turned towards the chair…only to hesitate. Her neck felt stiff, and she was cold. Not from the room's temperature, but chilled and shaky from emotional exhaustion.

Even in bed she couldn't get warm, and after what seemed an age spent tossing and turning she moved quietly out onto the gallery, contemplated going down to the kitchen to make a cup of tea, then changed her mind.

'Unable to sleep?'

She hadn't heard a sound or sensed any movement, yet Marcello was there, large and indomitable in the dim gallery light.

'I looked in on Nicki, and decided to check on you,' he offered quietly, and uttered a soft imprecation as a shiver shook her slim frame.

With an unconscious movement she wrapped her arms round her midriff in the hope it would minimise the shaking…without success, and the next instant he swept her into his arms and carried her to the master suite.

'I'm fine,' Shannay muttered as he slid into bed and drew her with him.

'Sure you are.' The soft oath whispered in the night air as he began smoothing his hands over her limbs, stimulating circulation with brisk sweeping movements, until the shivering slowly eased and warmth invaded her body.

She should leave, and she meant to…except she was reluctant to part from the compassion he offered, the security of being held in strong arms, and the touch of his lips against her forehead.

It felt so *good* to breathe in the familiar scent of him, the faint tinge of soap he'd used mingling with the muskiness of male.

It crept into her senses, as powerful as any aphrodisiac, stirring alive the hunger for his touch, and she murmured indistinctly as she pressed her lips into the warm skin, savoured a little, then slid her hand down his arm to rest on his hip.

Marcello tilted her chin and sought her mouth with his own, gently at first, taking it slow with an evocative slide of his tongue along her longer lip, felt her mouth part, allowing him entry, and the tentative welcome as her tongue moved to tease his own, sweetly cajoling in an elemental dance that could have only one ending.

He fought to control his arousal, knowing that if he didn't it would be over before it began, and she needed a slow loving, a subtle, drifting touch that took a leisurely path towards fulfilment.

This was all about comfort and reassurance, before need.

He could give her that.

And he did. With the slow drift of his hand, the soft caress of his lips as he traversed every sensitive pulse-point, each hollow, pausing to suckle at the tightened bud at the peak of her breast, the tender swell beneath, and low over her quivering stomach to the curls at the apex of her thighs.

Lower, as he explored the sweet moistness, the delicious scent of woman and the swollen clitoris pulsing beneath the erotic laving of his tongue.

Her fingers threaded through his hair, then curled into its length and tugged as sensation spiralled through her body. She arched, unconsciously craving more…and he obliged, cradling her hips between his hands as he held her still.

She was his, mind, body and soul, and still he held back, exerting taut control as she shattered beneath his touch.

Marcello eased her into his arms, cradling her shuddering form as she buried her face into the curve of his neck…and when she went to move, he tightened his hold.

'Stay,' he bade huskily. 'I need you like this.'

It was so easy to let her eyelids drift closed, to relax and let the darkness of sleep steal over her.

For a long time he simply held her, lulled by the evenness of her breathing, the soft sigh of her breath warm against his skin…and on the edge of sleep he wondered what the new day would bring.

CHAPTER TWELVE

DESPITE EVERY EFFORT to minimise the abduction attempt on Nicki, it still made the news, appearing on television stations and in the newspapers.

Marcello refused all interviews, requesting the media and public respect their privacy. He employed guards to ensure no media representative intruded into the grounds of his mansion, and Shannay kept Nicki indoors away from the zoom lenses of persistent cameramen well-known to use devious means in order to gain the slightest advantage.

Staff were reminded of their signed confidentiality agreement, and Marcello placed Sandro in a position of power in the city office while he worked from home.

Nicki's well-being was a prime focus, and Shannay rarely let her out of her sight. Thanks to Carlo's handling of the abduction attempt itself, his protective reassurance during their captivity in the van and counselling, Nicki appeared to be dealing quite well with the trauma.

Yet it became apparent the media refused to give up, and although they didn't get past the guards it was impossible to ignore reflected sunlight bouncing off the poised camera lenses, and a helicopter bearing a TV-station logo passed overhead at least three times a day in the hope of a photo scoop.

For Shannay, it was the last straw, and on the third day she drew Marcello aside soon after Nicki had settled to sleep.

'We need to talk.'

His eyes narrowed. 'Let's take it in the bedroom, shall we?'

Not the bedroom. It held too many memories, and she needed to be strong. 'I'd prefer the office.'

He regarded her carefully, examining her features and noting the darkness apparent in her beautiful eyes, the exigent determination, and prepared to do civilised battle.

With a smooth movement he indicated the direction of the office. 'By all means.'

On reaching his sanctum, he closed the door behind them and indicated a comfortable leather chair. 'Take a seat.'

And have him tower over her? 'I'd prefer to stand.'

Marcello crossed the room, leant one hip against the executive desk and held her faintly defiant gaze.

'There is something you want to discuss?'

His voice was mild, but there was a studied stillness about him that reminded her of an indolent predator.

Don't falter. Don't allow him to see the slightest chink in your resolve. 'I'm taking Nicki home to Perth.' There, she'd stated her intention. 'I can book a commercial flight, or ask you to organise your private jet.'

He didn't protest, merely stated fact. 'Your home is here.'

Shannay gave a slight shake of her head. 'We have an arrangement, and you gave me your word,' she reminded, holding his steady gaze. 'I insist you honour it.'

'Circumstances have changed.'

Her chin tilted. 'Because you persuaded me to have sex with you?'

Marcello was silent for a few measurable seconds, then one

eyebrow arched in deliberate query. 'Just…sex. Is that what you call what we share?'

'We scratched a mutual itch.' Liar. It was more than that. Much more.

She stood immobile beneath his deliberate appraisal, and she held his gaze as if her life depended on it.

'There's nothing I can say or do that will change your mind?'

Assure your love for me never died. That *love* is the reason you dragged Nicki and me back to Madrid…not a need to avenge the past.

But he remained silent. And she didn't have the courage to lay bare her emotions.

'No.' It was the only word she could manage without risking an inability to control the tremble in her voice.

'You intend to return to Madrid…when?'

This was the hardest thing she'd ever had to do. 'I'll accompany Nicki when she travels to visit with you.' And die a little every time, she added silently.

'That's your final word?'

She couldn't afford to back down, even though the decision was killing her.

Did he know? Or even guess?

Maybe he didn't even care. Sex was…well, sex. And for a man, without love to make it special, almost any woman would do. And any number of women would line up hoping to tempt him into their bed the instant news filtered out his wife had left him…again.

'Yes.' A determined if stoic confirmation.

She searched his features for the slightest sign her decision affected him…and failed to detect a thing.

When she thought of their lovemaking…and it *was* lovemaking, she wanted to burst into ignominious tears that he could brush it aside so easily.

'When do you plan to leave?'

He wasn't going to argue? Attempt to persuade her to stay? Yet what had she expected? For him to break down and beg? That wasn't his style.

'As soon as possible.'

He didn't move. He merely inclined his head. 'I'll instruct my pilot to have the jet ready tomorrow.'

'Thank you.'

She had to get out of here, away from him, before she broke down, and she turned towards the door.

'What do you plan on telling our daughter?'

It took tremendous effort to look back at him. 'The truth.'

With that she opened the door, passed through the aperture, then quietly closed the door behind her.

A week later Shannay conceded life had begun to slip into its former pattern.

The apartment was aired, cleaned, vacuumed and polished. The pantry, refrigerator and freezer stocked.

Anna appeared delighted to resume evening duties as Nicki's carer, and John was pleased to have her start back at the pharmacy.

She should be happy, content, *relieved* to have left a highly fraught situation behind.

It was, she silently assured, resolved. As originally intended. Hadn't she worked hard to hammer out a satisfactory custody arrangement suitable to Nicki's needs?

Her daughter appeared relatively relaxed, and was looking forward to resuming kindergarten, meeting up with her friends.

Each evening, at the same time, Marcello rang to speak to his daughter and bid her 'goodnight'.

Calls which Nicki eagerly anticipated and received with excited fervour.

The fact he rarely offered more than a restrained greeting to Shannay was immaterial…yet it hurt terribly.

Although what did she expect? Pleasant conversation?

How could he just…switch off, like that?

She shouldn't feel crushed, but she did. It affected her sleep and left her hollow-eyed and aching.

If she didn't soon pull herself together, she'd become a complete and utter emotional mess.

The second week in, she found it difficult to readjust to working the five-to-midnight shift, and John's voiced concern began to rankle.

'I'm fine,' she assured him, and refused to elaborate on the Madrid sojourn.

At the end of the second week confirmation her decree nisi had been granted arrived in the mail from her lawyer.

The decree absolute would follow in approximately one month.

It should have been good news, except it sent her into the depths of despair.

The third week she developed a stomach bug…a persistent one which showed no inclination to subside.

Combined with unaccustomed tiredness and mood swings, the obvious possible reason sent alarm bells skyrocketing through the stratosphere. Consternation provided the need for a pregnancy test, the result of which confirmed her worst fears.

Not so inconceivable when she hadn't used any form of contraceptive following Nicki's birth…nor had Marcello favoured protection.

Fool. What had she been *thinking?*

Worse, what had *he?*

Although, on reflection, *thinking* hadn't even entered the equation!

A fraught twenty-four hours later she redid the pregnancy test, only to have it show the same result.

Ohmigod, *no.* The silent scream seemed to echo inside her brain as she processed the implications in a stark replay.

OK, *think,* she bade shakily, and groaned out loud when she did the calculations and *possible* became *probable,* of which each passing day provided its own confirmation.

Then came the phone call on a week night when she'd cried off work, where Nicki unwittingly informed Marcello "Mummy is sick", and the words were out in spite of Shannay frantically shaking her head.

Seconds later Nicki held out the receiver. 'Daddy wants to talk to you.'

Well, I don't want to talk to him. 'Not now, darling, I'm busy.'

Nicki's eyes rounded in surprise, for Shannay was only folding clothes, and Marcello must have heard, for his voice came clearly through the mouthpiece.

'Take the phone, Shannay.'

She swore softly, and saw her daughter's eyes dilate even further, then she collected the receiver and prepared to play polite.

'Marcello.'

'Nicki said you're unwell.'

Whatever happened to *hello?* She kept her voice even. 'I'm fine.'

'Have you seen a doctor?'

'I'm a pharmacist, remember? I do have a reasonable knowledge of ailments and appropriate medications.'

'Are you pregnant?'

The query came out of left field, and surprised her…although, on reflection, she had to wonder *why*.

'I'm fine,' Shannay reiterated, refusing to fabricate or confirm, then she handed the receiver back to Nicki and exited the room on the pretext of delivering a small stack of folded clothes to the bedroom.

She could hear Nicki's voice in the background, and she moved into the bathroom and began running Nicki's bath.

Employing delaying tactics, she rearranged items on the marble-topped vanity until Nicki entered the bathroom.

'Why didn't you want to talk to Daddy?'

'We talk via email,' she explained carefully as she helped undress her daughter. Brief sentences conveying updates on Nicki.

It took a few days to gather the courage to arrange an appointment with an obstetrician, and she didn't know whether to smile or cry following his examination.

'Congratulations, my dear. You're about halfway through your first trimester.'

The remainder of the day passed in a daze, and she settled Nicki with Anna, then drove to the pharmacy, praying that if they weren't busy she might be able to persuade John to let her finish early.

Shortly after nine she was on the point of considering a tea-break when the electronic buzzer sounded as someone entered the pharmacy.

Shannay glanced up towards the entrance with a ready smile in place…and froze. For walking towards her was the last person she expected to see.

The tall, broad-shouldered male frame was achingly familiar. Attired in black jeans, a white collarless shirt undone at the neck and a butter-soft black leather collarless jacket, Marcello bore a distinct resemblance to a dark warrior.

Why was he here…and why *now?*

All her fine body hairs lifted in sensory recognition, and there was nothing she could do to prevent the surge of blood pulsing through her veins.

It was a magnetic reaction and, try as she might, she was unable to prevent the way she was drawn to him.

His eyes captured and held her own, his features sculptured into almost savage lines, his sensual mouth bracketed by slashing grooves.

He looked dangerous, his eyes almost obsidian in their darkness as he drew close.

Shannay's emotional heart went into meltdown, rendering her almost boneless as she experienced a mix of fear and elation, hope and dismay.

He didn't glance towards John when he spoke, yet the words were for him alone.

'My wife is ceasing work, as of now.'

It wasn't a question, merely a statement of his intent.

Shannay looked at him in shocked surprise. 'You can't just walk in here and—'

'You're leaving.'

'The hell I am.'

'You can walk, or be carried. It's immaterial.'

John started forward. 'Now look here—'

Marcello speared him with a forbidding glance. 'I understand you regard Shannay as a friend. But this is between me and my wife.' He shifted his attention back to Shannay. 'I suggest you collect your keys.'

'No.' The next instant she gave a startled yelp as he reached forward and lifted her over one shoulder, then he indicated the room at the rear of the pharmacy. 'Shannay's belongings are there?'

What was it between men? Silent signals, male recognition? Whatever, she became aware John retrieved her bag and passed it into Marcello's possession.

'Thank you.' He turned towards the door. 'We'll be in touch.' Then he walked calmly outside, paused beside a limousine, murmured something to the driver, then bundled her into the rear seat.

'What in hell do you think you're doing?' Her voice held restrained fury as he leant across and fitted her safety belt before tending to his own.

'Taking you to a hotel.'

Her face lit with scandalised disbelief. 'No, you're not!' She leaned forward. 'Driver, take me to Applecross.' She supplied the street address, and caught a glimpse of familiar features in the rear-vision mirror and was unable to hide her disbelief. 'Carlo?'

'I'm sorry. I have orders.'

Shannay turned towards Marcello and lashed out at him with her hand, uncaring where it landed…as long as it did.

Except he caught it mid-flight, and pressed their joined hands down to his side.

'Nicki is asleep, Anna is happy to stay with her overnight, and there's a bag containing a change of clothes in the boot.'

He'd already been to the apartment?

'Why?'

'I imagine it's self-explanatory,' Marcello drawled, and she curled her fingers into his, then dug her nails in hard.

'You can't *do* this.'

She caught a flash of white teeth as he smiled in the dim light. 'So—bite me.'

She wanted to, badly. And she would, the instant they were alone. Meantime she refused to speak to him, or even look at him during the drive into the city.

Carlo pulled into the entrance of one of the city's luxurious hotels, popped the boot, retrieved two overnight bags and handed them to the hovering concierge.

'I'll call you in the morning,' Marcello indicated as Carlo opened the rear passenger door for Shannay to alight.

For a moment she considered refusing to budge, except making a fuss would gain nothing at all.

'I hate you for this.' Her voice was little more than a sibilant whisper as he led her through the foyer to a bank of lifts.

'Let go my hand,' Shannay demanded tightly when they alighted on a high floor.

'Soon.'

He was taller, and indisputably faster on his feet…so where did he think she'd escape to? She threw him a dark look and stood in mutinous silence as he inserted the card, freed the lock, then drew her inside.

With economical movements he deposited both bags, removed the *do not disturb* tag and hung it outside the door, then closed the door and slid home the safety chain.

'You'd better have a good reason for behaving like a…' Words temporarily failed her. 'Barbaric beast,' she added with considerable heat.

He was too controlled, his eyes too impossibly dark, except she was too angry to heed their caution.

'Why don't you sit down?'

'I don't *need* to sit.'

Marcello shrugged out of his leather jacket and threw it over the back of a nearby chair.

'A drink? A cup of tea, perhaps?'

He was being too polite, and she sent him a venomous glare. 'Cut to the chase, why don't you?'

'Then you can leave?' His drawling voice resembled pure silk being razzed by a sharp steel blade. 'I don't think so.'

'What is this?' Her dark eyes flashed with latent fire. 'A duel to the death?'

He smiled, although there was a distinct lack of humour apparent. 'You possess a fanciful imagination.'

Her chin lifted in open defiance. 'You're holding me here against my will.'

Marcello regarded her steadily, his gaze that of a jungle animal watching its prey. 'Are you pregnant with my child?'

Shannay was suddenly speechless, and it took several seconds before she found her voice. 'You flew from Madrid to ask that of me?'

'If you recall,' he drawled with silky indolence, 'you refused to give me an answer on the phone.'

Angry beyond belief, she searched for words, any words. 'You're *unbelievable.*'

'You're evading the question.' His voice assumed the quality of silk, and her features became waxen-pale.

'What if I say *no?*'

'It won't make the slightest difference.'

'To *what?*' she demanded, almost at the end of her tether.

'How this plays out.'

So this was it…crunch time.

'In a matter of weeks the divorce will be finalised.'

'No, it won't. I've had my lawyer notify yours of our re-conciliation,' Marcello informed and obtained a degree of satisfaction at her shocked expression. 'Copies of the announcement in the Spanish media provided sufficient proof.'

'But that was merely a sham,' Shannay protested, eyes

wide with dismay as she searched frantically for the exact words quoted…hadn't Marcello simply acceded "anything is possible"? How could that be construed to be a positive confirmation?

She watched with startled surprise as he reached for his overnight bag, extracted a slim packet, opened the flap and handed the contents to her.

'I'd like you to look at these.'

Shannay told herself she wasn't interested, but the coloured photograph of a house caught her attention, and she felt herself drawn to it, unable to ignore her admiration for the beautiful, sprawling two-storeyed mansion set in spacious grounds overlooking what appeared to be a lake.

Underneath the photograph was another, even more magnificent, and there was a third with views out over the ocean.

Yet it was the first photograph she returned to, and she glanced up at him with open curiosity.

'Why are you showing me these?'

'The first house is at Peppermint Grove, the remaining two at Cottesloe and Cottesloe Beach respectively.'

Expensive real estate. *Very* expensive real estate, she perceived.

'We have an appointment to inspect them tomorrow.'

A soundless gasp escaped her lips. 'Excuse me?'

'You heard.'

She had, but the implication of them failed to compute. Why would he be interested in Perth real estate?

He watched her conflicting emotions and barely restrained himself from hauling her into his arms.

The past few weeks had been hell. He'd eaten at his desk, barely slept and literally turned his life upside down as he had liaised with Perth real-estate agents, selected three of the most suitable properties after viewing them via an internet visual tour, then he'd flown into Perth yesterday, consulted with lawyers, accountants, viewed the three properties and a few more purported to be worthy of inspection, organised Nicki's care with Anna…and had Carlo drive him to collect the reason for all this.

Shannay.

'We can do this by arguing half the night away,' Marcello began with deliberate patience. 'Or you can listen until I'm done.'

She looked at him, really looked at him, and saw the fine lines of tiredness fan out from each corner of his eyes, the faint shadowy smudges evident.

Heaven knew she was weary as pregnancy took hold of her body and drained some of her energy to nurture the tiny foetus developing inside her womb.

Together, what hope did they have?

Yet there was an instinctive feeling…some deep intrinsic knowledge hovering just beneath the surface.

His presence here…dared she even hope, let alone think what it might mean?

It was crazy, but the stress and tension that had consumed her for the past few weeks began to ebb, as if her subconscious recognised something she had yet to acknowledge.

Dared not envisage in case she might have it wrong.

'You have my heart, *querida*.'

For a few seconds she almost forgot to breathe.

'Always,' Marcello added gently. 'There has never been anyone else since the day I met you.'

She opened her mouth, only to close it again as he held up a hand.

'Please…hear me out. There are words I need to say. Not all of them good.'

She had nothing to lose. Absolutely nothing, and she simply inclined her head.

'Penè made things difficult for you, conspiring initially with Estella to cause trouble.'

Wasn't that the truth!

'I thought we could get beyond the resulting fracas, but you were adamant our marriage was doomed.'

'I left, because to remain would have been impossible.'

'I was angry,' Marcello continued. 'You ignored my phone calls and refused to respond to every one of my messages. Within a year Ramon developed pneumonia and suffered a heart attack. Soon after he was diagnosed with cancer, and it was necessary for me to take control.'

Marcello's responsibility would have been enormous. Remorse and a degree of guilt sat uncomfortably on her shoulders.

Timing, distance, misunderstanding. Each rational in hindsight, Shannay admitted.

'With your refusal to acknowledge any form of contact, I had little recourse but to accept you intended to make a life on your own.' He paused, and a muscle tensed along the edge of his jaw. 'Until fate played a hand with Sandro and Luisa's impromptu visit to Perth, their sighting of you at a local carnival and the discovery you had a child. Indisputably my child.'

Shannay relived that moment as if it were yesterday. 'I vowed revenge. Contriving to use everything in my power to have you revisit Madrid…and ultimately seduce you. To take hold of your emotions and crush them to dust beneath my feet.'

The knowledge sent pain arrowing through her body, and his voice softened as he glimpsed the shadows evident in her eyes.

'Except I couldn't do it. The woman I'd turned you into in my mind didn't exist. The reality was the young woman I fell in love with, the beautiful girl with integrity and a loving heart who fought against me and her own emotions…as I struggled to deal with my own.'

His mouth twisted with deliberate cynicism. 'Ironic, isn't it? When it came to revenge…I lost. As Ramon warned I would.'

Her eyes sharpened. 'Ramon?'

'My grandfather saw more than anyone gave him credit for. He'd glimpsed what was in your heart, and knew my own.'

What came next was painful. 'Nicki's abduction became the catalyst. I only had myself to offer in a bid to keep you with me.' He lifted a hand and let it fall to his side. 'And it wasn't enough.'

In his eyes, he'd failed yet again, and her sense of remorse returned.

'I didn't want Nicki to grow up shadowed by bodyguards, forever in fear of another abduction attempt.'

'Nor is it my choice,' he agreed quietly. 'Once is one time too many. Which brings me to my decision to relocate here.'

Shannay looked at him in disbelief. '*Perth?* How can you—'

'Easily. Sandro is now in control of the Madrid office. I've already signed a lease on suitable office accommodation in the city, and tomorrow we look at these houses.'

It was almost too much for her to take in. Yet any doubt fled as he took both her hands in his and lifted them to his lips.

'I love you,' he vowed gently. 'Stay with me, live with me. Let me love you, *mi mujer,* for the rest of my days. *Por siempre.*'

Forever.

They were only words, but they came from the heart, his soul…and were all she'd ever needed to hear.

Shannay withdrew her hands and cradled his face. Then she reached up, angled her mouth to his own and bestowed a lingering kiss.

'Yes,' she answered simply, and felt the tension ease from his body as he pulled her in close, then his mouth captured hers in a hungry, acutely sensual possession lasting long before he gradually eased to brush her swollen lips with his own, tracing their outline with a feather-light touch before lifting his head.

'I think this calls for a celebration.'

Marcello crossed to the phone and ordered a bottle of exceedingly expensive French champagne be sent up from the bar, and when it was delivered he eased off the cork and poured the sparkling, light golden liquid into two flutes and handed her one.

'To us.'

She lifted it and touched the rim to his own. Only to have her eyes widen in sudden consternation.

'What is it?'

'I—' there was never going to be a better time to tell him '—shouldn't have more than a sip of this,' she offered with obvious reluctance, and saw his eyes sharpen, then assume a lazy gleam.

'Because?' Marcello prompted gently, and glimpsed a mischievous smile teasing the corners of that lush mouth.

'It has to do with my being in the first trimester.'

She watched his expression change, and could only wonder at the joy, the love and an entire gamut of emotions flooding his features.

His eyes, she could die and go to heaven just on the look exposed there.

For her. Only her.

He laid the palm of one hand to her waist and splayed his fingers over her stomach.

'You don't mind?'

How could she mind?

She'd been fiercely protective of Nicki before and after she was born. Uncaring she'd chosen single motherhood over the alternative.

This time Marcello would be with her every step of the way.

'I'm delighted,' she assured gently.

'You gift me everything I could ever want, *amada*. All I need.'

The champagne went flat, which was total sacrilege.

Not that it mattered in the slightest, for there were more important matters to be taken care of.

Such as the leisurely removal of clothes, long, lingering kisses…and gentle tactile lovemaking far into the night.

CHAPTER THIRTEEN

IT WAS EARLY when Shannay woke, and she stretched, felt strong hands pull her in against a hard, warm, fully aroused male body, and gave a pleasurable sigh.

'Hmm,' she murmured as lips nuzzled the sensitive hollow at the curve of her neck. 'This is a very pleasant way to greet the morning.'

She reached for him, enclosed his hard length with light fingers, heard the faint hitch as the breath caught in his throat…and smiled.

'There's just one thing,' she began tentatively as Marcello's hand cupped her breast.

'And what's that?' he drawled close to her ear.

Oh, dear…not now, please. 'Morning sickness,' she enlightened as the nausea rose up in waves, and she made an undignified dash to the bathroom, clicked the lock, before being violently ill.

She barely registered the rattle of the door handle, and studiously ignored the double knock as Marcello demanded to be let in.

'I'm fine.'

The assurance didn't work, for she heard him utter a string of wicked-sounding Spanish imprecations. 'Open the door.'

'I'll be out in a minute.'

Not exactly an auspicious start to the day, and definitely not an enticing prelude to amorous activities, she grimaced as she washed her face and cleaned her teeth.

While there, she ran a brush through the tumbled length of her hair and twisted it into a knot atop her head, then she released the lock and emerged to find a concerned Marcello bent on dragging agitated fingers through badly rumpled hair.

A warm hand cupped her shoulder, while a firm thumb and finger captured her chin and lifted it as he subjected her to a dark-eyed scrutiny.

'Are you OK?'

Next he'll query if he should call a doctor…

He didn't disappoint, and he frowned as she rolled her eyes.

'What?'

'Morning sickness is a common occurrence during the early months of pregnancy,' she relayed with an impish grin. 'And not always confined to the morning.' She lifted a shoulder in a negligible shrug. 'It tends to wear off during the second trimester.'

'Is there nothing that helps?'

'Most often a cup of tea and a plain biscuit as soon as I wake will avert the physical symptoms.'

He crossed to the phone. 'I'll order Room Service.'

'Do that, for breakfast,' Shannay qualified. 'I'll make the tea.'

He looked appealingly disconcerted, and she had a difficult time hiding a smile.

Marcello Martinez, corporate head, entrepreneur and billionaire…master of many things, but a tad lost around his pregnant wife.

'I have a feeling I'm in for a learning curve,' he acknowledged with musing wryness.

She laughed, a low, throaty sound that was infectious. 'You'll do fine.' As he did with everything he chose to undertake.

He smoothed a hand over her cheek, cupped it, then traced her lower lip with his thumb. 'Starting now. Sit down and I'll make the tea.'

They showered, ate a leisurely breakfast, then checked out of the hotel and met Carlo, who drove them to Shannay's apartment in suburban Applecross, where Nicki greeted her father with unabashed affection.

'Daddy! Are you here for a visit?'

Shannay watched as Marcello swung their daughter into his arms and hugged her close.

'A very long visit.'

'Love you, Daddy.'

'Right back at you, *pequena*.'

Shannay swallowed the sudden lump in her throat at his smile.

'What would you say to me staying with you and Mummy?'

Nicki wound her arms around his neck and sank back in the cradle of his arms to regard him solemnly. 'Here, with us in Perth? All the time?'

'All the time,' he reiterated gently. 'Occasionally I'll need to visit Madrid, but I won't be away long, and sometimes you and Mummy can come with me.'

'I'd like it. Very much.' She leaned forward and kissed his cheek and assured plaintively, 'I missed you.'

'I missed you, too.'

It was enough knowing Marcello would be a permanent fixture for Nicki to go happily off to kindergarten while her parents met with real-estate agents.

The Peppermint Grove house won Shannay's vote. It was so *right* in every aspect, with its large grounds, spacious rooms and the most glorious curved staircase leading from an elegant tiled foyer to the upper floor.

All she needed to do was say "I love it", and Marcello closed the deal there and then.

Next came legal confirmation notification that the court would in all probability succeed in negating the processing of their decree absolute, thus voiding the existing divorce application.

The following few weeks proved hectic, as Shannay ordered furniture, furnishings and fittings, and, with Marcello organising delivery and placement, successfully orchestrated the move to their new home.

Shannay refused to leave John without a registered pharmacist, and worked a shorter evening shift for the week it took to employ a replacement.

Nicki loved her new bedroom, and delighted in the special playhouse Marcello had set up in the grounds for her.

By far, the baby news won out, with the future advent of a little sister or brother providing endless excitement.

Marcello was busy setting up a city office, employing staff and organising office space at home.

At his suggestion Shannay chose to lease her Applecross apartment, fortuitously to Anna's daughter and son-in-law, who had decided to relocate from Tasmania.

Everything seemed to fit into place with organised efficiency…mostly due to Marcello's influence, including a re-affirmation of their wedding vows to be held in the gardens of their Peppermint Grove home.

Sandro and Luisa flew in via private jet to attend the ceremony, while Penè declined on the grounds she was still mourning Ramon.

The day dawned with pale sunshine and a sky with drifting

cumulus, and caterers moved in mid-morning to prepare a sumptuous late-afternoon feast for the few guests Marcello and Shannay had chosen to invite.

It was the antithesis of the media circus their first wedding had become, and Nicki was in her element as Anna helped dress her in a miniature version of Shannay's gown. Wearing ivory shoes and a coronet of small flowers in her hair, she resembled a little princess.

Shannay chose a simple full-length gown in ivory silk with a long-sleeved slim-fitted jacket in matching fabric with a stand-up collar, ivory stilettos and a sheer scarf in ivory chiffon draped over her hair.

Her only jewellery was a diamond pendant and matching ear-studs.

There was an ornamental white gazebo in the grounds, decorated with white flowers, and Marcello stood resplendent in a dark suit, white shirt and ivory satin tie together with the celebrant as they waited for Shannay and Nicki to join them.

John and Anna acted as witnesses, and the vows were personally selected to endorse Shannay and Marcello's commitment to each other.

Guests were few, and consequently it was a very intimate gathering, with fine champagne, exquisite food, and much laughter.

Nicki was in her element, loving every minute of the day, and she made no protest when it came time for Carlo to take her with Anna for a sleep-over at Anna's apartment.

The caterers packed up, John departed, together with the remaining guests, and Sandro and Luisa left soon after for their city hotel.

Marcello closed and locked the door, then he drew

Shannay into his arms and touched his mouth to hers in a gentle salutation.

'Have I told you how beautiful you are?'

He had, when he'd slid her wedding ring in place, and again as the afternoon drew to a close.

A teasing smile curved her lips and she tilted her head slightly to one side. 'Should I commend how incredibly handsome you look?'

'Minx. Come dance with me, hmm?'

'That could lead to trouble.'

'Of the most delightful kind,' he agreed. 'But what's a wedding without a bridal waltz?'

She pressed a light kiss to his chin. 'Where?'

He activated a remote control and slow, dreamy music filtered through concealed speakers.

Together they barely moved, just held each other and drifted a little, swayed some, and Shannay felt boneless as the music crept into her soul, meshed with the overwhelming love she felt for the man who held her, and she rested against him, following wherever he led.

The track eventually concluded, and she pulled his head down to hers and kissed him.

'I love you.' The words drifted from her lips in a husky murmur. 'So much.' She thread her fingers through his hair, then caressed his nape, the sensitive skin beneath each earlobe, and rested against the pulse beating strongly at the base of his throat. 'I always have. Always will.'

He caught hold of her hand, unfolded it and laid his lips to her palm. '*Gracias.*'

She'd said the words before, but not quite like this, without accompanying passion, or in the dreamy aftermath of lovemaking.

'Let's go upstairs.'

Marcello placed a kiss to her forehead. 'Is that an invitation?'

'Do you need one?'

He placed an arm beneath her knees and lifted her into his arms, then began ascending the staircase.

'Isn't this just a little over the top?' she teased, and he chuckled.

'Perhaps I'm conserving your strength?'

'Next you'll suggest I lie supine while you do all the work.'

'It has been a long day.'

For which he received a thump on his arm from a very feminine fist.

'Wretch. Just as long as you remember I get to play payback in the early dawn hours.'

'Promises, huh?' They reached the main bedroom and he slid her down onto her feet, then they began removing each other's clothes…slowly, with infinite care.

Their love was everlasting, infinite and very special.

There was no need to hurry. They had the night, and all those remaining for the rest of their lifetimes.

Eternity.

Ramon Alejandro Martinez was born five months and two weeks later in the presence of his father, who cut the umbilical cord and handed him into his mother's arms.

With black hair, knowing eyes, he was the image of Marcello, and appeared to possess his mother's nature.

His sister, Nicki, adored him from first sight, and vowed to take care of him forever and teach him everything she knew.

MILLS & BOON®

Helen Bianchin v Regency Collection!

0316_MB520

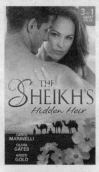